THE
WAKING WORLD

www.totallyrandombooks.co.uk

TOM HUDDLESTON

THE
FUTURE
KING

THE
WAKING WORLD

David Fickling Books

OXFORD · NEW YORK

31 Beaumont Street
Oxford OX1 2NP, UK

THE WAKING WORLD
A DAVID FICKLING BOOK 978 0 857 56045 2

Published in Great Britain by David Fickling Books,
a division of Random House Children's Publishers UK
A Random House Group Company

This edition published 2013

1 3 5 7 9 10 8 6 4 2

Copyright © Tom Huddleston, 2013

The Random House Group Limited supports the Forest Stewardship Council® (FSC®),
the leading international forest-certification organisation. Our books carrying the FSC
label are printed on FSC®-certified paper. FSC is the only forest-certification scheme
supported by the leading environmental organisations, including Greenpeace. Our paper
procurement policy can be found at www.randomhouse.co.uk/environment

MIX
Paper from
responsible sources
FSC® C016897

Set in 12.5/16pt Baskerville MT by Falcon Oast Graphic Art

Random House Children's Publishers Ltd
61–63 Uxbridge Road, London W5 5SA

www.**randomhousechildrens**.co.uk
www.**totallyrandombooks**.co.uk
www.**randomhouse**.co.uk

Addresses for companies within The Random House Group Limited can be found at:
www.randomhouse.co.uk/offices.htm

THE RANDOM HOUSE GROUP Limited Reg. No. 954009

A CIP catalogue record for this book is available from the British Library.

Printed and bound in Great Britain by Clays Ltd, St Ives plc

For Sarah

THE ISLAND
(NORTH)
SHOWING MAJOR
FARMSTEADS & PORTS

CROWDAL

HAWK'S
CROSS

FOURSTONES

BLEAKMOOR

KIPP'
TOWN

SOWERTON

BLACKPORT

THREE
MEN

WOODHEAD

LYEPOOL

N

W — *e*

s

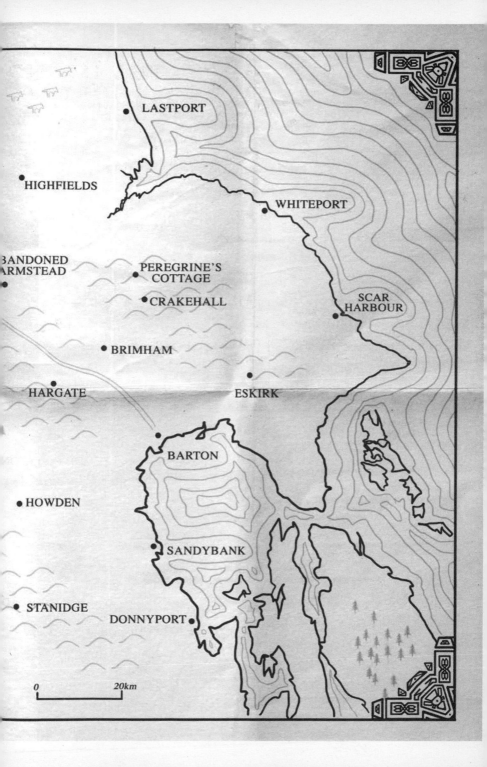

CHAPTER ONE

The Stranger in the Snow

They called it the Moon of the Wolf. It was rising now, over the crest of the ridge beyond the river, gleaming silver-grey through a fast-closing gap in the clouds. The third new moon after Exmus, the dying days of winter. The most treacherous time of all.

Aran pulled his scarf tighter around his face, thrust his hands deeper into the pockets of his battered hide jacket, and shivered. The forest was as sombre and silent as a tomb, the shadows deepening as the unseen sun crept below the horizon, making way for the prowling moon. The snow began to fall.

Aran didn't know how the third moon came by its name, but to his mind it seemed a perfect fit. This was the time of year when crisp blue skies could turn grey in moments, low clouds bringing flurries of sudden snow, as keen and deadly as a hunting pack. A time when the air was filled with howling, as torrents of wind rattled out of the north, felling trees, flattening buildings, sweeping strong men clear off their feet. A time when, in the uneasy quiet before dusk, a flicker of movement in the undergrowth could be the first tentative signs of life returning to the landscape, or it could be something far more threatening, something fanged and four-legged and hungry for your blood.

And any two-legged travellers were apt to be just as dangerous. Poachers, bandits and Marauders – only those with evil intent would be out on a night like this. Anyone with any sense would be sealed safe in their underground farmsteads, with a fire roaring in the grate and a hundred feet of solid earth between themselves and the elements.

Anyone with any sense – or anyone with a choice.

What would happen if a stranger did happen by? Aran thought. What would he find? One wiry fourteen-year-old boy and his even skinnier friend, all alone in the wild woods. Aran was bigger than he had been a year ago. He'd been admiring his muscles in the washroom mirror only that morning, trying to pull the sort of expression that he imagined might scare off a forest bandit. But the face staring back at him – soft brown skin, pale green eyes, his black hair only trimmed neatly, no matter how hard he tried to persuade his mother to let him shave it – was more likely to inspire pity than fear.

It was a curse, he thought, being born with a nice face. The women of Hawk's Cross might cluck around, squeeze Aran's cheeks and call him beautiful, but what good was that? He'd rather look ugly and tough any day.

Well, it would serve them right if he did get killed or kidnapped, his father most of all. It was Law Carifax who had ordered Aran to join the logging crew, sick of his son hanging around the farmstead, getting in the way.

So here he was, in this shadowy clearing between the snow-laden trees, scrabbling in the frozen mud for the remnants of a fallen oak. The tree itself had long since been hacked up and dragged off by the loggers, leaving the boys to deal with the scraps. In the gathering gloom, Aran could just make out the distant lantern above the farmstead's main gates, far away across the fields. Soon those gates would slam tight against the night, and woe betide anyone left outside when they did.

The same thoughts must have been going through Cas's mind as he peered up from beneath the peak of his cap, his thin black eyebrows huddling together as though for warmth. 'Come on,' he shivered. 'Let's get moving. It must be almost last bell, and I think I actually just heard a bowl of lamb stew calling my name. I'd hate to disappoint it.'

Cas's gold-tinged cheeks were almost blue, and he was trembling so hard Aran thought he could hear the bones rattling. They may have been the same age almost to the day, but Cas was a foot shorter than Aran and looked a lot younger. If someone did come looking for trouble, Aran thought, Cas'd be even more useless than me.

And then, almost as if his thoughts had made it happen, he heard the sound of approaching hoof beats. A twig snapped in the silence and Aran's hand strayed to the short blade which hung from his belt.

For a moment all was still, just the whisper of the wind

and the distant cracking of ice on the river. The boys stood frozen, scanning the shrouded trees.

Aran wanted to shout something, to let whoever it was know he wasn't afraid. The men in the stories always shouted 'Who goes there?' so he gave that a try. But something strange had been happening to Aran's voice lately, so instead of a bold challenge it came out like the squeak of a particularly nervous dormouse.

The hoof beats started up again, followed by the sound of harsh laughter. Shadows moved within the whiteness, coming closer.

'Who do you think goes there?' asked a voice. 'Bloody ice fairies, come to steal you away?'

A gust of wind parted the snow and Aran recognized his brother's black mare. His heart, which had begun to race expectantly, sank with dismay.

'Father told me you were on the twig run,' Akmid said. 'Must be a proud day for you.'

He slowed his horse with a tug on the reins. Though he was only three years older, Akmid already seemed twice Aran's size. He wore a battered leather waistcoat with a high collar, and his bulging arms jingled with iron bracelets. His bronze head was shaved and painted with a single red stripe, following that year's fashion. He had a pointed nose and piercing blue eyes which fell on Aran with disdainful superiority.

'Nothing like a bit of hard work to get the blood flowing,' he said sarcastically. 'And such important work too. Where would Hawk's Cross be without a steady supply of sticks?'

Another figure appeared, looming out of the darkness on a snorting steed which towered over the younger boys. Keller was Akmid's sergeant-at-arms: his mentor, his partner in crime and his only friend. He was still a few months shy of nineteen, but his immense stature and muscular frame made him seem a lot older. Keller's neck and arms were scrawled with intricate tattoos in black and red ink, and a ragged white scar ran from the edge of his lip to the back of his shaved head. There were conflicting rumours as to how he had come by the scar: a wolf, perhaps, or a bear, or even a Marauder. But whatever had attacked Keller, everyone agreed that it had lost.

Keller said nothing, his cold grey eyes regarding Aran implacably. A boar was strapped to the back of his horse, its tusks dripping red onto the white ground. In one hand he held a long wooden spear, its steel tip flecked with the pig's blood.

'Look what we've caught for your dinner,' Akmid said. 'I hope you're grateful.'

'We?' Aran shot back. 'Let's see your spear. I'll bet there's not a drop of blood on it.'

Keller's thin lips twitched into a smile, and Aran knew he was right. Akmid balled his fists, but Aran wasn't afraid of his brother. They'd grown up together, had even been friends once, long ago.

Akmid snarled. 'I'll show you blood,' he said. As Keller's horse came alongside Akmid reached out with one hand, grabbing the pig by the scruff of its neck. Then he turned and wiped his glove across Aran's upturned face, smearing him with a thick red sheen. 'Now you almost look like a hunter,' Akmid snorted. 'If you weren't three feet tall, that is.'

Aran spat, horrified, feeling sticky warmth on his lips. He grabbed a handful of snow and buried his face in it, mopping off with his scarf. He was about to scream a furious curse in his brother's face, but his breath caught when he heard the distant tolling of a bell.

Twice it rang, echoing in the stillness. Aran's heart began to pound. He hadn't realized how late it was.

'Warning bell,' Akmid smirked, digging his spurs into his horse's flanks. 'Best hurry along, or the ice fairies really will get you. Well, them or the wolves.'

And he kicked out with one steel-shod boot, tipping the little handcart over on its side, scattering sticks into the snow. Keller followed with his pig, which seemed to stare contemptuously back at Aran as it bounced away into the darkness.

Aran felt tears stinging his eyes. 'I hate him,' he muttered, stooping to gather the twigs and return them to the cart.

Cas knelt to help. 'He only acts like that because he knows it winds you up,' he said.

'Why does he get to spend his time trotting about the place, killing things?' Aran said. 'Playing war with that shaved bear of his? It's not fair.'

'He's the eldest son,' Cas pointed out. 'It's tradition. He'll get to lead Hawk's Cross, keep us all safe. You'll get to run the farm, keep us all fed. I know which job I'd rather do.'

6

'Well, that's because you're boring,' Aran spat back, and instantly regretted it. 'I'm sorry,' he said. 'You're not boring.'

Cas smiled. 'I am, a bit,' he said. 'I'd rather look at a book than fight a battle. But this is our place, you and me. You'll never be a warrior, and I'll never be a scholar.'

'That's not true,' Aran said. 'One of these days, you'll see. My father can't keep refusing to let me learn to fight. And one day I'll persuade him to let you take lessons too. Though I don't know why you'd want to.' He grabbed a handful of sticks and thrust them into the cart. 'Come on, let's leave the last of it. If the stores master says we're short, just tell him we decided not freezing to death was more important.'

'That's all right for you,' Cas said. 'He'll just give you a pat on the head and regards to your dad. I'll be back out tomorrow for the leftovers, just you see.'

But he took hold of the handcart nonetheless. They dragged it up the hillside between the trees, through prickly thickets of green gorse, over ice-crusted streams and slippery banks of mulchy leaves. Aran was soon sweating under his jacket. The moisture in his breath turned his scarf into a mask of ice, and his hands rubbed raw under his leather gloves.

It was full dark now, the moon hidden behind an iron roof of cloud. Aran could see nothing but the snow eddying all around, and the distant flicker of the lamp hanging over the farmstead gate. He swore under his breath, cursing his father and his brother, and all the other citizens who were safe underground. Hawk's Cross seemed a long, cold way away. He wondered what would happen if they really did get left outside at last bell. Would his father break the rules to rescue him?

He remembered a story Miss Crell liked to tell, a cautionary tale for boys who might feel the urge to go exploring on a winter's night. One Exmus, so the story said, an especially cruel, greedy Law rounded up all the boys from his farmstead and sent them out to steal food from their neighbours, to make up for a bad harvest. That night saw the heaviest snowfall they had ever known. The farmstead was buried. No one could get in or out. It was a long, hard winter, and many starved, never knowing what had happened to their loved ones.

But when the snow began to melt and the survivors stepped outside, there they were, right in the courtyard. Cattle and horses and young men, their hands filled with stolen bread, their mouths open in wordless cries. Frozen solid.

Suddenly the cart stopped moving. Aran turned back, cursing, and gave a hard tug. The back wheel was caught on something, refusing to budge.

Cas put a hand on Aran's arm. 'Wait, let me just . . .' He bent to take a look.

But Aran was in no mood to wait. It was late, he was tired, and he just wanted to get home. He gave a tug on the rope, as hard as he could. There was a crack and a snap, and the cart leaped forward on three wheels. The corner flew up, smacking Cas smartly on the forehead.

He staggered back, putting his arms out, then fell on his backside in the snow.

Aran ran forward. Cas looked stunned, a small trickle of blood leaking from his left eyebrow.

'Cas,' Aran said breathlessly, hurrying to his side. 'Are you all right?'

Cas blinked slowly, his mouth working. He reached up and touched his head, and his fingers came away shiny and black in the moonlight.

Fear rose like bile in Aran's throat. He couldn't carry Cas, not all that way. He could go back for help, but could he really leave his friend out here all alone?

He grabbed Cas by his shoulders and tried to haul him to his feet. Cas reached up, gripping Aran by the arm. 'Aran, wait, I just . . .' Then he slipped back down with a thump, looking confused.

Aran crouched, looking into his friend's eyes. They were wide but unfocused, and Aran didn't know what this meant.

Then he heard a twig snap nearby and his heart lifted. Akmid, it must be, sent back by their father to bring Aran home. He would smirk and gloat, but he wouldn't leave them out here. Not like this.

Through a curtain of falling snow, Aran could see the figure of a man on foot, coming closer. But it wasn't Akmid. In fact, it wasn't anyone he recognized.

It was a stranger, over six feet tall, clad in furs and leather. Aran could see a knife at his belt, a bow on his back. His hair was long and his brown-tinged face was all but hidden behind a tangled black beard. Deep within that thicket of hair shone a pair of wild eyes. They darted back and forth, finally fixing on Aran as the boy rose to his feet, standing protectively over Cas, his hand on the hilt of his knife.

'Who goes there?' Aran asked, and this time the challenge sounded almost convincing.

The stranger staggered towards Aran, his arms outstretched. Aran drew his knife and put his arms up to defend himself, then the man was on him.

In the courtyard of Hawk's Cross, the wind had almost abated. A watchman stood on duty at the top of the ramp which led down into the farmstead. He stamped his feet, impatient for the last stragglers to find their way home. There were two of them, he knew, the Law's youngest and that little friend of his. Both of them should know better.

In its glass case on the wall, the candle had almost guttered out. The wick was loose in a pool of wax, the flame barely a blue flicker. It had been lit when the gates were opened at daybreak, and when it died those same steel gates would seal shut for the night.

Hawk's Cross may have been the wealthiest farmstead in the region, with seven levels of living quarters and washrooms, brick-lined tunnels and winding stairwells. But they had rules like anywhere else, and it was the watchman's duty to make sure those rules were observed. If you didn't have rules, people died. It was that simple.

So he stood, scratching his chin and peering out across the courtyard, past the higgledy collection of stables and stockrooms and out into the valley beyond. He might be the last man on Earth, he thought. Alone within an endless sea of white.

Above his head towered the chapel, jutting from the cliff face like the prow of a ship. He could dimly hear a thin, metallic whisper as the wind howled around the great brass bell. Any moment now, he would haul on the rope and that bell would ring out one last, doleful chime.

He hoped the boy made it back, he really did. He might be a little Lawling, always finely dressed and well fed. But at least he didn't act as if everyone in the farmstead was put there purely to serve him, like that older brother.

The flame of the candle flickered, sputtered and died. The watchman sighed and took off his thick leather gloves. Then he spat on his hands and took hold of the knotted rope. When the bell chimed, his fellows inside the farmstead would haul on the lever, the cogs would turn and the counterweights would swing, then the gates would rattle shut.

He wondered what the Law would say when they told him that his son had not returned. And he wondered how strict those rules would turn out to be.

He raised his arms, ready to give the rope one mighty pull. But as he did so, he thought he saw movement, out beyond the courtyard wall.

Good lad, he thought. Cutting it fine, but better late than not at all.

Then the snow eddied and swirled, and through it he saw not a boy but a man, and a big one. He had something

11

slung over one shoulder, something limp and lifeless. The watchman swallowed hard and grabbed for his sword, ready to pull on the rope and seal the doors.

But a voice cried, 'Wait!' and now the watchman realized that there was more than one figure approaching. At the man's heels came a smaller shape, and in the lantern light he recognized the Law's boy.

'Hold the gate!' Aran cried.

The watchman held his sword out as the big stranger lumbered across the courtyard. He dumped Cas's limp body into the snow and stepped towards the watchman, who took a step back. The stranger's eyes rolled wildly, and his breath came hard and heavy.

'Have you seen her?' he demanded in a voice both harsh and distant. He swayed queasily from side to side, his eyelids fluttering. 'I have to find her. I found the boy but . . . She was there, and just . . . Wait, I don't . . .'

Then a look of confusion crossed his face and he fell, toppling on his belly in the snow.

There was a long silence. The watchman inched forward, prodding at the massive frame with the point of his sword. The figure stirred but did not get up.

'He saved us,' Aran explained through chattering teeth. 'I think he's lost his family.' He turned to Cas, who was lying on his back, his face pale and strangely peaceful. 'We need to get them inside,' he said.

The watchman frowned. 'I'll carry your friend. But we should check with the Law about the big fella. He could be trouble.'

'We can't just leave him,' Aran insisted.

'I'm not sure that—'

'I won't let him die,' Aran interrupted firmly. 'I'll clear it with my father.'

The watchman's eyes narrowed, then he nodded once. 'Your funeral,' he said, and hauled twice on the bell rope.

A pair of guards came hurrying up the ramp, muttering. But they stopped when they saw the stranger, lying prone. The watchman slung Cas over one shoulder and the guards half carried, half dragged the stranger down the ramp and into the entrance hall, where flickering lanterns framed the stone gateway. Gideon's banner hung overhead, emblazoned with the symbol of the falcon and the crucifix.

They strode down the spiral steps and through the maze of torchlit tunnels to the infirmary. Curious faces peered from doorways, whispering excitedly.

The guards heaved the stranger into a bed close to the infirmary door. Aran stood, studying his face. The man was old, he could see that now. His hair and beard were streaked with grey and fine wrinkles gathered on his brow and in the corners of his eyes. His clothes were tattered and many of them seemed to be handmade from the pelts of wolves, deer and even bears. But there was something in his face which spoke to Aran, even in this unconscious state: a noble quality belied by the man's ragged appearance.

A fire crackled in the grate. A white-robed sister bustled around the bed, unbuttoning the stranger's jackets and warming him with her hands. Behind her, Aran could see another nurse bending over Cas, mopping the blood from his forehead. Cas's eyes flickered open and he looked over at Aran, smiling faintly.

Aran was about to cross to him when a voice boomed through the open doorway. 'What do you mean, Aran gave the order?' it demanded. 'Since when has my son given you orders to do anything?'

Aran could hear the watchman's voice, explaining and apologizing. Then his father appeared.

Law Carifax ducked as he came into the infirmary, flanked by two of his personal guards. The lamplight gleamed on his shaved ebony scalp. His tight leather waistcoat squeaked as he bent and peered at the unconscious stranger.

'So this was your doing, was it?' he asked, fixing Aran with a stern stare, his massive grey eyebrows gathering at the bridge of his broad, flat nose. 'We have rules for a reason, Aran. You don't just bring strangers in from the forest in the dead of winter. That's how raids happen.'

Aran blushed. He was about to explain himself when the stranger stirred and his eyes fluttered. Aran, Law Carifax and the guards drew closer.

The man groaned and mumbled under his breath. Then his eyes widened suddenly and he sat up, staring about in confusion. 'Where am I?' he demanded. The guards leaped forward, taking the man by both arms.

'You're in the farmstead at Hawk's Cross,' said Carifax quickly. 'You're safe.'

The man struggled, kicking and baring his teeth. 'Let

me go!' he demanded. 'You don't understand. I have to find them. Are they here? Have you seen them?'

'Seen who?' Carifax cut in. He put his hand on the man's arm, holding his gaze.

The stranger calmed slowly, his fight subsiding. Then he shook his head, as though trying to recall something. 'I have to find them,' he muttered. 'They're lost and gone. All lost.'

'Who is?' Carifax asked softly. 'Who is lost?'

The man looked up, and there was infinite sadness behind his eyes. Aran almost gasped at the depth of it. 'My wife,' said the stranger in a weak, cracking voice. 'My wife and my boy. One moment they were there, the next . . . gone. They can't take care of themselves, not without me. They need me. I have to find them.'

He started up, but Law Carifax pushed him back with one firm hand. 'Listen to me,' he said. 'It's too dangerous.'

The man shook his head. 'No, you don't—'

'Listen,' Carifax repeated solemnly. 'Stay here tonight. Eat, get your strength back. In the morning I'll send out all the men I can spare and we'll find your family, if they're still alive. It's possible they've found their way to a neighbouring farmstead, or taken shelter in the forest. We know all the places to look. I'll not stop you if you insist on going, but you won't live to see the morning, I can guarantee that. For your family's sake, stay.'

The man looked long and hard at Law Carifax, as though deciding whether to trust him.

'We eat in one hour,' Carifax said softly. 'Take your

15

rest and I'll have my son find you some clean clothes. You should thank Aran. He may have saved your life.'

The stranger looked at Aran and smiled for the first time. Then he nodded and sank back, closing his eyes.

Law Carifax drew Aran outside, crouching in the hallway, his face grave. 'I'm giving you this responsibility, Aran,' he said. 'You brought him in, so you can take care of him. But you should bear in mind he could be dangerous. I think we both know that.'

Aran opened his mouth to object, but the Law quieted him with a look. 'I know he saved Cas's life, but he's a big man and we know little about him. There's no sense taking risks. When he wakes up, bring him to dinner. But make sure he's watched. Keep the guards with you at all times. Promise me.'

Aran nodded. 'I promise,' he said.

'Very good,' said Carifax, squeezing his son's arm. 'And if it makes you feel better, I like the look of him too. I don't know why. He seems oddly familiar. I'm trying to think, but . . .' A pensive expression came over his face, and he looked searchingly at his son. Then he shook his head. 'Most unusual.'

Aran returned to the infirmary, where both Cas and the stranger were snoring gently. He sank into a chair, and soon felt his head nodding as the warmth of the fire and the weariness in his bones overcame him.

CHAPTER TWO
The Dream

Aran woke with a start, looking towards the stranger's bed. It was empty, the sheets thrown back. His heart began to pound. With the exception of Cas, fast asleep in the corner, the infirmary was deserted. Where were the guards? Aran ran to the door, looking out into the corridor. Nothing. He had failed, and in such a simple task.

Then a noise made him turn round. The stranger stood in the doorway to the adjoining washroom. 'I wanted to change,' he said. The two guards appeared at his back. 'And these two take their orders rather literally. Sorry if we frightened you.'

Aran shook his head in disbelief. The stranger looked like a different person. His hand-stitched attire was gone, replaced by one of Carifax's best waistcoats. His hair was tied into a long ponytail which fell forward over one shoulder. His oak-brown skin, just a shade darker than Aran's own, had been scrubbed until it gleamed. Aran looked up at his face and felt an odd sense of familiarity, an echo somewhere in the very depths of his mind.

The stranger smiled and put out his hand. 'You're Aran,' he said, in a resonating voice. 'Pleased to make your acquaintance.' He held Aran's gaze for a long, silent moment, then let go of the boy's hand. 'I believe your father mentioned something about dinner?'

Aran led the stranger down the winding stone stairwell to the great hall. The sound of chatter and clattering cookware rose up to meet them. But as they reached the archway the sounds stopped dead, and every head turned.

Rumours of the stranger's arrival had swept through Hawk's Cross, and every one of the long oak tables was filled. People crowded into doorways and into the alcoves along the back wall, peering around the pillars to get a better view. Many had come straight from the brewery or the carpentry shop, still in their leather aprons and woollen leggings, their faces filthy with sweat and malt and wood shavings. Children stared with wide eyes, and even the servers stopped to take a look.

At the head table, Aran's mother got to her feet, her elegant cream-coloured robe sighing as she stood. Finding herself alone, she reached down and grabbed her husband's collar, giving it a sharp tug. Law Carifax looked up, startled, grease dripping down his chin. He spotted the stranger and put down his cup, clambering upright with a warm, genuine smile.

'Welcome, friend,' said the Law, wiping his hand

across his mouth then holding it out for the stranger to shake. 'Please, join us. Allow me to introduce my wife, Elena.'

Lady Carifax extended a tentative hand. The stranger smiled, bowing to kiss her thin white fingers. 'My Lady,' he said. The colour rose almost imperceptibly in the Lady's cheeks, and her pale eyes glittered beneath the straight black frame of her hair.

'Husband,' she hissed. 'Offer our guest a chair.'

Carifax gestured to an empty place at the table. 'Come,' he said jovially. 'Sit. Eat.'

The stranger took his seat, nodding to the other occupants of the table – Solly the Foreman, Aran's tutor Miss Crell, Akmid, Keller and a small collection of the Law's close advisers. He piled his plate with meat and tucked in heartily.

Aran sat opposite, unable to tear his eyes away. Looking around the table he saw others doing the same, watching as the stranger ripped into a leg of lamb. The hall rang with whispers.

Law Carifax filled the stranger's cup and put a hand on his arm. 'That's quite an appetite you have there, friend,' he said.

The stranger nodded. 'It's a while since I had the opportunity to satisfy it,' he said through a mouthful of meat. Then he paused, gazing appreciatively across the hall with its frescoed dome and chandeliers dripping with wax. 'This is a magnificent farmstead, the finest I've seen for many years.'

'I'm flattered,' said Carifax, beaming. 'And what exactly do you do, Mr . . .'

'I'm a hunter,' said the stranger. 'I trade furs and meat.'

Carifax nodded, but Aran could tell that his father didn't quite trust this explanation. There was a wildness in the man, but he didn't seem like a tracker. He was educated, and noticeably well spoken. It was as though he was several different people at once – part hunter, part family man, part scholar, perhaps even part Law.

Even Keller seemed impressed, his granite face growing almost animated as he discussed with him the best way to bring down a wild animal.

'With a wolf or a dog,' the stranger said authoritatively, 'you've got a chance to fight him one on one. He's quicker than you, and often stronger, but you've got wits he doesn't have, and hopefully weapons too.'

Aran realized the entire hall was hushed, hanging on the stranger's words.

'But when you're dealing with a bear,' he went on, 'that's a different matter. It doesn't matter how smart you are, or what weapons you've got. A bear is always bigger, always stronger, and he doesn't stop until one of you is stone-cold dead. Usually you. So if you want to hunt bears, you have to have him finished off before he even knows you're there. Lay a trap, dig a pit, use arrows if you can shoot straight. But don't let him near you.'

'Have you ever fought the Marauders?' Aran asked eagerly.

'Aran, for Ala's sake,' Akmid said. He turned to the

stranger. 'My brother's tutor loves to fill his head with these ridiculous stories.'

The stranger shook his head slowly. 'No, I don't believe I've encountered those particular individuals. I'm thankful. The tales I've heard . . . they don't bear repeating.' Then his expression grew deadly serious. 'I have fought men, though. Alone and in packs. In my opinion, they're more dangerous than any bear.'

'Why do you say that?' Aran asked.

The stranger fixed him with a penetrating stare. 'With a bear,' he said, 'with any animal, you know what it's after, and why. It wants to eat you, or it wants to protect its young. Either way, it's simple, and when it's over, it's over. But a man's motives are never simple. You could look into his face for a year and never know what he's thinking. That's what makes him dangerous.

'And a man never forgets,' he went on. 'He keeps coming back, compounding treachery with treachery, until you have no choice but to kill him, however horrible that idea might be to you.'

This is another side of him, Aran thought. The soldier, hard-faced and practical. The voice of cold reason and bitter experience.

'But in one thing, man and bear are alike,' the stranger finished. 'If you have to kill him, it's best done when he least expects it.'

Aran frowned. 'That doesn't sound very honourable.'

The stranger smiled. 'If it's a choice between honour and survival,' he said, 'I know which I'd prefer.'

Law Carifax looked uncomfortable. 'Let's hope none of us has to make that distinction any time soon,' he said, closing the subject.

After dinner, the hall was cleared and a band struck up. People began to dance before the fire, and there was a giddy atmosphere the like of which Aran had not felt since the coming of winter.

It was all down to the stranger's presence – he joked and told stories, sang songs and danced with the prettiest girls. Aran could see him now, his arm around the waist of a long-limbed cropper's daughter just a year older than Aran. Lissie, they called her. Aran could recall a game of Sardines down on the sixth level, crammed face to face in a broom closet, biting back laughter as Cas roamed the halls outside, calling their names. He'd felt Lissie's breath and seen her cheeks flush red.

But not as red as they were now, as the stranger whirled her from the stairway to the fireplace and back again. The girl bit her lip and clung on, letting out an involuntary squeal which turned to breathless laughter as the stranger bent her back over his arm, her crow-black hair tumbling loose and almost touching the stone flag floor.

Aran could not equate this carefree spirit with the man he had encountered in the snow only hours before. He sat on the sidelines, watching as the stranger turned to Lady Carifax with an exaggerated bow. He took her by the hand, waltzing her down the hall before spinning her into the waiting arms of her husband, who had been watching suspiciously. There was a round of applause, but the stranger waved it away, chuckling.

He collapsed onto the bench beside Aran, breathing hard. 'Oh, I'd forgotten the simple pleasures of good company,' he said. 'It gets lonely, the huntsman's life.'

'What about your family?' Aran asked.

The stranger looked at him quizzically, as though he had no idea what Aran was talking about.

'Your wife and son?' Aran insisted. 'Your family?'

The stranger shook his head, and his eyes darkened like clouds across the sun. His whole body seemed to tighten. 'I don't know what you're talking about,' he hissed, placing one hand on top of Aran's and squeezing hard.

Aran almost cried out, but something in the stranger's gaze made the breath catch in his throat. The big man's grip tightened, and his eyes flashed with fury.

Then a hand fell on the stranger's arm and he raised his head. Lissie was tugging on his sleeve. 'The fiddler says his arm is growing tired,' she complained, barely casting a glance Aran's way. 'He says this is the last one.'

In an instant, the stranger's expression broke. His eyes lit up and a grin spread across his face. He slammed his cup down on the bench. 'Nonsense!' he cried. 'That layabout, we'll see about him.' He leaped up and slipped an arm around the girl's waist. 'Another jig!' he bellowed. 'Come, fiddler, the night is young, and so are we!'

And he swung Lissie out into the centre of the hall, between the dancing shadows of the roaring fire.

Aran left the hall, feeling unsteady and confused.

Perhaps this was simply a part of adult behaviour which he did not yet understand. Worrying would not help find the stranger's family. Why shouldn't he try to forget his troubles?

But it was more than that. He lay in the dark of his bedroom, going over everything in his head. It was as if the man had forgotten his family altogether. But in those first moments, his need to find them had been so overpowering. How could it just disappear?

Aran fell into a troubled sleep, the distant sounds of music ringing in his ears. He dreamed that he was alone in the darkling wood, helpless and weary. But he could not stop because he knew that something followed close behind, something ravening and treacherous and thirsty for his blood. At last he could go no further and collapsed on his face in the snow, weeping and terrified.

Aran was suddenly awake. Something had disturbed him, a noise or a movement, but he had no idea what. All he knew was that his eyes were open, and that all was quiet. He yawned and rolled over, and almost cried out in shock.

There was a woman standing at his bedside. She was not looking at Aran; her eyes were fixed on a point in space somewhere above his head. She wore a long white gown which seemed to shimmer with its own light. Her skin was pale and her yellow hair fell tangled over her bare shoulders. She stood utterly still, seeming somehow far away, though Aran could have touched her if he had put out his hand.

'Who are you?' he began. 'What do you want?'

The woman did not seem to hear him. She turned slowly towards the door, moving as though underwater. Everything was hushed and still. Aran held his breath.

There was a pounding crash. The wooden door shuddered on its hinges. Aran sat upright. The steel bolt was shot, but someone was trying to break through. There was another thud. Aran scrambled backwards, pulling the sheets up to his chin.

The woman raised her hand, holding her palm upright, facing the door. Then the wood splintered and the handle flew free, the door crashing inwards. The stranger entered, a knife in his hand. He stood silhouetted against the torchlight from the corridor. Aran stared at him, helpless and terrified.

'Where is she?' the stranger demanded.

Aran's eyes darted to his bedside. The woman had vanished. He had not heard her move, but somehow she had disappeared. Had the stranger even seen her at all?

He advanced into the room, looking down at Aran with furious eyes. 'You tell me, boy. You tell me where she is.'

'She . . . she was here,' Aran spluttered. 'She just disappeared.'

'You're lying,' the stranger spat, coming closer. 'Tell me what you've done with her.'

'It wasn't me,' Aran said. 'Please. I don't even know who she was.'

The stranger laughed. 'You expect me to believe you didn't recognize your own mother?'

Aran was sure of it now: the man was insane. He looked

desperately around the tiny bedroom. He had stashed his belt in the wardrobe; there was no way to reach the dagger hanging from it. There was a bow on the back of the door, but that was little more than a toy. Aran had no way to defend himself, and no way to escape.

The stranger seemed to fill the room. His eyes darted wildly. 'Come out,' he demanded loudly. 'It's the boy. He wants to see you.' He looked at Aran. 'Tell her,' he hissed. 'Tell her you want to see her.'

Aran coughed. 'Come out,' he said uncertainly. 'I want to see you.'

The stranger nodded. 'Call her by her name.'

Aran looked at him helplessly. The stranger's face fell. 'Don't play games. How could you forget?' He turned and shouted out, 'Sara! Show yourself!'

'Sara?' Aran called out weakly. 'Sara, are you there?'

The stranger growled, turning on Aran. 'Sound like you mean it,' he said, 'or I'll make sure you do.' And he advanced, his sharp blade glistening.

'Get away from him!' came a voice. Law Carifax stood in the doorway, a flaming torch in one hand, a drawn sword in the other. A quartet of armoured guards clustered at his back.

The stranger backed away, looking around in desperation. 'Sara?' he cried. 'I can't see you. I know you're here. Please.'

The guards advanced, but the stranger fought, striking out with his knife and fists. One man fell, red gushing down his face.

Another guard moved in, taking hold of the stranger from behind. They careened off the walls, smashing into Aran's bedside table, scattering wooden soldiers. The guard was strong but the stranger was bigger, throwing himself back against the wall, squeezing the breath from the guard's body. He crashed to the floor, gasping.

The stranger's eyes darted around the room, fixing on nothing. 'Sara!' he cried again. 'I hear you! I'm coming!' And he let out a roar, barging past Law Carifax and straight into the last two guards, sending them flying.

He disappeared into the corridor and the guards gave chase, followed by the Law. Aran flung his blankets aside and pursued them, his heart hammering.

Sounds reverberated down the narrow spiral stairwell: pounding feet, followed by the clash of metal on metal. Aran ran headlong, his nightgown flapping around his ankles. He heard a cry of pain, followed by a chorus of shouts, all blending together to form an indistinct clamour. Then, over it all, the stranger's voice. 'Open it, or I'll cut his throat!'

Aran reached the top of the stairs and flung himself into the entrance hall.

The steel-plated gate stood shut against the night. At the bottom of the ramp stood the stranger, an unconscious guard headlocked under one arm, a knife to his throat.

Carifax's soldiers fanned out around their Law, swords drawn. One lay prone at the stranger's feet, blood pooling around his head. At the far end of the hall Aran could see the gateman, his eyes wide, one hand on the lever.

'I mean it!' the stranger cried. 'You let me go! I have to get her back!'

Carifax held out his hands in a gesture of conciliation. 'Be calm now, friend,' he said. 'You don't want to—'

The stranger jabbed with his knife, and a pin-drop of red bloomed on his captive's throat. 'Open it!' the stranger bellowed, his voice cracking.

Then he caught sight of Aran watching from the archway, and his face fell. He lowered the knife, looking directly at the boy who stood, shivering, on the cold floor. 'I'm so disappointed in you,' he said, and there again was that terrible sadness, flowing from his tear-stained eyes.

The stranger dropped the unconscious guard to the floor and turned. To Aran's astonishment he ran headlong up the ramp, barrelling bodily into the solid steel gate. The metal shook, but it did not bend or buckle. The stranger recoiled, shaking his head. Then he ran again, lowering his body like a battering ram. This time he left a thin smear of blood on the metal sheeting.

'For Ala's sake,' the Law cried, 'somebody stop him.' But when one of the guards tried to approach the stranger turned, baring his teeth and lashing out with his knife.

He ran at the gate for a third time, stumbling to his knees with the force of the impact. His blood ran in rivulets between the steel plates. Aran could see the pain and confusion on his face. He was like an animal, unable to understand what was happening to him.

'Please, Father,' Aran cried out. 'Open it. Let him go.'

Carifax saw his son and turned. 'Aran, get back to your bed. Now.'

There was another crash. The stranger's hair was matted with blood and he was becoming unsteady. 'Please,' Aran almost screamed, tears running down his face. 'Open it.'

Carifax looked at his son, then at the stranger. A battle raged behind his eyes. Then he turned reluctantly to the gateman and nodded. The man leaned on the lever and the cogs groaned and began to turn.

The stranger took a step back, looking up at the rising gate and the ragged, gold-trimmed banner hanging above it. Blood ran freely down his face, into his eyes and his beard.

A bitter wind howled into the farmstead, bringing gusts of snow. Aran shielded his eyes. The stranger stood alone. The wind rose, and it sounded as though the whole world was screaming; whether in rage or agony Aran could not say.

Then suddenly the stranger was gone. He had bolted through the widening gap and vanished into the night.

Aran ran to the bottom of the ramp, looking up into the midnight darkness. But the man had been swallowed by the shadows.

Snow caught in Aran's hair and melted on his upturned cheeks. His father stepped up behind him, putting an arm around the boy's shoulders. 'He won't live to see morning,' he said. 'You can be sure of that.' But there was an edge of sadness in his voice.

Aran nodded. He knew he ought to tell his father about

the mysterious woman in his room. But now he was no longer sure if he'd seen her at all. Perhaps he'd still been dreaming, and it was only when the stranger had broken in that he'd truly come awake. He was a madman, that was all. Just a simple, confused huntsman, looking for his lost family. His wife and son. His Sara.

CHAPTER THREE

The Wager

The Moon of the Wolf waned, giving way to the Moon of New Leaves. The snow melted and the weather turned. The farmstead rose from its slumber, threw open its gates and welcomed the sun. The cattle roamed through dead fields, barely able to recall the world out of doors. The people wandered too, luxuriating in the smell of fresh earth and the touch of the breeze. Soon it would be time for the real work to begin: the spring planting, and preparations for Carny. But for now, a moment's peace.

The memory of that winter night had already begun to fade from Aran's mind. If he thought about it at all it was as a distant dream, remote and unreal. But the fear still lingered. The helplessness he had felt when the stranger came crashing through his bedroom door. The knowledge that he had no way to defend himself. Very well, he thought. If his father refused to let him learn to fight, Aran would take matters into his own hands.

Which was how he came to find himself, late one golden evening, up in the armoury on the surface with Cas and their friend Mohanna, wondering where to start.

'Just look at it all.' Mohanna took a step back, marvelling at the racks of swords and spears, bows and pikes, armour and arrows. Her green eyes shone beneath the scarlet tangle of her hair. 'You could hold off an army of Marauders with this lot.'

She'd ridden over that morning from her home at Crowdale, and her tattered riding jacket was spattered with mud. Not that Mohanna seemed to care; she was far more interested in an iron broadsword with a blade longer than her arm.

'You don't have an armoury at home?' Aran asked. Crowdale was a poor farmstead, stuck out on the high moors, but surely they could afford to defend themselves.

Mohanna shrugged. 'A few rusty swords and a couple of old bows,' she admitted. 'Most likely stolen from your lot during the Long Vendetta. Nothing like this.' She hefted the sturdy blade. 'Do you ever imagine what it must have been like, our farmsteads at war? You two would have been my mortal enemies. And if anyone caught me in here they'd cut my throat without thinking twice.' She drew the sword across her neck with a grimace, crossing her eyes and sticking out her tongue.

Aran laughed. 'If Law Darnell heard you'd been playing in our armoury, the whole thing might start up again,' he said.

Mohanna smiled ruefully. 'If my father heard about half the things we get up to, he'd string me up by my ankles,' she agreed.

'So would Law Carifax,' muttered Cas bitterly.

'Then we'll just have make sure he doesn't find out,' Aran shot back irritably. Why did Cas always have to ruin things by being sensible?

The chapel bell tolled and they heard the sound of footsteps in the courtyard outside, the cattlemen and croppers wending their weary way back from the fields. The light had almost vanished from the sky.

'I just don't see what we're doing here,' Cas hissed. 'It's not like you're going to learn how to fight just by looking at a sword.'

'I'm not just going to look,' Aran told him. He scanned the racks for an appropriate blade, one befitting a beginner. 'Keller won't miss just one. Here, this looks—'

A noise cut him off. A creak like rusted hinges, followed by a scuffling thud. The colour drained from Cas's face and his lower lip began to tremble.

Aran stepped to the door, peering through a crack in the planks. The courtyard was empty except for the watchman, dozing in the slanting sunshine.

'There's no one there,' Aran said, but his voice had lowered to a whisper.

The noise came again. It was closer now, and definitely human. Two sets of feet, and hushed voices.

'I told you!' Cas hissed, his face turning pale. 'I told you we shouldn't be here!'

'There's no one there,' Aran insisted. 'I swear, the courtyard's deserted, I don't see how— Oh.'

But realization had come too late. In unison, their eyes lowered.

The access hatch was only used in emergencies, a back way into the armoury in case of a really severe storm. They didn't even bother to keep it bolted.

With a crash the hatch flew open and someone came clambering up the steps, breathing hard. Cas retreated instinctively behind Aran. Mohanna shrank back against the wall.

It was Akmid, glancing fearfully over his shoulder. He stopped as he saw the three children watching him, their mouths hanging open. 'What are you doing here?' he hissed. He was dripping with sweat and there was a tremor in his voice which made Aran uneasy.

Keller sprang up the steps behind Akmid, slamming and barring the hatch. He turned and saw Aran, and his eyes narrowed above his snarling, scarred lip. There was a long, awkward silence.

'How did we end up here?' Aran said, backing towards the door and trying his best to look innocently confused. 'We must have taken a wrong turning. Cas, honestly . . .'

'Stop,' said Akmid in a low voice, before Aran could lay a hand on the door. 'Just stay there. And keep your voice down. He might still be after us.'

'Who?' Aran whispered.

Akmid's face flushed. 'None of your business,' he said.

'The cook,' Keller grunted. 'Your brother tried to nick a

34

barrel of barley beer from the storeroom. Pretty stupid.'

'But you told me to do it!' Akmid protested, turning on him with a look of betrayal.

Keller shrugged. 'You do everything I tell you? I'm not your father. Anyway, I didn't tell you to get caught.'

Akmid fumed, and for a moment he looked just as he had when he and Aran were boys, being punished for stealing sugar twists. Aran couldn't help laughing.

Akmid glared and raised his fist. 'I'd like to see you do better,' he said.

Aran sneered. 'No problem,' he said. 'I pinch stuff from the storeroom all the time.'

Keller raised an eyebrow. 'Like what?' he asked.

Aran shrugged. 'Barley beer,' he said. 'Wine sometimes, fruit pies, um, cheese . . .'

Akmid scowled. 'Why would you steal cheese?'

Aran had no answer. He'd never stolen anything in his life. But it was too late now, the lie had been told. 'I like cheese,' he said weakly.

'Proper little crook,' said Keller appreciatively. 'Shame it doesn't run in the family.'

Akmid flushed. 'He's talking complete dung,' he said. 'My brother couldn't steal honey apples from a baby.'

'I could too,' Aran shot back, bristling. 'I could take anything I wanted. The cook wouldn't even know I was there.' He glanced at Cas and Mohanna. They stared back helplessly.

'Oh, this is ridiculous,' Akmid snorted. 'I bet you anything he'd be caught before he put one foot in the door.'

'A wager?' Keller said. 'That's not a bad idea. What do you say, boy?'

Aran's face felt suddenly hot. Everything seemed to be happening too quickly, and he had no time to stop and think. 'Sure,' he said, surprising himself. 'You're on.'

'What would you want in return?' Akmid asked. 'Besides bragging rights?'

Aran thought. If he was going to accept this ridiculous challenge, he might as well gain something from it. 'I get to come in here whenever I want,' he said. 'With whoever I want. We get to use all this stuff. And you don't tell Father.'

Akmid looked at Keller, who nodded. 'Fair,' he said.

'OK,' Aran said, not knowing if this was his greatest idea ever, or his most idiotic. 'Name your stake.'

Akmid leaned over and whispered to Keller. A broad smile spread slowly over his face and he began to nod. 'Perfect,' he said.

Akmid was barely able to contain his smugness. 'You said you'd get anything we asked for?' he said.

Aran nodded. What was it going to be? A crate of sweet wine, a keg of apple cider? The cook's special smoke-weed?

'You can fetch me . . .' Akmid said slowly, 'one side of beef.'

Aran's jaw dropped. 'That's half a cow!' he protested. 'What do you need it for?'

Akmid shook his head. 'Doesn't matter why,' he said. 'You said you'd get anything.'

'But . . .' Aran spluttered. 'But that's just . . .' If he tried to back out he'd be humiliated, or worse. 'All right,' he said. 'But I'll need some time to plan.'

Keller nodded. 'This time tomorrow,' he said.

Aran hung his head. Cas and Mohanna hurried to join him by the hatch. Then a thought struck Aran and he turned back. 'What happens if I lose?' he asked.

Keller's teeth gleamed in the dim light. He raised his hand, stretching the fingers so that his knuckles cracked one by one. Then he made a fist. 'Don't,' he said.

But as they crouched in the tunnel behind a stack of empty barrels, peering out towards the kitchen door, Aran knew that his biggest problem wasn't Keller's threat of punishment. It wasn't even the size of the prize, which he still wasn't sure they could lift between the three of them. No, his biggest problem was the cook.

If they'd agreed to steal from anyone else, Aran couldn't have cared less. Most of the citizens of Hawk's Cross – the planters and croppers, the brewers, blacksmiths and cattlemen – were so busy they wouldn't notice anything missing until it was too late. But not the cook. In addition to possessing the shortest temper in the farmstead, he was also renowned for his keen eye and precise knowledge of the storeroom's inventory. Akmid had barely taken three steps before the cook had noticed the missing beer. They had to get the meat to a safe place before he even knew it was gone.

Right now, however, there was no sign of him. The

entire second level seemed deserted. The only sounds were the distant hum of conversation from the dining hall below and the soft babble of water from the end of the tunnel, where a diverted stream ran through stone channels into the kitchen and the washrooms.

'I think the coast's clear,' Aran whispered. His eyes glinted in the flickering torchlight.

Cas shook his head. 'It's too soon,' he said, an edge of panic in his voice. 'He's still in there. You just can't see him.'

Crouched behind them in the alcove, Mohanna sighed. 'He said it's clear,' she said. 'Stop stalling, shrimp.'

Cas glowered. 'I'm the one who's been watching him all day,' he said. 'I think I know a little bit about his routine.'

Aran peered down at the piece of paper in Cas's shaking hand, a crude map drawn in charcoal. A circle with stick limbs represented the cook, and a line of dots marked the route they expected him to take: along the corridor to the main stairwell, then down to the great hall to dish up dinner. Their own location was marked by three little crosses.

Cas folded the paper and stuffed it back in his pocket. 'I don't like it,' he said. 'If we went with my plan . . .'

'Oh, not this again,' Mohanna sighed. 'You seriously want to string up a net so it falls on the cook? He'd murder us.'

'But that's the beauty of it,' Cas argued. 'He'll never know who did it!'

'Right,' said Mohanna. 'Because Hawk's Cross is filled

with people who make daft traps. I mean, when has one of them ever worked the way you wanted it to?'

'What about my pheasant-catcher?' Cas asked, bristling.

'The pheasant ran away!' Mohanna retorted incredulously. 'His feet were sticking out the bottom!'

'Yes, but he was still in the trap,' Cas pointed out. 'For all you know, he still is.'

'God's beard, stop bickering!' Aran snapped. 'I made this deal, and I intend to honour it. But I don't expect you two to put yourselves at risk if you don't feel up to it.'

'Don't be daft,' Mohanna hissed impatiently. All she cared about was the task ahead. They could worry about the consequences later. 'Let's just get on with it.'

'Cas?' Aran turned to his friend. 'This is my responsibility. You don't have to be involved.'

Cas held Aran's gaze. The consequences if they were caught would be most severe for him – he wasn't a Law's child, like Aran and Mohanna. The cook would demand punishment, and somebody would have to take the fall. But Cas knew that the plan couldn't work without him. And besides, this was his place, at Aran's side, making sure he didn't get into more trouble than he could handle. He sighed and lowered his eyes. 'I'm in,' he said.

Aran grinned. It would be worth it just to see the look on his brother's face. Whatever may come, let it come.

'All right,' he said. 'Let's go.'

They had almost reached the kitchen door when the cook's voice boomed out and sent them scurrying back to the safety of the alcove.

'I don't care if your fingers are worn to the bone, I want them clean!' the voice roared. 'Just because you're a lazy slob doesn't mean you should make the rest of us suffer.'

Aran thought his heart was going to burst. That had been too close.

'I told you he was still in there,' whispered Cas. Mohanna scowled at him.

'Put your back into it, for Ala's sake,' the cook barked from the doorway. 'Scrub, man! Scrub!' Then he marched from the kitchen with a sigh of disgust, his bulky frame filling the narrow corridor. There was a crash and a cry of 'Out of my way, cretin!' Then he was gone.

Silence descended. Cautiously, Aran led them back out into the open. Cas broke away, ducking into a side passage which led up to the surface. Mohanna and Aran took flanking positions on opposite sides of the kitchen doorway.

Aran peered inside. Through clouds of vapour he could see a lone kitchen hand, up to his elbows in filthy water. His back was to the door and he was muttering resentfully. Steam billowed from an iron pot suspended over an open fire-cage in the centre of the room.

Aran and Mohanna slipped inside, ducking under the chopping table on their hands and knees. Then they ran, pressing themselves against the storeroom door. Neither of them dared breathe as they inched it open and slid silently through.

Aran dropped the latch and they fell back, breathing hard. The storeroom was silent. In the darkness, a rich confusion of smells assaulted their nostrils: meat, smoked and raw; fish and poultry; herbs, fresh and dry – lavender, thyme and rosemary. They followed the wall with out-stretched hands, stopping when Aran felt a cool breeze on his face.

'Here,' he whispered.

It was the ventilation shaft, an almost vertical tunnel which ran all the way up to the surface a hundred feet above. All the rooms in the farmstead had one. Some were wide enough for a man to crawl through, others were just narrow chimneys connected to the central shaft. But the storeroom vent doubled as a delivery chute, so it was broad and lined with bricks.

Aran peered into the shaft, squinting at the tiny circle of daylight high above. Something moved against the light. He heard a rustling, coming closer. The end of a rope. He took hold and gave a firm tug. He felt an answering pull from Cas.

'Here's one.' Mohanna's voice floated out of the dark-ness. She'd located a sizeable side of beef hanging nearby, skinned and drained but not yet cured. Aran took hold with both hands and tried to lift it. The meat was clammy against his cheek and the smell of blood was sickening. Between them they managed to loosen the hook and lower the beef carefully to the ground.

Aran took the rope, tying it around the back leg. The plan was simple. Between them they would shove the meat up into the shaft, taking the weight while Cas tied the rope to a tree. Then they would sneak out of the storeroom and all three of them would haul it the rest of the way. Aran couldn't wait to see his brother's face when they appeared, carrying the prize aloft on their shoulders, their faces gleaming with victorious pride . . .

'Aran, stop dreaming,' Mohanna hissed loudly. 'Lift your end.'

Aran blinked. Together they dragged the meat up to the vent. Aran yanked on the rope and felt it pull tight. They shoved from beneath, forcing their burden up into the opening. Aran caught Mohanna's eye and grinned. They were going to make it. He pushed hard and the beef slid up another foot, and another, into the sloping shaft.

'Nearly there,' he said out loud, resisting the urge to laugh. This was just too easy.

'Nearly where?' came a booming voice from the doorway.

Aran and Mohanna whipped round. The door was open, but they'd been so wrapped up in their task they hadn't heard a thing.

'I thought I heard rats in my pantry,' growled the cook, stepping into the room. 'Scampering down the delivery chute to feast on all my goodies.'

He took a step forward, holding up a flickering oil lamp. His face was red and monstrous in the greasy light. A pimple on his cheek oozed oil.

'I know you, young master,' said the cook. 'Just because you're the Law's son doesn't mean I won't give you a solid thrashing. And you too, missy. Law Darnell's good name can't protect you down here. You're in my world now.'

'You lay one finger on me and I'll make sure you regret it,' Mohanna snarled back. Aran looked at her in astonishment. Her face gleamed defiantly.

The cook laughed wickedly and advanced another pace, his arms spread wide. Something shone at his belt – a freshly sharpened cleaver, the keen blade winking in the lamplight. Aran held his breath. The cook's face filled his vision: the dripping cheeks, the glistening teeth. 'You want to mind your tongue with me,' the big man spat. 'I've skinned and boned bigger fish than you.' He advanced towards Mohanna, his fingers grasping at her arm.

Aran backed away, glancing over his shoulder. The door stood wide. If he ran, he might make it. Then the cook's hand fell on Mohanna's sleeve, pulling her towards him.

'Let go of me,' she cried, lashing out. Her fingernails tore across the cook's cheek, drawing blood, and he let out a howl of pain, which swiftly deepened into a roar of rage.

'You little divvle!' he shouted, dealing Mohanna a vicious slap which knocked her across the room into a rack of hanging meat. Aran gasped. Mohanna slumped to the floor.

Aran looked down at her on the stone, unmoving. Then he looked at the cook, at the cruel, satisfied glint in his eye. He felt his blood boil.

'That's not fair!' he shouted. 'She's my friend!'

He ran at the cook, flailing with his fists and his feet. But his blows rained harmlessly on soft, yielding flesh, and the cook flicked him away as easily as swatting a fly. Aran fell back against the wall. The cook bent over him, drawing the cleaver from his belt.

'Now,' he said, 'we'll see what happens to thieving little rats in my kingdom.'

There was a scraping sound from the wall beside them. The cook raised his head.

Cas stood at the top of the shaft, the rope burning his palms, sweat running into his eyes. He knew something was wrong. The meat seemed to weigh more with each passing second, and his arms were trembling with the strain. What was happening down there? He could hear distant voices, but could see nothing.

His knees began to buckle. His feet were slipping on the cobblestones. He knew he would have to let go or be dragged down into the chute. With an involuntary cry of pain he took a step back and opened his palms. The side of beef vanished from view.

The cook raised his lantern and peered into the ventilation shaft. For the briefest second, all was quiet.

Then the slab of meat thundered from the opening, striking the cook full in the face. He put up his hands in a feeble attempt to protect himself, but the beef was unstoppable. He was pinned to the floor, his arms and legs flailing helplessly. The glass in the lantern shattered and they were plunged into darkness.

Aran pulled Mohanna to her feet. They staggered to the doorway, into the light.

'Are you all right?' he asked. She nodded gratefully.

They fled through the kitchen. The cook's voice pursued them down the tunnel, cursing and spitting and calling on the Trinity to strike them down.

But Aran had no fear of the Gods; he had more earthly concerns. He knew that his father's wrath would find them, wherever they tried to hide.

CHAPTER FOUR

Departure

He didn't have long to wait. By late afternoon, Aran, Cas and Mohanna had been ordered up to Law Carifax's summer room to receive their punishment. Aran didn't think he'd ever get used to rooms with windows. It felt unnatural somehow, to be able to see the outside world but not feel it. He was far more comfortable underground.

A group of riders came pounding up the track towards the farmstead. Aran's throat tightened as he recognized his father among them. Please, he thought. Whatever punishment he has in store, please don't let him stop me going to Carny.

Law Carifax entered the office, slamming the door behind him. The glass in the window shook. Aran turned to face him.

The Law sank into his armchair, flattening his palms on the desk and glaring at the three children. 'I don't appreciate having to curtail a perfectly good hunt to deal with this nonsense,' he said. 'What would three fourteen-year-olds want with a side of beef, anyway?'

'We would have put it back,' Aran muttered.

The Law's eyes widened in surprise. 'Put it back? Why would you steal a thing if you were only going to put it back? Did someone put you up to this?'

Aran felt himself flinch. 'Aha!' said Carifax. 'I thought so. I didn't think even you would be stupid enough to try something like this unprompted. I sense craftier minds at work. Your brother and Keller, no doubt. Looking to make a fool of you, and you walked straight into it.'

Mohanna frowned. 'But we'd have made it if the cook hadn't—' She broke off, silenced by Carifax's disappointed frown.

'Young lady, you are your father's daughter,' he said. 'And it is for that reason that I have no right to punish you. I'll leave it to Law Darnell. Good luck trying to explain away that black eye.' He gestured to the glistening multi-coloured bruise which covered the entirety of Mohanna's left cheek, up to the hairline. Her face turned pale.

Carifax turned to Cas. 'As for you,' he said, 'you're supposed to be the smart one, aren't you? What on earth made you think this was a good idea?'

Cas mumbled and spluttered, but the words wouldn't come.

'I know, I know,' said the Law. 'My son can be very persuasive when he puts his mind to it. He's too charming for his own good. But he doesn't think of the consequences. That should be your job. One day Aran will be Foreman of this farmstead, and I'd hoped you might make a good Second to him when the time came. But if you carry on like this, I don't see how you'll ever be more than a labourer like your father.'

Cas looked at the floor. 'I'm sorry,' he managed.

Carifax nodded. 'I know,' he said, his voice beginning to soften. 'And I know you only went along because you care about Aran. Well, if you really cared about him, you would have stopped this foolishness before it got out of hand. I did think about ordering your father to keep you home from Carny, but that would be as much a punishment for him as for you. So I've offered you up as a potboy for the next week. I've told the cook not to bruise you too much. Right, off you go, both of you. I want to talk to my son.'

They obeyed silently, and Aran was left alone with his father.

'Oh, Aran,' said Carifax in frustration. 'You are not your brother, you know. Akmid has a task ahead of him, to protect Hawk's Cross and everyone who lives here. Keller was the best I could find to make him strong, make him tough, the way he has to be. But you have different abilities; a different path is laid for you.'

Aran frowned. 'A boring path,' he said.

Carifax sighed. 'Yes, I suppose it must feel that way sometimes. But what am I to do? It's a second son's responsibility to look after the running of the farmstead. I'm not going to overturn years of tradition just so you can go off and be a soldier or a sea captain or a travelling player, or whatever it is this week. I mean, what is it you want, really?'

'I don't know,' Aran said in frustration. 'I just want . . . more.'

He turned back to the window. From here he could look out over the courtyard, past the armoury and the livery stable and down across a sprawling patchwork of corn and wheat fields, apple orchards and shimmering pastures. A line of people wound down to the riverbank, hauling sloshing casks to feed the irrigation hoses.

Aran cast his gaze to the far horizon, where a shelf of craggy rock lifted its head above the greenery. Beyond that were the open moors, and beyond that . . . who knew?

'More?' Carifax asked. 'More than your home, more than your family? This is a better life than most people can even imagine. You'll always be safe here.'

'What if I don't want to be safe?' Aran shot back.

Carifax threw up his arms. 'What, then? It's a cruel world, Aran. You have to make the best of what you're given.'

Aran tore his eyes away. Perhaps his future really was written. What was the point in trying to fight it? 'It isn't fair,' he said.

Carifax's face fell. 'Maybe not,' he said, taking Aran's hand and giving it a squeeze. 'But this is the way things are. Don't try to be something you're not. You have a good heart and a sharp mind, use them. Leave the rough stuff to your brother.' His voice lowered, and he sounded almost sad. 'Trust me, you'll come to appreciate him for it, one day. He's giving up a lot for you. For everyone in Hawk's Cross.'

Aran sniffed and wiped a tear away.

'Now,' finished the Law. 'Your mother wanted me to keep you from Carny, but I told her it's good training for any Foreman. I won't ask what Keller's threatened, because I know you won't tell me. But I ask for the last time, stay out of trouble. You've got your own friends, you don't need to go bothering Akmid. Next time I won't be so forgiving. All right?'

He held Aran at arm's length, looking him square in the eye. Then he shook his head. 'Get out of my sight,' he said.

A week later, the day of departure came. Aran rose at first light, unable to contain his excitement.

The courtyard was already crowded. Horses stood saddled and bridled, or lashed to carts laden with crates and casks. Children raced across the cobblestones, armed with sticks and whips to keep the livestock in line. Dogs bounded alongside, yapping ecstatically. Aran saw the Law's horsemaster struggling to control a skittish mare who kicked up her heels at all the commotion.

The gate was raised and a steady stream of people passed up and down the ramp – guards in dress uniforms emblazoned with the winged crucifix; young men in their finest leathers, clean-shaven and reeking of oil; old men with minds firmly on the matter, their experienced fingers running over chicken coops, barrel lids, packing crates, cartwheels, tie-ropes, horseshoes, reins and blinkers. The older women marshalled the young, parcelling them out among the carts and keeping them clear of the bright-eyed boys.

Aran took his place at the head of the procession beside Law Carifax. This was the first year he had been allowed to ride a full-grown horse, and he felt ungainly perched atop the wide-shouldered animal. Behind them stood a carriage carrying Lady Carifax and Miss Crell, followed by Akmid on a piebald colt he'd been given for Exmus.

The bell in the chapel tolled and the courtyard fell silent. The librarian stepped forward to read the blessing, a diminutive figure in black robes, leaning on a yew cane.

'We call upon the Trinity to guide your steps and bring you safe home,' he spoke in a clear voice, his fingers threading restlessly through his long white beard. 'In the name of God, Law of the Heavens, the ghost in the wind and the voice in the thunder, may your skies be clear. In the name of Ala, Law of the Earth, the giver and Protector, may you find shelter at day's end. And in the name of Jess the Child, Law of Man, the life in us all, may your feet never tire. Amen Akba.'

'Amen Akba,' the crowd repeated solemnly.

They wound slowly down the track into the valley's long shadow. In their train came the carts, and finally the herds of braying, bleating livestock.

Aran glanced back up the hill towards the farmstead. Groups of children and old folk watched anxiously from the gate, waving to their loved ones and drying uninvited tears. The party would be gone for less than a week, but for many it was the only time they would ever spend apart.

They followed the river, crossing at the shallow place called Foster's Ford. As they crested the far bank, Aran saw movement in the trees. Through the budding branches came a dapple-grey mare, and on its back rode Mohanna, resplendent in a sky-blue frock with feathery white trimmings. Her flaming hair had been arranged into an ornate decorative pile. She spotted Aran and her face flushed.

'Child, you rein that animal in right now,' a voice bellowed from behind. 'If I see a spot of dirt on that dress, you'll scrub it yourself.'

The party from Crowdale hove into view, a collection of carts similar to their own, if a little shabbier and more sparsely laden. They were led by Law Darnell, a heavily built man with sallow skin and an unkempt mane of greasy black curls.

'I mean it.' He grabbed Mohanna's reins. 'Just because we're away from home doesn't mean you can behave like some highland savage. Remember your breeding.'

Darnell greeted Law Carifax with a curt nod and the two Laws shook hands dutifully.

'My Lady.' Aran rode alongside Mohanna, unable to keep the smirk off his face. 'You look simply delightful.'

'Get lost,' she muttered. 'When I finally persuaded my father to let me come to Carny, I didn't think it meant I'd have to dress up like a fairy princess.'

'Someone should have told him it's a cattle market, not a dinner dance.' Aran laughed.

'He just wants me to look nice,' said Mohanna, eyeing her father with a mixture of reproach and adoration. 'He picked it out himself. I suppose it is quite pretty. If you like that sort of thing.'

'Run along, if you like,' Darnell barked, barely looking at his daughter. 'But keep that dress clean!' Then he turned back to Carifax, rolling his eyes as if Mohanna was the bane of his existence.

Aran and Mohanna rode towards the back of the line, seeking out Cas in his father's rattling carriage. He lounged on a bed of hay, a reed stem between his teeth. They hitched their mounts to the cart and clambered in. Mohanna wriggled out of her constricting frock and waved her stockinged legs in the air.

'So how many people do you think will be there, altogether?' she asked.

Aran shrugged. 'About fifty thousand,' he said, plucking the number out of the air.

Mohanna gasped, then remembered herself. 'That's not so many,' she said casually.

'Well, maybe it's more,' said Aran. 'I wouldn't be surprised if there was . . . a million.'

Mohanna snorted. 'That's not even a real number. You made it up.'

Aran shook his head. 'It's a number. Samson the tally-keeper told me it's the biggest number there is, a thousand thousands.'

'Why would anyone need to count that many of anything?' Mohanna asked.

Aran had no answer to this.

'You could be counting the stars in the sky,' said Cas dreamily. 'Or leaves in the forest. Or grains of sand on the riverbank.'

'Why would you want to count grains of sand?' Mohanna demanded.

Cas fixed her with a serious stare. 'To see how many there are.'

Aran smiled. He and Cas had been best friends their whole lives. But still there were times when Aran would look at him, far away in thought, and know that there was a whole world going on behind Cas's eyes, a world he could never reach.

Mohanna lay back in the hay, muttering. Aran rolled over and gazed into the woods as they passed. The track was bathed in sunlight, but a few feet into the trees darkness took over. The forest floor was a swampy bed of ivy and knotweed and rampant, brightly flowered rhododendron. There were no paths to follow in that tangled wilderness.

He looked at the oak branches arching overhead and tried to count the leaves. There must be even more than a million, he thought. It was lucky no one wanted to count them, because they'd soon run out of numbers.

CHAPTER FIVE

Law Darnell and the Bear

That night they camped on the high moors near a small tarn fringed with reeds. Aran slept in a canvas tent beside his snoring father, but most simply wrapped themselves in blankets and lay under the stars, shrouded in woodsmoke and the scent of roast rabbit.

They departed before the sun was up, wending across rolling moorland wild with heather and gorse. Sometime after midday they descended into a river valley with small farmsteads on either side. Here the main east–west way joined the Barton road, and the junction was clogged with horses and livestock and carts piled with goods for sale and trade.

To Aran it seemed there were more people on the road than ever before. He saw vintners from Three Men, brickmakers from Bleakmoor, big-bellied brewers from Fourstones and crook-backed slate miners from Stump's Cross. A team of wool-clad sheep farmers from the highland tenements were struggling to keep their flock from mingling with a parcel of prize pigs driven by gangs of ruddy-faced women from Sowerton.

Aran eased his mare into the throng. The sun beat hard and the air was choked with dust. His nose wrinkled as he passed a line of carts packed with salted fish and whale blubber from the port towns. The cries of herders mingled with the bleating panic of their animals, creating an unholy, deafening din.

Aran felt a touch on his leg and looked down. An old man stood in ragged trousers, his chest bare, ribs poking through the skin like the roots of trees. In his other hand he clutched a piece of string tied to a scrawny goat. His fingers scuttled across Aran's knee, then grabbed at his wrist. There was desperation in the man's eyes.

'Spare a bite, son?' he slurred. His mouth was almost toothless and his gums were red with blood.

Aran kicked with his spur and drove his horse forward. His heart thudded. He passed another man in rags, his leathery skin tight over dry bones. A woman hobbled alongside, a half-empty basket of grain strapped to her back. Beside them walked another couple, younger but just as poor, a mewling baby lashed to the woman's breast. Looking up, Aran realized that they were all around him, hundreds of dark faces, an entire farmstead on the move.

He thought about the dried beef and the apples in his pack, the fresh water in the bottle around his neck. These people needed those things more than he did. But there were so many. How could he tell who needed it most? The faces surrounding him were weary and expressionless, the bodies weak and slumped. But he could imagine them turning angry, resentful. Crowding him.

He scanned desperately around for a familiar face, but could see none. His knuckles whitened on the reins. The dark figures seemed to close in. Aran braced himself, ready to bolt.

'Aran!' a voice called out. 'Don't get too far ahead!'

Aran's head whipped round. He could dimly see his mother a few cart-lengths behind, waving at him. Somehow he had passed them in the dust and the din.

Aran halted his horse and let the crowd flow around him, like a rock in a stream. 'Honestly,' the Lady said, grabbing Aran's bridle as her cart drew alongside. 'You're as bad as your father, always leading the charge. One of these days you'll turn round and there'll be no one behind you.' She gestured at her husband, who rode upright at the front of the column, nodding graciously to each passing traveller. 'Look at him,' she said in a tone caught somewhere between annoyance and affection. 'Cock of the walk.'

Then her eyes narrowed as they fell on Carifax's riding companion. Law Darnell was speaking intently, gesturing with both hands.

'I wonder what poison he's pouring this time,' the Lady mused. She looked at Aran, and a gleam came into her eye. 'Here, make yourself useful. Go and make sure Darnell's not talking your father into something he'll regret.'

'But I was just going to see if Cas wanted to—'

'Do as you're told,' his mother snapped. 'It'll be good

for you. That Darnell is as slippery as a sack of snakes, and every bit as venomous. Just the sort of crooked customer a good Foreman needs to be on the lookout for, if he doesn't want to end up buying a herd of three-legged sheep. Go on, you can report back to me when you're done.'

She leaned out and gave Aran's mare a sharp slap on the behind. The horse whinnied and lurched forward, overtaking three ranks of house guards from Hawk's Cross and Crowdale.

Aran tugged on the reins as they came up behind the Law on his sturdy bay stallion. 'They can't live like this by choice,' Carifax was saying as he drew level. 'Either their land is not productive or their Law takes more than they can afford.'

Law Darnell sneered. 'It's a lower standard, that's all,' he said. 'The eastern farmsteads have always been . . . different.'

'That's so,' Carifax nodded. 'The Goatland moors are no place to raise crops. It must be a hardscrabble life.'

'They've no discipline,' Darnell went on. 'They don't respect others or themselves. They live like animals because they don't know any better.'

Carifax sighed. 'You must give respect before you can expect to receive it,' he said. 'What I don't understand is why they're here in such numbers. Why would people who have so little travel so far? It doesn't make sense.'

Darnell shrugged. 'Maybe they're fleeing the Marauders,' he suggested.

Aran's ears pricked.

'Nonsense,' said Carifax. 'Marauders would never come so far inland. They're just seafarers, scavengers.'

'But I heard—' Aran started, breaking off when the two Laws turned to look at him. Carifax gestured for him to continue. 'I heard they took people prisoner,' Aran finished. 'Stole them away on their black ships.'

Carifax smiled. 'That's just Miss Crell trying to scare you into behaving,' he said.

'Doesn't seem to have worked,' muttered Darnell. 'But the boy's right, there have been tales. Farms raided, people taken. We had a tinker at Crowdale this past week, said they'd burned a whole farmstead out east.'

Carifax frowned. 'I had a run-in with the Marauders when I was a boy. They were just raiders, scattered tribes living on the ocean.'

'You fought the Marauders?' Aran asked, amazed.

Carifax nodded. 'When I was little older than Akmid, my father sent Solly and me off to see the world. We spent some time on the eastern coast, and yes, there were Marauders. A ship would come in at night, take a few sheep or ransack an isolated trading post. But they were nothing to be afraid of – wave a sword at them and they'd run off.'

Aran grinned. He loved the thought of his father as a young man, riding out on adventures. 'Tell us more,' he asked eagerly. 'What else did you see?'

Darnell sighed. 'We were having a serious discussion,' he said. 'Why don't you ride back and play with my daughter?'

'Nonsense,' said Carifax. 'As far as I recall, Darnell,

you were merely making impolite comments about our fellow travellers.' His eyes glazed over and his voice took on a wistful tone. 'Aran, one day I will tell you the whole story. The great wolves of Whiteport. The wild men of Cumbree. The time I spent in Howden, at the court of Tarik Karn himself.'

Aran looked at his father. 'You met Law Karn?' he asked in wonder.

Carifax flushed, as though he'd said something he hadn't intended to. 'I did,' he said. 'He was quite a remarkable man.' A serious look came over his face. 'Quite remarkable.'

Darnell snorted with derision. 'Tarik Karn was a thug and a gangster,' he barked.

Aran bristled. 'That's not true,' he retorted bitterly. 'Law Karn was a great man. Why, he—'

'Aran!' barked Carifax angrily. 'Mind your manners. Apologize to Law Darnell, immediately.'

Aran hung his head, mumbling a feeble apology.

'As I was saying,' Darnell continued, shooting Aran a smirking grimace, 'Law Karn was nothing but a common hoodlum trying to control everything for himself. All this talk of uniting the people was nonsense then and it's nonsense now. I mean, look at them. Every man should look after his own, I say, and damn the rest.'

'Well, we may long for one like Karn if these Marauder rumours prove true,' said Carifax darkly. 'Perhaps it's time we started to think beyond our own farmsteads again.'

Law Darnell shook his head pityingly. 'There's absolutely no point in— Hey, watch where you're going!'

A young woman had strayed into the path of Darnell's horse and he had almost ridden her down. She wrapped her arms protectively around her skinny body, gazing up at the Law with wide, uncomprehending eyes. Darnell stuck out a booted foot and gave her a firm shove. The girl spun away into the jostling crowd, and Aran heard a shout as a cart pulled up short behind them.

'Bloody peasant,' Darnell muttered. 'Probably out of her mind on barley wine and glory seeds. I don't know, Carifax, why you have any sympathy for the likes of—'

Something whistled through the air and struck Darnell on the arm. A piece of dry soil which exploded on impact, showering the Law with dirt. Just for a moment, Aran thought he glimpsed a shadow beneath the line of tall, spreading oaks which bordered the road: a figure, darker than the rest, slipping silently through the crowd.

Darnell's cheeks reddened and he wrenched his horse's reins. 'Who threw that?' he shouted. His hand strayed to the sword on his belt. 'Somebody answer me.'

No one spoke. The carts had ground to a halt but the crowd still trudged alongside, ignoring Darnell as he sat, scarlet with fury. 'Animals,' he snarled. 'Ala-cursed, ignorant, inbred, skin-and-bone animals.'

At this several travellers stopped and stared at the Law. 'Get down off your horse and say that,' came a voice from somewhere in the crowd. 'Posh ponce,' yelled another.

Suddenly Aran felt afraid. He could feel the tension in the air, an ugly rage that seemed to swell up from all around. Every eye was on them now; every cart had ground to a halt. The party from Hawk's Cross and Crowdale was several hundred strong, and many were armed. But the walkers on the road must have numbered in the thousands.

'A yearling to the man who tells me who threw that filth,' the Law barked, sitting upright in the saddle. 'I'll find him anyway, someone may as well profit by it.'

'I'll tell you where you can stick your yearling,' came a shout. 'It'd probably fit too!' came another, sparking howls of laughter. Aran saw several of their own party fighting hard not to smile.

The flush in Darnell's cheeks spread to his neck, and his hands began to tremble on the reins. 'You craven bloody rabble,' he spat. 'Cowardly peasant scum.'

The smiles were wiped clean. Aran saw one man, barely ten feet away, reach for a cudgel on the backboard of his cart. Another slipped a knife from his robe. Everywhere Aran looked he saw teeth bared and fists clenched.

Then Carifax reached out, putting a gloved hand on Darnell's arm. 'My friend, I think this could get out of hand.'

Darnell whipped round, glaring. 'Carifax, you heard them,' he snarled. 'How could I possibly— Hey!'

Something had brushed against Darnell's horse, and the animal started to whinny and buck. He wrapped the reins around his hands to avoid being thrown. The horse reared and turned, and Aran watched in astonishment as Law Darnell came face to face with a giant bear.

The bear sat on its haunches by the roadside, staring implacably at Darnell. A loose rope around its neck extended to a tree some yards away. Its fur, which had once been white, was filthy with road dust. The other travellers were giving the animal a wide berth, but Darnell had been so indignant he hadn't seen the creature until it was too late.

He looked around, enraged. 'Who owns this . . . beast?' he demanded.

The travellers watched silently. Darnell took out a riding crop and flicked it in the bear's direction. The bear did not move.

There was a rustling from the bushes nearby. An old man appeared, pulling up his trousers. He had a scraggly beard and a skinny frame. He stopped in his tracks, realizing that several hundred people were staring in his direction.

Law Darnell approached. 'Is this your bear?' he demanded.

The old man looked at Darnell, then at the bear, which scratched its nose and grunted. He nodded. 'That's my Grizelda,' he admitted. 'I'm sorry if she's caused you any trouble.'

'You'll be more than sorry,' said Darnell and raised his crop, bringing it down on the old man's back. Aran gasped and Carifax started forward. But before they could act, a figure sprang from nowhere and knocked Darnell from his horse.

The Law hit the ground in a cloud of dust. The old man cowered behind his bear. Darnell sat upright, spitting dirt, looking around in astonishment. The man who had attacked him stopped a few feet away, glaring contemptuously. Three of Darnell's company rode in and surrounded him, spears at the ready.

The newcomer looked young, Aran thought, not much older than Keller. But there was something in his narrow face that spoke of time and distance and hard experience. His once-black robes were ragged and torn, his skin so pale you could see the blue veins beneath. His hair was jet black and spiked in every direction and his eyes were a deep red-brown, glowing beneath his sheer white brows like the dying cinders of last night's fire. He stood poised and motionless, as Darnell's riders circled warily.

'How dare you!' the Law demanded as soon as he could speak. 'How dare you assault me! Answer me, boy.' He struggled to his feet, brushing dirt from his tunic.

The pale man kept his eyes fixed on the riders, his fists clenched. 'I'm not your boy,' he said in a rough voice, strongly accented. 'And if you come one step closer you'll know you've been assaulted.'

Darnell spat on the ground. 'You wish to fight me, then?'

The newcomer shook his head. 'Me? No. I'm just a peaceful traveller on my way to Carny. You were the one walloping a defenceless old man.'

Darnell shot a glance back at the old man and his bear, who were hurrying off into the crowd.

'Look,' said the pale man sardonically. 'They're getting away.'

Darnell rounded on him. 'You will pay for your insolence,' he said. He gestured to his guard captain, Devin, a muscle-bound brute with a dirty red beard and scars on both cheeks. 'Take him into the forest and deal with him,' Darnell demanded.

The captain nodded, and the three riders circled closer. 'Don't make a fuss now,' Devin warned. 'It'll only turn out worse if you do.' And he reached down to grab the newcomer by his hair.

But as he did so, the pale man reached up and grabbed Devin by the wrist, flipping him effortlessly out of his saddle and onto the hard ground. Aran heard a crunch and Devin screamed, writhing in pain.

The remaining two riders wheeled their horses and advanced, spears raised. The traveller crouched. As the riders approached he uncoiled like a spring, leaping into the air. He spread his arms as he jumped, grabbing each man by the collar and allowing himself to be carried forward. Then he hammered their heads together and dropped to the earth. The unconscious riders slipped from their horses and toppled into the dust.

There was a round of applause. The pale man took a bow, then backed away as Law Darnell came storming towards him, his face red with fury.

Darnell looked over his shoulder, his eyes fixing on Akmid and Keller. 'Take him!' he demanded. Akmid looked at Law Carifax, who shook his head slowly. 'Take him, damn it!' Darnell screamed.

The pale man smiled, showing thin white teeth. 'What of it, Law Carifax?' he said. 'I can see by your face you've not forgotten me.'

Aran looked up in surprise. The pale man glanced in his direction and Aran felt those fiery eyes exploring every inch of his face. For a moment he was transfixed. There was such depth there, such boundless intensity. Then the man looked back at Aran's father.

Carifax turned away. 'Get out of here before you cause any more trouble.'

Darnell looked at Carifax in astonishment. 'What are you doing?' he demanded. 'This man assaulted me. He—'

'Let him go,' said Law Carifax quietly. The pale man grinned impishly, winked at Darnell, then backed away, vanishing into the trees. Darnell climbed onto his horse, kicked his heels and rode off at a gallop, scattering travellers as he went.

Aran looked at Law Carifax. He seemed tired and sad, as though reminded of some old, painful memory.

'Who *was* that?' Aran asked.

Carifax looked at him, and for a long moment he seemed far away. Then he shook his head. 'No one you need worry about. Come on, let's get moving.'

He flicked his bridle and the parade rumbled forward once more.

CHAPTER SIX

The Carny

A ran could not get the pale man out of his mind. He kept going over the incident in his head: how fast the man had moved, how purposefully; the way Law Carifax had refused to assist in his capture, over-riding Darnell's authority without a second thought. It all meant something. Aran couldn't begin to work it out. But he was left with the image in his mind of the stranger's eyes – those burning, ageless eyes.

The afternoon passed in silence as they were slowed by swelling crowds on the roads from Hargate and Brimham. The sun sank and the air cooled, and they moved in a deepening gloom of dust and shadows.

As night fell the torches were lit. The road seemed to Aran like a flaming river snaking through the dark, until it emptied at last into an ocean of light. They had reached Barton.

The town lay on the far edge of a wide expanse of scrub grass, by the shores of a great saltwater lagoon barely visible in the gloom. Every inch of the approach plain was crowded with tents and dwellings, and outside each one a cooking fire blazed. Sparks danced through the dusty air, and the night was filled with leaping shadows.

Aran felt a stirring in his heart. He had never seen so many people. So many lives, so many stories, and himself just a tiny part of it.

Faces loomed out of the darkness. Hands pawed at him, offering fresh bread, buttered corn and flavoured toffee, citrus tart from the lowland orchards and wild berry jam from the forest farms, steaming pies stuffed with anything that could be skinned and eaten. The proprietors of competing auction houses vied for the Laws' attention, while costumed barkers advertised shows and attractions, games and trials of skill and strength.

'Longball tickets!' a voice yelled in Aran's ear. 'Get your tickets here! Sellin' out fast so get 'em while they're 'ot!'

The Longball game was the most popular event at Carny, and this year Akmid and Keller had been chosen to play for the Moorland team alongside players from Crowdale and Highfields. The match was scheduled for tomorrow afternoon and Aran had been selected as his brother's Second, a responsibility he took very seriously.

They left the carts on the crowded outskirts and headed for their lodgings, weaving between brick townhouses, bustling auction shops and wooden pens crammed with livestock. The narrow, muddy streets of Barton were as rackety and crowded as the plain beyond, but the people here were noticeably better dressed, in leather leggings and jackets of deer hide and sheepskin.

Law Carifax owned the controlling share in an inn, the Trader's Rest, which stood on a main street close to the lakeshore, and each year it was cleared to make way for the Law and his entourage. Aran always enjoyed staying at the Rest; there was something cosily ramshackle about the place with its shadows and corners and little hidden passages.

But as they approached, Aran could see that great changes had taken place since their last visit. In place of the old stables stood a vast building constructed of brick and wood. It had three rows of windows and a high, sloping roof. Law Carifax sat back on his horse in amazement.

A door flew open and a red-faced man strode out, shaking Carifax eagerly by the hand.

'My Law, my Law,' said Parry, the innkeeper. 'Welcome back.'

Carifax nodded and muttered a greeting, but he was distracted by the edifice which had sprung up where the old inn used to be.

Parry grinned proudly. 'We just finished it this moon,' he said. 'The stables were pulled down after your visit last Carny and we put in the foundations then. Our lads stumbled over another lot of ruins in the forest, and the sifters have been working round the clock so we've not been short of bricks. There are twenty buildings this size in Barton now, and more going up. The world's changing, my Law. Perhaps in a few years we'll all be living above ground like the Ancestors did.'

Carifax snorted derisively. 'Legends and poppycock,' he growled. 'It'll never last the winter.'

Parry shook his head. 'It's a risk, I know, but things aren't like they were when we were boys. The storms aren't so savage, not any more. There hasn't been a real housebreaker in these parts for almost as long as I can remember.'

Carifax shook his head in amazement. 'Well, my family and I will take our usual rooms on the lower levels,' he said.

At this the innkeeper frowned. 'Well . . . that's, erm . . .'

'A problem, Parry?' demanded Carifax.

'Well, it's just that I expected you'd want to try out the new facilities,' Parry explained nervously. 'I've put you on the third floor.'

Carifax blanched, peering up at the high windows. 'All the way up there?'

Parry nodded. 'I already let out the underground rooms. Got a good price for 'em too.'

'I should think so,' snorted the Law. 'Very well, I suppose it can't be helped. The boys can take the top floor, my wife and I will remain on the ground. But if this entire structure comes crashing around our ears in the middle of the night, I shall be most aggrieved.'

Aran was soon ensconced in a corner room with a window overlooking the street. He didn't like it at all, neither the height of the room nor the size of the window. He could hear the clamour and din from the street below as deals were struck and fights broke out, and thousands upon thousands of terrified animals were herded back and forth. But he didn't feel a part of everything as he had before. Now he felt cut off, above everything but not connected to it.

The whole town was spread out before him, a maze of narrow avenues and alleyways all winding down to the Lake of York, which stretched grey and misty into the far distance. An old rhyme his nurse had sung claimed that the lake had drowned ten thousand men, but Aran didn't know if it was true.

Mohanna came hurrying in. She marvelled at the new building, standing at the window and firing imaginary arrows at traders passing in the street below.

'You could pick off anyone you wanted from up here,' she said.

Aran frowned. 'Come on,' he said. 'I'm starving.'

In the smoky, low-ceilinged drinking hall, Law Carifax and his wife were entertaining a large group of their peers. Most were members of the Laws' Council, a loose affiliation of local landowners who met each year to discuss the urgent matters of the day.

Aran and Mohanna were shunted off to a table under the stairs with the other Laws' children, most of whom were more interested in throwing their food about than in sharing news. So as the first course was being cleared away, Aran clambered up and, on the pretext of looking for the new facilities, began to listen in.

Most of the faces were familiar. Kindly old Law Ryder, who'd always had a joke and a piece of honey brittle for

Aran when he was small, sat on a bench by the big bay window with craggy Law Craven from Kipp's Town, who'd once mistaken Akmid for a servant and threatened to beat him if he didn't fetch his supper. Bushy, brawny Law Gorton from Three Men, the only Law who ruled more than one farmstead, leaned casually against a pillar with his sleeves rolled, comparing hunting scars with Lady West of Sowerton, who had left her husband at home this year. Barton itself had no Law, just an ever-shifting guild of tradesmen and auctioneers. They crowded the snugs and alcoves, whispering in the shadows and offering money-making schemes to the more gullible Laws.

But there was only one topic Aran wanted to hear about, and as he sidled closer to a pair of Laws seated on stools at the long, bronze-panelled bar, his persistence was rewarded.

'Fifty killed, they said,' muttered Law Hitchens from Highfields, his broad, veiny face looking considerably less jolly than usual. 'As many taken. Cattle too. What I want to know is, who's next? And what are we going to do about it?'

The other Law stroked his thick black whiskers. 'What can we do?' he mused. 'The Marauders have always been a problem. Sooner or later they'll have had enough, and they'll sail off to bother some other poor divvle. We'll just have to ride it out.'

Hitchens sighed. 'Whatever you say, Walden,' he said. 'If you tell us not to worry, we'll follow your lead, as always. But what about the men who haven't even shown up? I heard Law Little won't even leave his farmstead, he's so terrified the buggers'll come along and burn it down.'

'They'd never come so far west,' Walden said dismissively. 'Every attack has been within a few miles of the coast, and Eskirk's only, what? A day's ride from here? Little always was a worrier.' He leaned close to Hitchens and lowered his voice. Aran craned his neck. 'My fear,' Walden whispered, 'is Marauder spies.' Hitchens's eyebrows shot up. 'Eavesdropping on us. They could be anywhere, anyone. Maybe even someone we know.'

Then suddenly he turned, opened his eyes wide and roared in Aran's face. The boy shrieked and leaped back, catching himself on the hard edge of a table. Walden shook with laughter and Hitchens howled, looking down at Aran, who stood white-faced and trembling.

Carifax joined them, putting an arm around Aran's shoulders. 'This one not bothering you, is he, my Laws?' he asked.

Walden wiped his eyes with the sleeve of his shirt and shook his head. His eyes shone merrily. 'Not a bit of it, Carifax,' he said, and chuckled again. 'Boy's just interested. I don't blame him. What do you think, Aran, eh? Bet you could take on a Marauder or two if they came spoiling for a fight, couldn't you?'

Aran nodded keenly. But Carifax frowned and pulled him away. 'Come on, Aran,' he said. 'The Laws have business to attend to. This is no place for small boys.'

Aran trudged back to the children's corner, passing the circular table where Akmid sat with his Longball

73

teammates, laughing and drinking, showing no sign that they were the underdogs in tomorrow's match.

Beside Akmid sat Callum Ridge, a skinny, self-serious Highfields lad who had recently been named captain of the Moorland team. Aran had seen him ride the year before, already an accomplished sticksman. Keller was the only other veteran of that fateful game, when the Lowlanders from Three Men had driven the Moorland players back, leaving them beaten and shamed. Aran prayed it wouldn't happen when they met again tomorrow.

He watched as Parry's daughters hurried around the table, distributing flagons of wine. Akmid took two mugs, downing them both to a roar of approval.

Aran's frustration boiled over. He strode to the table, grabbing the last cup from Akmid's hand and tipping out the dregs. 'Don't you think you've had enough?' he demanded angrily.

The table fell silent. Akmid smiled up, his eyes straining to focus. 'Little brother!' he said. 'Come, sit. My brother, everyone. My little baby brother.'

'And your Second,' Aran reminded him. 'If you keep this up you're not going to be able to stand tomorrow, let alone play.'

'Lea' me 'lone,' Akmid grumbled, shoving Aran aside. 'You bein' Second was Father's choice, not mine. So I don' need you tellin' me what to do, 'kay?' He reached out for another mug, raising it happily to his lips. But before Akmid could drink, Aran had knocked it to the ground.

Akmid squinted at his suddenly empty hand. 'Hey!' he

said, and glared at Aran. 'Whajida . . . whadija . . . wha' did you do tha' for?'

'Because I don't want you to embarrass yourself out on that field tomorrow,' Aran snapped.

Akmid waved him away. 'Don't be daft,' he said. 'We're the best. Right?' He got to his feet. 'We're the best! Moors rule!' He grabbed a jug and clambered up on the table, to the delight of his teammates. He swayed back and forth, cracking his head on a hanging lantern. The shadows leaped and danced, and Akmid laughed and did the same.

Aran felt a hand on his shoulder. He turned to see Law Darnell smiling coldly down at him. 'Come now, Aran,' he said. 'Your brother needs to let off some steam, all right? Let him have his fun.'

Akmid stumbled off the table into the arms of a passing barmaid. He grabbed her by both cheeks and kissed her on the lips. His teammates cheered again.

Aran sighed and backed away. Mohanna smiled sympathetically as he slumped back into his seat. 'I'm sure they'll be fine tomorrow,' she said. 'A nice cold bath, a full breakfast. Good as new.'

But when the morning came, Akmid was pale and unsteady, and balked at the sight of food. A low mist clung to the ground as Aran helped him down to the Longball grounds on the edge of town. A crowd had already begun to gather, and the cries of ticket scalps rang in the chill morning air.

Inside the players' enclosure, the Moorland team were

slumped on their benches in apathetic silence. Their horses snorted impatiently. Aran's heart sank.

'We're going to get massacred,' he said to Cas, who peered over the fence from the seating area beyond. 'And in front of all these people.' The sloping ranks of wooden benches on either side of the field were filling up, and Aran had to shout over the din.

Cas looked around. 'Still, they've done the place up, at least.' The goalposts had been painted, the grass on the pitch was a healthy shade of green, and even the slatted pine walls of the players' enclosures had been sanded smooth. 'Seems like someone's making a fair bit of money on these games. Shame it's only twice a year.'

'There's only four teams,' Aran pointed out. 'It's Lake-siders versus Miners tomorrow.'

'Yes, but there are lots of people who want to play,' Cas argued. 'You could have a team from every farmstead if you wanted. They could all play against each other, and the best one could win a prize.'

Aran laughed. 'That'd be hundreds of games,' he said. 'Who'd go to them all?'

'I was just thinking,' Cas shrugged.

Aran shook his head. 'You should really stop doing that.'

Cas looked up. 'There's my dad and Mohanna,' he said. 'They've got honey apples. I'll see you after the game. Good luck.'

Aran sighed. 'We're going to need it.'

The Moorland players climbed wearily onto their horses, lining up before the gate. Aran held tight to his brother's reins. When the whistle blew, those gates would swing open and the team would ride out to victory or humiliation.

The seconds ticked by. A hush fell over the stadium. Aran gritted his teeth.

Then the whistle sounded and the crowd erupted into wild cheering.

The Lowlanders burst from their enclosure, seven determined-looking young men on horseback and one on foot, their breachpoles held aloft. Each pole had a scoop-shaped glove on one end for directing the ball, and a padded bolster on the other for knocking the enemy off his horse.

Aran joined his fellow Seconds astride the enclosure gate just in time to see Keller taking up his position in the goal mouth, swinging his pole over his head to the delight of the crowd. At least one of the Moorland team looked alive, Aran thought. The others limped onto the field, their horses sagging.

The ball was already waiting out in the centre; the first team to reach it would gain the advantage. The horses drove forward, players from both sides breaking away to protect the outer flanks. Akmid rode close behind Callum Ridge, his captain. Ridge extended his breachpole, hoping to knock the ball back towards his teammates.

But the Lowland captain was faster, scooping the ball up and putting the Moorlanders on the defensive. Akmid wheeled back, pursuing the captain, who was already charging down the field, weaving smoothly in and out of the opposing players. Two riders flanked him on either side, striking at anyone who came within range.

A wall of Moorland riders took their positions a few feet from the net, blocking it. But the Lowland captain knocked the ball between his horse's charging legs to another player, who scooped it up and flung it towards the goal mouth. Keller was caught off guard by the sudden switch. The ball rocketed past to grant the Lowlanders first blood.

Aran watched, his heart in his mouth. This Lowland team was tight and determined; the Moorlanders seemed sluggish by comparison.

Another goal came in the fifteenth minute as sloppy defending allowed three Lowland riders to slip through. Only Keller's speed and agility managed to save the team on four separate occasions. Aran could see him becoming enraged as his team fumbled the ball, fell from their horses and missed the easiest shots on goal. By half time it was three to nothing.

The Moorland team sloped off the pitch. Keller trudged at the rear, pulling the gate shut behind him and turning furiously on his fellow players.

'What's going on?' he demanded, red-faced.

The team stripped off their shirts and wet their faces. Callum Ridge shook his head. 'We're just having a bad day, that's all.'

'Bad day?' Keller barked. 'I waited a year for this.'

Some of the players seemed barely able to stand; they leaned against the fence, breathing hard.

Keller sank down onto the bench. 'May as well just give up,' he said bitterly.

'We're doing the best we can,' muttered Akmid. Ridge covered his face with his hands.

Before he could stop himself, Aran cried out. 'Listen to yourselves!' Every head turned. Aran swallowed. 'There's still an entire half to go, and you're talking like it's over!'

Akmid shook his head. 'Don't bother, Aran,' he said. 'It's not your place.'

But Aran was sick of it. 'Well, someone has to say it. This is pathetic. There's people out there cheering for you. At least try to give them a show.' He looked at their blank, exhausted faces and knew that, for a moment at least, he had their attention.

'Every one of those people is going to go back to their families and their farmsteads,' he said. 'And they'll ask, how was Carny? What did you do, what did you see? What do you want them to say? *Oh, it was fine. I sold some beasts and drunk some booze and then I came home.* Or do you want them to say, *Here, son, let me tell you a story.*'

He lowered his voice, and the enclosure seemed to grow still around him. '*Our boys looked finished, but they came out and drove the Lowlanders back, you should have been there. They may not have won, but they did themselves proud.* Wouldn't that be something?'

The team looked at him, doubt on every face. Aran met their eyes, one by one, all except Akmid, who turned to the wall, frowning but silent.

Aran shrugged. 'Or you can just give up. Your choice.'

He walked back to Akmid's horse, taking out a stiff brush and scrubbing the animal's mud-stained flanks.

For a long time, the only sounds were of buckles being tightened, saddles straightened and jackets strapped on. Then Ridge said, 'All right. Let's see what we can do.'

The riders remounted. Each face was firm, every hand gripping tight to their breachpole. The minutes ticked by in torturous silence, the tension rising until Aran didn't think he could take it any more. Then the whistle blew and the gates swung wide.

The change was not immediately apparent. The Lowland riders were still giving all they had, and an early breakthrough threatened to tip the score until a dynamic lunge from Keller saved the day. Aran clambered back up on the gate, clinging with both hands to the uppermost rung.

'Do you think they've a chance?' Lady Carifax was standing by the fence, looking up from the benches. 'Don't worry,' she said. 'I haven't suddenly developed an interest in sports. But your father was daft enough to lay a fairly sizeable bet on the outcome, and I want to know exactly what sort of odds we're facing.'

Aran looked at her with concern. 'What was the stake?' he asked.

The Lady pursed her lips. 'Twenty casks of ale,' she said sourly. 'Honestly, he'd bet the whole farmstead and everyone in it given half a chance.'

Aran's eyes widened. 'Twenty casks,' he said in disbelief. 'Who with?' Who was mad enough to bet such a fortune on a single Longball game?

'Who do you think?' the Lady hissed.

For a moment Aran was nonplussed. Law Walden was the wealthiest of the Laws, but he'd never been a betting man. Law Gorton could probably afford it . . . Then Aran looked at his brother, loping queasily down the field, and it all fell into place.

'Darnell was paying for the wine,' he said in amazement, and felt a rush of anger. 'The miserable little—'

'Quite,' his mother cut in. 'Not that your brother and his friends have anyone to blame but themselves. But still, it was a dog's trick, betting against his own side. I told you he needed watching.'

Aran nodded. 'Well, they're not beaten yet,' he said through gritted teeth.

And with that, a roar went up from the crowd. Aran looked to see Ridge thundering back down the field, his breachpole raised triumphantly. The Lowland goalkeeper stood red-faced on the line, shaking his head. Aran grinned and let out a whoop of joy.

A second goal followed swiftly on the heels of the first, and now the game was starting to get interesting. Aran looked into the stands to where Law Darnell sat, his fists clenched in his lap, grimacing with every Moorland strike. Lady Carifax had rejoined the party, sitting at her husband's side, her fingers crossed in her lap.

Akmid was riding hard now, the ball poised in his glove. Ridge and another player followed on his heels, striking left and right, forcing their opponents to yield. Then the Lowland captain joined the fray. One Moorland player fell back, slamming into the dirt with bone-crunching force. Now it was just Akmid and Ridge, driving towards the goal mouth.

The Lowland captain swung in on their left but Akmid flicked the ball away, flipping the breachpole over his shoulders in a practised move. The captain drove in, trying to trip his horse. Akmid swayed, then righted himself and kept control.

The crowd was cheering wildly. Aran felt his heart pound. If Akmid could make this strike, the game was anyone's. The Lowland captain drove in again, his breachpole catching Akmid in the ribs, almost tipping him. Akmid stumbled, about to fall. The crowd held its breath.

And then it happened.

A noise began to build, over by the main gates. People were shouting and backing away, pushing against each other. One by one, every eye strayed from the action on the field and turned to watch the commotion.

A man ran onto the pitch, hurtling blindly into the mass of players. Akmid's horse reared to avoid trampling him. Aran gasped. At first he'd thought the man was wearing a bright-red shirt; now he realized that he was soaked with blood. As he came closer his panicked cries became audible.

'They're coming!' he shouted as he ran, flinging his blood-stained arms wide, foam spraying from his mouth. 'They're coming! Run, run for your lives!'

CHAPTER SEVEN

The Marauders

Panic erupted in the Longball grounds. People running for the entrance were driven back by others shoving wildly in the opposite direction. Their faces were white with fear. What had they seen, outside the gates? A noise began to build, like thunder in the distance. The ground shook. Perched above the mayhem, Aran gripped his narrow rung and watched.

The players turned, the game forgotten. The fences broke and people flooded onto the field, a great tidal mass of blind terror. Aran glanced up into the viewing stands – he could see Law and Lady Carifax trying to hold fast as the mob drove them this way and that. He saw Devin barging bodily through the crowd, Darnell cowering at his back. Cas and Mohanna clutched tight to one another, struggling to keep up. The entrance to the Lowland players' enclosure stood open, and many seemed to be fleeing that way.

Keller stood by the gate below Aran's feet, waving his teammates back. Akmid came riding hard towards them.

He clung to his horse, trying to stay aloft, but the crowd swarmed around him. His horse reared, kicking its heels. Akmid was thrown back, head over heels. A flying, panicked hoof caught him on the chest, then he was driven down, the mob closing over him. Aran sprang up, craning to see, but his brother was gone.

Then a hand was reaching into the mass of people, pulling Akmid to his feet. Ridge had forced his horse through, whispering to keep her calm. He dragged Akmid up behind him. Aran's brother clung on weakly, his arms wrapped around Ridge's waist. He was bleeding from a cut on his forehead and his face was pale. Ridge turned and forced his way back towards the enclosure.

Aran looked towards the main entrance. The noise of hoof beats had been joined by another sound, a clamour of howling and barking. Through the gates came a pack of ferocious black dogs, their jaws dripping with foam, their eyes red with murderous rage. Snapping and biting, they fell on the crowd. Cries of panic turned to screams of pain as the dogs tore across the field, staining the grass red in their wake.

Then a horn sounded, and in rode the Marauders.

Their horses were black and gleaming with perspiration, eyes wild and agitated. The riders were clothed from head to toe in leather and animal skins. They carried swords and cleavers of iron and bone, and their saddles rattled with metal ornaments and trophies of ivory, whalebone and walrus tusk. Their teeth were bared and their baleful eyes showed no mercy.

They ploughed into the crowd with gleeful abandon, trampling anyone who came too close. Aran saw Law Ryder backed up against the fence, holding up his hands and pleading for his life. A leering Marauder reached down with one gloved fist, tearing the jewelled necklace from around the Law's neck. Then he swung back with a polished bone club and beat Ryder unconscious.

The Marauders at the entrance seemed to regroup and divide, opening a bloody avenue from the gate to the pitch. Along this path came a dark steed, and upon it sat the tallest man Aran had ever seen. He was bone-thin, his skin so white that he resembled a grinning skeleton. His long white-blond hair was bound into a single braid, with six-inch steel spikes woven along its length. He wore the hide of a white bear wrapped around his shoulders, and a shark's jaw rested on his forehead like a thorny crown. His saddle was festooned with gold, and three human skulls hung from a thread around his horse's neck.

A bodyguard of three rode at his back, each masked with the skull and pelt of a different beast – a walrus, a wolf and a horned stag. Their mounts were sleek and black and they moved with patient, undulating grace into the centre of the stadium.

Aran felt suddenly vulnerable, balanced above the teeming crowd. His eyes locked on the pale Marauder chief, who sat back and surveyed the scene, his lips drawn back into a scornful grimace. He barked an order and his men hurried to obey.

Aran tore his eyes away and dropped back into the

enclosure. Akmid now lay in the dirt, bloody and pale but still breathing. The cut on his forehead was nothing compared to the ugly black bruise spreading across his chest.

Aran helped Keller to pull the gate closed, barring it with a stout oak beam. He could hear terrified cries outside, fists pounding against the wood.

Most of the other players had already fled through the enclosure's rear entrance. Ridge sat upright in the saddle, calling to them to hurry. Keller dragged Akmid to his feet, gripping his face with both hands and staring into his eyes.

'Can you stand?' he demanded roughly. Akmid nodded, wiping the blood from his mouth.

'I can carry him,' Ridge offered.

But his horse looked ready to drop. 'She won't take two,' Keller argued. 'And you'd be exposed. Better to stay low, and stay together.'

Ridge frowned. 'Let me at least give you cover,' he said, and Keller nodded gratefully.

Ridge eased his mount through the narrow doorway, turning to beckon them forward. As he did so, a steel blade came out of nowhere and drove into his back. A Marauder horseman thundered past, yanking his sword free with a howl. Ridge toppled from the saddle, blood coursing from his mouth. Aran felt his knees weaken; he backed away in horror. Through the opening they could see Marauders patrolling the plain, riding down anyone who tried to escape.

Keller slammed the door shut, bracing it with his back. 'There's too many of them,' he said. 'We can't get out that way.'

They were trapped inside the circular enclosure.

Aran heard a crash as something heavy drove into the barred gate. There was a sound of splintering wood and the gate shook on its hinges. Then a sword slid through the gap, hacking at the beam which held it shut. They could hear the mad baying of the hounds.

'They're breaking through!' Akmid shouted, his voice cracking with terror.

Suddenly Aran had an idea. He grabbed one of the discarded breachpoles and used the knife on his belt to hack away the soft bolstering. Underneath, the pole was tipped with steel to keep it from cracking.

Aran drove the steel shaft into the wall of the enclosure, then again. The slatted pine shattered, boards splintering to reveal a dark passageway beyond. Keller picked up another pole, following Aran's lead. Together they broke a hole in the planking big enough to climb through.

Keller led the way, half carrying Akmid. Faint streaks of daylight filtered between the sloping benches above their heads, revealing a shallow forest of wooden pillars. They moved forward in silence. Aran brought up the rear, the pole under one arm, his dagger clutched in his hand. He jumped as something brushed against his hair. Looking up, he saw a hand reaching between the boards. Blood dripped from the outstretched fingers.

A din of snarling and growling began to swell behind

them. Aran looked back and saw movement around the ragged hole in the fence.

'I think they're coming,' he said.

Keller glanced back. 'Move!' he cried, shoving Akmid forward.

Three black dogs came bounding through the opening. Aran caught a glimpse of a Marauder face in the gap. The raider saw the boy and grinned, drawing his finger slowly across his neck. The dogs came on, howling and snapping.

Aran crouched low, weaving between the posts. He could see the outer fence just twenty feet away, but they were still going to have to break through. Akmid snatched the pole from Aran's hands. He reached the fence and started to pound furiously against it. The dogs were right on top of them.

Aran turned, brandishing his knife. One of the dogs drew close, circling him warily. Its jaws were ringed with bloody slaver, and its muscular body moved with terrifying, predatory patience. Aran swept his blade back and forth. The dog drew back its ragged red lips to reveal glistening teeth. Then it leaped, snarling.

Aran ducked and the dog bit down on nothing. It landed on all fours, turning to snap at Aran's bare legs. He sliced down with the knife and the dog retreated, whining, blood seeping from a gash on its snout. It shook its head, recovering quickly. Then it crouched low, ready to spring again.

The dog's leap was powerful and perfectly timed; if

Aran hadn't stepped aside, it would have torn his throat to shreds. But instead the animal crashed past him, tumbling into the pillars which held up the benches overhead. The force was so great that the pillar slid loose, bringing a whole section of the stands down upon the startled dog. Light flooded in. The dog was trapped, its body crushed, its jaws snapping feebly.

Another dog closed on Keller, leaping furiously. He brought his breachpole down in a sweeping arc, knocking the animal into the dirt. The dog howled and rolled back, but soon recovered and rejoined the attack.

Keller pulled out his knife as the dog sprang for his throat. He grabbed it by the scruff of the neck as it pounced, driving his blade deep into its belly, toppling back under the weight. The dog died with its teeth just inches from Keller's exposed windpipe.

Akmid had managed to break open a small hole in the outer fence. But his blows were growing weaker; he was exhausted and terrified. Aran stepped forward, taking the pole from his brother's hands and driving it into the wooden slats, widening the hole. But as he did so, he heard a cry.

Keller was struggling, the weight of the dead dog hampering his movements. The third animal had circled in, snapping at his legs. As Aran watched it took hold of Keller's foot, worrying with its jaws. Keller let out a howl, kicking wildly. The dog retreated, two of Keller's toes hanging from its mouth. Aran rushed in, pulling the dead animal off Keller and helping him to his feet.

Keller faced the last dog. His blood dripped from its exposed fangs. The dog growled, and Keller growled back. He held up his breachpole, the steel tip glittering.

'Come on!' Aran shouted.

But Keller was moving back into the shadows. He and the dog circled, neither willing to risk the first strike. Keller was limping, and the scent of fresh blood was driving the dog wild. It sprang, howling. Its teeth sank deep into Keller's shoulder, driving him to the ground.

Keller's grip tightened on his breachpole. He swung it round above the dog's back and drove it deep into the shuddering fur. The dog's jaws unlatched in a squeal of agony. Keller shoved the animal away, reaching up with his knife, driving it under the dog's chin and deep into its skull.

For a moment, all was silent. Aran could hear Keller's ragged breath, short and shallow. Then he saw him push the carcass aside and stagger to his feet. Keller's chest and arms were covered with blood and there was a reckless light in his eyes.

They crawled through the hole and into the open. The scene that greeted them was more dreadful than anything Aran could have imagined. The Marauders had swept through the town, slashing and burning everything in their path. Countless bodies lay strewn on the approach plain. The fires had been scattered, and everywhere tents and huts were ablaze, sending plumes of black smoke spiralling into the grey sky.

The Marauders had raided the animal pens, using

their dogs to drive the cattle and livestock back along the lakeshore. Now the bulk of their forces were following, leaving destruction in their wake.

Aran saw two men on horseback driving a group of terrified citizens along the shore. 'They're taking people,' he said.

Keller nodded. 'We have to get out of sight,' he growled.

Aran looked at Akmid; he was fading fast, his face pale and his eyes drooping. But getting back to Barton would mean crossing several hundred yards of open ground, exposed and unprotected.

'We'll never make it,' Aran said.

'We don't have a choice,' insisted Keller. 'He'll die if we don't get him to a healer.'

They began to move. All around, the noise of battle raged. Through the smoke Aran could see clashes erupting as the citizens regrouped and began to fight back. But it was too late. The Marauders were taking what they could and fleeing the field.

The buildings of Barton rose up above the haze. They were close, but Aran could feel his strength draining.

He heard a noise and whipped round. A black horse towered over him. A sword swept down, inches from his face. Aran staggered back.

The Marauder captain was instantly recognizable – one of the three who had ridden with their lord into the Longball grounds. His face was framed by a pair of sharpened ivory tusks, and between them Aran could see a fleshy mouth and flashing eyes. A leathery walrus pelt hung down his back, leaving his barrel-chest bare. His arms were spattered with blood and hair and what looked like scraps of bone.

Keller turned, Akmid's arm wrapped limply around his shoulder. His eyes met Aran's, and there was pity there, and regret. Aran realized in an instant what this meant. Keller was not going to help him. His responsibility was to Akmid and he couldn't risk that.

Aran faced the Marauder, lashing out with his knife. The warrior said something in a cold, cruel voice. Then he pushed the walrus mask back and looked at the boy appreciatively, as though admiring a strong bull or a well-trained dog. He sheathed his sword and took from his belt a whalebone club. He circled closer, his horse skittish and wary of Aran's blade.

Aran was shaking, his fingers sweaty on the knife. The heat rose all around him. Tears streamed from his eyes. He held up his blade and cried out, 'Come on, then! Come and take me!'

The Marauder spurred his horse. His club was raised, and as he passed he swept down, knocking the knife from Aran's hand. Aran turned as the horse came around for another pass. The Marauder let out a screeching, wordless battle cry. Aran braced himself. This time the club caught him on the side of his head and he tumbled into nothingness.

CHAPTER EIGHT

Captives

Aran woke in darkness. There was a searing pain in his head. The world shuddered around him and there was a din of rattling and clanking. His arms were pinned to his sides. He tried to open his eyes but saw only dim shapes rocking back and forth.

A hand touched his forehead, gently tipping it back. Cool water coursed down his throat. He spluttered.

'Ssshhh,' said a low voice. 'Don't try to move.'

Aran struggled to focus. A face floated in front of him and he fixed upon it, fighting the pain which hammered behind his eyes. It was a young man's face, he could see that now. Pale skin and black, unruly hair. Those eyes, fiery-deep and ageless.

Aran struggled upright. 'You!' he said.

The pale man nodded. 'Quiet,' he warned. 'We're in a bad situation.'

Aran looked around. He was in a barred cage of rusted steel with thirty other prisoners – men, women and

93

children – staring fearfully out into the blackness. The cage was strapped to a moving cart. A Marauder rode alongside, a broadsword hanging from his belt. Behind them stumbled a herd of livestock driven by a rangy boy who lashed cruelly at them with a pointed switch. A line of torches snaked into the distance, each carried by a warrior on horseback.

Aran fought to free his arms. He reached behind his left ear, feeling an egg-sized lump which was sore to the touch.

'You'll live.' The pale man extended a calloused hand. 'Peregrine,' he said.

Aran shook warily. 'Aran,' he said.

'It's good to meet you, Aran. You're Carifax's boy.'

Aran remembered the look that had passed between Peregrine and his father on the road. Carifax didn't trust this man, that much was clear. Aran was suddenly struck by the realization that he had no idea what had happened to his family or his friends. They could have been captured, thrown into one of these cages, or worse.

'I'm sure they're safe,' said Peregrine, as though reading his thoughts. 'Your father was closely guarded.'

'Well, they caught you,' Aran pointed out, remembering how the stranger had bested Darnell's guards.

'I don't abandon my friends in time of need,' Peregrine explained, looking down at what seemed to be a ragged bundle clutched in his arms. Then a pair of eyes opened, and Aran recognized the old man from the road, the owner of the bear. Peregrine pressed his water bottle to the old man's lips, and he drank gratefully.

'Bless you,' he said in a fading voice.

Aran gripped the bars. They were old and weathered, but solid. The gate at the far end was held shut by a massive iron clasp. 'You can get us out, can't you?' He turned to Peregrine in desperation. 'You're strong, I've seen it.'

Peregrine sighed. 'I wish it were so simple,' he said. 'I may be quick on my feet but it takes more than that to break steel bars. No, we're in a tight spot and no mistake.'

Aran felt hot tears springing into his eyes, and refused to let them fall. He had to be brave, like the heroes in Miss Crell's stories. But he knew that he had never been more scared in his life.

He gazed out into the dark woods lining the track. A pale ghost moon was rising above the swaying pines. A movement in the trees caught his attention. He only saw it for a moment, a flash of white in the very depths of the forest. Then it was gone.

He looked back at Peregrine. He too was gazing off into the darkness. He seemed lost in thought. His lips moved almost imperceptibly, making no sound.

'Where are they taking us?' Aran asked. Peregrine did not seem to hear him.

'Over the sea,' said a faint voice. Aran looked down. The old man was staring at him with wet, rheumy eyes. 'Over the sea in their black ships.'

'You've seen them?' Aran asked.

The old man nodded. 'Long time ago,' he said. 'Far

out at sea, beyond sight of land. Out where the storms are born. That's where they dwell.'

'Tell us,' Aran asked, eager for something to think about besides his terror. Perhaps if he knew more about these Marauders, he'd have a better chance of escaping them.

The old man took the bottle from Peregrine's hand and drank deeply, gaining strength. 'I was a seafaring man once, if you can believe it,' he began, his voice cracked and hoarse. 'Captain of my own ship, plying the trade routes between the Island and the shoals.' He pulled himself up, wrapping a threadbare shawl around his shoulders.

'Late one autumn, a rich Law paid me good money to fetch a load from up beyond the Gap. Salt beef, swords and wolfskins, a year's plunder from some backward mountain tribe. I knew it was a risk so close to the snows, but it had been a mean summer.

'My crew and I made the pick-up and were on our way home when a snowstorm blew up, driving us out beyond the Air Isle and into uncharted waters. We fought the storm for two nights and three days. Four of my lads froze to death at their posts. But just when we thought we could fight no longer, the storm blew itself out.'

Aran looked around the cage. Every eye was upon the old man as he continued his tale.

'I was woken that night by a hand over my mouth,' he said, his voice barely more than a whisper. 'One of my men, shaking me. I listened, but all I could hear was the howling wind. Then I heard it. Voices on the air, drawing nearer.

'There was no moon and the stars were behind the clouds, so we didn't see 'em until they were almost on top of us. But they'd seen us, and they were ready. Ropes came flying out of the darkness, with hooks that latched onto the sides of my ship, dragging her forward. I could see shapes on either side, shadows on the water. It was like we was being swallowed whole.

'Then a cry rose all around us. Torches flared. We'd been hauled into a harbour hundreds of feet wide, filled with tall black ships, and around it a great floating city. I knew we didn't stand a chance. They swarmed onto the deck, and when Charlie the bosun tried to fight back they cut him in two without breaking a sweat. That left just three of us. I never saw my ship again, nor that cargo. Those filthy beggars must've thought all their Exmusses had come at once.

'The men and me were thrown into a stinking cage like this one, only half underwater. They left us there for five days, until I thought they'd forgotten about us. On the third day the cold did for my first mate, so then there were two.

'We were allowed one night's sleep in a hard bunk, then they put us to work. We scrubbed decks, boiled fish guts, emptied latrines. Whatever our masters wanted. They gave us food enough to keep us alive, but we were always weak, always hungry. They treated us worse than dogs. Never one moment of kindness or mercy.' His voice was cracking, the memory still painful. 'I can't go back,' he said, his lip trembling.

Peregrine took the old man's hand, warming it with his own.

'But you escaped,' Aran whispered.

The old man nodded. 'Every winter we'd moor at a different port. That first year we travelled south and west to a land of green hills. That was when I found out there was more than one floating city. Another tribe was there ahead of us. The party lasted for three weeks and cost more than a few lives.

'But when spring came, we moved on. My old midshipman went soon after, taken by one of the sharks that used to follow the city, feeding on whatever we threw overboard. He was pulling in the lines when it came up out of the water and took hold of him. So then I was all alone.

'The next year we came back east. My heart rose 'cause I knew we was headed towards home. But we sailed north, past the Island, to a land of endless snow and ice. They put me in a hut on the edge of a little trading town. There was supposed to be someone guarding me, but he was usually sloshed or half asleep. I suppose they didn't think I'd bother to escape, there bein' nowhere to go. Or maybe they just didn't care.

'So one night I made a break for it. I had no food, no water, but I was past caring. For a week I lived on pine nuts and sorrel. I remember the day I killed my first rabbit, the first fresh meat I'd eaten in three years. I found a cave in the hills, built myself a little fire and waited.

'And it was about that time I found Grizelda,' he

remembered with a smile. 'It was early spring, and I'd decided to head back down, to see if the Marauders were still about. I was barely a mile out when I heard this roar. A bear was caught in a pit with wooden spikes on the bottom. Her pain must have been terrible. I crept closer and peered inside. She'd been in there for days, she was on her last legs. But there was a cub with her, just a week or so old. I don't know why, but I couldn't leave her behind. I just couldn't. I sat there on the edge of the pit until the mother passed away, then I climbed in and took the cub. She was just a little helpless thing.

'A few days later the Marauders had gone, so we stole a boat and found our way home. Now I don't suppose I shall ever see her again.' He broke into a heavy, racking cough, his whole body shaking.

'But you say there were only a few slaves back then,' Aran asked. 'What do they need all these people for?'

The old man shook his head. 'Something's changed,' he said.

Peregrine nodded. 'Someone has given them purpose,' he said, and Aran thought of the skeletal warrior he'd seen at the stadium.

'His name's Karik,' said a voice.

A woman was watching them. She was thin and hunched, with sharp, alert features and the accent of an Easterner. 'They call him "Destroyer", 'cause he shows no mercy. That attack on Carny were a show of his force. This is only the beginning. They're not raiders, they're invaders. Mark my words, they'll be ruling this land in a few years.'

'How do you know so much?' Aran asked. 'How do you know his name?'

The woman looked away. 'I made a point of learning Karik's name after he stole my little boy.'

'Hush, Kira,' said the man at her side. 'You'll only scare them.'

'Might be they could do with being scared,' she shot back.

'What will they do with us?' Aran asked.

'They'll put most of us to work,' said Kira. 'Making their weapons or manning their ships. Slaves, like your friend there.' Then her gaze fell on Aran, and her face hardened. 'But you're a strong lad. What are you, fourteen? They'll make you one of them.'

Aran was horrified. 'One of them?' he asked.

Kira nodded. 'They'll feed you, train you, beat the feeling out of you. Force you to do unspeakable things. A year or two of that, you'll be just like they are.'

'But . . .' Aran stammered. 'But they're animals.'

Peregrine put his hand on Aran's shoulder. 'You mustn't think that,' he said. 'They're cold and they are cruel, but they're as human as you or I. They choose to do this.'

'But why?' Aran asked.

Peregrine shrugged. 'I've long since learned not to ask that question when it comes to the things men do,' he said. 'Perhaps they think it's necessary for their survival.'

Kira shook her head, smiling coldly. 'Don't you believe it,' she said. 'They may be people as you say, but by Ala, they enjoy their work.'

Peregrine nodded grimly. 'Perhaps,' he said. 'Violence breeds violence, it has always been so.'

Aran huddled into the corner of the cage, shivering. He tried to imagine himself a year from now, carrying a Marauder sword. Could he truly become someone else entirely, someone brutal and heartless? No, it wasn't possible; he could never be one of them.

Then he looked at Kira's cold, unfeeling face, and realization flooded over him. Perhaps she had seen him, back at Barton – her boy, riding into battle alongside his new masters. Perhaps she had even seen him kill.

Aran felt sick inside. His longing for home intensified, and with it a desperate need for escape. He clutched the bars, muttering a silent prayer. There had to be a way.

CHAPTER NINE

The Traitor

Gradually, Aran was aware that he could see the
faces around him more clearly. The Marauders
were drawing to a halt by a farmhouse in a ring
of ragged birch trees. The doors were open and people
hurried out carrying trays of meat and mugs of pale ale.
They were skinny and subservient, reminding Aran of
the poor travellers they had passed the day before on the
road – the same tatty garments, the same windswept faces.
The farmstead itself was just a moss-covered stone house
surrounded by a huddle of tumbledown outbuildings.
East, he thought. We're going east.

The citizens did not look the Marauders in the eye as
they laid the food on a long wooden table. The warriors
gathered, pushing and scrambling and stuffing their
mouths.

The cart carrying the steel cage was wheeled into a
shadowed corner of the courtyard beneath a broad and
budding beech tree. The horses were unshackled and the

guards hurried off to fill their bellies, leaving the young herdsman standing watch. He amused himself by jabbing his stick through the bars at the helpless prisoners. Aran glared at him, and the boy put out his tongue.

'I know this place,' said Kira from the corner of the cage. 'Eskirk, they call it. My father sold pots all across this region and we ended up spending the winter here once. Most miserable season of my life. The Law was a nasty old bugger. Worked my pa to the bone, earning our keep. Still, I suppose he's dead now.'

'Or perhaps not,' Peregrine observed, and they all turned to look.

A figure had appeared in the farmhouse doorway; a man, aged beyond measure and bent almost to the ground. He hobbled into the courtyard, supporting himself on a crutch.

The Marauders parted and Karik strode through, steel heels clacking on the flagstones. His black leather garments gleamed in the lamplight, and his white hair shone.

The old Law bowed low, gesturing proudly at the feast before them. Karik nodded his approval, clasping his bony hands together and smiling through thin, ice-white lips.

'That's him all right,' Kira hissed. 'Law Little, they called him. Little sod, my dad used to say. Still, he's got the right idea, I suppose.'

'He's a Law,' Aran objected. 'How can he give shelter to these murderers?'

'Don't judge too harshly,' admonished Peregrine. 'I

imagine the price for refusal would have been his life, and the lives of those under his care.'

'He could still fight,' said Aran, feeling anger growing in his stomach. It felt good, better than the fear he'd felt before. 'He could make a stand.'

'Like Barton?' sneered Kira. 'How many died today, d'you think? He's doing the only thing any of us can do if we want to survive. Keep our mouths shut and our store-rooms open.'

Peregrine shook his head. 'As soon as the Marauders have taken what they need, these people's lives will be forfeit,' he said.

Kira shook her head. 'I don't think so,' she said. 'This isn't the first time these two have met.' Her eyes followed Law Little. 'I'd bet the old divvle gives them more than meat and shelter.'

'Such as?' Peregrine asked.

'Information,' said Kira. 'Who had a good harvest and who didn't, who's well defended and who isn't. How d'you think they knew exactly when and where to attack the Carny?'

Peregrine nodded grimly. 'It is a possibility,' he admitted.

Aran shook his head in disgust. 'He's no better than they are.'

Peregrine turned to him. 'And what would you do, if it was your loved ones facing death and torture?'

Aran looked at the Law grovelling, stooping, spittle on his lips. He didn't believe a man so twisted and heartless could *have* any loved ones.

A bellow of hoarse laughter broke the silence. A group of Marauders was approaching across the courtyard, their eyes bright with drink. One of them gnawed messily on a chop bone, his fingers gleaming with grease.

They stopped by the cage, peering in at the prisoners. The captives drew back, but Aran refused to be cowed. He stared defiantly at the Marauder band. They didn't seem to notice.

One stepped forward, and with a sickening lurch Aran recognized the sharpened tusks and leathery pelt of the captain who had captured him. The Walrus fumbled under his overhanging belly, producing a ring of jangling keys. He unlocked the clasp and the gate swung open.

Kira, closest to the gate, glanced uncertainly at the man beside her. He stared back, terrified.

'Move,' said the Walrus, in a thick, slobbering voice. 'You. Now.' Aran wondered if these were the only words he knew of their tongue.

Kira froze. Everyone was silent, waiting.

Then the Walrus reached up, took hold of Kira's arm and pulled her roughly over the threshold. She tripped and fell from the cart, sprawling on her face in the dirt. The Marauders cackled.

They took the prisoners from the cage and herded them into a row, prodding and groping, muttering to one another like a flock of carrion crows. The captives stood, some shaking, some sobbing, some holding hands, some staring rebelliously at their gaolers. Kira had her fists balled and her teeth gritted. The warrior with the greasy fingers paused in front of her, smirking and gesturing with his chop bone. Then he leaned in and tried to plant a kiss on her mouth. Kira pulled back, spitting. The Marauders roared with laughter.

Aran was the last out, taking his place at the end of the line, closest to the cage. The old man stood between Aran and Peregrine. Aran felt his cold, bony hand trembling where it clutched his arm, and he vowed not to let the old man fall.

Then a chill wind blew, and the Marauders fell silent. Karik was approaching. He strode lightly, almost gracefully, across the broken paving stones, dark robes rustling. Aran felt his heart skip as he gazed upon that sunken, skeletal face.

Karik paused to say a few words to his captain, then he turned to inspect the prisoners. He made his way along the line, his small, hard eyes falling on each of them in turn. None could meet his gaze.

He tapped a pale young woman on the shoulder. As the Walrus shoved her roughly out of the line and back towards the cage, Aran saw that she was clasping her hands protectively over a swollen belly. She stood a few feet from them, her eyes streaming.

Another prisoner was singled out, a boy half Aran's age clutching a stuffed pig made of stitched rags. The pregnant woman took hold of his hand and squeezed it tight. He looked up at her with wide, uncomprehending eyes.

Aran's stomach rolled. He knew what was happening.

The Marauders would never waste their food on those who couldn't survive.

'We have to do something,' he whispered to Peregrine, as loudly as he dared.

Peregrine shot him an urgent glance. 'No,' he hissed. 'There are too many.'

The Walrus shoved Peregrine in the back with the butt of his spear and he straightened, coming face to face with Karik. For the first time, the Marauder chief seemed to draw back. Peregrine offered no resistance, but there was something defiant, even threatening, in his calm, open gaze. Karik's lip curled and a small growl escaped his throat, like a predatory animal bristling at its rival.

Then Karik came to the old man. He reached out with one bony finger, as Aran had known he would. As the guards hauled the old man away, Aran glanced urgently at Peregrine. He has to do something, he thought. He *has* to.

Then Karik was towering over him. His white hair was bathed in moonlight and the bones in his necklace gleamed. He took hold of Aran's chin, turning the boy's head first to one side, then the other. His grip tightened, forcing Aran's mouth open. Then he reached in and tapped the boy's teeth with one long, black-painted fingernail. Aran tasted salt and shuddered, trying not to retch. Then the shadow was gone.

Aran looked over at Peregrine. The pale man's eyes were closed and he was mumbling under his breath, a strange singsong chant. The Marauders paid no attention, turning instead to the three they had singled out – the old man, the little boy and the pregnant woman. They lined them up against the cage.

Karik drew his sword, running the blade along his outstretched finger. The old man stared helplessly, his lip trembling. Karik met his gaze regretfully, muttering a few words. A prayer, Aran suspected. What foul Gods must he worship, that they would countenance this?

He wanted to cry out, to shake Peregrine from his trance, to force him to act, but something held him back. Peregrine's eyes were still closed and his mouth still moved, his voice so low that it was barely even a whisper, just the dry rustling of his lips and the hollow breath beneath. A stillness seemed to radiate from him, and to Aran it felt almost as though the air itself were listening. He had never felt anything quite like it.

Karik's sword flashed in the darkness. In the moment before it fell, the Marauder chief glanced back at Aran. Then his blade pierced the old man's chest above his heart.

The old man sank slowly to the ground and a soft sigh escaped his lips. Someone cried out. Aran thought it might have been himself.

For the briefest moment, everything was silent.

Then, with a roar, the forest erupted. Branches shook and cracked. Everyone turned and drew back, even the Marauders.

Something was coming out of the darkness. Something heavy and powerful, smashing the foliage with the force of its approach. Aran heard snorting breath and lumbering feet. He saw a flash of white between the trees.

The clouds parted and pale moonlight bathed the clearing. There against the dark forest stood Grizelda, the bear. She paced towards the cage, shaking the leaves and burrs from her coat.

Karik and his men retreated towards the farmhouse. The prisoners held firm. They didn't dare flee. The bear might decide to run them down.

Grizelda approached Peregrine. He greeted her with a smile, stroking her wet nose and scratching under her ear. Aran cowered behind him. Up close, the bear's size and strength were awe-inspiring. She growled, a deep sound from the very depths of her massive body.

'Now now, Grizelda,' whispered Peregrine. 'You found us.'

The growl rose in pitch and volume, and Peregrine pulled his hand away. The bear stamped her paw and looked at the petrified prisoners. She scanned each face in turn, but none belonged to her master. Her voice took on a demanding tone.

Peregrine took a single step towards the cage. 'I'm sorry,' he whispered.

The bear's nose caught the scent and her growling ceased abruptly. She came forward, sniffing at the lifeless bundle on the ground. She opened her mouth and licked the old man's dry hand, giving a little whimper of confusion. She tugged at his sleeve with her teeth, gently at first, then with increasing force. The jacket ripped and the bear spat a patch of cloth down into the mud.

Grizelda let out a roar of disbelief, turning on Peregrine

and the other prisoners. Some broke and ran. Aran saw the pregnant woman and the little boy vanishing into the woods. Peregrine pulled Aran back, facing the bear.

Then they heard the sound of approaching feet. The Marauders were returning.

The warriors drew their weapons as they advanced, jabbing at the bear with long spears. Aran saw the Walrus in the vanguard, a long pike upraised in his hands.

At first the bear merely batted them away. But when a mean thrust drew blood she reared up on her haunches. She lashed out with her front paws and three Marauders fell, tumbling into a heap.

Grizelda lowered her head and lunged, snarling. Aran saw the Walrus backing away, jabbing with his pike. The bear swatted it to the ground, the long stem snapping. The Walrus tried to scramble clear but his men were bunched up too tight behind him. He tripped and fell on his backside, and the bear was on him. Aran heard a frantic, high-pitched scream, abruptly silenced. There was a hideous wet ripping sound.

Peregrine put his hands on Aran's shoulders. 'Go,' he said. 'Run.'

When he reached the trees, Aran looked back. Karik had come riding into the fray, circling the bear at a distance. An arrow pierced Grizelda's hide. She howled, plucking at the shaft. Seeing her distracted, Karik swung in and dealt her a vicious blow with his sword. Grizelda screamed with pain and rage.

More Marauders came running to intercept the

escaping prisoners. Peregrine stood silhouetted in the light from the farmhouse. In his hand was a cleaver he'd taken from one of the bear's victims. Peregrine swung, and Aran heard a sickening thud as the axe sunk deep into a Marauder's chest. But reinforcements were approaching, and Aran saw that Peregrine would soon be overwhelmed.

He stepped clear of the trees, raising his arms to get Peregrine's attention. But before he could cry out, something struck him on the side of his head and he staggered into the dirt.

Aran dragged himself up, blinking. The young Marauder herdsman faced him, his fists raised. He had white hair and wiry limbs, towering over Aran with his fists balled. His face and arms were covered with scars, and he had that empty look in his eyes, just like the others.

They circled cautiously. The boy struck out. Aran ducked and the fist whistled over his head. His size was actually an advantage here, he thought as he ducked for a second time.

Then the boy reached out with lightning swiftness and took hold of Aran's neck. Aran felt his feet leave the earth. He kicked wildly as the boy shoved him to the ground, holding him down by his throat. The boy reached into his pocket and drew out his herding switch. He smiled cruelly. Aran was helpless, trapped in the boy's shadow. The switch lashed down towards his face.

Then suddenly the weight was gone, and Aran blinked as moonlight flooded his eyes. A hand on his shoulder was dragging him up, towards the safety of the forest. Looking back, Aran could see the boy lying prone in the grass, a startled look on his features.

'He'll live,' said Peregrine, waving his cleaver. 'I only hit him with the blunt end.'

When they reached the trees, Aran turned for one last look. Grizelda stood on her hind legs, paws swiping blindly. Her bloody coat glistened in the moonlight. Her eyes were wild, her lips drawn back in a snarl of rage. Her victims were scattered across the clearing. But cold-eyed Karik came riding hard, lashing out with his blade, thrusting with concentrated energy.

Aran allowed himself to be pulled away. They heard a deafening roar, a last scream of defiance and fury. Then there was silence.

CHAPTER TEN

Peregrine

They didn't rest until the sky was light. They had struggled through the undergrowth for hours, over muddy streams and sucking bogland. Finally they came to a sheltered glade beneath the arms of a hunched old oak, and Peregrine agreed to make camp.

Aran slumped to the ground, his head spinning. Peregrine drew his cloak up to his chin like a cocoon and lay back on the mossy earth, closing his eyes.

'Shouldn't we keep watch?' Aran asked.

'If you like,' Peregrine said without stirring. 'But you're flattering yourself if you think they'd chase us this far.'

'What about the dogs?' Aran asked. 'They could have tracked us.'

Peregrine shrugged. 'Maybe,' he said. 'If we wake up dead you'll know I was wrong.'

Aran spluttered. 'But what if . . . ?'

Peregrine opened one eye. 'Aran, seriously, do as you like,' he snapped. 'But do it quietly.'

Aran hunched against the trunk of the tree. In the stories it was always the children who slept while the gallant grown-ups stood guard. But Peregrine was already snoring.

Aran looked at his new friend and wondered. In the excitement of their escape he hadn't thought twice about following this pale stranger. But now his relief was tempered with unease. True, Peregrine had helped everyone to escape. But even that was unusual. Singing to a bear? What sort of person could do a thing like that?

When Aran woke some hours later there were beetles in his hair and roots digging into his back. He sat up, feeling like he hadn't slept at all.

Peregrine crouched a few feet away, the cleaver upraised in his hand. As Aran watched it whistled from his grasp, thudding into the trunk of a tree. There was a surprised squawk. Peregrine jumped up, returning with a neatly beheaded partridge.

'Good trick,' Aran said.

Peregrine shrugged. 'Spend as much time in the woods as I have, you learn a few things.'

'Don't you have a home?' Aran asked.

'Sometimes,' Peregrine replied. 'But I've done some travelling too. I've been to places you couldn't even imagine, let alone pronounce. One day I'll tell you. Not that you'd believe half of it.'

After breakfast they set off. Peregrine cut a switch from a birch tree and whittled off the twigs with his axe. He used it to beat the bushes aside, clearing a path through dense thickets of nettle and gorse.

By mid-afternoon they had left the woods behind, following a muddy sheep trail through narrow gullies of striated limestone up onto the high fells. Peregrine moved with a purpose, but did not feel the need to explain himself to Aran. Eventually the boy could take it no longer.

'Where are we going?' he asked. 'I'm completely lost.'

'I know,' said Peregrine.

'Will you take me back to Hawk's Cross? You do know how to get there, don't you?'

'I do,' said Peregrine.

'So is that where we're going?' Aran asked again.

'Eventually,' said Peregrine.

Aran fell back. Eventually? What did that mean? He felt a knife blade of uncertainty twist in his gut.

'You don't trust me, do you, Aran?' Peregrine asked suddenly, turning to face him.

Aran shook his head. 'Yes, of course, I—'

'It's all right,' Peregrine said. 'I know I'm not the sort you're used to dealing with. You're thankful that I got you out of that cage, but you suspect I might be a bit loopy. A few chips short of a fish supper. Am I right?'

Aran opened his mouth and closed it again.

'I'm no happier about this than you, believe me,' Peregrine told him. 'I thought I'd at least have a couple more years to get my act together before it all started up again.' He looked down with an expression of annoyance tinged with sympathy. 'It's not your fault,' he said. 'But if this is going to work, we're going to have to be completely honest with each other.'

Aran swallowed. If *what* was going to work?

'It's just . . .' he started. Peregrine was looking at him expectantly. 'It's just that I don't know where I am, or who you are, or what you're talking about. And you seem to know all about me, and exactly where we're going.'

Peregrine smiled. 'There,' he said. 'That wasn't so hard, was it?' And he turned on his heel and marched on, humming softly.

Aran hurried at his side. 'So?' he said.

'So what?'

Aran fought back a wave of frustration. 'So where are we going?'

'Right now?'

'Yes, right now.'

'We're going to my cottage. We'll rest there tonight, and in the morning I'll take you back to Hawk's Cross. But jog on, I want to be home before nightfall if I can help it.'

Aran shut his mouth and set himself to walking. He wasn't sure about this cottage business – Miss Crell's stories had been full of kids who were lured to strangers' homes and baked into pies. But somehow he couldn't picture Peregrine as the child-eating type. For all his strangeness, there was something familiar about him. And besides, what choice did he have? If he tried to run he'd still be lost in the wild, only this time he'd be all alone.

They crossed the low edge of a line of rolling hills which stretched into the far distance. The air was warm, even as the sun crept down towards the horizon. Soon they were descending too, following a narrow stream which carved its way down the hillside to meet a rocky, winding river. Meadows opened out on either side, dotted with nodding daffodils and sleepily grazing sheep. On the far side of the valley a long pinewood barn jutted from the grassy slope, surrounded by a stone courtyard, and beyond that a patchwork of tilled fields. To Aran it almost looked like home.

'That's Crakehall,' Peregrine explained. 'My neighbour Law Maddon lives there. I expect he's still off at Carny. Good thing too, he doesn't like me much.'

Aran could see the citizens staring narrow-eyed at Peregrine as they passed. One of them hurried her children inside.

'Why don't they like you?' Aran asked.

Peregrine shrugged. 'Long story,' he said. But he did not elaborate.

They followed the track along the riverbank, through woody hollows carpeted with bluebells and reeking of damp earth and wild garlic. Then suddenly they struck off into the undergrowth, following no trail Aran could make out. He followed as quickly as he could, scrambling over mossy stones and rotted roots. As the last light faded from the day, they reached Peregrine's home.

The cottage was unlike any dwelling Aran had ever seen. It stood alone in a brake of trees, surrounded by a tangled garden of weeds and thorny bushes. Looking up, Aran could see crumbling red-brick walls thrusting above the greenery, capped by a roof of cracked tiles and a toppling chimney. Thick vines of ivy hung in knots around a rusted drainpipe, and collected in tangled clumps beneath the eaves.

Peregrine took his stick and began to beat at the weeds, clearing a narrow path to the flaking, red-painted front door. A rusted plaque over the lintel bore a word which Aran could not read, and beside it a number: 1926.

'What does that say?' Aran asked.

'It says "Fiveacres"; that's the name of the house,' Peregrine explained. 'The numbers mark the year it was built.'

Aran was confused. Years didn't have numbers or names, not like moons and days. They just came and went, and no one bothered to number them.

Peregrine opened the door and pushed inside. Dust rose in a sooty cloud. The floor was tiled with cracked squares of black and white. There was a wardrobe against the wall, and as Aran watched a chubby rat scuttled under it.

'Sorry it's such a tip,' said Peregrine, taking a strange lamp down from the wall and lighting it with a click. 'I never was much for housekeeping, and I haven't been home in a while.' Aran could believe it. It looked as though no one had crossed the threshold in years.

He followed Peregrine into the living room. There was a leather sofa covered by a moth-eaten throw, and a battered armchair bursting with yellow stuffing. The walls and fire-place were thick with cobwebs and the once-white carpet was filthy with droppings.

Aran looked up, and his eyes widened. Books were a luxury – even Law Carifax could only afford a few. But here there were hundreds, crammed together on the collapsing shelves.

In the corner stood a black box with a glass front. Aran wondered if it was some kind of display case, but all he could see was his own reflection in the dusty glass. Leaning against it was a triangular frame of metal poles holding a pair of spoked wheels. Aran put his hand on the wheel rim. It squeaked rustily.

'Could probably use a spot of oil,' said Peregrine. 'Even so, it was a pretty good racer in its day.' Then he clapped his hands and looked around. 'One of these days I'll have a big spring-clean, and you won't recognize the place. In the meantime try to make yourself comfortable. How about a spot of supper?' He shuffled off into the next room and began to clatter and mutter loudly to himself.

Aran continued to look around. Above the door were two wooden rods, like broom handles with metal plating. He took one of them down and inspected it, peering into a hole which had been bored into the wood.

Peregrine appeared in the doorway and let out a screech. He wrenched the rod from Aran's hands, replacing it above the door. 'I'm going out for supplies,' he said. 'Don't touch anything until I get back. Just read a book or something.'

'I can't read,' Aran said, thinking it should have been perfectly obvious he wasn't a scholar.

'Of course you can't,' said Peregrine, an edge of irritation creeping into his voice. 'I'll find you one with photographs. Here: *A Child's Treasury of Animals*. This'll give you something to think about.' And he thrust the book into Aran's hands, pushing him down onto the sofa.

On the front of the book was a more lifelike picture

than Aran had ever seen. It was as though the very thing the artist was looking at had been frozen on the paper. He must have been a great painter, Aran thought. The picture depicted a beast of some kind, like a bear with a shaggy mane.

Aran opened the book and laughed out loud. The artist was a joker. Here was a mouse five times taller than a man, but with huge papery ears and a snake attached to its face. On the opposite page was a hairy woman with red fur and broad, flat features. She wasn't wearing any clothes. Aran wondered if Peregrine had drawn the pictures himself. He was certainly weird enough.

After a while Aran became aware of a pleasant smell drifting in from the next room. Peregrine followed, carrying two plates piled with cooked vegetables and chunks of roasted bird. 'I left the coop open before I went away,' he said, handing a plate to Aran. 'I suppose they must just like it here.'

He rested his supper on the mantelpiece and took up a poker to clear the worst of the cobwebs out of the fire-place. Then he threw in a bundle of sticks and some coal, and set light to it.

'I've an idea,' said Peregrine. 'How about a tune while we eat?'

He pulled out a tiny black object, showing it proudly to Aran. 'Thank God for solar batteries.' He tapped the device with the tip of his finger and a light came on. 'Here we go.'

When the music started, Aran almost jumped out

of his seat. It seemed to come from all around them, a glittering, thrumming sound backed by a pounding beat. A man began to sing; a deep, gulping voice with an accent entirely foreign to Aran's ears.

'Hail to the King,' said Peregrine, sinking into the armchair and tucking into his supper.

Aran looked around. The music was coming from a pair of long black cases, high up on the wall. Perhaps the singer was actually somewhere in the farmstead, below their feet, and his voice was being carried up through a vent. It sounded suitably boomy and distant.

'I've confused you,' Peregrine said. 'I'd try to explain but there wouldn't be much point. But don't fret, I haven't trapped a little man in a box or anything.'

Aran tried to eat, but his thoughts were overwhelmed by the music. The man seemed to be having some trouble with a baby, and had moved into a hotel filled with sad and desperate characters.

'So?' Peregrine asked, as the song faded. 'Are you a fan?'

Aran wasn't sure what to say. 'He sounded terribly unhappy,' he offered.

Peregrine frowned. 'Well, it's better than that modern music your lot seem to enjoy,' he said. 'Every song I heard at Carny this year was about people killing each other. And they all seemed to go on for about half an hour.'

'They're about great deeds,' Aran argued. 'They need to be that long or you wouldn't get the whole story.'

'Well, we had proper music in my day,' Peregrine sighed. 'Three chords and the truth.'

Another song had started. 'It doesn't make any sense,' Aran argued. 'Why would he stop being friends with the dog just because it hasn't caught any rabbits? It's just mean.'

Peregrine rolled his eyes and didn't reply.

When they were finished eating, Peregrine cleared the plates and poured himself a drink from a small glass bottle. He yawned mightily, and Aran found himself doing the same. He felt the weight of a restless night and a long walk sinking into his bones.

'Take the sofa,' Peregrine said as the music faded for the last time. He settled into the armchair, stretching his long legs out before the fire. 'There's a bed upstairs, but I wouldn't like to imagine what's been nesting in it while I was away. This'll do for tonight. I know it's been a big day, but try to get some sleep. We'll be making an early start in the morning.'

He switched off the lamp and the room was bathed in the fiery glow. Aran lay back, listening to Peregrine's steady breaths. He knew he should try to think things through. Somewhere in all the confusing things Peregrine had done and said there must be some kind of clue, a key that would make sense of all this. But the room was too warm and the sofa was too soft. Before he could figure any of it out, Aran was fast asleep.

CHAPTER ELEVEN

The Museum

Aran woke in the night with his bladder bursting. For a moment he didn't know where he was, then the memories came and he was wide awake.

The fire had sunk to smouldering cinders. The house lay in a deep well of silence, broken only by Peregrine's wheezing breaths, soft and regular in sleep. A breeze stirred the ragged curtains and the thorned stem of a rose bush tapped lightly but insistently against the window pane.

Aran sat up, cursing himself for not asking where the piss-pit was. At home there was one on every level, but here it could be anywhere. He thought about waking Peregrine, but pushed that idea aside. Who knew how he might react if startled?

There was only one thing for it. Aran got to his feet and tiptoed to the door. He opened it gently, shivering as he heard a squeak which could have been a rusty hinge or a hungry rat. His feet were bare and the tiles were cold.

He reached the front door, turning the handle and

tugging firmly. Nothing happened. The door was stuck fast. He turned back, hopping from one foot to the other, feeling the pressure build inside him. There was no way he could go back to sleep, and the thought of waking Peregrine was equally unappealing. A pale shaft of moonlight came leaking through the far door from the kitchen. Aran crept towards it.

The kitchen was as cluttered and cobwebbed as the rest of the house. Two dusty glass receptacles stood empty on the counter, beside a pair of strange metallic knobs which sprouted above the sink. Aran looked for a bucket or trough, but could see none. For a moment he considered just going in the sink, but his conscience wouldn't let him. It was bad enough that he was creeping around a stranger's house in the middle of the night, never mind peeing in his kitchen. There must be a proper pit, either in the garden or under the house.

A door to his left stood open, revealing a dark flight of stairs. It must be on one of the lower levels; that made sense.

He crept down the steps. On a shelf halfway down he found candles and a tinder box, and took them along. There didn't seem to be any vent shafts down here; it was pitch black. Aran lit the candle and held it up in front of him. The steps seemed to go on and on.

At last he came to the bottom. He turned a corner, and almost dropped his candle.

He was standing on the edge of a vast room, bigger than his feeble little flame could illuminate. From floor to ceiling, a sprawling, irregular labyrinth of dust-covered objects stretched beyond the limits of his vision, eventually dissolving into shadows.

There were wardrobes and shelves overflowing with boxes, many of them packed with books or shiny metal discs. There were bulging black bags with words scrawled on them. There were hanging drapes and carpets which had once been colourful, now ravaged by moths and mould. There were rusty white upright coffins with gleaming steel handles, and grey cubes with clear screens and wires trailing, all made from some smooth, shiny material.

Aran jumped. A pair of eyes was watching him blankly. It was only a dummy – a human figure formed from that shiny, unfamiliar substance, its jointed body slumped in a corner. Its face was a featureless mask, and its glassy eyes stared emptily as Aran picked his way around the room.

Set into the wall beneath the stairs was another door and Aran crossed to it hopefully, putting down his candle and giving the handle a sharp tug. There was a crash, and Aran was almost swept off his feet by a landslide of bags and boxes and paper. He had to bite his lip to suppress a cry.

Looking down, he found himself up to his knees in small, colourful pieces of stiff card. He picked one up to inspect it more closely, and this time he did cry out.

The card was painted like the animal book, but with a scene beyond anything Aran could have imagined. There were towers hundreds of feet high, canyons of steel which dwarfed the tiny figures in the foreground. He picked up another. Here was a silver bird with broad metal wings, soaring through high white clouds.

He grabbed a handful, leafing through. There were mountains like the ones in Miss Crell's stories, and endless sandy deserts stretching beyond the frame. There were carriages of iron and glass, people waving happily from the windows. There were buildings covered with colourful signs emblazoned with writing and drawings, pictures within pictures within pictures. The detail was astonishing. It must have taken a thousand master artists working their whole lives to create so many.

And then he realized. These weren't paintings at all. Somehow, the paper had acted like a mirror, trapping the reflection of something which had really happened. Aran's mind reeled. Could this be another world he was looking at? He'd heard a story once about a man who went to the moon and had adventures with the people who lived there. Perhaps that was where Peregrine had come from, travelling in one of these metal birds.

But alongside his sense of wonder, his old fear began to creep back in. Why had Peregrine brought him here? And what would he do if he caught Aran snooping?

Panic ran like a cold finger down the back of his neck. He began to scoop up the pieces of paper, thrusting them back into their boxes, trying to shove the whole mess back into the cupboard. But it was no use: it just toppled out again, making things worse.

Aran's heart hammered. Perhaps he should just run. Slip out while Peregrine was asleep. He could make for that nearby farmstead, ask them to send word to his father. He knew it was cowardly and rude, but what choice did he have? If he was quiet, and with a little luck, he could make it.

'How do you like my museum?'

Aran whipped round, dropping the papers. Peregrine was standing at the bottom of the steps , his face unreadable. 'Just having a poke around, were you? Forget your manners?'

Aran gaped. 'I wasn't . . . I didn't . . . I was looking for . . .'

'Fine time of night to go sneaking about.' Peregrine crossed purposefully towards Aran, who drew back instinctively. Peregrine scowled. 'Oh, for God's sake, I'm not going to yell at you, or anything worse. I'm just putting the lights on. Here.'

He flicked a switch and the room was suddenly flooded with light, streaming from a line of glass tubes on the ceiling. Aran felt his knees weaken. The room was hundreds of feet from end to end, and every inch was heaped to the rafters with boxes, cupboards, storage crates and some larger shapes which he couldn't quite make out.

'So?' Peregrine asked. 'What d'you think?'

Aran was at a loss. 'I . . . I don't understand,' he said at last. 'What is all this?'

'It's history,' Peregrine told him. 'All that remains of a forgotten world. Photographs, music, films, books. Clothes, computers, cookers, fridges. Bikes, boards, buggies . . . I think there's even a bus down here somewhere. The

127

washed-up flotsam of a lost civilization. The Ancestors, you call them.'

Aran had heard tales of the Ancestors all his life, but nobody took them seriously. The stories were so fanciful – how the Ancestors could fly without wings, and fight battles with the push of a button.

Yet at the same time, he had often wondered why the world was as it was. He knew that neither his father nor his grandfather had built Hawk's Cross, that deep warren of rooms and tunnels. So who had? And he'd seen things neither he nor anyone else could satisfactorily explain – piles of rubble in the forest, cages of twisted metal piled one upon the other, rusted and cracked with age. And here in this room, the strangest sights of all.

'I tried to salvage all I could,' Peregrine went on. 'But so much was lost. So many beautiful things gone. Still, it's amazing how well it's all lasted down here. I think maybe there's a little bit of magic in this house. My mother . . . well, that's another story.'

'So how did . . .' Aran began. 'What did—'

'Where did that world go?' Peregrine asked. 'Well, partly it was down to machines like these.' He pulled back a sheet, uncovering a hollow object about Aran's height, with curved metal sides and murky windows through which the boy now peered. Inside were leather seats and a series of complicated levers and handles.

'It's called a Ford Focus,' said Peregrine. 'I'd take you for a spin, but we'd have a hell of a time finding a petrol station.'

Aran looked at him, his mouth hanging open. 'I don't understand,' he said again.

'I know,' Peregrine said. 'You don't have to, really. Here.' He took down a wooden ball with a colourful painted surface. 'This is the world as it was. The blue bits are the sea, the other colours are the land. This, here' – he pointed to a tiny pinkish mark on the top half of the ball – 'is the Island, or Britain, as it was known.'

'But it's tiny!' Aran protested. He wasn't convinced. He'd heard people say the world was round, but if that was the case, why was everything flat?

'It's even smaller now,' said Peregrine. 'A globe today would look very different. I won't bore you with the details, you wouldn't understand them anyway. Suffice it to say that the Earth grew hotter, and it was all the fault of men. They built factories and produced chemicals and . . . Oh, I know, the words mean nothing to you. But as the Earth began to heat up, the ice melted. These white parts here, you see? And many countries went down beneath the waves. That's what the different colours mean, by the way,' he explained. 'Countries.'

Aran looked blank. Peregrine scratched his chin. 'It's an area of land ruled over by a person, or a group of people. Sort of.'

'Like a farmstead,' said Aran, trying to be helpful. 'Only bigger.'

'Yes, I suppose so,' said Peregrine. 'But a lot bigger. For example this country here' – he pointed to a large greenish expanse – 'had over a billion citizens.'

Aran stared at him blankly. 'A billion is a thousand million,' explained Peregrine.

Aran's head span. That must be more than all the leaves on all the trees in the world. 'That's not possible,' he said.

Peregrine put down the globe. 'I think I may've just blown your mind,' he said with a sympathetic smile.

Aran shook his head. It was as though the world itself were expanding before his eyes, revealing more of itself with each passing moment. So many people, so many lives. But he was staying the same, shrinking in the face of such vastness.

'Come on,' Peregrine said softly. 'The sun's coming up, and we've a long road ahead. I promised to take you home, remember?'

He clicked the switch. The room was plunged into darkness, except for Aran's flickering candle and a thin shaft of daylight filtering down the stairway.

Aran was almost reluctant to leave. His eyes had been opened, just a little, and going back to Hawk's Cross would mean closing them again.

Then he felt a tightening in his belly and remembered why he had come down here in the first place. The Ancestors may have been strange and powerful, but they must have needed to answer the call of nature.

He followed Peregrine up the steps into the pale light of morning.

CHAPTER TWELVE

Homecoming

The sun was peeking above the treetops as they set out, striking west around the bottom of Crakehall farm and down into the flatlands beyond. Aran felt a growing sense of expectation. The sun shone and life seemed filled with possibilities. A line of hills rose blue and hazy in the distance, and they followed with a purposeful step.

That afternoon they became bogged down in a peat mire, and Aran's shoes were almost lost. Some hours later they were forced to scale a rocky ridge that lay across their path, the bottom of which was thick with hawthorn and holly bushes that grazed their skin and tried to snatch their bags away. Nightfall found them on the high moors, hunched in the lee of a sparse, knotted ash as a drizzly rain hampered Peregrine's efforts to light a fire. Eventually he gave up and they went hungry.

But by the next afternoon the weather had brightened, and as they walked Aran began to recognize features of the landscape around them – a rocky stream where he and Mohanna had played guards-of-the-crossing, leaving Aran soaked and bruised; the sycamore tree he and Akmid had climbed when a tribe of wild dogs caught them hunting in the woods. They had perched in the branches for a day and a night, blaming each other bitterly, before their father's men came along and scattered the pack.

Then, most familiar of all, the wide, rippling river, its rocky banks gleaming in the last light of the sinking sun. Dragonflies darted across the surface and a heron stood sentry in the shallows, lifting on great flapping wings as they approached. Even the swarms of black midges seemed to whine a welcome home.

They struck the road just as the sun touched the horizon, and as they crossed the ford Aran heard hoof beats echoing close behind. Law Carifax came riding hard, scooping Aran up in his arms, clutching him tight as the horse whinnied and bucked beneath them.

'Oh, my boy,' he said, his voice cracking. 'Don't you ever do anything like that again.'

'I won't,' said Aran tearfully. 'I promise.'

The Law had scoured the battlefields of Barton for any trace of his youngest son. Then, when the healers told him that Akmid was fit enough to travel, Carifax had sent the carts back to Hawk's Cross without him. With his family and advisers out of the way, the Law had embarked upon a dangerous plan, offering ample reward to anyone desperate enough to join him in following the Marauder band that had taken Aran.

After a hard night's ride they'd had the good luck to run into Kira. She had been paid handsomely for the information she gave – that a strange man had helped them to escape, that a boy was with him, and that the two of them had gone off together. Kira's description of the stranger may have given Carifax a moment's pause, but at least he knew that Aran would be safe. He had turned for home with a happy heart.

There was commotion in the courtyard as the Law came riding up to the gate, Aran perched in the saddle behind him. Lady Carifax ran from the summerhouse, practically dragging Aran down from the horse.

'You little wretch,' she muttered lovingly, cradling his head. 'Cruel, heartless child. Putting your poor mother through so much worry.'

They bundled Aran down to the dining hall, where the evening meal was about to be laid out. Word had spread and the hall was soon crowded with people, clambering around the pillars and over the tables to take a look at the Law's prodigal child. They plied him with food and drink, making him tell the story over and again. Akmid was still confined to quarters, but Keller watched from an alcove, the relief plain on his face. The Law hadn't taken kindly to his decision to abandon Aran on the battlefield.

Lady Carifax told Aran about their own escape, how she and her husband had survived thanks to Carifax's guard captain, who had lost two fingers and half an ear for his trouble. But they were all recovering well except for Miss

Crell, who had taken to her bed and was not expected to resurface any time soon.

Looking out at the sea of welcoming faces, Aran realized that his was but one tale among many. Of those who had made the trip, none had emerged unscathed. Faces he had known since birth bore red scars and black bruises. Many were swathed in bandages or supported themselves on makeshift crutches, while others could not walk at all but had to be carried into the hall by their families and friends. And as Aran looked, he realized that some faces were simply gone, whether captured or killed he could not say. But he knew that the people gathered here were the lucky ones, himself most of all.

And he had only one man to thank. Peregrine stood alone, watching as the people petted, poked and prodded the boy proudly. But they did not speak to the newcomer, or even acknowledge his presence – for although Aran left out the most peculiar parts, his story was still too mysterious, too unsettling. The people of Hawk's Cross had had enough of outsiders to last a lifetime.

Law Carifax, however, could not in good conscience remain silent. 'Peregrine,' he said at last. 'You have delivered my boy to me. I'm not sure how I can ever thank you. Anything I own is yours.'

Peregrine smiled inscrutably. 'Well,' he said, 'I'm glad you brought that up, actually. Much as I'd love a nice milking cow or a smashing leather waistcoat like that one, I had something else in mind.'

Carifax's face clouded. 'Anything,' he said, less certainly.

'Well, I've been thinking,' Peregrine said. 'It gets lonely, the travelling life, and my home is just a wreck, as Aran will attest. So I thought it might be nice to stay somewhere new for a little while. Have a spot of company. What d'you think?'

Aran's mouth dropped. Lady Carifax clutched her husband's arm. The Law was looking at Peregrine with an expression poised somewhere between disbelief, horror and outrage. 'You mean . . . stay here?' he asked. 'With us?'

'If it's convenient,' Peregrine said.

The air seemed to have been sucked out of the room. Aran distinctly heard someone on the very far side of the hall cough into their sleeve.

The Law's mouth worked soundlessly. 'Very . . . very well,' he said at last, clearly unable to think of a reason why not. 'I'll . . . I'll have someone find you a room.' And he glanced apologetically at his wife, who pursed her lips and said nothing.

'With a desk, if you don't mind,' Peregrine said, as though nothing out of the ordinary had happened. 'I may as well earn my keep, and with the boy's tutor out of action it would seem like perfect timing.'

Carifax's cheeks reddened further. 'Well, I don't know if . . . I'm not sure that . . . This seems awfully sudden, and—'

'Please,' Aran found himself interrupting, before the thought had even formed in his head. 'I'll bet Peregrine knows all about crops and livestock and all those boring things.'

'I've forgotten more about farming than your Foreman will ever know,' Peregrine said. 'And I mean that literally.'

'Please, Father,' Aran repeated. Suddenly the thought of studying with Peregrine seemed incredibly exciting. Who else could teach him all about the Ancestors and the world before?

Carifax let out a strangled *humph*, and looked defeated. 'Well,' he said. 'Well, then.' He coughed and fell silent.

They found a disused storeroom beneath the carpentry shop on the sixth level, filled with brooms and broken furniture. Aran helped to clear out the worst of the clutter and they dragged a bed and a desk down from the infirmary.

Peregrine seemed quite satisfied with his lodgings. He fumbled around in the bottom of his pack, pulling out a stray sock, a piece of mouldy cheese, a penknife and three huge leather-bound books.

'What are those?' Aran asked.

Peregrine placed the books on the desk. 'They were my mother's,' he said. 'There's nothing in them that would interest you. Boring stuff. Not like the exciting lessons in farming and trade that we're going to be enjoying together over the next few months.'

Aran smiled. 'I'm sure my father will get used to the idea,' he said. 'I like how you asked him right out in front of everyone, so he couldn't say no.'

Peregrine shrugged. 'It's his own fault. He said he'd give me anything.'

'And the thing you wanted was to teach me?' Aran asked.

Peregrine frowned at him. 'Don't get a big head,' he said. 'What I want doesn't come into it. The time has come. And there's nothing you can do about time.' He folded up his jacket and hung it over the back of the chair. 'But look,' he said. 'Go easy on your father. Law Carifax and I . . . well, we have a complicated history. Though I think he'd prefer I wait until you're older before we go into that.'

Aran frowned. 'Why do I get the feeling there are all sorts of things you're not telling me?'

Peregrine squinted at him. 'Because you're a bright boy,' he said. 'Run along now. I need to unpack.'

Aran shut the door and trudged back up the stairs. He staggered into his room with a sigh. It seemed small after three days outdoors, and he was aware of the oppressive weight of earth above his head.

There was a knock at the door. Aran lay on his bed, hoping whoever it was would go away.

'Maybe he's asleep,' said a voice.

'Rubbish,' said another. 'He's faking. I'm going in.'

The door opened and Mohanna entered, closely followed by Cas.

Aran sat up. 'What are you doing here?' he asked.

'I live here,' said Cas reproachfully.

'Not you,' said Aran, and looked at Mohanna. 'You.'

She shrugged. 'I rode over to see if there was any news, and there was.' She smiled and embraced him warmly.

They told Aran all about their own trials with the

Marauders; how they had been separated from Darnell's men during the escape and had to take refuge in a cattle pen, up to their knees in sewage and bull's blood. Still, Mohanna counted herself lucky compared to her father, who had disappeared for a day and a night before being found wounded, witless and wandering on the outskirts of town.

'But enough about us,' Mohanna said. 'Aran, you've been gone for four days. You must have all kinds of stories.'

'Cartwright the butcher told me you fought five bears single-handed,' said Cas. 'But Solly said he heard it was just two bears, but five Marauders.'

'News travels fast,' said Aran ironically. 'They're exaggerating slightly.'

'I thought as much,' admitted Mohanna. 'What was it? Three bunny rabbits and an old woman on crutches?'

Aran glared. 'I did my share of fighting,' he said. But they weren't about to let him get any peace until he'd told the whole story. 'Come on,' he said. 'Let's get some fresh air.'

They took the winch lift to the surface, stepping out into the quiet cool of almost-night. Then they clambered up behind the chapel to their favourite spot, a rocky lookout which jutted above the farmstead. They perched on the edge of the cliff, dangling their feet over the edge.

The courtyard below was silent and deserted. A faint stripe of liquid gold lit the western horizon and the waning moon hung suspended above the outline of the trees. Aran looked at the dark patches on the moon's surface. Were those countries too?

He recounted everything Peregrine had told him, and all that he had seen in the cottage. This time, he left nothing out. By the time he finished it was full dark, and their amazed faces shone in the silvery light.

'He could be mad, you know,' Mohanna suggested. 'He could have spent years in there, making this junk and painting those . . . foter graps.'

'But why?' Aran asked. 'It doesn't make sense.'

'That's where the mad part comes in,' she muttered. 'I don't know, it all sounds very odd to me. What do you think he wants? Why you? Why now?'

'He said he and my father had a history,' Aran offered. 'He wouldn't tell me what it was. But you should have seen my father's face when Peregrine invited himself to stay.'

'I'm not surprised,' Mohanna said. 'Just think how mine's going to react when he finds out. Tell you what, I bet this Peregrine knows something. Some secret Carifax doesn't want people to know. Why else would he let a violent ruffian stay in his farmstead?'

Aran laughed. 'He was only violent to your father,' he said. 'And let's face it, he had a good reason. Anyway, I don't think he's mad. He's just . . . different. And I mean it fits, doesn't it? The world before. The Ancestors.'

'I tell you what,' Mohanna said. 'You get him to make a giant metal bird and we'll see how far it flies.'

Cas smiled to himself. 'I always knew the world was round,' he said.

'No you didn't,' Mohanna retorted. 'Just last year you were completely taken in by that storyteller who said we all rode on the back of a giant codfish, swimming through space.'

Cas flushed. 'Well, he was very convincing,' he said. They all laughed.

'Oh, it's good to be home,' said Aran, looking down over the dark, familiar valley. Lights twinkled in the windows of the summerhouse, and down in the fields a single lantern swayed as someone kept watch over their sadly depleted flocks.

Aran breathed a great sigh of relief, glad to be safe and out of danger. But there was a new feeling growing inside him too. He felt a stirring in his belly, a thrill of anticipation. Perhaps the future might hold a few surprises after all.

CHAPTER THIRTEEN

Lessons

The heat in the room was stifling, and the librarian's voice droned on and on. '. . . Whose father was Law Caswell Carifax, the builder,' he was saying. 'By his command our great chapel was constructed. His eldest brother was Devin Carifax, who was murdered by the Darnells of Crowdale during the Long Vendetta. The present Law Darnell's uncles were killed in retaliation. Devin and Caswell were of course the sons of your great-grandfather, Law Akmid Carifax, for whom your brother is named, and he—'

'Aran, sit up straight!' Peregrine's voice barked.

Aran scrambled upright in his chair, brushing away the tatters of the dream he had almost slipped into. Peregrine glared at him, tapping his staff on the ground. 'I don't know what you were used to under Miss Crell,' he said. 'But in my classroom you pay attention. Please, sir, continue.'

He gestured to the librarian, who sat in a high chair, his rheumy eyes regarding both of them with some confusion.

'I'm sorry?' the old man asked, craning closer to Peregrine, grasping at the large leather-bound book which lay open on his lap.

The Tale of Laws was one of five books housed in the Hawk's Cross library, the largest in the region and the pride of the farmstead. The others were *The Tale of Records*, a list of trades and deals; *The Book of the Father*, a religious text transcribed from the teachings of a holy man; *The Book of Songs*, with words and music for more than fifty ballads; and *Advanced Mathematics for Engineers*, an ancient and mystical tome which even Peregrine had declared to be completely incomprehensible.

'Please continue!' Aran's tutor repeated, his voice rattling off the narrow stone walls.

'Are you sure?' the librarian asked, his hands shaking. 'Perhaps we . . . Perhaps Law Carifax could . . .'

'As you know, Law Carifax has gone to attend an emergency meeting of his Council,' said Peregrine, loudly and slowly. 'I have no intention of waiting until he gets back. I want the boy to know his history. What there is of it.'

'But why?' the librarian responded, scratching at the backs of his liver-spotted hands. 'He's a second son, he should be out in the fields. I'm sure if we speak to the Law . . .'

'Your Law has given me the task of teaching his son,' Peregrine snapped. 'And I will fulfil that obligation any way I see fit. If I want to teach him history, or mathematics, or how to read and write, I will do so, and I don't expect to be questioned at every turn.'

The librarian's mouth hung open. 'How to . . . how to read?' he managed at last. 'Why on earth . . . ? That's my job!'

Aran would have found it comical if he hadn't witnessed precisely the same argument with every one of the citizens Peregrine had invited into the classroom over the past few weeks. Everyone from the tally-keeper to the stores master had felt obliged to point out that Aran's future was as a Foreman, not a trader or a scholar.

'Oh, for God's sake,' Peregrine cried. 'It's like living in the bloody Dark Ages!' Aran had no idea where that was, but Peregrine said a lot of things he didn't understand, particularly when he was annoyed, which was fairly often. 'The concept of a rounded education just means nothing at all to you people, does it?'

The librarian glanced at Aran, seeking confirmation that this furious stranger was, indeed, completely mad. Aran just shrugged.

'Please, good man,' said Peregrine in a tone of steely calm. 'Just finish *The Tale of Laws*, then you can go back to doddering about in your study complaining about how it's not like it was in your day. All right?'

The librarian shot Peregrine a reproachful stare, then turned to his book with a disgruntled cough. 'Akmid's brother was Fredrik Carifax, the voyager, who led a party of traders across the Western Sea to the Isle of Air and was never heard from again . . .'

Aran slumped back in his chair. The fun was apparently over.

When Law Carifax had reluctantly agreed to give Peregrine this job, he had extracted a solemn promise that they would stick to the basics. Aran knew that Peregrine could be teaching him about the Ancestors, about the stars and the moon, even how to fight and use weapons. Instead, they had spent day after day in the cattle sheds learning to pick out a healthy cow or a productive bull, or out in the fields inspecting the crops. But even that was better than being cooped up here, as yet another peevish citizen sweated and seethed under Peregrine's implacable gaze.

'. . . who in turn were the sons of the first Law,' the librarian finished at last. 'Gideon Carifax, the beginner, who came from outside with his people and named this place Hawk's Cross, for the birds which still nest above the crossroads. And that is the Tale of Laws.' He closed the book with a dusty thud.

'Where did he come from?' Aran asked, a bit surprised that the tale had ended so abruptly.

The librarian peered down at him, nonplussed. 'I'm sorry?'

'You said Gideon came from outside with his people,' Aran pointed out. 'Where did they come from?'

The librarian shrugged. 'From outside,' he repeated.

'But where?' Aran went on. 'Were there people at Hawk's Cross before he came? Who built this place?'

'Well, I . . .' the old man spluttered. 'I suppose he must have come from somewhere, but I don't . . . The book doesn't . . . What do you care?'

Peregrine smiled. 'Good question, Aran,' he said. 'Why does it matter to you?'

Aran knew that Peregrine was expecting him to come up with a clever answer, but he didn't have one. 'I suppose it doesn't,' he said.

The librarian shot Peregrine a look of triumph. 'Good,' he said. 'Well, if the boy has no further questions . . .' He slipped down from his chair, tucked the book under his arm and shuffled to the door.

Peregrine looked at Aran with disappointed eyes. Aran fidgeted with discomfort. 'What?' he asked at last. 'They're all dead. Why does it matter?'

Peregrine sighed, then shook his head. 'You can work it out for yourself. That's the whole point. Come on, we've got an appointment with Solly. Let's hope he's in a better mood.'

As they trudged up the winding stair to the surface, Aran felt as though he hadn't lived up to his tutor's expectations. That too seemed to happen a lot.

When they reached the entrance hall, Aran's eye was caught by the banner which hung over the archway: Gideon's banner, the falcon and the crucifix. He had passed it every day of his life, yet he had never really looked at it before. Who had made it, and how long ago? Had Gideon himself carried it, perhaps into battle with an enemy farmstead, or even against the people of Hawk's Cross, the first ones? How else would he have become their leader, except by force? That dark stain just under the eagle's claw, that might be blood. Aran wondered if there was anyone alive who knew the answers to these questions. And he wondered again why it mattered.

Then they passed from shadow into sunlight, and the heat drove all thoughts from his mind.

There had been hot days since Aran's return, but nothing like this. The sun was a molten disc in a white-hot sky, and he could feel the stones in the courtyard cooking through his leather boots. He followed Peregrine down through the apple orchard, where the dry soil kicked up in clouds around their feet and the screech of corn crickets cut through the windless air.

When they reached the valley bottom, Peregrine allowed Aran a few moments' rest in the shade of a leafy oak. The river ran low and sluggish, shrouded in swarms of black flies. A group of women huddled beneath an overhang, scrubbing sheets and laying them on the rocks to dry. Children splashed in the shallows, their laughter reaching Aran as he sat, dripping with sweat, wondering if Peregrine would mind if he stuck his head in the river and left it there for the rest of the afternoon.

Hearing footsteps, Aran looked up. Solly, his father's Foreman, was approaching across the fields. Law Carifax's father had borne two sons, but Aran's Uncle Dex had died when he was a boy, stumbling into a bees' nest while the brothers were out climbing. Solly was Law Carifax's closest friend, a slender, quiet man with a wide forehead and a shy smile.

But he wasn't smiling now. Solly stepped into the shade of the oak, mumbling an awkward greeting. Aran was getting used to this kind of reaction whenever Peregrine was around. Even the Foreman, as friendly a soul as any in Hawk's Cross, didn't know how to respond to this stranger in their midst.

'Scorcher,' he said at last. 'We've had three fall out already, and it's barely noon.'

He was referring to the workers, Aran knew. Falling out meant fainting in the heat, and it was a common occurrence on a day like this. They would be carried back to the farmhouse, given water and a place to rest, but they'd be out again the next morning, or face the Law's questions.

'It'll get worse before it gets better,' said Peregrine un-helpfully.

Solly led them along the bottom edge of the corn fields. The irrigation crews were hard at work, filling barrels with river water and carrying them back up the hill. 'On a day like this, we're fighting a losing battle,' the Foreman said, kneeling. One of the irrigation channels had cracked in the heat, spilling much-needed moisture uselessly into the dirt. He took out a red flag and waved it above his head. A young man came hurrying down the path carrying a length of replacement pipe. 'But no water, no crops,' Solly went on. 'No crops, no food. And every year there are more mouths to feed. The day will come when there simply isn't enough to go around.'

'Why don't you plant more?' Aran suggested. 'Widen the fields?'

'And how would we irrigate them?' Solly asked. 'We're

overstretched as it is.' He ruffled Aran's hair. 'You see, it's not just about chucking seeds in the ground and waiting until they grow,' he said. 'A Foreman has to keep watch over every aspect of farmstead life. Since your grand-father signed the pact with Crowdale we've had thirty years of peace. Some say that's a good thing, but it also means more of us are living to a ripe old age. And they need feeding, even when they're too old to work. So where does it all come from?'

Aran knew that Solly was doing his best to get him interested in his future as a Foreman. But try as he might, he couldn't bring himself to care. He knew it was impor-tant, but the thought of waking up every morning thinking about cattle and crop rotation seemed to Aran a complete waste of a life. Was that what Law Carifax meant when he told Aran to grow up?

He followed Solly and Peregrine up the dusty path, the sun beating on his back. A pair of big men thundered past, barrels carried high on their shoulders. Aran could hear water sloshing about inside, and felt his throat cry out. His head was throbbing and he stopped, his hands on his knees, the sweat from his forehead dripping and vanishing into the dust.

'Here, take this.' A hand held out a tin cup of dark, dirty water. Raising his head, Aran saw Cas looking at him with concern. His face was swaddled in wet cloth, only his eyes peeking out. There was a barrel at his feet.

'How do you stand it?' Aran asked, handing the empty cup back.

'You get used to it,' Cas replied, his voice muffled. 'Today's bad, though.'

'I'm supposed to be helping out on the crews this afternoon,' Aran told him ruefully.

Cas laughed. 'I heard,' he said. 'Sim's taking bets on how long you'll last. He said twenty minutes. I told him he was being stupid.'

Aran smiled. 'Thanks,' he said.

'Don't get too cocky,' Cas returned. 'I bet him tonight's pudding you'd go at least twenty-five. But now I see you I'm not so sure.'

Aran punched him on the arm. 'Some friend,' he said. He looked at the lines of men and women staggering to and from the river. 'How do they do it?' he wondered aloud.

Cas frowned. 'They don't have a choice,' he said. 'It's either this or face your father.'

'No, that's not—' Aran said, realizing how it must have sounded. 'I mean, it doesn't seem fair. There has to be a better way.'

'It's funny you say that,' Cas said. 'Just the other day, I was thinking—'

'I've warned you about that before,' grinned Aran.

'No, seriously,' Cas said. 'What's the sense in all these people carrying all these buckets? Surely we could rig up some kind of pulley. All it would take is a lot of rope and some kind of turning mechanism, like on the winch lift. You'd need people at either end to—'

A hand fell on Cas's shoulder and he looked up to see

Solly leaning over him. His face was friendly but stern.

'Enough talk now, lads,' he said. 'There'll be people in the east pasture wondering what's happened to their water boy.'

Cas nodded, and just for a moment Aran caught a glimpse of the deep weariness his friend had been trying to conceal. 'Yes, Foreman,' he said, hooking the tin cup onto his belt and grabbing his bucket by both handles.

Solly turned to Peregrine, who had been inspecting a ladybird which had landed in his open palm. 'If you're ready,' the Foreman said.

Peregrine nodded, brushing the insect away. Then his eyes wandered, and he seemed to notice Cas for the first time. He put out a hand. 'I'm not sure we've been formally introduced,' he said. 'You're Cas. Aran's told me a lot about you.'

Cas's cheeks reddened and he looked at the floor. 'Yes, sir,' he said.

'No need to sir me,' said Peregrine. 'I'm Aran's tutor, not yours. You can call me Peregrine. I'd like us to be friends.'

Cas flushed again and mumbled something inaudible.

'That bucket looks heavy,' Peregrine went on. 'You must be exhausted. Listen, here's a thought. Why don't you join us? Solly was just teaching Aran about irrigation. Perhaps he'll learn better with a friend along, especially someone with hands-on experience.'

'I'm afraid the boy's got other duties to attend to,' said Solly apologetically.

'Nonsense,' said Peregrine breezily, but there was an

150

edge creeping into his voice. 'It'll do him good. All boys need food for the mind as well as the body. And I've heard that Cas here is a bright one. The brains of the outfit, you might say.'

Cas blushed to the roots.

'Why don't you tell Solly what you were just telling Aran?' Peregrine went on. 'About the ropes and the pulleys?' Aran hadn't even realized his tutor was listening.

'I don't . . .' spluttered Cas. 'I haven't . . . I really should get back to work.'

'Come on, it sounded like a good idea,' Peregrine pushed. Aran was starting to feel uncomfortable, as Cas muttered and blushed and Solly's eyes darkened.

'Please, leave the boy alone,' the Foreman cut in. 'He's got work to do.'

'He's fourteen years old,' Peregrine snapped suddenly. 'He should be down in the farmstead with his nose pressed into a really boring book. But you people don't believe in all that, do you? You call five books a library.' He looked down. 'Cas, I'll not ask again. Put that bucket down.'

Solly's bright demeanour had blackened into a scowl. 'That isn't how we do things,' he said. 'Who'd work the land if everyone was allowed to sit around all day reading?' He spat the last word with venomous disgust. A small crowd had begun to gather, and they murmured their agreement.

'Perhaps if you allowed them to learn, they'd come up with an idea that'd do the work for you,' Peregrine shot back. 'But no, Cas had to figure it out on his own. And he's so ashamed of himself that he won't even admit it! I wonder how many others had the same idea, but were so busy working like slaves they never thought to put it into practice? A pulley system, it's hardly rocket science.'

'For your information,' Solly thundered, 'we have tried it. There was no one in the farmstead strong enough to haul the rope. And we wasted valuable man hours trying to get it working.'

Peregrine opened his mouth to reply, then closed it again. For a moment, all was silent. Then a voice broke in.

'Well, actually,' said Cas, so quietly that Aran had to crane his neck. 'I was thinking we could use horses. Three or four ought to do it.'

Peregrine placed one hand on Cas's shoulder. 'Out of the mouths of babes,' he said with a victorious smile. 'Right, come on, Cas, let's start drawing up the plans. Aran, with me please. This time you might actually learn something.'

And he set off up the hill, pulling Cas with him. Aran followed, hoping this meant he wouldn't have to spend the afternoon hauling buckets. But before he had gone twenty paces, he heard hoof beats approaching. He glanced back, and his heart sank.

Aran's brother had turned his horse off the main track, followed by Keller and a pair of sweating guards. Akmid's left arm was still in a sling so he was forced to ride one-handed, guiding the black stallion through the fields towards the small crowd of indignant workers. 'What's going on here?' he barked.

Solly leaned close, muttering and gesturing angrily at Peregrine and the boys.

Akmid's lips pursed. Aran could imagine the struggle going on behind his eyes. Like everyone else, Akmid tended to give Peregrine a wide berth. But if he let this go, the workers would have even less respect for him than they did already.

Clearly, he didn't see a choice. Akmid dismounted, calling Peregrine's name in the most commanding voice he could muster. 'Come back here, please.'

Peregrine fixed a smile onto his face, the same one he had worn during his argument with Solly. The smile of a man who knows things are about to turn nasty.

'Akmid,' he said brightly, coming back down the hill. 'Or should I call you my Law, in your father's absence?'

Akmid stood with his legs apart and his fists clenched. Aran had seen his father adopt the same pose. It must be something they're taught, he thought. Lessons for becoming a better Law. But when Carifax stood that way, no one argued. Akmid just looked ludicrous, like a small boy trying on his father's shoes.

'It's not . . . I don't . . .' he began, then gathered himself. 'It's not important,' he finished. 'What's been going on here? Solly informs me you were having a . . . disagreement.'

Peregrine's face showed no sign of tension, which only made Akmid's nervousness more apparent. 'I don't think so,' he said. 'I just offered to let Cas join one of our lessons. The Foreman had his doubts, but I pointed out it wasn't

153

healthy for a boy so young to be working out in this heat. I'm sure you agree.'

Solly's face reddened and he opened his mouth, but Akmid silenced him with a glance.

'Sir,' Akmid began. 'Peregrine. I know my father invited you into Hawk's Cross to educate my . . . to educate Aran, but you must understand, we have a system here. We need our boys to work.' He's really trying, Aran thought. If this was anyone else, Akmid would have yelled until he was blue in the face.

'You're not working,' Peregrine pointed out. 'Neither's Keller. Your guards are just sitting there. One of them could distribute water if it's so important.'

Akmid's face began to turn the same colour as Solly's. 'I . . .' he spluttered. 'I am in training to be the next Law of Hawk's Cross,' he managed. 'Keller is . . . Listen, there's no reason why I should have to explain any of this. You're here for a purpose. Keep to it.'

'But that's precisely what I'm doing,' Peregrine said, his tone laced with humour. He's enjoying this, Aran realized. 'I'm teaching your brother perhaps the most important lesson of all. A practical study in the value of independent thought. I'm teaching him that small-mindedness and an uncontested acceptance of tradition are worthless. I'm teaching him to question everything and everyone, particularly those who claim to have the answers. I'm teaching him that true power lies up here' – Peregrine tapped his forehead with one bony finger – 'not in the strength of a man's arm or the length of his sword, whatever his brother and his father might say.'

Akmid's eyes widened. 'You're teaching him to . . . to question our father?' he asked, amazed.

'Oh, absolutely,' Peregrine smiled. 'How else can he become his own man? You, Akmid, you question your father all the time. Admit it. You don't approve of all that he does. Sometimes you even think he's weak.'

There was a gasp from the assembled audience, and Akmid's clenched hands began to shake. 'How do you . . . ?' he spluttered.

'Oh, it's obvious,' Peregrine laughed. 'Every son doubts his dad. And a boy like you, so sure of yourself, of course you'd look at a fair man like Carifax and see weakness.'

'This . . . this is some dark trick,' Akmid spat.

'You admit it, then?' Peregrine chuckled again. Then he saw the rage on Akmid's face and his voice softened. 'I'm sorry, that was cruel. But listen. Cas here came up with an idea for a machine that'd do the work of twenty men. It's a brilliant plan, and it could change everything for this farm-stead. Why not join us? Imagine how proud your father'd be if he came back to find both his sons working together, and on something so useful.' He took a step closer, putting out his hand.

Akmid looked at him, and his anger was replaced by confusion. For a fleeting moment, Aran thought that his brother might actually accept Peregrine's offer.

But he brushed the hand aside, taking a step towards Keller and his guards. 'Don't come any closer,' he said. 'I don't know what you want with us, but stay away from me and my family. You're here to educate the boy. Do your job.'

Peregrine's face twitched. 'I'd watch your words if I were you,' he said, and Aran noticed that the friendly tone in his voice had utterly vanished. 'Before you say something we'll both regret.'

Akmid blanched. 'Is that a threat?' he asked, his hand straying towards his sword hilt.

'No,' Peregrine replied coldly. 'More a caution.'

Akmid grimaced. 'My father was right,' he said. 'You are not to be trusted.'

Peregrine nodded. 'From your perspective,' he said, 'that's probably true.'

Akmid held his gaze for as long as he could, then placed one foot in the stirrup. 'Put the boy back to work,' he said. 'I won't ask again.'

'And if I say no?' Peregrine asked.

'Then I shall inform my father that you disobeyed my direct order,' Akmid shot back, pulling himself upright in the saddle. 'He can deal with you himself.'

'Very well,' said Peregrine. And he turned on his heel and began to walk away.

Aran watched his tutor go. He was almost disappointed. He knew Peregrine couldn't afford to stir up trouble, but he knew how much Cas would have wanted this. Sadly, Aran prepared to say goodbye to his friend and follow Peregrine back to the classroom.

But Peregrine had paused. He turned back, fixing Cas with a gentle but genuine smile. 'Come on,' he said. 'Both of you. We've got work to do.'

Aran wanted to laugh out loud. He walked backwards up the hill so that he could enjoy the look on his brother's face. Akmid sat, the sun pricking beads of sweat on his bronzed head, his eyes staring with pure hate at Peregrine's retreating back.

'This isn't over,' he called. 'Mark these words, my father will hear about this.'

'Why wait?' Peregrine called, without turning. 'Unless I'm much mistaken, that's his horse down there.'

Shielding his eyes, Aran saw that he was right. They had all been so preoccupied, no one had noticed the team of riders approaching along the riverbank.

Akmid spurred his stallion along the path towards the riders. Keller and the guards followed.

Aran drew alongside Peregrine and Cas. 'I figured it out,' he said. 'Why it's important.'

His tutor nodded. 'Go on,' he said.

'You knew Akmid's thoughts before he did,' Aran said. 'You knew everything he was going to say.'

'I've met boys like him before,' Peregrine said. 'Many times.'

'So if we know what people did,' Aran said, 'we can guess what they'll do next. We can be ready.'

Peregrine's eyes brightened. 'Good lad,' he said. 'See, I knew you weren't as dumb as you pretend to be.' Aran blushed. 'I've studied people for longer than I care to admit,' Peregrine went on. 'The one thing I've learned is, they don't really change. They make the same mistakes, again and again. Jealousy, guilt, greed, and eventually

157

hatred, violence and war. History repeats, but those who learn its lessons are best placed to guide the future. You'll need to remember that, these next few months.'

Aran looked up at him. 'Why?' he asked. 'What's going to happen?'

Peregrine shook his head. 'Nothing good,' he said, and turned.

Aran followed his gaze to the valley bottom, where a cloud of dust marked the passage of the Law and his men. They must be riding hard, Aran thought. But that made no sense. This was the road home. What could make them so impatient?

Akmid reached the track just as Carifax and his riders came alongside. Aran could see the strain on his father's face as he brushed Akmid's complaints aside.

'Something's happening,' he said. 'Something's wrong.'

The workers began flocking towards the Law. Others were already hurrying away, back towards the farmstead, their faces pale. Word was spreading. Men ran through the fields, stopping others, calling them back to the courtyard. Soon everyone began to move, dropping their barrels and their tools and turning towards home, crying out as they went.

Aran listened. A single word lifted on the breeze which gusted up from the valley bed.

'War!' they cried. 'War! We're at war!'

CHAPTER FOURTEEN

The Militia

From beside his father on the dais, Aran could see every face. All the seats in the hall were filled, the alcoves jammed, the spiral stairway crammed with people. The fields were empty, the beds unmade, the cattle untended. Aran could even make out the cook, standing in the shadows at the back of the room. Somewhere, he thought, a pot was boiling over.

'My friends,' the Law began. 'As you know, I've just returned from Barton, where I met with the Laws' Council. I know some of you have been disturbed by the rumours that have been flying around these past weeks. You have every right to be. As far as we can tell there have been three Marauder raiding expeditions carried out since Barton. Nine farmsteads have been attacked. Over seven hundred people have been killed or taken.'

There was a collective gasp. 'There's no need for panic,' Carifax went on. 'The attack on Carny was still the furthest west they've dared to come, and the furthest inland. It seems to have been a show of force, to let us know what we're up against. Well, now we know. They are strong, and they are ruthless. We have no idea of their numbers. But we know their purpose, and that is to take everything we have. We cannot let that happen.

'Some Laws think they're far enough inland to be considered safe. I don't share such illusions. Sooner or later they'll find their way here. Others wanted to build an army, to go over the sea, to find and destroy the Marauders before they can do the same to us. This course of action is simply too risky. Until we know how many of them there are, we can't make any such plans.

'So we have decided upon a middle way. We intend to form an armed militia, ready to respond to any reports of Marauder activity. Forty farmsteads will contribute, and we hope to build a standing army of five hundred men, with another five hundred in reserve. The barracks will be located in Barton, and we'll provide horses, food, weaponry – everything the militia needs to stay fighting fit.' He propped his fists on the table and looked seriously around the room. 'It won't be an easy task,' he said. 'Not all the men we send will be coming home. But hopefully we can give these Marauders something to think about.

'On a personal note,' he finished with a gleam in his eye, 'I'd like to announce that my own son has volunteered to be among the first to go. Akmid, I'm proud of you.'

Akmid beamed, his cheeks flushed. His father patted his back and smiled. Lady Carifax averted her gaze, her face pale.

The hall erupted, as all the young men and several women rushed forward to volunteer. The Law was swamped beneath a tide of waving, excited arms. Aran flung his own hand high, his heart leaping.

But Carifax smiled apologetically down at him. 'Not you, Aran,' he said, laying a hand on his head. 'Akmid will have to represent the family for now.'

In the end, forty men were chosen to fulfil the farmstead's commitment to the militia. They would leave for Barton in a moon's time, and until then their training was to be handled by Keller and, to Aran's surprise, Peregrine. A special red tunic was designed bearing the symbol of Gideon's banner. Akmid seemed to wear his everywhere he went.

'I bet he even keeps it on in the bath,' observed Aran darkly, as he sat with Cas and Mohanna a week later in the shade of the courtyard wall, sipping lemonade and watching the trainees going through their paces.

Aran had tried to join in, arguing that an early start would stand him in good stead when he came of age. But Keller had laughed and sent him away, and an edict from Law Carifax had forced Peregrine to do the same.

And now that he saw them in action, Aran couldn't help feeling just a little relieved. The courtyard was like a furnace. Peregrine stood barking orders – 'Stand fast! Turn about! Attack! Parry! Atten . . . *shun*!' – and the recruits struggled to obey. They may have been the best Hawk's Cross had to offer, but under Peregrine's unforgiving

161

eye even the strongest of them seemed clumsy and incompetent.

Aran and his friends weren't the only ones enjoying the spectacle. A group of women huddled in the shade of the armoury door, mothers and daughters both, nudging one another and giggling. Aran saw Lissie among them, fanning herself with a folded cloth. Her skirt was tucked into her waistband, revealing long, freckly white legs. Aran hunched in the shadows, feeling the sweat run down his back.

Trying to make an impression, one trainee lunged too vigorously and fell flat on his face. The onlookers erupted into gales of laughter. 'For Ala's sake,' barked Peregrine as the red-faced recruit picked himself up from the cobbles. 'These fine ladies want heroes, not clowns.' And he tipped a wink to the women, who blushed and looked away.

'At least someone's enjoying himself,' said Mohanna. 'Peregrine hasn't looked so happy since he got here.'

'I think people are starting to get used to him,' Aran said. Then he saw Akmid at the head of the column, glaring at his instructor with undisguised loathing. 'Some of them, anyway.'

'I suppose he's forgotten all about our irrigation plan,' said Cas sadly. 'I really think it would have worked too.'

'My father says Carifax has gone mad,' Mohanna told them. 'Allowing a ruffian like Peregrine to train his army. He says he won't show his face at Hawk's Cross until he's gone.'

'Big loss,' muttered Cas.

'It's just because of what happened on the road,' Aran argued. 'If Law Darnell could actually talk to Peregrine . . .'

Mohanna snorted. 'Fat chance,' she said. 'He thinks Peregrine has put some sort of spell on Carifax. And you.'

'He doesn't do spells,' Aran retorted. Then a look of doubt came on his face. 'At least, I don't think he does.'

'I just think you should be careful,' Mohanna said. 'Keep your eyes open. I don't trust a man who reads like a scholar but talks like a field hand.'

'You're such a snob,' hissed Cas. 'Just because somebody's common doesn't have to mean he's uneducated. Perhaps in the farmstead where Peregrine grew up, everyone learned to read.'

'And where is this farmstead?' Mohanna retorted. 'Aran said he lived on his own. That's just not normal.' She leaned closer to Aran. 'You know, just once I'd like to find out what he's really up to, down in that room of his. You said he's got all those weird books. I'd like to take a look at them. We could go in there when he's not—'

'Don't even think about it,' Aran hissed back. 'Peregrine's just a teacher, all right? Stop being so suspicious.'

'Right, just a teacher,' Mohanna said sardonically. 'A teacher who has a cellar full of Ancestor artefacts, and talks to bears, and can fight better than anyone I've ever seen. My father has a point. You don't know a thing about why he's here. He could be sacrificing kittens to the divvle for all you know. Or he could be in league with the Marauders, softening you up so they can come in here and—'

'Stop it!' Aran snapped. 'That's my friend you're talking about. Anyway, why would he be training the militia if he was in with the Marauders?'

'Perhaps he's training them badly on purpose,' said Mohanna. 'Not really trying.'

Peregrine had all of the recruits on their backs, clapping in time as they sat up straight, then slumped back down, then sat back up again.

'No, he's definitely taking it easy on them,' said Aran sarcastically. 'Why don't you join in, show him how it ought to be done?'

Mohanna scowled.

Peregrine rounded on the trainees. 'Right,' he said. 'On your feet. Let's end with a five-mile run to the waterfall and back. Last one home cleans my boots.'

The children propped themselves on the wall and watched as the recruits slogged wearily into the valley, forty staggering figures with Peregrine in the lead, his robes flapping around his ankles.

'Just look at him,' Mohanna said as the crowd began to disperse. 'No ordinary person has that much stamina.'

'For Ala's sakes,' said Aran. 'What will it take to convince you he's not a divvle-worshipping spy?'

Mohanna looked at the floor. 'I've told you,' she said. 'I want to know what he's up to. I want to see his room. And most of all I want to see those books. They won't be back for at least an hour, it's the perfect time to—'

Aran sighed and threw up his hands. 'All right,' he said. 'Let's go, if it'll shut you up.'

Cas frowned. 'You're joking,' he said. 'That's someone else's property.'

Mohanna turned on him. 'Peregrine is a citizen of Hawk's Cross now,' she said. 'His property is everyone's property. That's the rules. And Aran is the Law's son. He can go where he wants.'

'We won't take anything,' Aran insisted. 'We'll just have a quick look. I don't see how it can hurt.'

Cas looked at him, flustered. 'I know Peregrine's a bit strange, but that doesn't give you the right to go messing with his things. Just because your fathers are both high and mighty Laws doesn't mean you can just do what you want, when you want. You said he was your friend. You wouldn't go into my room and dig around, would you?'

'We would if we thought you were up to no good,' Mohanna retorted. 'And Aran's right, we'll be in and out. He'll never know we were there.'

Cas dropped back onto the wall. 'Well, I want no part of it,' he muttered.

Mohanna took Aran by the hand and led him down the ramp. The farmstead was unbearably hot, the walls running with condensation. In a normal year the furnaces would have been banked through the summer, but now they had been pressed back into service making swords, armour and arrowheads for the militia. The workshops rang to the sound of hammering, and great clouds of reeking steam came billowing up to greet Aran and Mohanna as they descended.

But down on the sixth floor, the corridors were oddly

deserted. The lanterns had gone out, usually a sure sign that no one had been there for days. There were barely any vent shafts so far down, so the tunnels were thick with shadows. A musty wind whistled up from the floor below, the lowest cellar where only the ratcatcher lived.

And as they approached Peregrine's room, Aran noticed the doors on either side standing ajar. These should be living quarters for the carpentry workers, yet the rooms seemed unoccupied. His sense of unease deepened.

Peregrine's door was closed but unlocked. Aran's doubts crowded in, clamouring to be heard. But before he could speak Mohanna was pushing in, and he was following.

The room was dark and silent. Sallow light leaked through a narrow vent high up on the wall. Peregrine's bed stood in the corner, a tangled mess of sheets and blankets. His grubby, unwashed robes were piled in a black heap. The room was dominated by the sturdy desk, scattered with papers and books, a half-eaten apple and a mug of flat beer.

'What a mess,' Mohanna breathed, wrinkling her nose. 'Was his house like this?'

'Worse,' said Aran softly, remembering the rat which had scuttled under the wardrobe.

Mohanna slid the door silently shut and crossed to the desk. She peered down at the leather-bound book which lay flat and open, a stick of charcoal marking Peregrine's place. Aran forced his fears aside and joined her.

To his surprise, the pages weren't filled with words, or at least no language he'd ever seen. Instead they were covered with signs and symbols, scratched in heavy black ink. Some of the symbols were almost recognizable – one looked like a star, another a sword. But most were simply shapes and scrawls, heaped haphazardly across the dry, age-worn pages.

'Do you think he drew these himself?' Mohanna whispered.

'He said they were his mother's,' Aran recalled.

Mohanna leafed through, but each page was the same. 'What do you think it means?' she asked.

Aran shook his head. 'Maybe it doesn't mean anything,' he said. 'Maybe you're right. Maybe he's just crazy.' He'd expected something like the books in Peregrine's house, pictures of outlandish creatures and Ancestor artefacts. Somehow, this was even stranger.

Mohanna turned to the loose papers scattered between the books. These, at least, were slightly more understandable. Some bore charcoal sketches of plants, animals and faces, including a few Aran recognized. Others were merely lesson plans written in Peregrine's recognizable, looping handwriting.

But some seemed to refer back to the books – the same symbols were repeated, but beside each one was a scribbled word or a sentence. Peregrine had begun to teach Aran his alphabet, so he was able to sound out a few of the words: 'moon', 'fire', 'stone'. One comment in particular gave him pause. Beside a symbol which looked like an upturned figure eight standing on the crest of a wave, Peregrine had written 'boy?'.

'It's like he doesn't know what the books say,' Aran whispered. 'As if he's trying to work them out. But why would he bring them if he doesn't know what they mean? It doesn't make any sense.'

'None of this makes any sense,' Mohanna pointed out.

'I don't know if this is a good idea,' Aran said suddenly, feeling a chill run through him despite the heat. 'Maybe we should go and tell my father.'

Mohanna turned. 'Tell him what?' she asked. 'That we happened to be snooping about in Peregrine's room and we found all this weird stuff? Come on, five more minutes.' She held up another handful of papers. These too were filled with Peregrine's writing. Mohanna squinted closer. 'Here, read this,' she said.

Aran squinted closer, trying to make out the words. 'But . . .' he read. 'But it . . . it's imp . . . impo . . .'

' "But it's impossible to know if he is the One," ' said a voice.

They whirled round. Cas was peering over Aran's shoulder.

'He's written One with a big O,' he observed. 'That's odd.'

'Where did you . . . ? Don't sneak up on us like that!' Mohanna cried out. 'You could have given me a heart attack.' Then realization made her eyes widen. 'Wait a minute, how did you know what it said?'

'I read it,' said Cas, and smiled at them. 'With my eyes,' he added.

'Who taught you to read?' Aran asked, incredulous.

'No one,' Cas explained. 'A little while ago I . . . well, I decided it might be a good idea to . . . to teach myself.'

'How?' Aran asked. 'Where did you get the books?'

Cas looked at him. 'You've met the librarian?' he asked. 'Elderly chap, half-blind, sleeps about twenty hours a day?'

'You stole them!' Aran realized. 'But when? I thought they kept you too busy working?'

'I suppose I started when I was about . . . five,' Cas admitted. 'By the time they put me in the fields I'd already memorized all the books in the library. Apart from *Advanced Mathematics for Engineers*, but that's just gibberish.'

'Five?' Aran asked, his mouth open. 'You've known how to read all this time and you never thought to tell me?'

'It never came up,' said Cas defensively. 'Anyway, I didn't want you to get jealous.'

'Jealous?' Aran asked. 'Why would I be jealous?'

Cas blushed. 'Well, because I . . . because I'm cleverer than you.'

Aran snorted. 'Being able to read doesn't make you cleverer than me,' he said.

Cas put a hand on his arm. 'You're right,' he said. '*Wanting* to be able to read makes me cleverer than you.'

Aran scowled.

'When you two are quite finished, I'd like to know what this says,' interrupted Mohanna.

Cas leaned in, peering at the paper in the dim light. '"How can I tell him the truth when I don't even know myself?"' he read on. '"It could destroy him. I am not my brother, and I should not try to be." Wait, Peregrine has a brother?'

'He never mentioned one,' Aran said.

'"I do not have my mother's power, that much is certain,"' Cas read aloud. '"So why do I continue to search? Because the threat is so great. Because so many could die. And I can't let it happen again." What is this, a story he's writing? Or some kind of diary?'

But Aran wasn't listening. Something had caught his eye, a dull glint of metal spilling from the mouth of a cloth bag on the edge of the desk. Reaching out, he drew forth a tiny silver locket on a sparkling chain. The metal was cold against his skin.

He held it up in the light, suddenly aware of a feeling inside him, eerie and unfamiliar. As if the locket had some kind of power within it, something strange and mystical. Something *other*. He reached in to unlock the clasp.

But as his fingers touched the metal he saw movement from the corner of his eye. The door to Peregrine's room was swinging open. Aran took a step back and dropped the locket. It clattered to the floor.

Law Carifax entered the room. His face was red, and wore an expression Aran had never seen before – anger, yes, but something more. Fear? Could that be it?

'What in all the hells do you think you're doing?' the Law demanded. Cas dropped the papers he was holding and Mohanna took an instinctive step back, coming up against the edge of the desk.

'M . . . My Law,' she said breathlessly. 'We were only . . .'

'Don't even start,' said Carifax, looming over her, his lip curling back. For one horrible moment, Aran thought he was going to strike her. But the Law merely took Mohanna by the arm and pulled her roughly towards the door.

'Out, all of you,' he barked, shoving them into the corridor.

'We were just d-dropping off some schoolwork,' Aran attempted, stumbling over the words. 'A test that Peregrine set. He said he wanted it on his desk before he—'

'Don't lie to me!' Carifax yelled, his voice reverberating off the narrow stone walls. 'Did you honestly think you could come down here without someone seeing you?'

Aran looked at his father. Carifax's breath came in great heaves.

'I didn't think . . .' Aran began. 'We just wanted—'

'We just wanted to know what was going on,' Mohanna cut in. 'People are talking, my Law. They don't trust Peregrine. We wanted to know what he was up to.'

Law Carifax turned to her. 'You're a stupid girl,' he said coldly. 'And that's your father talking. What business is it of yours what goes on in my farmstead? Honestly, Mohanna. I allow you free rein because I believe that you are, at heart, a decent child, and because I think you're better off here than you are at home. Don't make me regret that generosity.'

Mohanna flushed, and Aran could see brittle sparks of hurt and anger light up in her eyes. 'But . . .' she began. 'But my Law, you don't trust Peregrine either. I've seen the way you look at him. Everyone has. If *you* can't trust him, how can you expect anyone else to?'

'You speak for my farmstead now, do you?' Law Carifax retorted. 'You know nothing about this, and neither does your fool of a father. My problems with Peregrine are not problems of trust. He saved my son's life. You can't possibly know what that means.'

'Then what?' Aran heard himself breaking in. 'Why do you avoid him? That day on the Barton road – you knew each other before.'

But Carifax shook his head. 'No,' he said. 'Not yet. You're still too young. I think you've just proved that.'

'Too young for what?' Aran demanded.

But his father would not look at him. 'Aran, I'm telling you for the last time, stop asking questions. I can promise, you won't like the answers.'

And he stormed away down the corridor, his heavy boots echoing.

Aran and Mohanna looked at one another. Aran had no idea what had just happened. But he knew there was much more to this than he could possibly figure out. He wasn't even sure if he wanted to.

CHAPTER FIFTEEN
The White Flower

The Moon of Dry Grass waxed and waned, passing into the Moon of Long Shadows, and still the heat did not subside. At night the people gathered in the courtyard, sipping lemonade by torchlight. Children raced to the river to splash in the luminescent shallows. Bats skimmed over the water, their sonar song sounding across the moonlit valley. Great moths scorched their wings in candle flames, and sometimes the broad-winged shadow of a hunting owl would fall black upon the silver grass, and a thousand furry, crawling things would hide their heads and pray for deliverance.

There were few travellers passing through Hawk's Cross that summer, but those who did brought news of farmsteads raided and burned, citizens killed or taken. And with each tale the threat seemed to come closer to home, the names and places more frighteningly familiar – Brimham, Hargate, Highfields. Aran began to feel as though this valley, his home, was an island of calm in a world tearing itself apart. And there was nothing he could do to stop it.

At last the day came for Akmid and his fellow trainees to leave for their barracks in Barton. Aran stood dutifully in the entrance hall as one by one the recruits took their leave of the Law and his Lady, and the only home they had ever known. Akmid came last, his head high. If he had any sense of uncertainty or apprehension about the task ahead, Aran could see no sign of it.

'Be careful,' their mother said softly, kissing Akmid on the cheek and trying not to seem hurt when he pulled away, blushing and glancing at his men. 'Don't take any unnecessary risks. I want you back safe. Or there'll be trouble.'

The Law grabbed his son by both shoulders and his face shone. 'You show those Marauders whose Island this is, all right? And never forget how proud I am of you.'

Akmid bit his lip, and just for a moment Aran saw tears brimming in his brother's eyes. But he wiped them away and forced a laugh. 'We'll be home in a month,' he said. 'Once the Marauders realize what they're up against they'll run back to their boats with their tails between their legs.'

Carifax grinned, and brought his son in for a massive hug, clapping Akmid on the back with his big flat palms. 'That's the spirit,' he said.

He relinquished his grip and now Aran found himself face to face with his brother. For a moment, neither of them spoke. Akmid did not wear his usual dismissive sneer, not in front of their parents. He simply stood, looking down, his face blank. Not knowing what else to do, Aran stuck out his hand. Akmid took it uncertainly, and they shook in silence.

'Boys,' Lady Carifax hissed. 'Is that the best you can do?'

Akmid flushed, placing his arms awkwardly around Aran's neck and giving him a half-hearted squeeze. Aran smelled leather polish and lanolin. Then Akmid released him and hurried away, up the ramp and into the light. Aran watched him go, and heard the clatter of hooves and the jangle of armour out in the courtyard.

Lady Carifax let out a deep sigh, turning to her youngest son. 'That was pathetic,' she said. 'I hope you realize what your brother's doing. He's risking his life for us, you know. That means you too.'

Aran frowned. 'I'd have gone too if you'd let me,' he said.

The Lady shook her head. Aran could see the strain on her face. 'That's not the point,' she said. 'Akmid is your brother. How will you feel if he . . . if he doesn't . . .' And she marched away towards the stairwell, her shoulders trembling.

Law Carifax looked down at Aran and smiled through thin lips. 'Don't worry about your mother,' he said awkwardly. 'She's just upset. Come on, let's go and see them off.'

The recruits rode from the farmstead in a single formation, banners limp in the heat. Aran sat beside his father on the courtyard wall, watching them go. He knew that life in the militia would be arduous, but at least they'd be out there in the world, battling the Marauder threat. All he had to look forward to was another year of work and study, growing older and going nowhere.

But when he reported to his classroom later that morning, he found Peregrine standing in the hallway. To Aran's delight, his tutor was carrying none of the usual books and papers, but only his polished oak walking stick.

He led the boy up the ramp and across the courtyard. A thin gust of wind blew down from the moors, and the weather vane on the chapel roof creaked and span. Peregrine swung south, leading Aran through the cattle meadow and into the silent woods.

'Where are we going?' Aran asked.

Peregrine marched on without speaking. Aran hurried behind him, along a narrow poacher's path between thickets of bramble and rhododendron. Here in the shade it was almost cool.

'Are you going to teach me how to talk to animals?' he asked hopefully.

'No,' said Peregrine.

Aran looked at the knife hanging from his tutor's belt. 'How to make a bow and arrow?'

'No.'

'We're going to see some kind of Ancestor ruin that no one else knows about?'

'No, and hush.' Peregrine stormed on through the undergrowth, until they were far out of sight of the farmstead. Then he turned and laid both his hands on Aran's shoulders. 'All right,' he said. The boy looked around. He could see nothing but forest on every side of them.

'What d—' Aran started.

'*Shush*,' said Peregrine vehemently. Aran's mouth clamped shut.

They stood for a long time in the stifling silence. Aran began to get annoyed. What was this supposed to be teaching him, how to stand still?

At last Peregrine looked down. 'What d'you hear?' he asked in a whisper.

Aran shrugged. 'Nothing,' he said. 'It's quiet.'

Peregrine sighed. 'That's what I thought you'd say. Here I was, trying to teach you something useful for a change, and you won't even try.'

'But I . . .' Aran protested. 'I don't . . . It's just quiet!'

'Listen again,' Peregrine ordered.

Aran stood, red-faced and irritable. He drummed his fingers on his sleeve until an angry glance from Peregrine stopped him. His breath echoed in the stillness.

Then, slowly, he became aware of a faint tapping, somewhere off to the left. It repeated, a hollow *tock-tock*. Then a high chirruping, and the rustle of disturbed branches. Another sound arose: a scratching, far off and low to the ground. An insect whined in Aran's ear and he resisted the temptation to wave it away.

One by one, other noises revealed themselves. The lilting song of a skylark, high above the treetops. The steady *drip-drip* of dewdrops collecting in leaf pools and falling to the earth. The distant shout of a human voice, shrill and distinct. And beneath it all the thrum of the river, deep in the valley, rolling on.

Aran listened to each in turn. He found that he could tune out certain sounds in order to focus more clearly on others. He looked up to see Peregrine watching him.

'What d'you hear now?' he asked softly. Aran told him. Peregrine's face broke into a proud grin. 'That's better,' he said. 'Now you have to learn to hear those sounds without them hearing you.'

They took off their shoes and placed them in Peregrine's pack, then set off again. Now that Aran was better attuned, his own blundering passage seemed deafening.

As they went, Peregrine whispered the names of the creatures they could hear around them. 'A woodpecker, over to the left,' he said. 'A rabbit . . . no, a fox. Down in the valley aways. There's the rabbit. Do you hear him? Oh, he'd better run.'

Aran held his breath. The sights, the smells, the heat in the air and the weight of his clothes, all of this seemed to fade and let him bend his mind entirely to the task, listening for the telltale scramble and screech of a hunter bringing down its prey.

Then he could relax and let the other sounds, sights and scents come flooding back. Time passed. He could feel the kick and business of the forest all around him, the movement and activity, the surging struggle of life coursing through.

He opened his mouth to express these thoughts to Peregrine, but found his tutor looking back over his shoulder, one finger pressed to his lips. He beckoned to Aran and they crept up to the base of an oak tree on the edge of a sheltered clearing ringed by tall trunks and hawthorn bushes.

'Right on schedule,' muttered Peregrine.

Aran dropped to his belly, peering over a hollow log. In the centre of the clearing stood Cas and Mohanna, looking at the wall of dark trees.

'Well, I think you've been given bad information,' Mohanna was saying, 'because I don't see any sign of them.'

'Cartwright wouldn't lie to me,' said Cas defensively. 'He saw them come this way.'

'You know what,' Mohanna snorted. 'I'll bet that Peregrine's magicked him off somewhere.'

'Oh, not that again,' said Cas. 'You're obsessed.'

Aran glanced sidelong at his tutor, but Peregrine didn't seem to have heard. He was polishing a small pebble on the sleeve of his jacket. With a flick of his wrist, he launched it into the clearing. It struck the earth inches from Cas's leg. Both children whipped round.

'What was that?' Mohanna asked. Another tiny projectile kicked up a cloud of dust beside them. She raised her voice. 'Come out, whoever you are. This isn't funny.'

'Shut up!' hissed Cas. 'What if it's . . . you know . . . *them*. You might make them angry.'

'They're making *me* angry,' said Mohanna loudly. 'They should know that's not a good idea.'

They stood back to back. Mohanna raised her fists

defiantly. Cas jumped at every sound, even the ones he made himself.

Aran looked at Peregrine, who was counting silently on upraised fingers. On three, they jumped from their hiding place with a roar. Cas and Mohanna shrieked and clutched one another.

Aran fell to the ground, laughing. Mohanna ran over and kicked him in the ribs. 'That's for being a sneak,' she said. She glared at Peregrine. 'I don't know what you're smiling about. Some teacher.'

Aran clutched his sides. 'You should have seen your face,' he cried.

Cas sat in a bank of ferns, shaking. Aran crossed to his friend and put an arm around his shoulders. 'I'm sorry,' he said. 'It was just too easy.'

'How did you manage to sneak up on us like that?' Cas asked.

Aran looked at Peregrine. 'It's a secret,' he said.

'No, it's not,' said Peregrine. 'I'll teach you.'

They sat together in the clearing, and Peregrine made Cas and Mohanna listen as Aran had done. Mohanna soon proved herself a natural, able to pick out noises that were right on the verge of Aran's hearing. Even Peregrine became suspicious when she claimed to hear a barn owl waking in its nest, but a low hooting in the distance confirmed it.

'Ears like a bat, this one,' said Peregrine. Mohanna blushed into her hand.

Then Peregrine led them back into the tangle of the

forest, and showed them the telltale traces of animal comings and goings; the broken stem of a fern, the clustered droppings of a fleeing hare. Cas uncovered a hoard of nuts hidden away by a conscientious squirrel who knew that winter would soon return. A fox darted out of sight, his white tail-tip flashing in the fading light. Looking up, Aran realized that the shadows had grown long and edged with gold. They must have been sneaking around in the undergrowth for hours.

At last they returned to the clearing, hungry and tired. Peregrine crouched down and plucked a white, five-petalled flower from the forest floor. He twirled it between his thumb and forefinger and tiny droplets of dew sparkled and span.

'One more lesson,' he said. 'Do you know what this is called?'

Aran shrugged. 'A flower?'

Peregrine frowned. 'But what kind?' he asked. He looked at Cas. 'Who would you go to if you wanted to know the name and properties of this flower?'

Cas thought for a moment. 'The harvest master?' he said at last.

Peregrine shook his head. 'He's good with crops and fruit, but he wouldn't know anything about flowers of the forest.'

'My father, then,' Aran suggested.

Peregrine snorted. 'He wouldn't know a carrot from a cucumber.'

'Why do we need to know their names?' Mohanna asked. 'They don't know ours.'

Peregrine sighed. 'Don't try to be clever, it doesn't suit you.' He looked at them each in turn, and his face grew very serious. 'You need to know these flowers because they are part of the world around you. This world is changing, children. It has slept for almost a thousand years, but now it is coming awake once more. It is yours to discover.

'So much has been forgotten, so much knowledge lost. For the better part of a millennium, the struggle for survival has taken precedence over the quest for enlightenment. But no more. You three are in a unique position. You have time to learn, to explore. To make a new world on the ruins of the old. And you have the grand privilege of studying with the only living creature left on this earth who knows the true, old name of this insignificant little white flower.'

There was a long silence. Peregrine looked down at the flower lying on the palm of his hand, then with a single breath he blew it away.

'So?' Aran asked.

Peregrine blinked slowly. 'So what?' he said.

'So what was it called?'

'The flower? Columbine.'

Aran repeated the word. It was strange, the way it felt in his mouth. As though part of him had already known the name, even though his ears had never heard it before. It sounded *right*.

'Pretty name,' said Cas. 'What does it mean?'

Peregrine shook his head. 'It doesn't *mean* anything. It's a name.'

'Your name means something. It's a bird.'

Peregrine sighed. 'Do you always have to be so literal?'

Cas thought for a moment. 'Yes.'

'Oh, for God's sake, the name isn't important,' Peregrine said. 'It's the knowledge that matters, and it's high time somebody began to relearn it. What better place to start than right here?'

'So you're going to teach us the names of flowers?' Mohanna asked. 'Sounds fascinating.'

Peregrine gritted his teeth. 'You can call them anything you like,' he said. 'But these flowers, these trees, these creatures are a part of the world around you, and this knowledge cannot be lost. So I'll make you a deal.' He took off his pack and reached inside. To Aran's surprise, he drew out a pair of wooden training swords.

'Now that my commitment to Carifax's militia is done,' Peregrine went on, 'I'll have a bit more time on my hands. If the three of you will agree to spend half the day learning whatever I ask, without question, I'll teach you everything I taught Akmid and the others. With all these Marauder rumours, it's high time you learned to defend yourselves.'

He pressed one of the swords into Aran's hand, folding his fingers around the hilt. The weight felt good in his palm, but Aran shook his head. 'My father will never agree,' he said. 'He says teaching a Foreman to fight is like teaching a crow to swim. A waste of time.'

'Then it'll have to be our little secret,' Peregrine said. He looked at the wall of sturdy trunks and knotty bushes surrounding them. 'I didn't bring you to this clearing by accident. It's far enough from the farmstead to be safe and secret, as long as we stay alert. We'll stash these swords in that hollow log, and no one will be any the wiser.'

Cas looked worried. 'What about me?' he asked. 'I don't want to fight. Anyway, how am I supposed to get out of field duty?'

'Oh, that was taken care of weeks ago,' said Peregrine. 'When I agreed to train the militia, part of the deal was that you be allowed to study with Aran once they'd gone off to Barton. Another was that the two of us start on your pulley system. If we work at it, I think we can have something ready by next summer.'

Cas's grin was so wide that Aran thought his jaw might fall off.

'I'm serious, though,' Peregrine said. 'About the learning, and about the secrecy. Mohanna, this goes for you most of all. I know your father's feelings about me, and I know the history between Crowdale and Hawk's Cross. I won't be responsible for starting another Long Vendetta. But I also believe in self-defence, especially now. And I don't know why, but something tells me you might have a knack for violence. I've always tried to encourage young talent.'

He handed Mohanna the other sword, which she took eagerly. 'My father won't hear it from me,' she said. 'I promise.'

The horizon deepened to warm orange then fiery red, the stars began to prick the sky and now a true silence fell over the forest.

'Right,' said Peregrine. 'Let's start with the basics.' He

crouched on the edge of the clearing. Aran and Mohanna faced one another within the ring of hushed grey trees. 'The first rule of combat is always observation. Judge your opponent's strength. How does he move? Too fast, too slow? Too careful, too reckless? Does he carry any hidden weapons – a knife in the boot, a dagger on the wrist? Start at the top and work down. Take in every detail.'

Aran stared at Mohanna, scanning her up and down, realizing he didn't even know if she was left- or right-handed. He could see a bulge at her ankle that was probably a blade, another in her jacket that was more likely a sandwich. Her fists were clenched, her stance firm, her legs slightly apart.

Mohanna tried to focus, to read Aran the same way. But she found herself blushing and looking away, trying not to laugh. 'Mohanna, this is serious,' Peregrine snapped. 'Do it properly, or not at all.'

Mohanna nodded quickly and took a deep breath. Then she held up her wooden sword as a challenge. Aran did the same.

'All right,' said Peregrine softly. 'Let's see what you can do.'

They circled, rustling through dry leaves. Maybe it was Peregrine's solemnity or his own weariness, but Aran felt like a vibrating string. His heart was pounding and his palms were sweaty on the wooden hilt.

If only to break the tension, Aran lunged. Mohanna parried, and battle was joined.

Aran swung round but Mohanna deflected, forcing him

back. Aran stumbled, but righted himself in time to fend off a high swing, Mohanna's sword just inches from his cheek. Aran bit back a laugh. He felt suddenly giddy and altogether alive.

The hollow knock of the blades rang out in the forest stillness. Peregrine sat on his haunches, munching an apple. Cas knelt in the dirt beside him, flinching with every blow.

Aran swept his blade low, striking for Mohanna's legs. She thrust down, blocking him. Aran was ready; he shifted his feet and drew the sword back, then jabbed forward once more, aiming for her chest.

But Mohanna was too quick. She arched her back, lifted her blade and deflected Aran's attack. He was startled. Mohanna swung out with her right leg, sweeping him off his feet. Aran hit the ground hard, and when he opened his eyes her sword was at his throat.

Peregrine clapped. 'Bravo,' he said. 'I think we have a natural.' Mohanna's eyes flashed.

Aran picked himself up, brushing the dirt from his jacket. 'What about me?' he said. 'How did I do?'

Peregrine smiled kindly. 'Let's just say it was a perfectly good start,' he said.

'Let's go again,' Aran said. 'I'm ready.' And he faced Mohanna, his sword raised.

Peregrine laughed warmly. 'Well, you're keen, I'll give you that much,' he said. 'Most boys your age wouldn't respond so well to being beaten by a girl. OK, one more before last bell. This time, show her who's in charge.'

Within moments, Aran was flat on his back again. The trees spun around him.

'Who's in charge?' Mohanna demanded.

'You,' Aran said hoarsely, clutching his ribs. 'Definitely you.'

Peregrine reached out a hand and helped the boy to his feet, wrapping an arm around his shoulders. 'Poor Aran,' he said. 'It's going to be a long summer.'

CHAPTER SIXTEEN

Bows and Arrows

And so it proved. In the weeks that followed, Aran's ambitions were slowly chipped away. At first he had visions of greatness: he would impress Peregrine with his skill, then go on to astound his father. Before long he'd be signing up to join the militia, ready to take on the Marauder army.

Now he considered it a major victory if he managed to stay upright. Aran's instincts were good and he was quick on his feet, but he was clumsy and far too reckless. And Mohanna was a predatory animal, always on the hunt. In two months he had managed to knock her down just once, and that was only because she had thought she heard someone coming. Aran tried his best, but he was hopelessly outclassed. And today would be no different.

He rolled on his back in the dirt, clutching his wooden sword. 'Peregrine, did you see that?' he asked excitedly. 'I nearly had her that time.'

Mohanna looked down at him, her tangled hair

silhouetted against the icy sky. 'Not bad,' she smiled. 'Perhaps I've finally beaten some sense into that thick head of yours.'

'Let's not get ahead of ourselves,' Peregrine warned. 'That was an improvement, but there's a big gulf between almost knocking her down and actually doing it.' He stretched. 'Right, five-minute break. I have some . . . business to attend to in the forest.'

Aran and Mohanna leaned their backs against the trunk of a leafless birch. This would be their final day of training until spring. They had spent the morning dutifully learning the attributes of three kinds of lichen, all of which looked the same to Aran. But now that winter was here, Peregrine was struggling to find subjects for study – all the forest creatures were safely tucked away, and the plants had shed their leaves. The skies were clear and the air was dry, and that morning had brought the first hard frost. In a week, maybe less, it wouldn't be safe to wander so far from the farmstead.

Aran sighed. 'I know I'm rubbish, but I'm still going to miss this,' he said.

Mohanna shook her head. 'You're not that bad,' she said. 'He's only teasing. If you keep up your exercises, next year you'll be as good as me. Well, almost.'

Aran sighed. 'But still not good enough to join the militia,' he said. 'Not that my father would agree to it, even if I was.'

'I don't know why you'd want to,' Mohanna said. 'Living in some smelly barracks in Barton with five hundred boys. Sounds horrible.'

'At least I'd be doing something,' Aran pointed out. 'At least I'd be helping.'

'Maybe,' said Mohanna. 'Or else you'd be dead.'

At first, tales of the militia's exploits had been recounted excitedly, whispers passing through the farmstead of how one local lad had taken on three Marauders single-handed, or how another had protected a convoy of traders from attack. But then riders had begun to arrive from Barton, bringing lists of the dead and demanding replacements from the training pool. After that the stories dried up, and when people spoke of the militia now it was with guarded pride and desperate hope, and a mounting sense of dread.

'What do you think of this Randle business?' Aran asked.

That morning, one of Lady Carifax's handmaidens had reported that her fiancé, Randle, a poacher who often provided pheasants for the Law's table, had seen a group of men sneaking about the forest between Hawk's Cross and Crowdale. Randle had hailed them, intending to see them off for hunting in his woods, but the strangers had fled before he could catch up to them. But in the dirt where they'd been, he had found a bone necklace the like of which he'd not seen before.

'I think the Marauders are a long way from here,' Mohanna said dismissively. 'I also think Randle would do anything for a profit. If everyone's too scared to go into the woods, he gets to hunt for both farmsteads.'

Aran shrugged. She had a point.

'And even if it's true, he said there were only a few of them,' Mohanna went on. 'Let them try anything with me and they'll soon get a taste of what I've been giving you all summer.'

Aran touched the fresh bruise on his cheek and smiled.

Mohanna dragged him to his feet and pressed the sword into his hand. 'Come on,' she said. 'I think we've got time for one more.'

Aran gave his limbs a good shake. He held the sword out, inching towards Mohanna. He took a breath and tried to centre himself. One last bout, one last chance to prove himself. This time he could beat her, he knew he could. He took another deep breath. One . . . two . . .

Mohanna's head whipped round. Footsteps in the undergrowth, coming closer. Aran felt his heart quicken. Perhaps it was just Peregrine, back to yell at them some more. But perhaps not. There was a downside to being this far from the farmstead. What if Randle's stories were true?

He heard a rustling and a muffled twang. Something whistled past his cheek and thudded into the trunk of an oak tree. It was a short arrow with a wooden shaft and a blunted steel head. Aran recognized it immediately.

'Hey!' he shouted. 'That was a bit close.'

'Sorry!' came a familiar voice. 'I still haven't got the sights lined up right.' Cas stepped into the clearing. 'I was aiming just past your feet.' He shouldered his quiver and smiled apologetically.

The saga of Cas and his bow had been going on for

weeks. The project had begun as a way for him to stay involved even though he had no interest in physical combat. He'd always wanted to be able to shoot, but the longbows in the armoury were too unwieldy to use without risk to his fingers. And so, with a little help from Peregrine, Cas had begun to build a bow which would be smaller but equally powerful, using a winding cog and a length of strong twine attached to a wooden frame which locked to his wrist. The result was undeniably potent, as the steel head sunk into the oak tree proved. But somehow, Cas couldn't quite get the aim right.

'This time I really thought I had it,' he said, raising the bow to eye level and inspecting the sliding steel sights. 'Something's off, I can't work it out. Maybe Peregrine can have a go. Where is he, anyway?'

Aran jerked a thumb towards the forest. 'He's doing what bears do in the woods,' he said. 'Though he's been gone a while. He's probably found a particularly interesting sort of toadstool.'

'Or he's stopped to chat with a squirrel,' said Mohanna.

'Maybe he's run into your father,' Cas said to Aran. 'That's why I came up here, to tell you to pack up. He's out on a hunt – I'm surprised you didn't hear the horns.'

Aran sighed. 'We were almost done,' he said. He didn't want to be cheated out of his final fight. 'You keep watch, it'll be fine.'

'You really want to risk it?' Cas asked. 'They were by the stream when I saw them. Law Darnell seemed to be leading the charge.'

'What was Darnell doing there?' Aran asked. 'I thought he and my father weren't speaking.'

'Well, they seemed on good enough terms,' Cas told him. 'Mohanna, do you know any— What's wrong?'

Mohanna's face had turned pale. 'Get everything covered up. Cas, put that bow away. Now!'

'Calm down,' Aran laughed. 'They've got a whole forest to hunt in. What are the odds they'd stumble in here?'

'I'm serious,' she shot back. 'We need to get out of sight. Right now, or I'll beat you bloody, I swear.'

Aran grinned. 'What would your father say if he could hear you talking like that?' he asked. 'Threatening a Law's son is most unladylike.'

'Aran, honestly, we don't have time to—'

She broke off. Something was moving inside a thicket of rhododendron bushes on the edge of the clearing. The branches rustled and swayed, and they heard the scrabble of running feet. Mohanna backed away, her eyes widening.

A ferocious black shape emerged from the trees. It was a dog, its lips drawn back and its teeth bared. It dashed into the clearing, spotted the children and began to bark madly, running towards Mohanna with wild eyes.

Aran stepped into the dog's path. The animal leaped at him, and Aran brandished his wooden sword. The dog snarled, snapping at Aran's legs. He stumbled back, tripped over a root and let out a cry as he lost his footing. He fell on his backside in a cloud of dust. Then the dog was in his face, howling and barking, its spittle hot on his bare skin.

In the confusion, he heard Mohanna's voice. 'No!' she cried. 'No! Down!'

Then there was a clack and a twang, and a wet, fleshy thud.

The dog's cries turned from furious snarling to aggrieved howling. It forgot Aran, snapping instead at the arrow protruding from its rump. It rolled in contorted circles, chasing its own tail. Then it lay back, emitting great yelps of distress.

'Bessa!' Mohanna cried, kneeling at the dog's side. 'Oh, Cas, what have you done? You've shot my father's best hunting dog.'

Cas's eyes widened. 'I thought it was going to eat him!'

Aran scrambled to his feet, steadying himself against a tree. His head span.

Mohanna cradled the dog's head. 'It doesn't look too serious, it must just hurt,' she said. The animal's cries showed no signs of abating. 'Oh, shush, Bessa, shush. You'll bring the whole farmstead running.'

She attempted to cover the dog's mouth with one hand but only succeeded in getting covered in drool. The yelps continued, each more piercing and pain-filled than the last. 'What am I supposed to do? Should I pull the arrow out?' She looked around in distress.

'What in God's name is going on?' Peregrine came striding into the clearing, looking down at the injured animal. 'What have you been doing, target practice?'

'It's Darnell's dog,' said Aran. 'We had a bit of an accident.'

Peregrine rolled his eyes. 'Oh, nice work,' he said. 'What's wrong, Cas, you couldn't find one of our own dogs to shoot in the bum?'

'It was going after Aran!' Cas cried, tears springing to his eyes. 'I'm not even sure how I managed to hit it. Everyone was yelling and I just fired. It's not my fault, you have to . . . you have to understand . . . Wait . . .'

Cas's voice trailed off and a confused look came over his face. The dog's cries had ceased and a strange hush had fallen over the clearing. Peregrine was kneeling over the stricken beast, his hands outstretched. He was mumbling in a low voice, that peculiar singsong chant which Aran remembered all too well – it brought back images of iron bars and sharp swords, and the claws of a great bear.

Peregrine plucked the arrow easily from the dog's hide. Bessa whimpered but did not cry out. Peregrine smoothed her brow, whispering gently and evenly. All was still.

And that was how Carifax and Darnell came upon them, moments later. The Laws' horses crashed into the clearing, pursued by Devin and a pair of Darnell's guards. They saw Peregrine on his knees, cradling the dog in his lap, the bloody arrow in his hand. They saw Mohanna at his side, and Aran and Cas standing over them, held by the unearthly power which filled the clearing. They saw the crossbow on Cas's wrist, and the wooden swords scattered across the mossy ground.

'What in Ala's name is going on?' Carifax demanded.

Peregrine snapped to attention and the spell was broken.

'My Laws,' he said, climbing to his feet. 'We had a little accident, but it's all taken care of.'

'That's your Bessa, isn't it, Darnell?' asked Carifax, climbing off his horse.

Darnell peered down at the dog. She lay peacefully on her side, the wound seemingly forgotten. Mohanna looked up at her father, her face pale. The Law ignored her, looking at the arrow in Peregrine's hand. 'This was your work?'

Peregrine nodded. 'As I said, a regrettable accident. I take full responsibility.'

Darnell frowned. 'I didn't ask if you take responsibility. I asked who fired the bolt.' He turned to the two boys. Aran tried to shield Cas, but the unwieldy contraption strapped to his wrist was impossible to hide.

Darnell beckoned to Devin, and the burly red-bearded guard captain stepped forward. 'The little one,' Darnell ordered. 'Don't be too rough if you can help it. You can drop him back at Hawk's Cross when you're done.'

Cas blanched. Devin started forward, reaching down with black-gloved hands, but Peregrine stepped in, joining Aran. He put up a hand and Devin's horse shied.

'Do we really have to do this again, my Law?' Peregrine asked Darnell. 'You remember what happened last time?'

Darnell reddened. 'Is that a threat?' he asked. He turned to Law Carifax, bristling. 'Did you hear that? Your man threatened me.'

Carifax looked uncomfortable. 'Cas did shoot the Law's dog, Peregrine,' he said.

'Accidentally,' said Peregrine. 'And the animal will be fine. It's barely a flesh wound.'

'So Darnell should simply forego punishment?' Carifax asked.

'By all means, punish,' Peregrine said. 'Put the boy on half rations. Put him back in the fields. But turn him over to this brute? Not on your life.'

Darnell's eyes widened. 'Carifax, you allow this man to openly contradict you?'

Law Carifax looked at Peregrine in frustration. 'Darnell has the right of this,' he said. 'The crime was against his property. He gets to choose the punishment.'

Mohanna got to her feet. 'Father,' she begged, her voice thick with fear. 'Peregrine's right, it was an accident. I'm as much to blame as—'

'Be quiet,' Darnell snapped. 'Don't you dare contradict me. You've already betrayed me enough.' He bent, picking up one of the wooden swords and inspecting it. 'What's the meaning of this, I wonder?' he asked. 'Carifax, any thoughts?'

Law Carifax looked at the blade, then back at Peregrine. 'I'd been led to believe the children were up here to study plants,' he said. 'Isn't that what you told me, Peregrine? That they were here to learn the . . . how did you put it? . . . the secrets of the forest?'

'Peregrine knew nothing about it,' Aran attempted desperately. 'He was off in the woods, finding plants for us to . . . you know . . . study.'

'That'll do, Aran,' Peregrine said with a sigh. 'Thanks

197

for trying, but somehow I don't think it's working. My Law, you may as well know. I've been teaching Aran to protect himself. I thought it was time.'

Carifax's face reddened. 'Time?' he asked in a bitter tone. 'You just decided, against my instructions . . . We talked about this, Peregrine. My farmstead, my rules.'

'So we did,' Peregrine replied. 'But I won't leave the boy defenceless. I know you think you have your reasons, but—'

'Stop,' said Carifax. 'Stop right now. Don't say another word.'

Aran looked from one to the other. This is it, he thought. It's all connected. The books, the training, his father's fear, this strange bond between them. And somehow, he was in the centre of it all.

'The Marauder threat is real,' Peregrine insisted. 'Every day they get closer. You must have heard the stories this morning . . .'

Carifax shook his head. 'Rumours,' he said. 'Women's gossip.'

'Maybe so,' Peregrine countered. 'But we were all at Barton. How can you think these children aren't in danger?'

Law Darnell took a step forward. 'So this . . . threat gives you licence to do whatever you like?' he said. 'Flout your Law's wishes? Train his son to fight, and teach my daughter to play with swords?'

Peregrine glanced his way, and realization flooded his face. 'The dog,' he said. 'You put her on the scent. You weren't hunting boar at all, you were hunting us.'

Darnell smirked. 'She couldn't keep coming home with bruises and think I wouldn't notice,' he said. 'I knew she'd never betray her friends, so I decided to see for myself what was going on. I might have known you'd be behind it.'

Peregrine shook his head. 'I wonder if you have any idea, Darnell, what will happen if the Marauders find their way here? It'll be bad for the boys, they'll be killed or dragged off to one of these slave ships we've heard about. But what do you think will happen to the girls? Have you even thought about that?'

Darnell's lips drew back in a sneer of pure hatred. 'If they manage to find their way this far inland,' he said, 'I can guarantee you it won't be my daughter fighting them off.'

'*When* they come this far inland,' Peregrine spat back. 'Only a fool would assume it won't happen. When they come, each one of us will be forced to fight.' He looked up at Devin and his fellows, a pair of young thugs with shaved heads. 'Don't pretend you're unaware,' he went on. 'Don't think it's gone unnoticed that Crowdale sends only the old and weak to join the militia, and keeps the best at home. How do you feel, Darnell, when they bring those brave men home in a box?'

Law Darnell snarled, his fists clenched. The urge for violence was plain on his face. But instead he marched across the clearing, taking Mohanna by the wrist and hauling her towards his horse. Her feet slipped and she cried out, but Darnell did not stop. Mohanna's knees scraped bloodily across jagged roots and rough stones.

'Stop,' Peregrine cried out. 'For God's sake, let her go, you heartless—'

Darnell turned back, dropping Mohanna. She sank, sobbing, to the ground.

'How dare you speak to me this way, boy?' Darnell demanded. 'In my household you would be whipped for such impertinence.'

'I told you before,' Peregrine said, drawing himself up to his full height. 'I am no boy. Clearly you've forgotten the lesson I taught you that day on the road.'

'You will regret your insolence,' Darnell spat. Aran suddenly noticed that he held a short, bright-bladed knife which he had surreptitiously drawn and concealed in the folds of his robe.

Darnell lunged at Peregrine, but he was too slow. Peregrine took a single step, chopping down with the side of his hand, knocking the knife from Darnell's grip. He grabbed the Law by the throat, shoving him back against a tree.

'Peregrine, stop!' Law Carifax called out, as Darnell's guards prepared to charge.

But before they could act, Mohanna was on her feet. To Aran's amazement she flung herself at Peregrine, battering with her fists. 'Don't touch him!' she shouted.

Peregrine released his grip and Darnell dropped to the ground. But Mohanna's attack did not cease, her feeble blows raining down on Peregrine as he staggered backwards.

'You don't touch him!' Mohanna cried. 'You villain. You . . . you . . . Marauder!'

Darnell climbed to his feet and grabbed his daughter, pulling her away. Mohanna crumbled, her eyes streaming with tears.

'You stupid, stupid girl,' growled Darnell. Then he glanced at Aran, who stood watching helplessly. 'Say goodbye to your friend. You won't be seeing him again for a very long time.' He yanked his daughter roughly towards the waiting horse. Mohanna did not resist. Darnell hauled her up behind him, looking back at Carifax.

'My Law, if you value my friendship, you'll keep these two away from my daughter,' he said. Then he spurred his stallion down into the valley, followed by Devin and the guards. The sound of hoof beats receded into the trees.

Silence followed. Aran looked at his father, who suddenly seemed very tired and very sad. He stood on the edge of the clearing, one hand clutching his horse's bridle, the other limp at his side. 'You betrayed my trust,' he said to Peregrine. 'You disobeyed my orders. You've done potentially irreparable damage to my relationship with Law Darnell, a man who is not to be trifled with.'

'He knew,' Peregrine argued. 'He set this up to drive a wedge between us.'

'Apparently so,' Carifax admitted. 'But though his methods may be questionable, the result is the same.' He pointed one gloved finger at Peregrine. 'I see you clearly now. You have your agenda, and nothing I can say or do will sway you. I wanted to believe you'd changed, but I can see it isn't so. But then, you don't change, do you?'

'I'm trying,' said Peregrine, in a quiet, regretful voice. 'I really thought that this time—'

'It's clear this isn't working,' Carifax cut in. 'I'm grateful for all you've done for Aran. You saved his life, and for that I can never repay you. But I just can't trust you, Peregrine. He's still so young.'

'He's old enough,' Peregrine insisted. 'Old enough to defend himself. Old enough to learn what I have to teach him. Old enough to know the truth about—'

'No.' Carifax's voice fell like a stone. 'Need I remind you that Aran is my responsibility, and mine alone? That was the agreement.'

Peregrine nodded. 'I remember,' he said.

The Law climbed wearily onto his horse. 'I won't force you to go,' he said, wrapping the reins around his fingers. 'I doubt I could if I wanted to. But I want you to stay away from my son. Miss Crell is quite fit enough to resume her duties. If you've any sense you'll leave, before you cause any more harm.' And he kicked his spurs and rode from the clearing.

Aran stared after him in disbelief.

'What was all that about?' he asked. 'What did he mean?'

'Exactly what he said,' Peregrine replied. 'He wants me gone.'

'Because of a stupid dog and some wooden swords?' Aran said in disbelief. 'There's more to this, I know there is. What agreement? What did he mean, you don't change? You said we had to be honest, so why won't you tell me the truth?'

202

'Because it's not my place to tell,' said Peregrine, almost angrily. 'I've told you before, your father is not a man who does a thing without reason. And this time he feels as though the threat of my being here is greater than the benefit.'

'What threat?' Aran demanded. 'What have you done?'

Peregrine shook his head. 'No,' he said. 'I must respect his wishes. But Aran, one day, in a year, or five, or ten, I'll tell you everything you want to know. I promise.'

Tears sprang unbidden into Aran's eyes. 'Go, then,' he said. 'And maybe in a year, or five, or ten, we'll all be killed by Marauders, and it won't matter anyway.'

Peregrine crossed the clearing, picked up his bag and vanished into the trees. Aran sank back, his heart pounding and his head raging. Part of him wanted to go after Peregrine, to defy his father's wishes and face the consequences. But another part was furious at the two of them, how they treated him like a child, keeping their secrets and breaking their promises, leaving him alone again, here in the dirt.

Or, not quite alone. Cas looked at Aran with scared, sorry eyes. He crossed to his friend and put his arm around his shoulders, holding Aran tight as he broke into uncontrollable tears.

CHAPTER SEVENTEEN
The Break-In

The farmstead at Crowdale was buried deep in the side of a shallow, rocky valley dotted with emaciated pines. An icy wind howled through the patchy scrub as Aran and Cas approached on horseback. The lonely call of a hunting bird sounded high among dark clouds heavy with snow.

'I must be mad,' Cas moaned, wrapping his scarf tighter and shivering. 'Why do I always let you talk me into these things?'

'Because you know I'm right,' Aran retorted, his breath billowing. 'Because she's your friend too. And because you know that she wouldn't think twice if you were in trouble.'

'Have you thought . . .' Cas began, then stopped. 'Have you thought that maybe she won't want to see us? After she . . . After what happened with Peregrine?'

'Of course I've thought about it,' he said. 'I don't care. She's my friend.'

For the past week, all Aran had done was sit and think – about Darnell's trick, about Peregrine's secrets, about Carifax's stubbornness. He'd thought back, all the way to his first meetings with Peregrine, trying to piece it together, to figure out what it all meant. He was totally lost, and no one would give him any answers. His father was avoiding him, and he knew that Peregrine was under strict instructions to keep away.

But with Mohanna it was different. Aran could imagine how lonely she must be, how scared, locked away with little hope of ever seeing her friends again. And he knew what he had to do.

'Just promise me,' Cas said, the wind dropping as they descended into the sheltered vale. 'You only want to make sure she's OK. No raids, no prison breaks. No stealing from Darnell's storerooms.'

'I promise,' Aran said. 'Just remember everything Peregrine taught us.' He lowered his voice to a whisper. 'Silent and stealthy.'

Cas shook his head. 'You're completely mad, aren't you? You and Mohanna both. Honestly, I don't know what you'd do without me around.'

They tethered their horses in a pine coppice and approached the farmstead on foot. It was late and the sky was swiftly darkening, taking with it the last lingering warmth of the day. Aran found himself shivering despite the layers of wool and leather under his jacket.

They moved closer, picking through thickets of wind-battered bracken. There was a small collection of low, stone buildings up on the surface and an unevenly paved courtyard with tufts of grass sprouting between the slabs. A pair of watchmen huddled by the hatch, throwing dice. Several cows stood by, chewing patiently.

'I don't see how we're going to get past those guards,' Cas said. 'They'll recognize you right away.'

Aran's brow furrowed. He remembered Mohanna mentioning a secret entrance she used to get in and out without being spotted, but he had no idea where it might be. Then he spotted a faint glow in a nearby cluster of trees. 'Vent shaft,' he guessed. 'Let's take a look.'

They crept closer. The shaft was walled with dry earth. A flickering light emanated from it, but there was no sign of smoke. 'It's just a short one, down to the first or second level,' Aran said. 'Maybe a stable or a storeroom. Have you got a rope in that pack of yours?'

Cas shook his head. 'I didn't think we'd be going climbing,' he said.

'Well, what have you got?' Aran asked. 'Anything useful?'

Cas shrugged, slipping off his knapsack. 'Couple of apples. Water bottle. My crossbow.'

Aran's eyes widened. 'What did you bring that for?'

'You've got your short blade,' Cas replied. 'I should be able to defend myself too.'

'Great,' Aran laughed. 'So if Darnell's men come at you, you can shoot another one of his dogs.'

Cas scowled and Aran cuffed him on the arm. 'I'm only teasing,' he said. 'Come on, we should still be able to climb down. It doesn't look too steep. Why don't you go first, then if you fall you won't take me with you.'

Cas swung his leg over the side of the shaft, clinging to an overhanging branch with both hands. He braced his feet on the crumbling sides. 'This is a really stupid idea,' he said.

Aran nodded. 'You're probably right,' he said. 'Good luck.'

Cas descended into the stinking hole. It was only steep for twenty feet or so, then it began to level out. The light was growing.

At the top of the shaft, Aran shivered. It looked warm down there, cosy and quiet.

'Cas?' he called out. 'Are you at the bottom?' He began to lower himself into the hole.

'Just a second,' came Cas's voice from below. 'Don't come down. It's trickier than it looks.'

'It's too late,' Aran called out, letting go of the branch above his head. 'But I'll be fine. I just—'

And then his feet slipped.

He slid down several feet, clutching at the sides. There was nothing to hold onto except dry, flaky soil. For a moment he seemed to be slowing, and he clutched at the earth in an attempt to halt his decline. But it was too late – he could see light rising towards him, Cas's startled face coming closer.

'No, Aran, stop—'

They crashed through the tunnel mouth into a large pool of something warm and wet. Aran surfaced, gasping for air. Cas came up beside him, spluttering and cursing. They were standing knee-deep in an enormous vat of raw sewage. It was caked on the walls, on the ceiling and all over their clothes.

Aran wiped his face with his hand, looking angrily at Cas. 'Why didn't you warn me?' he demanded.

Cas glared at him. 'I didn't really expect you to drop in like that,' he said.

They clambered over the side of the vat and stood dripping in the shed. A lamp hung above the door and three cows watched cautiously from their hay-lined stalls.

'At least there's no one around,' Aran pointed out.

'I doubt they could stand the smell,' muttered Cas. He took a filthy rag from a hook on the wall and cleaned his face and hands before handing it to Aran. 'Well, this adventure's off to a fine start,' he said.

Aran grinned. 'We're inside, aren't we?' he said. 'And in disguise. No one will come near us, looking and smelling the way we do.'

'So this was all part of your plan, was it?' Cas asked.

'I'm just being resourceful,' Aran protested. 'It's like Peregrine says – when life gives you lemons, make lemonade.'

'That wasn't lemonade we just got covered in,' Cas muttered.

Aran crept to the door. A torch guttered in a brace on the wall outside. He could hear the distant sound of footsteps. He stepped out into the winding tunnel. Cas followed.

'Do you know where you're going?' he whispered.

'Not a clue,' Aran replied. 'And don't whisper, it's suspicious. Just talk in a low voice, like this.'

They followed the corridor to an intersection. An archway to their left led to a descending flight of steps. Crowdale was a mazelike burrow, very different from Hawk's Cross. The soil in these parts was pitted with boulders, and the farmstead had been built around these natural impediments. Passages suddenly turned aside, sloped steeply or stopped altogether. The tunnels were low and claustrophobic, the rooms small and uninviting. No wonder Mohanna always wanted to get away.

'We'll just have to keep our eyes and ears open,' Aran said. 'There's no way we can avoid being seen. But try to look inconspicuous, like you've been working all day.'

'I have been working all day.'

'Well, it shouldn't be that hard, then, should it?'

They joined a busy corridor. The air was hot and still. Aran was beginning to sweat beneath his clothes. People glared at them as they passed, holding their noses and grimacing. They turned into a steep, descending stairway, following the flow of the crowd.

A blow on the arm startled Aran and he looked up. A man was pushing past him up the stairs, against the tide. He was tall and lithe, with long greasy hair tied back with a length of leather twine. He had a cut on his forehead, the kind you'd get from a whipping tree branch. It wasn't quite healed. The man looked down at Aran, and for a second their eyes met. The man's irises were ice-clear. He looked away hurriedly, as though he too was afraid of being recognized.

Aran watched him go. He thought back to Carny, to the party from Crowdale who had joined them on the road. He was sure this man hadn't been among them. It wasn't as if he'd blend into a crowd. Aran couldn't think of the last time he'd seen such a stern face, or such hard eyes. Not, he thought, since his capture by the Marauders.

But now the man was gone, vanishing round a bend in the stairway. The people on either side were quickening their pace, eager to get somewhere. One sniff of the air and Aran knew exactly where they were going.

The stairwell opened out, leading down to a large, unevenly shaped hall. The sound of conversation echoed from the walls, creating a muddy, disorienting din. The kitchen doors on the near side were flung wide. Clouds of steam billowed out, rising towards high vent shafts in the walls and ceiling. The air was stifling.

Through a hatch in the kitchen wall a red-faced old woman ladled spoonfuls of dark broth into waiting bowls. The smell was rich and meaty.

'We should try to blend in,' Cas suggested. 'Get in line.'

'We didn't come here to have dinner,' Aran frowned.

'Well, we can listen in,' Cas said. 'See if we can hear news of Mohanna.'

They grabbed bowls and joined the queue. Hearing a brash voice, Aran turned. The back wall was one huge boulder with alcoves carved into it, housing flickering candles. The wax ran in rivulets down the rock, giving it a liquid sheen. Seated at the base of the rock was Law Darnell, with Devin and a party of fawning advisers. A steaming bowl was placed in front of him and the Law tucked in eagerly. Aran hid his face.

'Bowl!' said a voice. Aran's head snapped up. The old woman was glaring at him through the hatch, with a pinched expression like she'd seen something disgusting on her shoe.

She looked him up and down. 'What do you think you're doing?' she demanded loudly.

Aran shook his head. Had she recognized him? 'What—' he began.

'You stink!' she cried, snatching his bowl. 'I'm not serving you like this. Come back when you don't smell like a pig's bum.'

Aran backed away, pulling Cas with him. They ducked behind a pillar, peering towards Darnell. He hadn't noticed the woman's outburst; he was too busy attacking his supper.

'What are we going to do?' Cas demanded. 'The smell is drawing attention.'

'I want to keep an eye on Darnell,' Aran said. 'He's bound to go back to his quarters. Mohanna's room won't be far.'

'We can't stay here,' said Cas. 'We need to find some-where to get cleaned up.'

'Then someone will recognize us,' Aran argued. 'They all know I'm Law Carifax's son.'

'They'll just think you're here to see Mohanna.'

'Even though she's being punished?' Aran objected. 'Think how fast news travels at home. I bet everyone here knows all about what happened. Just let me—' He broke off, glancing towards the kitchen doors. A tall, pale-skinned woman stood there, carrying a wooden tray. 'Lady Darnell,' said Aran.

The Lady was slender and somehow sad, her long yellow tresses turning to grey. She crossed the room towards an open archway. As she passed the head table, Law Darnell reached out and took her by the arm. He said something insistently but she shook him off. Darnell got to his feet and went after her. He didn't notice Aran and Cas slipping silently through the archway behind him.

'Clare,' Darnell cried out. 'Clare, stop!'

They followed him down a flight of steps and along a winding corridor. He was muttering and cursing under his breath. Soon he caught up to his wife. She turned, her face pallid in the lamplight. Aran and Cas ducked into a doorway.

'Don't walk away from me,' Darnell barked. 'I've told you I want her left alone.'

'She needs to eat,' his wife replied frostily.

'I had the guards take her something this morning,' Darnell said. 'Now she needs to stay in her room and think about what she's done.'

'Then let me at least take her some clean clothes.'

Darnell's patience snapped. '*No*, I said!' he yelled. 'I don't know why the women in this family feel the need to disregard my wishes. The girl has lied to me for the last time, do you understand? I'm very angry with her.'

'I think you made that clear.'

Darnell snorted. 'I barely touched her,' he said. 'Why, my father would have beaten me black and blue for such a crime. But force means nothing to that girl. She's so stubborn, she just grits her teeth and lets you get on with it, then she carries on doing exactly what she's been doing all along.'

'I wonder where she got that from?' spat his wife.

Darnell frowned. 'Well, it's going to stop,' he said. 'If I can't trust her to obey me, I'll have to make sure she can't get into trouble. I'll have to know where she is at all times. If I let her out for one moment she'll be straight back to Hawk's Cross and that . . . criminal.'

'Maybe you just could find someone to keep an eye on her?' Lady Darnell suggested meekly. 'One of the nurses could—'

'You think my daughter's not smart enough to outwit one simple-minded nurse? No, she'll stay locked up, it's the only way.' The Law's voice became softer. 'Clare, I know this is hard. But she's too wayward, too independent. What kind of man would want to marry her like this?'

Aran and Cas looked at one another, wide-eyed.

'She loves you so much,' Lady Darnell said quietly. 'She fought to protect you. Doesn't that mean anything?'

'It's not her place to fight, even for me,' Darnell said with a sigh. He took his wife in his arms. 'Clare, I have big plans for this family. If my negotiations go well, we won't be stuck out here, at the back end of nowhere. I know the other Laws laugh at us. Carifax and Walden and their cronies on the Council. Well, not for long. Mohanna must understand she has a part to play. I'm making her a good match, but she'll need to learn to be an obedient wife, like her mother.'

Lady Darnell lowered her eyes. 'Why won't you tell me who the suitor is?' she said. 'Is it Carifax's son? Is that why you're so angry?'

Darnell barked a short, pointed laugh. 'Don't be ridiculous,' he said. 'No, if I'm going to give up my only child, I'll be asking more than a few acres of land. A lot more. You'll see.' He held her close, stroking her hair. 'If you want to feed her, I suppose it's all right. But for now, she stays in her room. My word is final.'

He turned and marched back along the corridor. Lady Darnell gazed after him, her eyes filled with tears. Then she hurried on, her long dress rustling around her ankles.

Cas and Aran ducked back as Darnell passed. Then they slipped out of hiding and followed the Lady. 'Did you hear that?' Aran whispered incredulously.

'I wonder who it is?' Cas asked. 'It might be Law Walden's youngest, or maybe one of the Ryder brothers—'

'That's not the point!' Aran hissed. 'He's going to sell off his own daughter. We have to get her out of here.'

Cas's face went white. 'Now, wait a minute,' he said. 'You promised, no prison breaks.'

'But that was before!' Aran protested. 'Come on, we have to at least warn her.'

'You should just be thankful it isn't you,' Cas whispered. 'Imagine that. She'd beat you black and blue every morning before breakfast.'

But Aran didn't want to imagine it. He pressed a finger to his lips, spotting Lady Darnell just ahead. She had placed the tray on the ground and taken a key from her pocket. She opened a door and stepped inside.

'I brought you some dinner,' she called out. There was no reply. Aran tiptoed to the door. 'Come on, don't be like that,' the Lady was saying. 'Here, try to eat a little.'

Mohanna's bedroom had a low sandstone ceiling covered with coloured draperies. There was no vent shaft, and the air was still and close. The Lady placed the tray on a table next to the mahogany four-poster bed. Aran could see nothing but a single bare foot hanging over the side.

'There's no need for any of this,' the Lady went on. 'If you'd only listen to your father, it'd make all our lives so much easier.'

Aran turned, beckoning to Cas. He gestured to the bed, and the dark space beneath. Cas nodded. Aran ducked into the room, scrambling under the bed on his hands and knees.

'You're your father's daughter,' Lady Darnell continued. 'He'll never understand that. He wants you to be like me, quiet and respectful. He'd never admit that it's his fault you are like you are.'

Cas scuttled in behind Aran. They huddled against the wall, trying not to breathe.

They saw the Lady's feet pause beside the bed, heard her

215

bend down and kiss her daughter. 'Try to eat something,' she said, her voice filled with regret. 'It'll all seem different in the morning.'

They heard Mohanna sigh. 'I'll still be stuck in here,' she said.

Lady Darnell left the room. They heard the key rattling in the lock.

Aran and Cas lay silent. They heard Mohanna sniff the air, then let out a grunt of disgust. 'Mother, you stink,' she said under her breath.

'How dare you!' said Aran, in a girlish falsetto.

Mohanna sat bolt upright, looking around. 'Who said that?'

Aran put his head out from beneath the bed. Mohanna's face broke into a huge smile. 'You!' she cried. Cas appeared beside Aran. 'And you!' she squealed excitedly.

They rolled out, coated with grey dust which had stuck to the sewage on their clothes. Mohanna grimaced, holding her nose.

'We had a bit of an accident,' Aran said. He looked at Mohanna. Her face was red and blotchy. There was a bruise on her left cheek and her upper lip was black with dry blood. She lowered her eyes, her cheeks flushed.

'What happened?' Aran asked. 'What did he do to you?'

'It's my fault,' Mohanna said quickly. 'I should never have lied to him.'

'We shouldn't have asked you to,' Aran said, perching

on the edge of the bed. He told her all that had happened after Darnell had carried her away.

'So Peregrine's gone?' Mohanna asked in horror.

'Not yet,' Aran said. 'But my dad won't let me speak to him, and no one else wants to. I don't see how he can really stay.'

'Well, at least my father will be happy,' Mohanna said. 'He's always going on about *that criminal, that vagrant.* Maybe once he's gone I can come back.'

Aran's face fell. He and Cas looked at one another. 'I don't think that's very likely,' he said.

They recounted all they had heard in the passageway. Mohanna listened with mounting dismay, her face going from red to white as Aran described the conviction in Law Darnell's voice. Then she fell back on the bed, her body shaking with silent sobs.

'Maybe he'll change his mind,' said Cas hopefully. 'You never know.'

'Yes I do,' said Mohanna through her tears. 'My father doesn't change his mind. He's worse than me.'

The wind howled along the corridor outside, rattling the door. Mohanna's weeping gradually subsided and she wiped her face with a handkerchief.

'So what do you want to do?' Aran asked.

She looked at him. 'What do you mean?' she asked.

'You can come with us,' Aran said. 'Right now, tonight. My father will look after you, I promise. He wouldn't refuse.'

Mohanna looked up and Aran could see the struggle

taking place behind her eyes. 'What if my father takes up arms?' she asked. 'Starts another Vendetta?'

Aran laughed. 'We've got twice the men and twice the weapons,' he told her. 'You don't think we could beat a piddling little farmstead like Crowdale?'

'That's not the point,' she said. 'People could die because of me.'

'Do you honestly think Darnell cares enough to risk his men?' Aran asked. 'He's going to keep you locked away until he's ready to ship you off to some rich farmstead. Does that sound like love?'

Mohanna blanched. 'He's my father,' she said. 'This is my home.'

'And we're your friends.' Aran looked at her seriously. 'You don't seem to understand. If you don't come with us now, you might never see us again.'

She nodded, and realization seemed to hit her with visible force. She reached out, taking Aran's hand in both of her own. 'You have to promise me,' she said. 'Promise me it'll work.'

Aran nodded quickly. 'I promise,' he said.

'No.' Mohanna's grip tightened, and Aran could feel her pulse pounding. 'Listen. If this goes wrong, he'll hurt me. You know that, don't you?'

Aran nodded again, more firmly. 'I know,' he said.

'So promise me. Even though you know what a risk this is, even though you know that I might never be able to come home, I want you to promise this is the right thing to do. That if you were me, this is what you'd do.'

Aran looked away, unable to hold her gaze. Mohanna was right, this was her whole future they were playing with. What if they got caught trying to sneak out? What if Law Carifax refused to take her in, even after he knew what Darnell would do? But the alternative was worse. He couldn't bear the thought of never seeing her again.

'I promise,' he said.

CHAPTER EIGHTEEN
The Poacher

In the end, breaking out was easier than breaking in. They waited until a kitchen hand came to clear away the dishes, then Mohanna jumped him and stole the key. She apologized profusely, locked him in and they snuck out through her secret staircase. It led to a hatchway above the main farmhouse, high on the moor.

The valley was silver-black in the moonlight and the night air was thin and ice-cold, refreshing their spirits after the heat of the farmstead. They ran through the heather, leaving Crowdale behind. Aran felt a wave of joy crashing over him and he leaped and tumbled through the grass, hooting and laughing.

'We're free!' he cried out to the night.

'You're barmy,' retorted Cas.

Aran tackled him, dragging him to the ground and tickling him mercilessly.

Cas struggled loose, staring at Aran with laughter in his eyes. Aran rolled onto his back, his arms spread wide.

Mohanna dropped beside him and the three of them lay in the rustling ferns, staring up into the night sky. The stars wheeled overhead.

'I wonder . . .' Mohanna began, then stopped.

Aran turned. Had she begun to regret her decision already? 'What?' he asked. 'What do you wonder?'

A slow grin spread across Mohanna's features. 'I wonder how many times I can kick your backside between now and Exmus?'

Aran laughed and kicked his feet in the air. 'You don't understand,' he said. 'You see, I've been letting you win. Peregrine's been telling me for ages that it has to stop. He says you're old enough to live with failure.'

'Oh, is that right?'

'Yes, I'm afraid so,' said Aran. 'From now on, I'm going to have to win every fight.'

'Every single one?' Mohanna asked, her voice filled with mocking fear.

'Yes. I wish there was something I could do. I'm sorry.'

Mohanna propped herself up on her elbow. 'Oh, you will be,' she said, and drove her fist into his stomach.

Aran doubled over, wincing and laughing at the same time. 'I'll give you that one,' he said through his tears. 'But from now on, you'd better watch out.'

Mohanna clambered up on the back of Aran's horse and they turned for Hawk's Cross. The waning moon rode high among the fast, scudding clouds, and the rocks and bare trees cast long shadows over the barren moor.

They descended into another valley, following a narrow, ice-encrusted stream which tumbled down through a swift, racing course to meet the river that would lead them home.

The wind had picked up, rustling the branches and finding its way inside Aran's woolly coat. But he could feel the warmth of Mohanna's body against his back and her arms tight around his chest. Cas trotted behind, yawning fitfully as the lateness of the hour and the excitement of the day overcame him.

Suddenly Aran felt Mohanna's grip loosen. He tugged on the reins.

'What is it?' he asked.

'I'm not sure,' she whispered, gesturing at Cas to halt. Aran listened. He could hear nothing but the water on the rocks and the wind whistling through a brake of huddled willows. 'I thought I . . . there!' Mohanna gripped his shoulder. 'There it is again.'

Aran listened. Still he could hear nothing.

The shadows seemed to deepen around them. Aran was suddenly aware that, even though the country was familiar, they were miles from home and far from help. He felt Mohanna slip down from the horse.

'What are you doing?' he asked. She glared at him and pressed a finger to her lips. The seriousness of her expression was enough to send fear fluttering through him. Mohanna crept to the bank of the stream, peering into the dark woods on the far side.

Aran glanced back at Cas. He was wide awake now,

climbing silently down and following Mohanna. Aran did likewise, and soon the three of them were crouching by the rushing water, their hearts pounding.

'What did you hear?' Aran asked.

'It sounded like voices,' Mohanna said softly. 'There!' She pointed into the darkness. At first Aran could see nothing, then for the briefest second he thought he saw a flicker of light between the branches. Then it was gone.

Mohanna stepped onto the rocky bank. Aran grabbed her arm, pulling her back. 'What are you doing?' he demanded.

'Taking a closer look,' she whispered.

Aran did not let go of her arm. 'Are you cracked?' he hissed. 'What if it's them?'

'It's probably just poachers,' Mohanna told him. 'I bet it's Randle, out looking for something for Carifax's pot. He should know better than to hunt on my father's land.'

'And if it is?' Aran shot back. 'What are you going to do about it? You've just run away from home, remember?'

'I don't care,' she said. 'I want to pay him back for spreading all those rumours. Come on, the least we can do is give him a good scare.'

'I don't think he'd take too kindly—'

'When did you become such a coward?' Mohanna cut him off. 'Randle may talk tough, but he'd never mess with a Law's kin. And if it is Marauders, imagine if you were the first to raise the alarm. Akmid wouldn't be the only one doing his bit then, would he?'

Aran thought about this. 'All right,' he muttered. 'We'll

take a look. Cas, stay here with the horses.' Cas nodded, trying not to look too relieved.

They crossed the stream in silence, hopping carefully across the ice-slick stones. Mohanna led Aran into the trees, clambering over roots and ferns until they were close enough to see that the mysterious light was in fact a low, guttering bonfire.

They huddled in the shelter of a leafless oak, peering through a cluster of bracken. It certainly looked like a poachers' camp. They could see two men wrapped in heavy blankets, their faces turned away from the fire. One of them let out a long, rattling snore.

'Is it him?' Aran whispered. 'Is it Randle?'

'It's hard to tell,' Mohanna replied. 'They're too far away. I wonder where the third one is?'

Aran hadn't noticed the third blanket lying unoccupied by the fire. But now he saw it, and the rusty unsheathed sword beside it. No poacher would carry a sword like that.

'I don't like this,' he said. 'I think we should get—'

A noise cut him off. It was a low whistle, like breathing, but ragged and wet-sounding.

'What was that?' Mohanna asked, shrinking closer.

They scanned the dark trees, trying to discern the source of the sound. It came again, a thick, bubbling wheeze, tortured and twisted but recognizably human. This time there were almost words in it, as though whoever made the sound was struggling to speak. Listening hard, Aran could almost make out their meaning.

'Help . . .' the sound seemed to say. 'Help me . . .'

Aran looked around. Nothing moved.

Then he felt something touch his head. He reached up instinctively. There was something in his hair, something wet and sticky. His fingers came away red in the firelight. He looked up, and gasped.

Strapped with thick ropes to the trunk above their heads was the body of a man. He was upside down and blood leaked in a thin trail from the side of his mouth, over his half-closed eyes, and dripped from the tips of his lank, sodden hair.

'Help . . .' the man repeated.

For a long, sickening moment Aran felt as though he'd wandered into a nightmare. The moon filtered coldly through the branches, his breath shimmered in a white cloud around his head, and he couldn't quite make himself believe that any of this was real.

The bound man shifted slowly, almost sleepily, but the ropes were too tight. He tried to speak again, but the words caught in his throat and he coughed blood.

Mohanna's voice broke Aran from his trance. 'Randle?' she whispered.

His face was covered with cuts and black bruises, but Aran recognized the infamous poacher. He reached for the knife at his belt and got to his feet. Mohanna pulled him back down. 'What are you doing?' she hissed.

'We have to cut him down,' Aran insisted.

'And do what?' Mohanna shot back. 'Drag him through the woods? There's no way he can walk, not in that state.

You really think we'll be able to get him to the horses without the others hearing us?'

'What, then?' Aran retorted, the fear welling up in his mouth. 'Just leave him to die?'

'He's dead already,' Mohanna insisted. 'The only thing we can do is ride as fast as we can back to Crowdale and fetch my father.'

Aran nodded, trying to fight down his panic. Mohanna was right. It was the only way.

Then a movement caught his eye and he turned back towards the fire. A third man had entered the clearing, buttoning his trousers and yawning mightily. But even in the dim light, Aran recognized him right away. Those hard eyes, that stern face. That long, wiry frame. And this time, he knew the man for what he was. A Marauder.

Mohanna had already begun to scuttle away through the undergrowth, but Aran pulled her back, pointing with one trembling figure. 'I've seen that man,' he whispered. 'Today. In Crowdale.'

'Are you sure?' The Marauder lay down in the firelight, pulling the blanket up to his chin. Mohanna grabbed Aran's arm. 'Then there's no time to lose. We have to warn my father, right away.'

She pulled on Aran's sleeve, but he did not budge. A thought was surfacing in his mind. 'No,' he said. 'No, you don't understand.'

'Aran, if they're in my farmstead, we have to tell—' Then she stopped, her mouth dropping open. 'No. Aran, don't even think it. He must have broken in, like you and Cas.

226

Come on, we'll go to my father and tell him everything. I'm sure there's another explanation.'

'And what if there isn't?' Aran asked. He remembered everything Darnell had said in the corridor. *Big plans . . . negotiations . . .* 'What if he already knows?'

'Impossible,' Mohanna replied. 'How dare you—'

'I'm sorry,' Aran cut in. 'I don't know what it means, but I'm not going to take the risk. We ride for Hawk's Cross.'

Mohanna looked at him, and Aran knew he'd never seen anyone so frightened in his life. 'I . . .' she began, stumbling over the words. 'I don't . . .'

Then a cry broke the night and they flung themselves to the ground.

Randle had managed to twist his head so that he was looking directly downwards, and the sight of the children huddled at the base of the tree had stirred him from his stupor. He began to shriek, his words catching in his blood-filled throat.

'Boy,' he cried out. 'Boy, cut me down!' He began to buck and kick but the ropes were too tight. 'I know you. Boy, help me!'

'Please,' Aran whispered, as loudly as he dared. 'Please, sir, you don't understand, you have to—'

'It hurts!' Randle cried out. 'Help me, please, O Gods, help—'

He was cut off by another, harder sound. Looking up, Aran saw an arrow protruding from the poacher's neck, feathers quivering. Randle's head dropped back, his eyes staring at nothing.

The tall Marauder stood in the firelight, his longbow raised. His companions were beginning to stir, rising to their feet, drawing their swords. For a moment they looked at one another, the three warriors and the two terrified children.

Then the bowman reached down, lifting something in both hands. It was a mask, grey and furred, with snarling lips, pointed teeth and a long pelt that ran down his back. Aran knew then that he had seen the man before – at the Longball grounds, riding as one of Karik's honour guard. The Wolf.

The mask's hard glass eyes gleamed in the moonlight as the Marauder lifted his head and let out a howl, an inhuman bellow which echoed through the midnight forest. Then he began to lope towards the two children, his long legs crashing through the undergrowth, his two companions closing ranks. The hunt was on.

Aran turned, stumbled, almost fell, but righted himself. Then he was running, headlong, his feet slipping on the dew-soaked ground, roots tangling around his feet. A bowstring twanged and an arrow pierced the night, passing overhead with a barely perceptible hiss.

Aran and Mohanna broke from the cover of the trees, hurling themselves towards the stream. They could see Cas on the far side holding two sets of reins, his eyes widening. But the Marauders were too close – now that Aran and Mohanna were out in the open, their pursuers would be able to pick them off before they could get near the horses.

Aran felt cold water soaking his boots. He grabbed Mohanna and pulled her aside as an arrow careened off the rocks in front of them. They splashed through the ice-covered stream, keeping low, using the bank for cover. Glancing back, Aran saw Cas duck as an arrow whistled over his head. Then he leaped onto his pony, pulling Aran's horse behind him, following the course of the water.

Aran clutched tight to Mohanna's hand, crashing through the thin sheets of ice which clung to rocks and roots in the water. He could hear the Marauders reaching the bank and turning in pursuit. He put his head down and ran, the water soaking his clothes. The cold was bracing and he felt energy course through his body, driving the weariness away.

They reached a narrow part of the stream where the water broke into channels and tumbled over a pile of scattered granite boulders. They leaped onto the rocks, bounding from one to the next, then splashed back into the freezing water on the far side.

They couldn't be far from the river, Aran knew, but that was a problem in itself. The banks would be open on both sides. They'd have to lose their pursuers before they got that far.

They reached the place where another shallow brook joined the first, and now the water began to deepen. They kept to the bank furthest from their pursuers, ducking under low-hanging branches, clambering over beaches of scattered rocks. From the sounds behind, Aran knew that the Marauders were having an even rougher time

– the bank on that side was knotted with brambles and stinging nettles, and the ground underfoot was marshy and treacherous.

Aran glanced at Mohanna. 'Are you all right?' he asked, through heaving breaths.

She looked at him and nodded, and for the briefest moment a smile flickered across her lips. By Ala, Aran thought to himself, she might actually be enjoying this.

He caught a movement in the corner of his eye and looked up. The banks of the stream were rising steeply, piled with mossy rocks and clinging weeds. At the top of the slope, Aran could see a familiar face. Cas had reined in his horse and he was waving at them, pointing downstream and shouting.

But somehow, Aran couldn't hear him. At first he thought it was just the pounding of his heart, or the splashing of his feet in the water. But then he realized there was another sound, building in intensity. And he knew they were in trouble.

He had known that there was something important he had missed, one detail of the stream's course that had eluded his confused mind. And here it was, drawing closer as they ran between the narrowing banks. The waterfall.

How could he have forgotten? The falls had been his favourite place when he was a boy. He, Cas and Mohanna would meet there on hot days to splash in the shallow pool and sun themselves on the bank. It wasn't a huge fall, perhaps thirty or forty feet, but none of them had ever dared to jump it. There were stories of kids who had tried, and none of those stories ended well.

Aran glanced back over his shoulder. The Marauders had taken to the water, legs pounding as they waded relentlessly through the shallows, closing the gap. There was to be no escape that way. And if they tried to scale the banks, the wolf-headed bowman would shoot them down before they got halfway. Even now, he was plucking another arrow from the quiver on his back, taking careful aim. Aran dodged and the arrow clattered and fell, inches behind.

The sound of the falls was a steady roar. Aran could taste the spray on his tongue as they leaped over a last barrier of boulders and found themselves standing on the precipice. The jagged, spray-slick cliff face curved outwards to join the woods on either side. But there was nowhere to climb to, no sheltering overhangs to hide behind. There was only one way down.

Aran peered into the dark woods, but he could see no sign of Cas. He must still be picking his way down the slope, along the narrow path through the trees. On foot it was steep; on horseback it must be terrifying.

The pool itself was placid and almost inviting. But Aran knew it was barely two feet deep, except at the point right below the falls. Still, there was no other way. The Marauders were almost upon them. Even over the din of the water, Aran could hear their guttural speech, their heavy footfalls, and the clanging of their swords.

He looked at Mohanna, her eyes flashing in the moonlight. 'I'll go first,' he said.

She smiled and shook her head. 'Don't be silly,' she said, and jumped.

Aran saw her vanish into the foamy spray. Peering down, he could make out nothing but the ribbon of falling water, ice-white in the moonlight.

For a moment, all was still. Aran waited for Mohanna to surface, to signal that it was safe to jump, but she did not. She was simply gone. Aran's heart seized. Should he leap anyway, and trust to fate? What if the stories were right – what if Mohanna was . . . No, it didn't bear thinking about.

Then he saw her. A shape on the surface of the pool. Face down, her hair fanning out like a red halo. Floating. Spinning. Drifting downstream towards the river.

Aran was about to cry out with horror when a hand fell on his shoulder.

It wasn't the Wolf but one of his subordinates, a stocky brute with a yellow beard and overhanging brows. His eyes shone with glee as he took hold of Aran, pinning his arms. He turned to his captain, who clambered, long-limbed, over the last wall of rocks, the bow clutched in his hand.

The Wolf smiled, a second set of sharp white teeth to match the ones in his mask. His narrow chest rose and fell with the exertion of the chase, and his eyes gleamed with triumph.

'Just a boy,' he said softly, almost tenderly. 'Just a dead boy.' Then he drew an arrow from his leather quiver and slipped it into the bow. Aran could hear his burly captor laugh and felt hot breath against his cheek.

The Wolf drew back his bowstring, and Aran heard the wood creak. Mohanna was most likely dead. In a second, he would be too. The Marauders would leave no witnesses to warn of their coming. He shut his eyes, seized by hopelessness.

'No,' said a voice. 'Open.'

Aran felt a hand on his face. His captor reached up, forcing Aran's right eye open.

At first he didn't know what he was looking at. A small grey shape, floating in space. Then he realized it was the point of an arrow, trembling just inches from his eye. The bowman's arms strained, his eyes shone and his mouth opened in a strange sort of gloating half-smile.

Aran wondered if he would feel the bolt as it passed into his brain. A sharp pain, he supposed, then it would all be over.

'Good, quiet,' hissed the bowman softly. 'Just another dead boy.'

Aran's mind rebelled.

No, said a voice inside him, cold and clear. You're not just another dead boy; you're Aran of Hawk's Cross. Law Carifax's son, Peregrine's pupil. Whatever end is meant for you, it isn't on the sharp end of some Marauder's arrow, out here in the wild. And he knew what he had to do.

Aran threw himself back. The man holding him let out a grunt of surprise and Aran felt his grip slip momentarily. Then the hands tightened once more.

Good, he thought. At least I'm not going to die alone. And he dragged them both over the edge.

The white water surrounded them, forcing the breath from Aran's body. For a moment he was weightless, twisting in the violence of the falls, the Marauder's arms around him like an embrace. Then they struck the bottom.

Aran felt the impact all the way to his bones, but it wasn't the hard hit of stone. The grip around his chest loosened and was gone. The Marauder had broken his fall.

Aran kicked with all his might, breaking the surface. He dragged himself free from the waterlogged body, pushing for the bank. Glancing back, he saw the man rising to the surface, his open eyes fixed on the sky, his broken limbs splayed as he floated slowly out into the centre of the pool.

Then Aran remembered, and looked around desperately. There was a shape in the darkness by the bank, a movement in the shadows, and his heart leaped. Mohanna was dragging herself onto the grass with one arm. The other hung limp, trailing blood into the water.

Aran pulled himself up beside her, spitting river water. 'I thought,' he managed at last. 'I thought you were . . .'

Mohanna smiled through gritted teeth. 'My arm,' she spat. 'I think it's broken. I passed out. Sorry if I gave you a scare.'

Aran looked around for any sign of Cas and the horses, but he could see nothing. The woods were dark.

'Dead boy!' The Marauder's voice cut through the silence. 'Good try, dead boy.'

Aran rolled onto his back. The two men stood on the lip of the falls, their eyes gleaming. The Wolf had his

234

bowstring taut, and once again he took careful aim.

Aran sighed. So it had all been for nothing. There was nowhere to hide. Even if he could run, he couldn't carry Mohanna. He was pinned, exhausted, and his luck had finally run out.

Then there was a sound from the trees, a hollow *thock* which rang loud in the stillness. Aran saw something whistling through the dark, a black shape shooting straight towards its target.

The Wolf clutched his chest, his eyes widening as he felt the bolt pierce his heart. Then he fell, the bow dropping from his hands.

He missed the main falls, his body slamming into an overhanging rock with a hideous crunch. His mask was knocked free, spinning into the trees. Its owner splashed into the pool. He bobbed to the surface, and Aran saw with a shudder that his face and his feet were pointing in different directions, his broken teeth winking in the moonlight. He turned in the current, following his companion downstream towards the river.

The last Marauder looked down at Aran where he lay on the bank. Then he turned from the edge and vanished into the night.

Hearing hooves, Aran looked up. Cas emerged from the treeline, leading the horses. He hurried to Aran's side, kneeling on the wet grass, the crossbow strapped to his wrist.

'I'm sorry,' he said. 'I would've been quicker, but I wanted to make sure I didn't miss.'

Aran smiled. 'You were brilliant,' he said. Cas blushed proudly.

Together they helped Mohanna up onto Aran's horse. She was passing in and out of consciousness. Aran swung up behind her, grabbing the reins with one hand and clutching her tight with the other.

He spurred his horse and followed Cas down the last slope to where the river waited to greet them, its wide and placid course leading them home.

CHAPTER NINETEEN

The Accused

B y the time the pale sun rose over Hawk's Cross, the farmstead was ready to fight.

Aran and Cas had made good time over open ground, thundering into the courtyard to the surprise of two dozing guards. Mohanna was rushed to the infirmary while Aran recounted his story to Law and Lady Carifax, their faces clouding with worry.

Tall fires were lit in the courtyard. Men huddled around them, swords drawn, faces set against the darkness and whatever might emerge from it. They were boys and old men mostly, Aran saw. Those too elderly or inexperienced to join the militia. Perhaps Darnell was wise to keep his best behind. But the very thought of him still made Aran's blood boil.

He wanted to talk to Peregrine. If anyone would know what to do, it was him. But his father's orders still stood, and all Hawk's Cross knew it. If anyone saw him going down there, they'd run straight to Carifax. Later, he thought, he would sneak down and tell Peregrine everything. But for now, the situation was too fragile.

So he leaned against the courtyard wall as the sky lightened, wrapped in his woollen coat. A watchful silence fell. The skies had cleared, and that was a blessing. There would be no snow. But the cold was hard and absolute – Aran's breath froze in his nostrils, and he kept having to rub his eyes as the moisture in them began to harden.

He was about to slip away to bed when hoof beats sounded in the still air. To Aran's astonishment, he saw the familiar shape of Law Darnell riding purposefully up the track, Devin at his back. Aran was about to throw himself forward, to scream that here was the traitor. But a strong hand on his shoulder stopped him.

Aran looked up into his father's unsmiling face. 'I know what you're thinking,' Carifax said, wrapping a fur-lined greatcoat around his shoulders. 'But let's see what he has to say. If nothing else, think of Mohanna.'

Darnell swept into the courtyard, dismounting in a flurry of robes and fury. 'What is the meaning of this?' he barked, brushing aside the Law's offered hand and glaring in surprise at the armed men grouped around the gateway. 'Carifax, where is my daughter?'

'She's downstairs, resting peacefully,' said Law Carifax calmly.

'Take me to her,' Darnell demanded. 'Your messenger told me her arm was broken. Is this true?'

Carifax nodded slowly. 'It is,' he said. 'And you can see her, if you like. But we have more important matters to attend to first.'

Darnell's eyebrows shot up. 'More important?' he shouted. 'What could be more important? If I find out your boy had anything to do with this injury, I'll—'

'Marauders have been sighted in the woods between here and Crowdale,' said Carifax, cutting Darnell off. 'I think that's more pressing, don't you? Please, if you'd come inside. Your man can wait out here.'

Darnell frowned but obeyed, leaving Devin behind. Aran followed them through the deserted summerhouse and into the Law's study, where he found his mother waiting with a small group of armed men.

Darnell bristled when he saw the party that had been arranged for his welcome. 'What is this?' he demanded. 'My Law, if these rumours prove true, I fully understand your need to be on the alert. But there's no need for—'

'They're not rumours,' Carifax said flatly. 'Aran saw them with his own eyes. As did your daughter.'

Darnell stole a glance back at Aran. 'They were together?' he hissed. 'After I strictly forbade them from seeing each other?'

Carifax sighed. 'Again, I must insist that we keep our focus on the matter of real importance,' he said. 'Darnell, have you not been listening? Or do you simply not care that there are Marauders within reach of both our farmsteads?'

Darnell looked around the room, realizing that every eye was on him. He puffed out his chest. 'But of course,' he said. 'I simply . . . This is a lot to take in, you must understand.'

'I do,' Carifax said. 'And I appreciate your fatherly concern. But please, be seated. Take a drink. Mohanna is out of danger, they tell me. There's no cause for alarm.'

They took seats on either side of the Law's desk. 'Now, Aran,' Carifax said, ushering his son into an upright chair. 'I'd like you to tell us precisely what happened last night. Leave no detail out. We're not here to judge you.'

Aran began to speak. At first his tone was cautious as he recounted his frustration at Mohanna's absence, and how he and Cas had broken into Crowdale. Darnell simply stared at the floor, unable to look Aran in the face.

But when Aran mentioned the man he had encountered on the steps, the Law looked up, his eyes narrowing to little points. And when they reached the part where the same man appeared in the clearing, Darnell could stand it no longer.

'What is this?' he demanded. 'What exactly are you accusing me of?'

Carifax put out his hands. 'We're not accusing you of anything,' he said. 'We're here to get to the bottom of this.'

'Simply because a man is sighted in my farmstead doesn't mean I had any knowledge of his presence,' Darnell spat hurriedly. 'He might have broken in like your boy did, or done some kind of deal with my guard captain to—'

'You're not doing yourself any favours, you know,' said a quiet but commanding voice. Lady Carifax had kept silent throughout Aran's story, but now she fixed Darnell with a penetrating expression. 'Getting flustered. Defensive. It only makes you look guilty.'

'Now now, my dear,' said Carifax calmly. 'As I said, we're not here to judge.'

'Then why are we here?' the Lady shot back. 'Say for the sake of argument that Law Darnell was contacted by the Marauders. What do you suppose he'd tell them? *Well, I've got nothing you could possibly want, but there's a lovely farmstead just down the road, richest in the region, they say.* Wouldn't that sound like an enticing prospect?'

'Now,' said Carifax gruffly, 'I think that's a big leap. Darnell and I have been friends for a long time.'

The Lady sneered. 'My love, you always were terribly naive,' she said. Then she glared at Darnell. 'We ought to cut his throat right here, save ourselves a lot of bother.'

Darnell had been looking from one to the other with mounting horror, his mouth working soundlessly. 'These accusations are . . . are . . . scandalous!' he managed at last. 'Carifax, on our friendship, I demand a fair hearing. This is all just rumour and hearsay!'

'A hearing?' Carifax said thoughtfully. 'That's an idea.' Aran thought he caught a sly glance between the Law and his wife. 'I suppose we could take this before the Council, see what they have to say.'

'What could they possibly do? Slap his wrist and send him home? This man is a direct threat to my family and I want him dealt with.'

'Yes!' Darnell cried out, before she could go on. 'The

241

Council! I shall submit to their ruling, and no other.'

'Then it's settled,' Carifax said. 'I'll send out a rider this morning. I'd imagine an issue like this will bring a few heads to the table.'

Lady Carifax frowned. 'Very well,' she said. 'I suppose that will have to do.' Then she fixed Darnell with a piercing gaze. 'My Law, I know you think my husband is weak. He lets people get away with things which other Laws, such as yourself, never would. So you must be tempted to think this Council business is just a question of buying time, perhaps to finish whatever deal you've struck with the Marauders, perhaps just to get your farmstead ready in case this . . . disagreement between us turns nasty.

'So let me make you aware of a few hard truths before you leave. My husband may be kind, but I am not. If you lift a hand against my family, or anyone under my care, you will live to regret it. But not for very long.' Darnell's eyes widened. 'Now,' she finished, 'you may go. My husband, make sure he leaves.'

Law Darnell got to his feet slowly, as though confused as to what, exactly, he'd just agreed to. 'And my daughter?' he asked.

'She'll be well looked after,' the Lady said. 'But she won't be coming home until this is all over.'

'A hostage?' Darnell asked.

'A guest,' smiled Lady Carifax.

Darnell's eyes flashed, but the fight had gone out of him. Law Carifax took him by the arm. 'There's no need to worry,' he said. 'I'm sure we'll get it all straightened out.'

And he ushered Darnell to the door, closing it firmly behind them.

Lady Carifax slumped against the wall with a sigh of relief. 'Good grief,' she said. 'I honestly never expected that to work.'

Aran looked at his mother in confusion. 'Expected what to work?' he asked. 'Why didn't you just arrest him?'

'And start a vendetta that could claim lives?' she asked him. 'We've no proof. It would have led to bloodshed, I've no doubt of it.'

'So what?' Aran shot back. 'I'd fancy our chances against Darnell's people more than I would against the Marauders. Most of them hate him anyway.'

'But it wouldn't have been one or the other,' the Lady pointed out. 'Think, Aran. If you're right, we would've been fighting both. We're not strong enough for that. At least now we have a bit of breathing room while we call in the Council.'

'And what if he really *is* working with the Marauders?' Aran demanded. 'What if he's already told them about this place? What if they're already on their way?'

'Then there's not a lot we can do except be ready,' she said. 'Your father already sent a rider to Barton requesting militia reinforcements. They should be here by nightfall.'

'But you let him get away!' Aran protested. 'Why didn't you make him tell the truth?'

'How, exactly?' Lady Carifax asked, her voice suddenly cold. 'Tie him up, torture him? I suppose you'd have wielded the nail-pullers yourself, Aran? No?'

Aran shrank back. The Lady put an arm around his shoulder. 'That's not the way we do things,' she said, her wrath already passing. 'This is a tricky situation we're in now. One wrong step and we fall. And it's not just ourselves we risk. It's everyone in Hawk's Cross, and everyone in Crowdale too. We tried to find the best way through this without putting anyone in danger.'

'But we don't know the truth,' Aran said softly. 'We don't know which side Darnell is really on.'

The Lady shrugged. 'Would it make a difference?' she asked. 'I've never trusted him. Neither has your father. And you got Mohanna out. That took guts.'

'We wouldn't have stood a chance if it hadn't been for Peregrine's training,' Aran told her. 'Surely Father must see that.'

The Lady nodded. 'He knows,' she said. 'But it's just not that simple. One day you'll understand.'

Aran pulled away, getting to his feet. 'And what if things had been different?' he asked. 'What if we'd not been fast enough, in the woods or at the waterfall? Then all of your secrets and your wait-until-you're-older would have been for nothing.'

She looked at him, a slow realization seeming to unfurl behind her eyes. Then she grabbed him with both hands, wrapping him in a warm embrace.

When at last the Lady let him loose, her eyes were full of tears. 'I just want you to be my boy for a little while longer,' she said, and kissed him.

In the silence that followed, Aran became aware of a

sound in the courtyard. Men were shouting, feet clattered on the cobblestones, and beneath it all he could hear the hammering of hoof beats. Panic grabbed him and he thought, This is it. They're here.

He ran for the door, his mother behind him. They emerged in time to see a dark phalanx of unfamiliar horses come crashing through the gates, scattering the defenders. A wiry figure, clad head to toe in brown leather, hopped down from the foremost stallion. He stood on the flagstones, looking around with a superior sneer. With a start, Aran recognized his brother.

Law Carifax strode forward, his arms spread wide. He clasped Akmid in a suffocating hug, spinning him off his feet. Then he took him by the shoulders and looked proudly into his face. 'My son,' he said. 'My brave son.'

The Lady rushed in, grabbing Akmid and kissing him furiously on both cheeks. His fellow soldiers looked down from their horses, nudging one another and smirking. Akmid gently pushed his mother away, smoothing his uniform. He seemed to have grown a foot taller since Aran had last seen him, and every ounce of fat had been burned from his bones. He was lean, muscular and rough-shaven, his skin several shades darker.

'Mother, Father,' Akmid said. 'May I present the Fourth Platoon of the Island militia. My platoon.' And he puffed out his chest, gesturing to a tiny silver medal which glittered as it caught the light.

Law Carifax insisted on shaking every hand, bidding them welcome. The soldiers wore suits of leather, and many had breastplates or helmets of iron and steel, some emblazoned with symbols: a snapping crab, a kneeling stag, even a smiling pig. Most had scabbards strapped to their belts, a few carried longbows or axes, and one held a six-foot pike with a sharpened steel head. In age they ranged from white-bearded men to boys not much older than Aran, but each had the same resolute expression, the same air of weary, battle-hard determination.

A group of citizens hurried forward, greeting three Hawk's Cross lads who pushed their way clear of the crowd. Hands were proudly shaken and a few tears shed. But one man stood alone, watching implacably as his fellows accepted the hospitality of Hawk's Cross: mugs of hot wine, fresh rolls and places by the fire. No one came forward to welcome Keller home.

'We were near Hargate when your summons came,' Akmid told his father, looking around at the hastily constructed defences and the small gang of bleary, haggard citizens who manned them. 'We'll give you all the help we can.'

'Have you heard anything?' Carifax asked. 'Do you think an attack is imminent?'

Akmid shook his head. 'We've had no word,' he said. 'In fact, they've been quiet for weeks. We had a rumour that ships had been sighted south of Whiteport a few days ago, but there was nothing to back it up. It could have been fishermen. Or perhaps someone made it up just to make himself seem important. You'd be surprised how often that happens.' And he shot a lingering glance at Aran.

'And what of Darnell?' Carifax asked. 'Do you think he could be working with them?'

'It's possible,' Akmid said. 'It's happened before. But Darnell? I thought the two of you were friends.'

'So did I,' said Carifax. 'But Aran's story . . . I don't see what other explanation fits.'

Akmid pursed his lips. 'I can think of a few,' he said. 'I'm right in thinking no one saw these Marauders except Aran and his friends?'

'Well, there was the poacher,' Carifax pointed out. 'Randle.'

'But no one's seen him since,' Akmid argued.

'I have,' said Aran, unable to stay quiet.

'Of course,' Akmid said, finally acknowledging his brother. 'He was strapped upside down to a tree. Seems an unusual method of tying up a prisoner, doesn't it?'

Aran shut his mouth. It wasn't worth it.

Akmid turned back to his father. 'Anyway,' he said, 'true or not, every rumour is worth investigating,' he said. 'Tomorrow, Aran and I will go out to the woods and take a look. If we find something to back up his story, we'll think about calling for backup.'

Law Carifax looked at the thirty men who stood brushing down their horses and unbuckling their packs. 'So this . . . There aren't any more coming?'

'This was all we could spare,' Akmid said. He looked at Carifax's disappointed expression and his face softened. 'Father, I'm sorry, but I don't think you understand what we're dealing with.' He placed his hand on the hilt of his sword. 'They have this leader, Karik. Tall, thin. Ruthless. He knows we're based in Barton, and he picks his targets so we'll get there right after he's left, so we can see exactly what they're capable of. The buildings are still burning when we arrive, the dead and wounded lying out in the open. Sometimes he'll leave a few behind to ambush us, kill as many as they can before we finish them off. But that's the way he thinks. He'll leave his own men to die, just to make a point.

'Even if Aran's story proves true, it could simply be a diversion, distracting us from the real attack elsewhere. If there was any solid evidence, I'd have more men up here like a shot. But I'm afraid my brother's word just isn't enough.'

CHAPTER TWENTY

Fathers and Brothers

That night the soldiers were given positions of honour in the great hall, plied with food until they could take no more. Law Carifax drank steadily, determined to celebrate his son's return. But Akmid seemed in no mood for a party – he sat at his father's side, his face grim, knocking back cup after cup until his eyes were swimming.

After dinner, Carifax called for music. He stood in the middle of the hall, clapping his hands, a strained smile on his face. 'Dance, damn you,' he cried, and a small group of citizens climbed to their feet and began to shuffle awkwardly across the floor.

Aran's eye strayed to the stairwell. He still hadn't forgotten about Peregrine. He'd planned to find time to speak to Carifax, to beg him to change his mind in the light of all that had happened. But the Law had been far too busy to listen to Aran. And now he was far too drunk, holding tight to his wife and lumbering gracelessly around the room, exhorting the band to play louder, faster, better.

Aran could bear it no longer. In the morning he would talk to Carifax, and Peregrine, and anyone else who demanded his attention. But for now he was simply exhausted. His body was bruised, his bones were aching and his mind was overrun.

But as he climbed the spiral stairs and turned into the corridor which led to his room, he heard footsteps behind him, and turned. Akmid was standing against the light, swaying from side to side. 'Little brother,' he slurred, 'I want to talk to you.'

He stepped closer, placing a hand on the wall to steady himself. Aran could smell the wine on his breath.

'We came a long way on your word,' Akmid said. 'We'd better find something in those woods tomorrow, or you're going to be in a lot of trouble.'

Aran held his gaze for a moment, then he turned away, shaking his head. 'Our father believes me,' he said over his shoulder. 'Why can't you?'

Akmid let out a sharp, barking laugh. 'Oh yes,' he said. '*Our* father.'

There was something in his tone that made Aran stop short. He turned back and found Akmid fixing him with the steadiest stare he could manage. There was a light in his eyes, that familiar look of disdain mingled with something else, something dark and cruel.

'Where's your friend?' Akmid asked. 'You don't think he left without saying goodbye, do you?'

'If you mean Peregrine,' Aran said, 'he wouldn't do that. Anyway, don't talk about him. You don't know him.'

'And you do?' Akmid smiled. 'I swear, if you knew half the things I've heard about him . . .'

'I don't care what you've heard,' Aran spat back. 'I don't—'

'Where does he come from, your friend?' Akmid interrupted, sliding along the wall towards Aran. 'Does he have any family? How old is he, do you think? I met a man in Kipp's Town, must have been eighty if he was a day. Could barely see, let alone speak. But he told me about a man he met when he was a boy, a stranger, all in black. Talked to animals, he said. Could fight better than he'd ever seen. Does that sound like anyone we know?'

Aran shook his head. 'You're mad,' he said. 'It could have been anyone. Maybe it was Peregrine's father.'

Akmid nodded. 'Maybe,' he said. 'Awful coincidence, though.'

Aran stared at Akmid, searching his face for signs of the brother he'd once known. 'What happened to you?' he asked, after a long silence.

Akmid looked confused. 'What do you mean?' he asked.

'What happened?' Aran repeated. 'Why do you hate me so much? We're supposed to be family.'

Akmid pulled himself upright. 'Family?' he said, as though the very word tasted foul in his mouth. Then his voice exploded into high volume. 'Family? I'm out there risking my neck, day after day, and you're back here, safe,

251

protected . . . Until one night you think you see something in the woods and it's, *oh, call Akmid, he can sort this out*. I haven't been home in moons, not a word from Mother or Father, and I'm summoned on what, the strength of your word?'

'I saw them,' Aran repeated. He pulled up his shirt sleeve, showing the bruise on his arm where the Marauder had grabbed him. 'I killed one. Cas killed another. The third ran, probably back to his people. Why won't you believe me?'

'Because I don't want to!' Akmid shot back, his voice hitting a high, quavering pitch. Aran realized his brother was more drunk than he'd ever seen him before. 'Because why do you get to be the hero of Hawk's Cross when you don't even belong here? You don't deserve any of this! None of it! This is my home. My family.' He reached out and cuffed Aran across the head. 'Father told me he kicked your friend out for teaching you how to fight. Talk about a hopeless task.' He put up his fists and thrust out his chin. 'So come on, show me a few moves. Hit me. I can tell you want to.'

Aran balled his fists but kept them at his sides. 'Don't be stupid,' he said. 'I'm not going to fight you.'

Akmid nodded solemnly. 'That's what I thought,' he said. 'What was it really, in those woods? A pack of angry badgers?'

Aran swung his fist. Akmid pulled back, but he was too slow. He took it square on the jaw, his teeth clacking together. He stepped back in surprise, shaking his head.

Then he put his head down and ran, grabbing Aran around the waist and throwing him to the floor.

Aran struggled, striking out with his feet and his fists, but Akmid's hold was too strong. His fists battered against Aran's head and his back, pummelling him into the dust.

Akmid sat astride his brother, leaning in and pressing his mouth close to Aran's ear. 'As soon as Father dies,' he hissed, 'as soon as this place is mine, you're finished. Out. Go travel the world with your weird friend. You don't belong here.'

And he pushed Aran's face into the floor. Aran tasted blood, and he felt the world spin around him as the air was driven from his body.

Then suddenly the pressure was gone. There was a cry and the thud of something heavy slamming into the wall. Aran fought for breath, rolling over on his back.

Peregrine stood over him, a pack on his back and boots on his feet. Akmid hung in Peregrine's grip, his cheeks reddening. He kicked out, making contact, but Aran's tutor did not seem to feel it. He stood motionless, staring at Akmid. 'You should play nicely,' he said in a flat, emotionless tone.

'Get . . . your hands . . . off me . . .' Akmid managed between breaths.

'I don't think so,' Peregrine replied calmly. 'Not until you tell me what you were fighting about.'

'None of your . . . business . . . freak,' Akmid hissed. 'Why did you . . . have to . . . bring him here? Tell me . . . that. Why don't you . . . just take him . . . back where you

. . . got him?'

Aran heard, but he didn't understand. His head was ringing.

'You want to watch your words,' Peregrine warned Akmid. 'I don't think your father would approve.'

'Did he . . . tell you?' Akmid managed, through gritted teeth. 'Did my father . . . tell you . . . he was here?'

Peregrine's brow furrowed. 'Who was here?' he asked.

'Him,' Akmid hissed, as the breath left his body. 'Before you came . . . last winter. In the . . . snow. Law . . . Karn.'

Peregrine's eyes widened. His grip loosened and Akmid crashed to the floor, landing in a heap beside Aran, his chest heaving.

Aran knew instantly who his brother meant. The images came flooding back. The stranger in the woods, the words he had spoken before he disappeared into the snow. *You're such a disappointment* . . . But what did Akmid mean when he called him Law Karn?

'Your father told you this?' Peregrine asked.

Akmid nodded feebly, rubbing his neck.

Peregrine looked down at him for a long, tense moment. Then he turned on his heel and marched down the stairs towards the great hall. Aran picked himself up and followed.

The hall was quiet, the band slumped over their instruments. The tables had been cleared and the citizens sat in silence. At the far end of the room beside the sputtering fire, Aran could make out the hunched figure of his father, gazing into the flames.

'Carifax!' Peregrine's voice boomed across the hall, startling everyone to wakefulness.

The Law looked up, his eyes bleary. Aran scrambled down the steps behind his tutor. Glancing back, he saw Akmid following unsteadily.

'Carifax, get up!' Peregrine barked, his robe billowing as he strode across the room. The Law did as he was bade, climbing wearily to his feet.

'Why would you keep this from me?' Peregrine demanded. 'Karn was here, and you didn't think to tell me?'

Carifax's mouth tightened. 'How did you . . .' he began. 'Where did you . . .'

'Your son,' Peregrine explained, shooting a glance back at Akmid. 'Couldn't keep his mouth shut, though I'm sure you told him to.'

'No,' Carifax said, in a voice edged with desperation. 'He was just some wild man, some hunter in from the snow. I thought, perhaps . . . but I wasn't sure. I couldn't be sure.'

'You were sure enough to tell Akmid,' Peregrine shot back. 'Sure enough to keep it from me.' He gritted his teeth, his dark eyes reflecting the light of the fire.

Carifax looked at him, and seemed to gather his strength. 'No,' he said calmly. 'I am not going to have this conversation with you, not here in front of . . . all these people.'

'And if I don't give you a choice?' Peregrine asked.

Carifax balled his fists. 'I will not let you tear this family apart,' he said. He turned to the remnants of Akmid's platoon, those who weren't passed out on the floor. 'I want this man out of here,' he said. 'Now. I don't want him saying another word.'

The soldiers climbed to their feet.

Peregrine backed away, holding up his hands for calm. 'Gods, Carifax, it doesn't have to be like this,' he said. 'It's time. I know it. You know it. Your wife certainly knows it. All these lies, they'll tear this family apart far quicker than the truth ever will. This whole business, breaking into Crowdale, rescuing his friend . . . He's his father's son, right to the bone. He needs to know what that means.' He looked pleadingly at the Law. 'When it's done, when I've said my piece, I'll leave. That's a promise. But if one of these men lays a hand on me, I won't be responsible for the consequences.'

Carifax shook his head. 'That's a risk I'll take,' he said, and gestured to the guards.

Peregrine stood stock-still, his whole body coiled. The soldiers moved in, unsheathing their swords, circling him cautiously. There wasn't a man among them who hadn't heard the tales about Peregrine, Law Darnell and the guards. Silently, they drew closer.

One lunged forward, his gloved hands reaching for Peregrine's arm. Aran saw his tutor grab the man's wrist, arch his back and pull. The soldier flipped over Peregrine's shoulder, crashing to the flagstones. His head smacked back and Aran heard a crunch.

Another soldier moved in, raising his fists like a boxer. Peregrine ducked then struck out with one leather boot, sweeping the soldier off his feet. He too hit the tiles with a resounding crack.

'This really isn't necessary,' Peregrine said as three men glanced at one another and moved forward in unison. 'My Law, call them off before someone gets seriously hurt.'

Carifax said nothing. The three advanced, two drawing their blades, the other wielding a dirty serving pan. Peregrine sighed and raised his fists. Aran held his breath.

Then a voice said, 'Stop!' and everyone turned.

Lady Carifax took hold of her husband's arm. 'Please, just stop. He's right. My love, you know he's right. I know how much you want to protect Aran, but not like this. Call them off.'

'No,' Carifax repeated, his voice thick with wine. 'It's too soon. He's our son.'

The Lady put her arm around her husband's neck and gazed deep into his eyes. 'He'll always be our son,' she said. 'Are you really willing to risk lives over it? The time has come. We just have to be strong.'

Carifax closed his eyes and sank back into his chair. The Lady motioned to the soldiers and they stepped back, sheathing their blades. Aran ran to his father's side, wrapping his arms around the Law's neck and holding on for all he was worth.

He felt his father's hands on his shoulders, pushing him gently away. Carifax held Aran at arm's length, looking up with tearstained eyes. 'My boy,' he said. 'Perhaps we should have told you a long time ago. I just wanted you to be safe. To be happy. To be my son.

'But the truth is, you never were. That man, the one who came out of the snow. At first I didn't recognize him, he'd changed so much. So many years had gone by since the last time I saw him . . . the time I ate at his table. But then, when I heard him in your room, I knew. I knew his name, and I knew why he had come, even if he didn't know it himself. His name was Tarik Karn. He was your father.'

CHAPTER TWENTY-ONE

The Rise and Fall of Tarik Karn

O n Law Carifax's order, the room was cleared. Aran saw Akmid slipping silently away, his face a mask of guilt and anger.

Lady Carifax took a seat by the fire and drew Aran close. He could feel her heart beating against his cheek, her arms linked tight across his chest. The real world felt very far away. He could hear his father's voice, Law Carifax's voice, telling Peregrine about that night, how Karn had broken into Aran's room, chasing a ghost. He shivered despite the warmth.

'How much do you know of Law Karn?' Peregrine asked, turning at last to Aran.

Aran searched his memory. 'He brought the farmsteads together, stopped them fighting. He was a hero.'

Peregrine smiled faintly. 'That's the legend,' he said. 'The truth is a little different. He did bring peace, for a little while. But at what cost? No, I'm afraid Tarik was no hero. He was, however, my friend. My greatest risk. And my greatest failure.'

He sipped his drink, staring into Aran's eyes as though searching for something, something he'd lost a long time ago.

'The story begins about . . . I'd say forty years ago. The world was a different place, even then. The society you know barely existed. People had only really been back on the surface for a century or so, and they were learning how to deal with each other again. I was wandering—'

'Wait,' Aran interrupted. 'You said forty years. How could you have been alive?'

Peregrine thought for a moment, then shook his head. 'No, this isn't the time for my story. That can wait. For now, just accept that I'm a little older than I look.'

Aran glanced uncertainly at Law Carifax, who did not speak.

'As I said, I was wandering,' Peregrine went on. 'Learning all I could about this new world. Old hierarchies of power and privilege were re-emerging. Laws attacked one another over a few acres of ground. Petty religions sprouted up out of the soil, exploiting the downtrodden for their own cynical gain. I thought perhaps I could help to bring about a change. Well, I learned my lesson.

'When I first saw Tarik he was just another Lawling, not much older than you. The Karn farmstead was remote, way up on the highlands beyond Stanidge. They had one close neighbour, the Morin clan, and of course the two families were always fighting, that was the way of things in those days. But this fight had been going on so long everyone had forgotten what the original argument had been about. Battle had followed battle, atrocity piled upon atrocity. The previous year, Tarik's father had slaughtered an entire herd of Morin cattle that had strayed over the border of his land. Just killed them and left them in the sun to rot. It was that kind of conflict, petty and vicious.

'Law Karn knew I had a reputation as a man of letters, so he hired me to be his son's tutor. He was ahead of the curve in that respect, he recognized that the best way to lend Tarik the edge was to give him a good education. Not that he didn't train Tarik in the martial arts as well. He was a tough kid; he had to be. I don't think I ever saw him without a bruise, whether from sparring or sword practice.

'But he was a bright boy. I saw that right away. He was a natural student of people; he had watched them all his life. It made him a formidable fighter, and a wonderful pupil. I loved teaching him, and he was eager to learn. So as the years passed, I began to think of Tarik as more than just another future Law. Perhaps, I thought, this boy could help to heal this shattered world. This could be what I had been sent for, the fulfilment of my purpose.'

Peregrine coughed and looked at his feet, and Aran realized that his tutor had somehow said too much. He tucked that word away for later. *Purpose.*

'Foolishly, I shared my thoughts with Tarik,' Peregrine continued. 'You can imagine his reaction. Like any boy born into power and privilege, he'd always thought he was a cut above the crowd. He was smarter and stronger than anyone else in the farmstead. Of course he should be a leader. And I—' Peregrine broke off, shaking his head. 'I *encouraged* this,' he said in a tone of disbelief. 'I didn't try to bring him down to earth. I wanted him to feel invincible. I taught him down all about the great rulers of old: Caesar, Napoleon, Churchill. I showed him where they'd gone wrong, the choices they should have made. And Tarik lapped it up, every word.

'The old Law died when Tarik was nineteen, killed in a skirmish with two of Morin's sons who'd been raiding the storehouse. It was expected that Tarik would wreak bloody revenge for his father's murder. But he and I had discussed this exact scenario, and our plans were already in place.

'Tarik called a meeting of the local Laws. This hadn't been attempted before, and there was a lot of suspicion. But the meeting was held on neutral territory and Morin received assurances that he would not be harmed. Forty Laws attended, every landowner in fifty miles. Tarik and I brought them together. We were very pleased with ourselves.

'Our proposal was simple. A council of representatives from each farmstead, headed by an elected leader who would unite all the Laws present, and eventually the entire Island. Tarik did not make it a secret that he believed himself to be the best candidate. And he was a passionate speaker; by the end of the first day more than half the Laws were on his side. He promised prosperity, a period of calm in which they could all rebuild. Old scores would be settled with fairness and diplomacy. And to prove his willingness to make it work, he would forgo any revenge against Law Morin for the murder of his father.

'Most of the Laws respected his position; they saw it as a real commitment to peace. The others, Morin included, took it as weakness, and refused to join us. This was exactly what we'd predicted. We knew we wouldn't be allowed to establish our new society without a certain amount of bloodshed. But we'd underestimated quite how nasty things might get.'

Peregrine passed a hand over his eyes. 'The Council of Laws was formed, with Tarik at its head. He established a court at Howden, after the example of the old English kings. He didn't crown himself outright – we knew better than to risk such a bold move – but he was in charge, and everyone knew it.

'Morin and the other rebels weren't giving us an easy time. So Tarik decided to form a standing army, requisitioning young men from all the farmsteads on his Council. He trained them himself, taking the best and brightest for his personal guard. The Laws were pleased. As long as someone else was doing the fighting, they could sit back and get rich.

'And get rich they did. These were the glory years: the summers were mild, the crops tall and the cattle fat. Law Karn's army patrolled the land, quashing any hint of rebellion. In over a hundred skirmishes he never got a scratch. Many of the rebel Laws were forced to change sides, unable to stem the tide of progress. Soon there were only Morin and a few others holding out, and they just kept their heads down and plotted.

'Things seemed to be working exactly as Tarik and I

had predicted. He was firmly in place as ruler. I was his counsellor. I could keep him in line, manage his excesses. Or so I thought.

'You see, Tarik was already beyond my control. As peace settled he began to grow restless. He just loved danger too much, I suppose. The thrill of combat. It was an addiction. That was a side of him I could never have predicted. Everything I'd hoped for was coming true, but now our great society was beginning to rot from within.

'At first I barely noticed. Tarik was always off with his royal guard, and when he was back at court he tended to stay in his room, alone. His moods had always been unpredictable, but now they spiralled out of control. He challenged one Law to a death duel for accidentally stepping on his robe.

'Karn's weakness was soon obvious to all. He was pale, restless. He didn't bother with the details of government. But there was no one else to take his place – he was a young man, he hadn't married. And there was still the problem of Morin and the rebels. They were growing in strength, and soon they had gathered an army powerful enough to take on Law Karn.

'All we'd worked for was coming apart. Men had died for this, and it was crumbling. I went to Tarik and demanded an audience. I was shocked by what I found. He looked like he hadn't slept in weeks, pacing the room like a caged animal. I tried to talk to him, I told him he needed to come out and connect with his people. He just laughed.

'He said they weren't his people, they never had been. They weren't worthy of him, all they did was hurt one another, steal from one another, blame one another. He'd tried to show them the way but it was useless. People didn't change, they were petty and cruel and always would be. The only way they'd ever improve was in the grave.

'I couldn't believe what I was hearing. There was a madness in him. He hated everything, himself most of all. Because if humanity was worthless and he was their ruler, what did that make him? I tried to convince him there was still a future worth fighting for, but he wouldn't listen. He had his guards remove me. They threw me into the street with nothing but the clothes on my back. I let them. What choice did I have?

'I passed Morin's army on the road that afternoon. They'd heard Tarik was weak so now they were advancing on Howden, intent on replacing him with one of their own. But once again they'd fatally underestimated him. Because the only thing guaranteed to bring Tarik Karn back from the brink of insanity was the promise of a good scrap. His army marched out and faced the rebels on the Hollow Field, and Tarik rode at their head.'

Aran sat up. The Battle of Hollow Field was the most famous in living memory. He'd heard tales of it his whole life, but never from someone who was actually there.

'God, he was magnificent,' Peregrine said. 'It had been barely twenty-four hours since I'd seen him, broken and feeble. This was a different man. You must have witnessed a similar change, Aran, that night he came out of the

265

snow. I think it's part of his madness, part of his strength. The ability to transform himself simply by force of will. He rode tall in the saddle, his sword gleaming. He had a suit of golden armour, with a great plume of feathers that streamed out behind. His royal guard rode with him, and the earth shook.

'Morin's forces were dumbstruck. They'd been led to believe Law Karn was practically crippled, yet here he was, bigger than life and twice as dangerous. I watched from a high hill overlooking the plain. All I could see was his sword flashing in the sunlight. He was the eye of the storm, out of control, showing no mercy. His armour was soon caked with blood, but still he went on, until Morin's army was cut to shreds.

'Law Karn's forces began to celebrate, believing their leader had returned. They would regain their old strength, and he would lead them to even greater victories. He rode from the field in triumph, as the last light shone across the bloody landscape. I couldn't watch. There was so much pain, so much dying. The grass was red. This was everything I'd tried to prevent. More men died in that one day than in twenty years of fighting between farmsteads.

'The next morning Law Karn's advisers came to his tent, hoping he'd ride in a victory parade through the streets of Howden. But Tarik was gone. His bed was empty, it hadn't even been slept in. He just vanished.

'A society which had taken years to build fell apart in a few days. Without him to hold it together, the court simply collapsed. Nobody wanted to take responsibility for anything, it was chaos. Our great experiment was over.'

He sighed and sipped his drink. 'And that's where the official records end. Most presumed Law Karn dead. There were occasional sightings, rumours and gossip. He became a folk hero. His deeds were embellished until he could fight three hundred men single-handed, and everything he said or did was right and just. People need to believe that things were once better than they are today, because maybe that means they could be better again. It's rarely true. Trust me, I should know.'

Peregrine got to his feet and stoked the fire, sending sparks dancing into the chimney. 'I took to the woods and the quiet places, and tried to forget. It wasn't easy. The guilt ate at me. I've long since stopped trying to count how many good men would be alive if I hadn't interfered. I returned to my cottage and spent some time with the remnants of the past. And twenty years went by.

'One day there was a knock at the door. A man was standing there. He was covered in mud and twigs, and he had this enormous beard. But still I recognized my old pupil. I took him inside and made him a cup of tea, and for a long time we just sat and looked at each other. Then eventually he began to talk.

'He'd changed, he said. He'd been haunted by everything he'd done, the men who'd died. He had seen their ghosts in his dreams, and sometimes when he was awake. They'd spoken to him, guided him. Brought him back to the world. He'd fought for so long; had hurt men, killed them. Now he was ready to try something new.

'He'd decided that what he needed was a child. Someone to live after him, to carry his name and his likeness, but not make all the mistakes he'd made. It would learn to cherish humanity, not despise or pity them. All he had to do was find an appropriate bride.

'I didn't know how I was going to do it, but I was determined to help him. It would lift some of the burden of guilt if just one story could end happily.

'There was a young woman on Law Maddon's farm, close to my cottage. She was bright and solitary, interested in plants and wildlife. She wasn't as mistrustful of me as some of the others. A lonely creature, too gentle for the world she'd been born into.

'The next week I introduced them, Tarik and Sara. It was almost too easy. They were both isolated people who'd lived their whole lives without love. A week later they were inseparable. Sara moved into the cottage, and to all intents and purposes they were man and wife. She was pregnant by the end of the year. We were all very happy.

'But Tarik was the happiest of all. He began to look to the future, seeing in his child all the potential he'd failed to fulfil. He would be a leader of men, a champion. It amazed me that he still had these dreams, after all that had happened. He told me that the same problems still afflicted mankind, the same weakness we'd vowed to overcome. His child could be the one to change it all. Not with violence, but with love.

'I don't think Sara quite believed her good fortune. Suddenly she had a man at her side who seemed to love her absolutely. Soon she would have a child to care for. It was as if all of her dreams had come true. Then everything fell apart again.'

Law Carifax leaned forward, looking from Peregrine to Aran. 'Please,' he said. 'He doesn't have to know all of it. Not yet.'

But Aran shook his head. 'I do,' he said, feeling sick and a little afraid. 'Please, Father.'

Law Carifax winced at the word. Aran felt his mother's heartbeat quicken.

Peregrine smiled sadly. 'The truth is, your mother loved you from the moment you came into the world, Aran. But she was a fragile soul, you must understand that. And what he did to her . . . it was more than she could bear.

'It was a long labour, and by the time you were born Sara was exhausted, emotionally and physically. She barely noticed when Tarik came into the room. When she realized what was happening she tried to stop him, but the blow he dealt knocked her unconscious.

'I was out gathering strengthening herbs when Tarik came through the trees, carrying you on his back. He'd undergone another one of his transformations. All the uncertainty was gone. He was smart, clean-shaven, ready to take on the world. He was leaving, he told me. He'd find a place to raise you, give you all the opportunities you deserved. Sara would understand, he insisted. She'd get over it in time.

'And then I knew. I could see it in his eyes. The madness

had returned. In fact, it had never gone away. It had been there all through our time together, as I trained him, shaped him, turned him into a warrior. It had been there through his brief reign, allowing him to look the other way when atrocities were carried out in his name. It had been there the day I confronted him at Howden, it had shone in his eyes as he muttered his defeated curses, but it had also given him the strength to come back, to fight on, to pound Morin's army into the dust. And it was there that night in your room, Aran, when a vision of his long-dead love stirred up all the guilt and pain he carries locked away in his heart.

'It took all my strength to wrest the baby from Law Karn's grasp, but I did it, leaving my old pupil bleeding in the dirt. Then I ran back to the house, with you screaming in my arms. But it was too late. Sara thought she would never see her beloved or their child again. Believing she had nothing left to live for, she had put the rope around her neck.

'Tarik broke, for good this time. He ran to lose himself in the wilderness. I think that if he'd been brave enough he would have followed Sara into death. But he was too weak even for that. I never saw him again, never heard any rumours. This time even I believed him dead.

'I brought you here, to Law Carifax, who I knew to be a decent man. After Akmid was born, the Lady was told she would never bear another child, so they were happy to take you as their own. I told them about your parentage, and I also said that one day I would come back to check on you. When we met that day on the road, I think your father was afraid I would take you away. I have tried to assure him that this was never my intention. He is the best father you could have hoped for. All I wanted was for you to know the truth.'

He reached into his pocket and drew something out. Aran recognized the locket he had seen in Peregrine's room, small and silver, on a fine chain. Peregrine unfastened the clasp and showed it to Aran. Inside were two pictures, a man and a woman. Right away, Aran recognized the stranger, with his piercing eyes and proud features. Years had passed, but the face was the same. He turned his attention to the woman and nodded.

'I think that's her,' he said. It was the same long, flowing hair, the same faraway eyes. 'The one who was in my room.'

Peregrine pursed his lips. 'I don't have an answer for that,' he said. 'I buried her myself. But there are more mysteries in this life than even I can comprehend. Here, I think this should belong to you.'

He closed the locket and handed it to Aran, who held it tightly in his hands, feeling the cold metal against his skin. He didn't know what he should think or feel. Lady Carifax's heart was pounding, fast and regular against his back. Aran disentangled himself and she let him go, looking at him sadly. 'We should have told you sooner,' she admitted.

Aran looked from her to Law Carifax, who sat with his head in his hands, his body heaving with each breath.

'Why didn't you?' Aran asked softly. 'Why didn't you tell me?'

'What good would it have done?' Carifax replied, looking up at last. Tears glistened on his ebony cheeks. 'You were so young.'

'But you told Akmid,' Aran said.

Carifax shook his head. 'Akmid found out on his own, many years ago. He had heard too many rumours not to believe them. But he promised never to tell you, not without my permission.'

How had Akmid managed to keep his mouth shut for so long? Aran thought about his brother as he'd been when they were boys. However hard Carifax had tried to stress the importance of keeping this secret, the brother Aran knew would have been unable to resist. He might have been able to keep quiet for a week, a month, even a year. But sooner or later, in the heat of an argument, he would have blurted it out.

Unless there was something holding his tongue. But that only led to another question – what had changed? Why had he chosen tonight? Of course he was drunk, but Akmid had been drunk before. He'd transformed since he joined the militia. He was tougher, that was clear. More confident. Braver.

And then Aran realized, and it all made sense.

'You were afraid of me,' he said in amazement. 'That's why you never let me learn to fight. Why you got so angry when you found the swords. You thought I might be like Law Karn. That I might be . . . wrong.'

'No, Aran . . .' The Lady reached out for her son's hand but he drew back, looking at each of his parents in turn, the knowledge flooding through him.

'You forget,' Carifax said. 'I was there. I was only a young man, but I understood that the choices Karn made, the way he used his power, could only lead to more blood-shed. That's not what I wanted for you. All we ever wanted was to keep you safe.'

'To keep me weak,' Aran protested, pulling his hand back. 'You were scared of Law Karn. And you were scared of me. Because he's in me.'

'No,' Peregrine interrupted. 'Aran, you are not Law Karn any more than you are Law Carifax. You're Aran. The things you do and say come from you, not from anyone else. That goes for the bad as well as the good. It's very important that you understand that. Whatever madness drove Tarik Karn, it's not in you. I'd know it.'

'How?' Aran asked, his confusion turning to bitter dismay. They had lied to him, all of them, his whole life. 'How can you possibly know?'

'Because I know you,' Peregrine replied. 'I know what you are.'

'And what am I?' Aran asked. 'What am I, Peregrine? I'm not tough like Law Karn or patient like Law Carifax. I'm not smart like Cas or quick like Mohanna. What am I?'

'You're just a boy,' Peregrine said. 'A good, scared boy. You have to have faith that all your answers will come.'

'So does this mean you'll stay?' Aran asked, glancing uncertainly from Peregrine to his father. 'Now that the truth is out, there's no reason for you to leave, right?'

Peregrine looked long and hard into the fire. Then he shook his head. 'I've thought a lot these past few days,' he said. 'And I've come to the conclusion that your father is right. I have to go.'

'But you—' Aran began, unable to believe what he was hearing. 'I don't understand. I thought we were friends.'

Peregrine frowned. 'Oh, Aran, we are,' he said. 'More than I ever expected. But look where it's got us. My meddling has almost destroyed this family. I tried to teach you to defend yourself, and the next thing I know you're breaking into farmsteads, fighting Marauders. You could've been killed.'

'But . . .' Aran spluttered. 'But it was your training that saved us.'

Peregrine sighed. 'Maybe,' he said. 'I'm not so sure. Anyway, you need time to think, to come to terms with everything I've told you. To become strong, become the man I know you can be. But I can't fail you the same way I failed Tarik.'

'Fail me?' Aran asked. 'How would you fail me?' Then he knew. 'There's more, isn't there? There's more you're not telling me?'

Peregrine shook his head, unable to look Aran in the eye. 'No,' he said. 'It's too soon. I have to go.'

'But you can't!' Aran said, louder than he'd intended. 'We need you here. And anyway, it's too dangerous. The snows could come, and you'll freeze to death. I won't let you. I won't—'

'Aran, please,' Peregrine said firmly. 'I promise, this won't be the last time we meet. One day you'll understand. I'm sorry. I'll leave tonight.'

Aran looked at him, his heart pounding. He felt like he was coming loose from the world, as though everything he thought was real and true was being slowly, painfully stripped away. Tears sprang into his eyes. 'That's not enough,' he said.

And he leaped to his feet and ran. Up the spiral stairs he went, his breath loud in his ears, his heart thundering. But neither of these could compare to the noise in his head, the clattering and crashing of a hundred conflicting thoughts.

He threw himself into his room, slamming the door behind him and sinking onto his bed. Looking up, he saw pale light filtering through the vent and knew that dawn was fast approaching. Suddenly the thought of a future at Hawk's Cross seemed too much to bear. Here, where everyone knew his secrets before he knew them himself. Where no one trusted him enough to tell the truth. Where even his parents were not who they appeared to be. Akmid was right – he didn't belong here. The walls seemed to tighten about him, pinning him to the bed, his future closing in, dark and lifeless and empty.

It was impossible. He couldn't forget all that he had learned. And he couldn't stay here, pretending that everything was still the same. He knew what he had to do.

Aran slipped out of bed, grabbing his pack from the back of the door. He stuffed some underclothes into it, some dry bread and an apple from his bedside table. The smell of breakfast rose temptingly up from the kitchens, but he ignored it. He struggled into his warmest jumper, then pulled another on top of that, and another, topping it all off with two scarves, two pairs of gloves, his peaked deer hide cap and his warmest jacket. Then he peered out into the corridor, made sure the coast was clear, and hurried up the stairs.

The sky was the colour of ice on the river as he ducked out into the courtyard from the armoury, glancing back to check he'd closed the hatch. Men gathered around flickering fires, their eyes fixed on the valley beyond. Nobody noticed Aran as he slipped through the shadows, over the wall and into the frozen fields. As soon as it was safe he began to run, making for the shelter of the orchard. There he paused, looking back at his home, twinkling brightly in the grey dawn. He wondered when he would see it again.

CHAPTER TWENTY-TWO

Fire and Fog

There was something in the shadows, and it was growling. Aran drew his knife. The faintest glimmer of moonlight filtered through the trees, but otherwise it was pitch dark. He saw movement from the corner of his eye. It might have been branches whipping in the breeze or shadows shifting on the frozen ground. Or it might have been something more. Aran was lost, he was exhausted, he was chilled to the bone. It was long past his bedtime. And something was growling.

It was hours since he'd had any sign of Peregrine. He'd kept him in sight all through the long day, but that had been over the high moors where Aran could stay a mile or more back and not lose the trail. The sky had been wide and empty and the land much the same, endless expanses of grey-green scrub and limestone dotted with patches of heather.

Peregrine had walked quickly, his robes flapping. Aran had scrambled in his wake, using all the tricks his tutor had taught him. The sun had been pale and distant, but

Aran had felt it on his back – between that and his layers of clothing, he had managed to stave off the worst of the cold. But now the sun had set.

He knew they were not making for Peregrine's cottage. That lay to the east, beyond Hawk's Cross. They had headed west and north, towards the silent lands beyond the last farmstead. Aran couldn't begin to imagine what Peregrine might be seeking out here.

The events of the previous night had already begun to seem unreal. Aran's head was so foggy, his emotions so conflicted that it was almost as if he felt nothing. His anger, his resentment and his fear all boiled into one great cloud of confusion. One day those feelings would have to be dealt with. But for now, his focus was on the matter at hand.

Towards evening they had descended into a steep, stony valley. Aran had seen no signs of human life, not even sheep or cattle. A hawk circled overhead, its keening cry echoing on the bare stones. A pine forest carpeted the lower slopes of the valley, and through the opening at its mouth Aran had seen a wide plain glittering emerald green, cut by a shimmering silver river.

Peregrine had quickened his pace, hurrying towards the wall of pines. Aran had scrambled over the rocks, suddenly aware that he might lose Peregrine once he entered that tangled darkness.

It was too late. By the time Aran reached the treeline his tutor had vanished. The sun had set, a heavy peace descending. Aran had stood at the edge, looking into the forest. The narrow path which snaked between the dense, forbidding pines would be hard to follow once the light faded. But what choice did he have? It was either press on, or turn back. He couldn't go back.

Now it was hours later, and Aran was hopelessly lost.

The growl came again, barely audible over the wicked wind. Fear settled on Aran's heart. He could die out here, he knew that for a fact. If whatever was making those sounds didn't get him, the cold most certainly would.

He needed to think, make a shelter, build a fire. Defend himself. But he was so frightened, and so very tired. Where was Peregrine? He must have passed him in the dark. But he'd seen no campfire, smelled no smoke.

Perhaps if he just closed his eyes, the solution would come to him. He huddled against the trunk of a tree, trying to clear his thoughts. At least it was warm inside his jacket. He could just slip into sleep. In the morning he'd know what to do.

The clear, crisp snap of a twig broke Aran from his reverie. He jumped up, lashing out with his knife. Suddenly he saw movement, off to his left. Low to the ground. A shadow in the dark, drawing closer.

'Come on, then,' Aran muttered feebly. 'Come and get me.'

The wolf moved sinuously through a patch of moonlight. Aran saw shining eyes, lips drawn back over white teeth. He heard ragged breath and smelled rotten meat.

He held up his knife, his hands trembling. The wolf growled again, a deep rumbling sound welling up from deep within its massive body. Aran tried to growl back, but it came out as more of a whimper.

For a moment, the wolf seemed to draw back. Then Aran realized it was preparing to spring. He gripped the handle of his blade.

There was a dry rasping sound. A spark flared and something caught fire. The wolf recoiled, its green eyes glistening. It snarled, muscles tensing under grey-white fur.

Then a voice said, 'Get lost.' The wolf turned tail and fled, vanishing into the trees.

Peregrine faced Aran, a flaming branch in his hand. 'Who's your friend?' he asked.

Aran flung himself at his tutor. 'Thank Ala,' he said. 'Thank Ala you're here.'

Peregrine disentangled himself. 'Calm down,' he said. 'You only saw me yesterday.'

'I was so scared,' said Aran.

'I'm not surprised,' said Peregrine. 'You were about thirty seconds away from being a dog's dinner. Honestly, I really didn't think you'd be idiotic enough to follow me all this way. I kept hoping you'd give up.'

'What, you knew I was there?' Aran asked.

'Since about lunchtime,' Peregrine admitted. 'I knew someone was after me. I thought it was probably you, but I wasn't sure until we came down into the valley. Then I got a good look at you.'

'I tried to stay out of sight,' said Aran.

'You didn't do a bad job,' said Peregrine. 'I'm your teacher, so I know your tricks. But someone else wouldn't have spotted you.'

'So why didn't you stop?' Aran asked.

'I did,' Peregrine said. 'As soon as I got inside the forest. Ever since then *I've* been following *you*. I've been sitting by that stump over there for the past two hours.'

Aran's face fell. 'Why would you do that?' he said, punching Peregrine on the arm.

'To teach you a lesson you should've learned two nights ago,' replied Peregrine angrily, rifling through his bag and pulling out a small pan. 'You can't just go wandering about the countryside alone. A small boy can be a big meal if you're hungry enough. And I don't just mean the wolves.'

He dropped two chunks of raw meat into the pan. They sizzled noisily.

They ate in silence, then Peregrine pulled out his blanket and lay under it, close to the crackling fire. 'So where are we going?' Aran asked.

'We?' Peregrine asked. 'You're going home. Where I'm going is my business.'

'You can't send me back,' Aran protested. 'I'll get lost!' It sounded more like a promise than a warning.

Peregrine scowled. 'Then I'll have to go back with you,' he said.

'Fine,' Aran said. 'But only if you'll agree to stay. You can't just tell me all those things then run away. I won't let you.'

Peregrine sighed. 'I'm not running away,' he said, though his voice lacked certainty.

'Then where are you going?' Aran asked. 'Not back to your cottage.'

Peregrine shook his head, looking almost sheepish.

'There's something I'm supposed to do,' he said. 'It's . . . well, it's important to me. It shouldn't take long.'

'Great,' Aran said. 'I'll come with you.'

Peregrine looked into the fire, and let out a grunt of resignation. 'But after it's done, I'm taking you home. No arguments, no questions.' He lay down, wrapped in his woollen blanket. 'Now shut up and let me sleep.'

Aran lay back, huddled inside his jumpers and his jacket. He could hear his tutor breathing in the dark beside him. The forest didn't seem so terrifying now. It was almost beautiful, in the light of the fire and the glow of the Timber Moon.

Something was digging into his side. Reaching into his pocket, Aran pulled out the locket. He must have stuffed it in there without thinking. He unhooked the clasp and gazed at the pictures within. Law Karn, with his wide, flat features and deep set, deep blue eyes, and Sara, with her faraway smile and melancholy mouth.

He wondered how they had felt, each of them, at the end. Did his mother know she was abandoning him as she slid the rope around her neck? Did his father feel the madness when it came, or did he just slip into it softly, like going to sleep? Aran tried to picture them together, walking in the woods, falling in love. Raising their child, his family as it should have been. But somehow, he couldn't. The years had passed, the chance had gone, and that was another life.

They left the forest just as the sun was cresting the hills. The plain ahead lay in shadow, wreaths of mist clinging to the hollows and along the banks of the river. As they watched, the pale line of dawn came creeping back across the landscape. The fog melted and the land was revealed, shades of brown and green and gold, jewelled with sparkling frost.

Peregrine pointed towards a bank of dark shapes on the horizon. 'That's where we're going,' he said. 'Those mountains. And we must be there by nightfall, so keep up.'

They fell into a quick march, following the river. Aran kept his eyes peeled for signs of human habitation, but there was nothing – no fences, no smoke. This country was altogether deserted.

As they walked, he noticed that the grass beneath his feet was getting sparser and more ragged. The few trees they passed looked sickly and withered, and the sound of birds faded. He mentioned this to Peregrine, who nodded.

'This is a bad place,' he agreed. 'There's poison in the earth.' He gestured off to the west. That way even the grass petered out, leaving only dry soil. 'I've seen the ruins,' Peregrine went on. 'On the edge of the sea. Nothing but black earth and concrete. Chernobyl was a firework compared to Sellafield.'

They made good time across the rolling ground and soon the hills had grown large on the horizon. In the early afternoon they passed a row of rusted steel-frame pyramids, towering over Aran and Peregrine like guardians keeping watch over the scarred land. A bright-eyed hawk sat on a metal perch and watched them pass.

The land began to slope as they came to the feet of the

mountains. These were the tallest hills Aran had ever seen, rising jagged and uneven. Some were thickly forested with oak, ash and windswept pine, while others were simply walls of bare granite, pale green with moss. The sun was dipping and Peregrine tried to hurry Aran forward.

'All right, all right,' he complained. 'I'm going as fast as I can.'

They followed a narrow path up onto a short expanse of boggy moor. The hills rose sheer on either side. They came to a copse of pines and descended into another valley. The shadows lengthened and Aran found himself almost running to keep up.

Suddenly the trees parted and they were standing on the lip of a wide, placid lake. Ripples cut the surface, lapping at the rocky shore. The lake was fringed by a dense wall of firs. In the centre stood a solitary island, a spare protrusion of stone topped by a spinney of ragged trees.

Peregrine made his way along the shore, his boots crunching on the shingle. He rooted around in the undergrowth, uncovering a small wooden boat which lay upended on the rocks, tied with ropes to the trees on either side. Together they turned the boat over and dragged it down to the water. Inside were stashed a pair of sturdy oars and two rusted rowlocks.

'Push off,' Peregrine ordered, climbing in. They skidded away from the shore and Peregrine dipped the oars. The boat sliced cleanly through the water, sheets of ice splintering around the prow and spinning like tiny islands in their wake.

'I suppose you want me to tell you what we're doing here,' said Peregrine as he rowed. 'Truth is, I'm not even sure myself.' He strained on the oars, angling towards the island. Aran trailed his fingers in the black water.

'I come here every year, if I can,' Peregrine went on. 'To perform a sort of . . . ritual, I suppose. I know it sounds ridiculous. The thing is, I'm not the man I appear to be, Aran. I think you've figured that out for yourself. My mother was . . . well, I may as well just tell you, now that we've come this far. My mother had power. Magic, you'd call it.'

Aran looked at him, startled. 'You mean she was . . .' He felt slightly ridiculous even saying it. 'She was a witch?'

Peregrine shrugged. 'That's one word for it,' he said. 'A touch medieval, but it'll do. Anyway, when she died, one of the only things my mother left was an envelope with my name on it, containing a single sheet of paper. On it was a map to this place and the instructions for this ritual. I don't know what it does, or if I'm even doing it right. But it has to be performed on the night of the last full moon before the snows come. I've been doing it for a long time, longer than you can imagine. So far, nothing. I suppose I'll only be successful when I'm truly ready, when the time comes to fulfil my purpose.'

Aran's eyes narrowed. 'That's the second time you've said something about a purpose,' he observed. 'I suppose you're going to tell me I'm not old enough or something.'

Peregrine's face reddened. 'Or something,' he said. 'Besides, it's rude to interrupt. Let me finish my story.'

'I thought you had finished.'

'Had I?' Peregrine looked away. 'Oh, look. We're here.'

There was a crunch and the boat stopped moving. They had run aground on the pebble shore of the little island. Peregrine clambered over the rocks and Aran followed. The stars were out overhead and Venus glowed bright and low in a black velvet sky.

The island was capped with a damp plateau of scruffy grass and a cluster of sorrowful pines. In their centre was a circle of smooth, wind-carved stones barely a foot high. They looked almost as old as the hills surrounding them.

Peregrine pointed to a dry spot beneath the trees. 'Sit there,' he said. 'Don't say anything, don't do anything. OK?'

Aran nodded. Peregrine reached up into the pines, using his knife to trim a few branches. He laid them within the stone circle, forming a tight two-armed spiral. Then he knelt in the centre, bowing his head.

Aran wrapped his jacket around his shoulders and shivered. The only sound was the lapping of the waves on the shoreline. His teeth began to chatter.

Peregrine turned on him. 'Please, Aran. I'm trying to concentrate.'

'I'm cold,' Aran protested.

'I don't care,' Peregrine snapped back. 'You promised to behave.'

'I am behaving,' Aran shot back. 'What do you want me to do, freeze to death?'

'If it'll shut you up.'

Aran scowled. 'What are you even doing, anyway?'

'You wouldn't understand,' Peregrine snapped.

'Do you?'

Peregrine's face darkened, his fists clenching. Then his anger seemed to subside, and he sighed deeply. 'Oh, maybe you're right,' he said. 'Who am I kidding? It's not like anything's going to happen. We should probably just go home.'

Aran hurriedly shook his head. 'I'm sorry,' he said. 'Your mother sounds like the kind of person who knew what she was doing. I'll be quiet, I promise.' He locked his mouth with his fingers and threw away the key.

Peregrine couldn't help smiling. A shaft of light fell across his face and he looked up. The full moon was rising. The lake rippled and all the world was silver-black. He got to his feet, facing the moon, then began to mutter under his breath, caught in a trance like that night in the cage, running over and over the same mysterious words and phrases. Aran felt the same strange awakening, as though the trees, the lake, the air itself were listening.

Something was changing. He could feel it, but he didn't know what it was. He looked up at Peregrine; his back was turned, his arms flung wide to greet the rising moon. His voice seemed to fill the air, his whispered incantations echoing all around, mingling with the sigh of the wind and the lapping of the water.

Something moved at the very lowest edge of Aran's vision. Looking down, he realized it was his own hand. It was reaching out towards the circle, fingers spread. He tried to pull it back but the hand would not obey. There was no pain, no fear, just the knowledge that his hand was not his own, that some other force had taken control.

Before he knew it, Aran was on his feet. He almost laughed, there was something so peculiar about this feeling – his mind was perfectly clear, yet his body would not respond. He took one step towards the circle of stones, then another. He felt like a sleepwalker, but one who was awake. He knew that didn't make sense. He wanted to call out, to get Peregrine's attention, but found that his mouth wasn't obeying his orders either.

A twig snapped beneath his foot. Peregrine turned, and the look which crossed his face was one of pure annoyance. 'Right,' he said. 'This is ridiculous. If you can't sit down and stay quiet, I don't see why I should make a fool of myself. Come on, get your things.'

Aran stood, his arms outstretched. He could feel something on the surface of his skin, an electric charge like static on wool. Only this feeling was all around, filling the air.

Peregrine seemed to notice it too. 'Aran?' he asked, his brow furrowing. 'What . . .'

Then Aran's hand crossed the border of the stone circle, and the spiral of branches burst into flames.

Aran was thrown back into the dirt. The flames roared upward, a pillar of fire sending sparks into the black sky. The air was sucked from his lungs. He tried to cry out but no sound came.

Peregrine was standing in the circle, his eyes flashing.

The flames licked at his legs and arms, but he did not seem to notice. He turned sharply, took a single step back into the centre of the spiral, knelt on the ground and raised his eyes to the sky.

The full moon shone above his head and a beam of light descended from it, enclosing Peregrine in a spectral glow. His skin gleamed white and his mouth opened in a noiseless cry. The flames rose to their highest, their thunder ringing in Aran's ears. And then, as suddenly as they had arisen, the flames died. For a moment, all was still.

A sound was building, outside the stone circle. The waters of the lake began to boil and churn. A column of steam rose from the surface, twisting and writhing into the air. Soon the island was swallowed in a bank of thick fog. Aran could barely see the stones in front of him. Peregrine was just a dark shape in a sea of whiteness. Aran wanted to step forward, to take hold of his tutor and shake him from his trance, but he could not.

Something was coming. He couldn't hear it or see it, but he could feel it. A presence in the mist, approaching fast. A shadow swept past him, stirring the fog, and just for a moment Aran thought he smelled horse-sweat and heard the sound of hoof beats and clanking armour. A distant whinny rose and fell on the still air.

Now here it came again, and this time he saw it clearly: a man on horseback, no, two, riding hard, their horses' hooves not even touching the ground. The mist swirled around them. One wore polished silver armour and carried a sword whose blade shone like the moon. The other had golden armour and his helmet was shaped like the head of a wild stag, but with a flattened, almost human face. There was something sickening about it, and Aran felt his heart pound.

The two figures came around for a third pass, and Aran could see now that the golden rider was pursuing the silver, thrusting from behind with a steel-tipped lance. The blade struck home, and the man in the silver armour crashed from his horse. But as he did so, he managed to reach back and, with both hands, drag his enemy with him.

They rose again in fury, swords drawn. They came together, armour clashing, swords swinging, stumbling back and forth. The man in the silver armour held a gleaming blade which flashed like a beacon in the mist. He drove forward, pounding his enemy like water against a rock.

But as he raised his sword for the killing blow, his opponent thrust viciously with a short knife, piercing the skin where the breastplate broke at the waist. The warrior in the silver armour clutched his gut, letting go of his sword. His opponent toppled back, the sword projecting from his chest, its trembling hilt pointing directly at the rising moon.

As Aran watched, the man in the silver armour staggered forward, putting his foot on his defeated adversary's neck and pulling the sword free. The blade glimmered red. Then he too fell back, breathing hard, blood seeping from the wound in his stomach.

But as he died he looked up, and just for a moment it seemed to Aran that their eyes met. Even though he knew this was only a vision, Aran realized that what he was seeing was real. Whether it was the past or the future he had no idea, but all he was being shown was the truth.

Now the vision was fading, as the mist itself began to break. The silver armour lost its lustre, and the man seemed to ripple and dissolve. But to Aran's astonishment, the sword stayed clear and whole. And now it was falling, end over end, until blade-first it disappeared beneath the still waters of the lake.

A single mirrored ripple cut the surface, broadening until it crested on the rocky shore of the island. And from its centre, something began to rise, barely visible through the clouds of vapour which clung to the water like a shroud.

Then a ghost-wind blew, and the mist dissolved into tattered shreds which danced raggedly away into the darkness. A figure was revealed, standing on the shoreline. It was a woman, clad in shimmering robes which seemed to move like liquid across her body. Her hair was as white as moonlight and in her hand she clasped the sword. Drops of water sparkled on the blade. Her image was broken and distorted, like a reflection glimpsed in a rippling stream. She glided across the rocks towards them.

She reached the ring of stones, approaching the kneeling figure of Peregrine. He was pinned, helpless, trapped in the moonbeam that encircled him. The woman looked down, and her ageless face showed no expression. She swung the sword effortlessly, as though despite its massive size it weighed less than air. She cut a circle in the darkness, once, twice, the keen blade humming in the silence. Peregrine's eyes were fixed upon her, gazing up in terror.

Then she raised the sword above his head and brought it down in a perfect arc. Aran watched in horror as the blade struck Peregrine, cleaving through his skull. He did not fall, but stayed upright in the shaft of light. His head had been sliced cleanly in two, allowing the moon's radiance to penetrate directly into the open bowl of his skull. Shapes moved within the beam, dancing motes entering him and departing, filling him with iridescent light. Piercing, luminescent blades leaped from his wide-open eyes.

Aran cried out, and the spell which held him seemed to break. He staggered to his feet, leaping into the circle. The woman faced him and her black eyes were as deep and dark as a bottomless pool, cold sparks glittering in the depths like reflected starlight. Aran stopped, trapped in her gaze. Suddenly the fear within him melted away, and he smiled.

The woman nodded. She threw the sword into the air, and it flashed in the moonlight. She caught it by the blade, extending the golden handle towards Aran. He reached out to take it. A deafening roar rose all around them and the woman began to pulse and glow with a spectral light. The glare was blinding, and Aran could hardly see to take the sword. He felt with his fingers, grasping the hilt. The light intensified until it seemed to blaze inside his very skull. The sword was heavy in his hand and he staggered back, shielding his eyes. Then the noise and the brightness overcame him and he fell into the black.

CHAPTER TWENTY-THREE
A Column of Smoke

'**R**ise.'
A voice was calling Aran back to the world. For a long moment he didn't know where he was. He felt a soft breeze on his face and heard the lapping of waves.

'Rise!'

The voice was more urgent now. Aran opened his eyes. He was lying on his back, his jacket covering him. At first all he could see was a green blur, then his eyes fixed and he found himself looking up into a swaying canopy of trees.

'Rise!' said the voice again, and Aran realized that it was not speaking to him. 'Oh, forget it.'

There was something lying beside Aran on the rocks. A golden sword, its steel blade reflecting the white light of the sky. With a start, he recalled the events of the night before. The fire and the fog, the vanishing warriors and the woman in the water.

He sat up, smelling smoke. Peregrine was seated a few

feet away, across a small fire which crackled in a ring of stones. They were back on the shore. Aran could see the island, a distant black shadow among glittering waves. The sun was up but hidden behind swollen grey clouds.

Peregrine had constructed a small pyramid of pebbles. He held out his hand towards them, palm first. He closed his eyes, screwing up his brow in concentration. 'Rise!' he commanded angrily. Nothing happened.

'What are you doing?' Aran asked.

Peregrine jumped. 'Nothing,' he said quickly. He brushed the rocks with his hand and the little pyramid collapsed.

'What happened?' Aran said. 'Your head . . .'

'I know,' said Peregrine. 'I can't explain it either.'

'Who was she?' Aran asked. 'I thought maybe it was your mother. Until she hurt you.'

Peregrine shook his head. 'That was definitely not my mother,' he said. 'And she didn't hurt me. See?' He parted the hair on the side of his head. There wasn't even a mark.

'Do you think that's what the ritual was supposed to do?'

Peregrine shrugged. 'I always imagined it would somehow unlock my mother's power, but it doesn't seem to have worked. I can't levitate pebbles, as you can see. I couldn't make the boat move by itself, and I can't light fires with my mind.'

'What about that one?' Aran asked, indicating the flickering blaze.

'I used a flint,' Peregrine admitted sadly.

Aran looked at the sword. 'So what does it mean?' he asked.

Peregrine looked searchingly at him. Then he squinted up into the steely sky. 'We should get moving,' he said. 'I don't like the look of those clouds.'

'But . . .' Aran protested. 'But this isn't . . .' Then he sat back down, crossing his legs. 'Forget it,' he said. 'I'm not going anywhere until you tell me exactly what's going on. I'm sick of all the sneaking around and wait until you're older. I want to know now.'

Peregrine sighed. 'All right,' he said. 'But at least let me tell you while we're walking.'

Aran eyed him suspiciously. 'If I think you're holding anything back, I'm just going to sit right down and not move another inch.'

Peregrine nodded. 'You'll be up to your neck in snow by nightfall,' he said. 'But suit yourself.'

They followed the path up through the pines, between steep grey-green slopes of scree and mossy rock. Ahead they could see the poisoned plain, and beyond that the distant moors. A dark canopy of clouds sucked all colour from the landscape.

Peregrine took one last look at the valley, at the lake rippling gently under the dull sky. Then he set himself to marching.

'First,' he said, 'my own beginnings. I know I don't look it, but I'm an old man, Aran. Perhaps the oldest who has ever lived. For over a thousand years I have walked this Earth.'

Aran's first instinct was to laugh. Peregrine raised an eyebrow. 'You doubt me? After what you saw last night?'

Aran shrugged. Peregrine had a point. 'Go on,' he said.

'As I said, my mother had great power, the nature of which I've never fully understood. But it had something to do with matter and mind, a binding connection at the most basic molecular level . . . It's probably easier just to call it magic. I don't know why it is, or how it is. But I do know where it comes from. Its source is the Island itself.

'There are places of power all across the globe. Centres of mystical force. I've visited most of them, and each is different, in some inexpressible way. Each has a different . . . flavour, almost. The power of this Island is elemental; it's wild and earthy and ancient. It comes from the rocks, the soil, the metal that forged the sword you're carrying. The rain and the rivers, the forests and the fields, everything living. It's all bound together, and we're bound to it.

'My mother was the last and greatest of an ancient clan of wise women whose task was to stand guard over this remote corner of the Earth, this Island that they loved. She had been born with the gift inside her. It lent her sight and strength, and the power to protect. There were others like her, perhaps there still are, charged with watching over that part of the world most beloved to them.

'But the forces ranged against them were mighty and uncomprehending. And as the Island itself became corrupted, as poison leaked into the earth and sky, as the clouds blackened and the water rose, so my mother's power weakened. It was a time of great but reckless discovery, you see. A headlong race for dominance over nature, with no thought for the consequences. And the Earth was falling into chaos because of it.

'My mother had many gifts, but the one she prized above all was her ability to part the veil of time. She practised prescience, future prediction, but also sense memory, reliving the past through the experiences of her ancestors. In her visions she had seen time laid bare, had seen the ribbon circling, repeating, revolving and resolving. The past and the future, inextricably intertwined. And she had discovered that there were two points which had the greatest importance for the Island she loved. Two moments at which people had the greatest chance to influence the destiny of the land, for good or ill. One lay in what we call the past. The other lay far in the future.

'She herself was mortal, unable to affect things outside her own short span of life. So she used the last vestiges of her power to cast a spell upon herself, to weave a magic within her very flesh. Nine months later she gave birth to twin boys. The bells of midnight had just begun to ring when I took my first breaths. And as the chimes faded, my twin brother came into the world.

'The spell was too much for our mother to endure, and she drifted into a peaceful sleep from which she would not wake. But before she died, she whispered to her midwife the names she had chosen for us. The names of wild birds, wise and perilous. My name was to be Peregrine, for the falcon. My brother's name was Merlin.'

He looked expectantly at Aran. 'When I was a boy,' Peregrine said, 'there wasn't a man, woman or child on this Island who didn't know that name. He was to become the most famous wizard of all time, my brother. We were together in the womb for nine months, but our time on Earth lasted just two minutes, between my own birth and his. We gazed at one another as we lay on our mother's breast, each of us knowing a special awareness of the bond that would always exist between us. Then he was gone, his life playing out in reverse, sending him back into the past.

'Merlin's story has been told time and time again, embellished and altered until it's impossible to say how much of it is true and how much is myth. But the basics remain unchanged: at a time when the Island was under threat, from invaders on her borders and squabbling between her rulers, a boy came to unite the people and bring them into an age of peace and enlightenment. The boy, whose name was Arthur, was advised by a powerful wizard who wove spells to protect him, and taught him how to be a just ruler.'

Peregrine shook his head. 'But for me, things were very different. I grew to manhood in a world tearing itself apart, with no one willing or able to prevent it. I inherited all my mother's books and possessions, but the words were written in a language I couldn't understand and the trinkets she left were useless to me. Then when I reached the age of seventeen I stopped growing. It was embarrassing. I had to sever ties with many of my friends because they began to ask too many questions.

'So I travelled the world, seeking out those who could help me understand. I met witches and wizards, shamans and gurus and men of vision. They taught me about my mother's magic and what it could do, but they couldn't show me how to use it. I just didn't have the gift. They could teach me tricks, how to harness my physical strength and communicate in simple terms with wild beasts, but they couldn't tell me what my mother had meant for me.

'I had to learn to live alone. One by one my friends grew old and passed away, while I stayed the same. And now the world itself was changing beyond recognition, and my troubles seemed insignificant. The sun blackened the land and people were forced north, great waves of refugees searching for a better life, or any life. Storms swept in, tearing whole cities apart. The water rose, driving people from their homes. But where could they go? Millions died, and the survivors retreated underground, into basements and bunkers and mines and railway tunnels. Governments crumbled, societies shattered. The people hid themselves away and forgot about the world as it had been.

'And I too sank into the dark.' Peregrine's voice had grown sad and weary. 'I'll admit, Aran, there are times when I curse my mother for making me this way. She has allowed me to live through many lives of men, but she hasn't given me the power to save them. I saw so many die. And for seven more centuries I waited for the day when my purpose would be revealed. And now, I believe, that day has come.

'You see, my brother's story gives clues to my own purpose. All this time I've lived in the shadows, piecing together scraps of legend and half-truth, wondering how I would bring peace to this troubled land. But now I know. The legends foretold that Arthur would be reborn and rule again. At a time of great peril, a boy will come whose destiny is to reunite the Island under one banner, in peace.'

Aran looked up at him. 'When?' he asked.

Peregrine looked at the sword in Aran's hand. 'In the stories, King Arthur was given the sword Excalibur by the Lady of the Lake. She was supposed to be some sort of spirit, a living embodiment of the power of the Island. The sword was Arthur's emblem; it bound his kingdom together. Until at the last he was betrayed and murdered by his own son, Mordred.'

Aran remembered the figures in the fog, the struggle he had witnessed. He told Peregrine what he had seen.

Peregrine nodded. 'The final battle,' he said. 'They slew one another and the sword was lost. Until now. Excalibur has returned, Aran. She gave it to you.'

Aran blinked and looked up slowly. 'You think it's me?' he asked.

'Oh, I no longer have any doubt of it,' said Peregrine. 'The Lady, the sword. It all fits.' He placed his hand on the boy's shoulder. A strand of sunlight pierced the clouds and for a brief moment the world was all aglow. 'Aran, you are the once and future King.'

Aran swallowed, looking up at his tutor. The sun slipped

back behind the clouds, and in the grey gloom Peregrine's face was as serious as a statue, his eyes gleaming like dark jewels.

Aran shook his head. 'How am I supposed to become King? I'm not even a Law's first son.'

'Oh, but you are,' Peregrine reminded him. 'The greatest Law of them all.'

'I may be Law Karn's son,' Aran admitted, 'but I won't become a Law. Akmid's going to inherit Hawk's Cross, and when that happens he'll throw me out on my ear. I don't see how you're going to persuade everyone that I'm their ruler.'

'I don't, either,' said Peregrine. 'But you've been given the sword. Your destiny is written, so it's only a matter of time.'

Snow had begun to fall, fine white flakes that melted as soon as they touched the skin. Peregrine refused to stop for lunch, pushing on towards the line of hills that rose in the distance. Gusts of wind swept down from the moors. Aran felt his cheeks stiffen.

'I don't know,' he said at last, almost to himself. 'I suppose I did always feel . . . different, somehow.'

'Like you're special? Meant for great things?' Peregrine asked.

Aran's eyes lit up. 'How did you . . . ?'

'Every boy your age feels like that,' said Peregrine. 'I did. But then again, I lived to be a thousand, which just goes to show.'

The snowflakes fell thicker and heavier, blown in their

faces by the strengthening wind. The light vanished, the sky fading from white to grey and finally to black, the blackest night Aran had ever known.

The sword hung heavy at his side. The cold sank into his bones and the snow clung around his ankles. His shoes were full of bricks, his legs wooden. He could stop, just for a moment. Sit down, get his strength back. The snow would make a nice soft bed . . .

Then he felt Peregrine's hand on his collar and was almost yanked off his feet. 'Not yet,' his tutor shouted over the howling of the wind. 'If we stop now, we'll die.'

Aran tried to force himself forward. 'I thought you couldn't die,' he yelled.

Peregrine grinned, his brows and his hair gleaming with ice. 'Maybe so,' he shouted. 'But I don't particularly want to test that theory.'

He drove through the deepening drifts, his legs working like pistons, dragging Aran behind him. The wind seemed to fight against them, making every step a battle.

But at last Aran felt dry leaves underfoot and saw broad trunks looming out of the darkness. They had reached the forest. Peregrine found a dry space between the trees and made a fire. Aran wrapped himself in his jacket and shut his eyes, shivering hard.

They rose before first light and moved on. They came up into the rocky valley just in time to greet the rising sun. The snow had stopped falling and a few scattered rays managed to break through the blanket of cloud. Aran felt his spirits lift as warmth touched his upturned face.

They trudged across the moor in silence. That same hunting hawk watched them from the branches of a bare, crooked tree. Again they did not stop for lunch, but chewed on the last of Aran's dry bread.

The land rose to meet the clouds and they found themselves wreathed in clinging tendrils of freezing mist. They couldn't see more than a few feet, lost in a world of grey and formless shadows.

Despite everything that had happened before he ran away, Aran was eager to be home. He had visions of roaring fires and crackling pork, and hot mugs of camomile sweetened with honey. He didn't know how he was going to explain all this to his parents, but he'd think of something. And now that the whole truth was out, there was no reason for Peregrine to leave. He thrust his hands into his pockets and hurried onward.

Soon familiar landmarks began to appear: a gap in the wall, an overhanging rock. A rotted tree where Aran and Cas had once buried valuable treasure: a bronze medallion and a dead mouse in a pine box.

'It should be just over that—' Peregrine began, then broke off. 'That's odd,' he said, squinting into the distance.

Aran followed his gaze. There was a texture in the air ahead, a dark shade of grey clearly definable against the paler clouds. A column of smoke rising.

'Is it Hawk's Cross?' Aran wondered.

'I think so. It must be.'

They walked on. 'Perhaps it's another celebration for Akmid,' Aran suggested.

'I'm sure that's it,' said Peregrine, but his voice was uncertain.

They struck the main track. They could smell the smoke now, dry and acrid. Snow was falling once more, big heavy flakes that settled on the wet ground. They rounded the last bend in the river and saw something lying on the bank. A pile of blue and red rags.

Aran gasped and ran forward. It was a man, his body broken and lifeless. Cartwright, the blacksmith. A sword was in his hand, a look of surprise on his face. Aran looked up towards the farmstead. The smoke was rising thick and black into the darkening sky.

'Aran, wait—' Peregrine began, but it was too late. The boy was running up through the barren fields, the snow pelting his face. His weary legs found new strength as he ran, blind with terror, up to the courtyard gate.

CHAPTER TWENTY-FOUR

A Calling

The cattle sheds were on fire. The hay was burning, sending up churning pillars of black smoke, and Aran could hear the desperate screams of the animals trapped inside. All the windows in the summerhouse were broken and the chapel door hung on its hinges. Three more bodies lay twisted on the flagstones. There were no signs of life.

Peregrine caught up to him, breathing hard. 'Marauders,' he said.

'Where is everyone?' Aran asked. He drew Excalibur from his belt. The farmstead gate had been torched, battered and finally smashed to pieces, leaving a trail of blackened steel and shattered wood. Aran picked his way through the debris, peering down the dark ramp. He felt tears sting his eyes, and fought them back.

Peregrine unbolted the stable doors, allowing herds of terrified, smoking cattle to stampede out into the courtyard. Then he threw his cloak over his face and ran in to drive out the horses, bolting the door behind him as they scattered in panic.

Aran held the sword in front of him and descended the ramp into Hawk's Cross. At the foot of the slope Gideon's banner was a mud-stained rag, trampled by countless feet. The entrance hall was empty. The guards' table lay in splinters and beside it sat the watchman, staring sightlessly into the daylight. A scarlet spray painted the wall behind his head.

From somewhere below, Aran heard a low moan, then silence. Water dripped steadily. He reached for a lighted torch on the wall. As he did so, he heard a sound. Footsteps approaching. A voice said, 'Stop.'

Aran's head snapped up. A figure appeared from the passageway, clutching something in its hands. A crossbow.

'D-don't move. I'll shoot.'

Aran took a step forward. 'Cas?' he called out. 'Cas, is that you?'

'Aran?' Cas rushed forward, throwing himself at his friend. He began to sob. His clothes and skin were black with ash and smeared with blood. 'I'm so sorry,' he said. 'I was just . . . I nearly shot you!'

'It's all right,' said Aran, pulling Cas up. 'What happened? Where is everyone?'

Cas bit his lip. 'Marauders,' he said. 'They took them.'

'Everyone?' Aran asked incredulously.

Cas shook his head. 'A lot. Your parents. My father. Mohanna—' He broke off, shaking. 'The rest are downstairs. Lots of injured. Some dead. I was told to watch the steps. Just in case they—' He broke down, his body racked with sobs.

Aran held him, stroking his hair. 'I'm here,' he said. 'Peregrine's upstairs. There's no sign of them now. Tell me what happened.'

'Akmid and the others left at dawn,' Cas explained. 'He said there was no reason to stay, that once you ran away there was no reason to believe the story. I tried to make him listen, but . . .'

'It's all right,' Aran said softly. 'I'm sure you tried.'

'The Marauders must've been watching,' Cas went on. 'I was with Mohanna in the infirmary; we heard horses and people screaming, this awful . . . Someone came running down, covered with blood. I've never seen so much . . . And then they were coming down the steps, and Mohanna was fighting. She got one, I saw her, took his arm clean off, but then the next one . . . All I could do was hide. I could hear them, taking whatever they could find. I think they wanted to be gone before the militia could figure out what was happening. They'd planned it, Aran. Timed it, so they'd be able to . . . so they could see . . .' Cas wiped his nose on his sleeve. 'Then things got quiet. I came back upstairs. Akmid was back, he'd seen the smoke. He and his men were going after them. He told me to guard the steps, so that's what I was doing. Guarding the steps so no one could get in.' He sank back against the wall, sobbing hard.

'You did a fine job,' Aran said. He wondered how long Cas had been hiding in the shadows, terrified and alone. He could imagine the Marauders tearing through Hawk's

Cross like a vengeful wave, cutting down all that stood in their way. He had never loved his home as much as he did in that moment.

Peregrine descended the ramp, looking around in horror. Aran repeated what Cas had told him, and Peregrine nodded. 'I need a drink.'

As they descended the stairs, Aran could hear the muttered moans of the injured and the dying. Women moved along the tunnels with bloody rags and steaming buckets. Aran ducked through Peregrine's door and closed it behind him. Cas stood by the cold fireplace, jumping at shadows.

'This is my fault,' Aran said, dropping the sword on the table like the useless lump of metal it now seemed to be. 'I should never have left.'

Peregrine shook his head. 'Don't be daft,' he said. 'What could you have done?'

'I could have forced Akmid to stay,' Aran said. 'I could have made him believe me.'

'You tried,' Peregrine said wearily. 'He didn't want to believe you.'

What would my father do? Aran found himself thinking. What would each of my fathers do? Law Karn would go after the Marauders, risk his life to save his family and his friends. He wouldn't think twice, he'd just act. But Law Carifax would caution just the opposite. *You're a child*, he'd say. *The only thing you can do is get yourself killed. Best to stay at home, be safe.* But how safe were they? And what could he possibly do, here, alone?

All he knew was that he had never been so afraid. And if he let this happen, the fear would never end. It would dominate every day of his life from then on.

'We have to go after them,' he said.

Cas gasped.

Peregrine turned on Aran. 'And do what?' he demanded. 'Take on the whole Marauder army – two scared boys and one useless old man?'

'We can catch up to Akmid,' Aran said. 'We have to do something. This can't be the way it happens. It can't be. I can't become who you say I'm going to become, not without my family.'

Peregrine shook his head. 'I won't let you risk your life on some—'

'Won't *let* me?' Aran barked. He was shaking, close to tears. 'How are you going to *stop* me? I'm going, with you or without you.' He reached out and grabbed the sword.

As he did so he felt some sort of spark touch his hand, an eager, familiar quickening. He jumped, pulling his hand back.

Peregrine looked up quizzically. 'What is it?'

Aran eyed the sword uncertainly. 'I don't know,' he said. 'I was thinking about going after them, and I reached out for the sword, and something . . . changed. Did you feel it?'

Peregrine shook his head. He crossed and looked down at Excalibur, lying on top of the pile of books. He reached out gingerly, touching the blade. Nothing happened.

'I think . . .' Aran began. 'I think it wants me to go after them.' He felt ridiculous even as the words were leaving his lips.

'It's a sword, Aran,' Peregrine said. 'It doesn't want things.'

'How do you know?' Aran asked. 'You said the Lady in the Lake was part of the Island, part of its power. If this sword came from her, maybe it has some of that power too. Maybe this is what the Island wants. What it needs me to do.'

Peregrine shook his head. 'Nice try,' he said. 'But if you think you can use my own stories against me, you've got another thing coming.' He poured himself another drink, looking dubiously at Excalibur.

'I think you're jealous,' Aran objected. 'Because I got a magic sword, and you didn't get anything. You've been doing that ritual for years, and now you're miffed because it didn't do what you thought it was going to.'

Peregrine looked at him through slitted eyes. 'Mind your tongue,' he said. 'Anyway, I'm not miffed. I have complete faith that my mother knew what she was doing, and that whatever she meant for me will come to pass in its own good—'

'But you don't,' Aran interrupted. 'Not really. You were looking for any excuse to get out of that ritual. Ever since we met you've been grumpy half the time, as if this whole thing was just a huge burden for you. And now we've got the sword, and your purpose has been revealed, and you don't even seem all that pleased about it.'

'Aran, you wouldn't understand—'

'Stop saying that!' Aran yelled, surprising even himself. 'The very first day you said the only way this is going to work is if we're honest with each other, but you've never once told me the truth until it was forced out of you. Well, why not just try it for once?'

Peregrine looked down into his whisky glass, then drained it with a snarl. 'It's not that simple,' he said. 'I've lived so long, Aran. I've seen so much. Disaster, disease and death. People at their absolute best, and their absolute worst. And every time I think I'm coming close to some kind of understanding, some kind of answer, it turns out to be just a whole lot more questions.

'When I first met Tarik, I was sure he was the One. I even went so far as to tell him everything I've told you. And he did unite the Laws. He did bring peace. But then it all began to fall apart, and neither of us could understand why.' His expression softened. 'Oh, Aran, if I've ever treated you like a burden, I'm sorry. But I've come to care for you, much more than I ever wanted to. And if I take all this as a sign, if I let you take that sword and follow the Marauders, and something happens to you . . . I don't think I could live with myself.'

'So you won't even try?' Aran protested quietly. 'Listen, you said your mother's power was about the mind as well as the magic. Maybe you need to trust it before you can make it work. If you believe that only bad things are going to happen, then maybe you won't be able to do any good.'

Peregrine glanced up at him, wondering. 'When did you get so wise?' he asked.

Aran shrugged. 'Maybe I'm growing up,' he said. 'I hope not.'

Peregrine smiled. 'I don't think you need to worry about that quite yet,' he said. 'Anyway, I suppose I do have a tendency to look rather on the grim side. It's hardly surprising, given everything that's happened. But maybe I ignore the possibility that things might go right every once in a while.' He gritted his teeth. 'Well, if it'll make you feel better, I suppose I can give your way a go. My mother brought me into this world, so the least I can do is give her the benefit of the doubt.' He looked up at the ceiling and took a deep breath. 'Come on then, Mother,' he said. 'Wherever you are. I'm open. Show me.'

And with that, something happened. One of the books which lay in a jumbled heap on the table top slowly flipped open. The pages fluttered for a moment, then lay flat.

Aran looked around. There was no wind, the room was utterly still. In the silence, he became aware of a low, insistent hum. It seemed to come from all around them, a vibration in the air. Peregrine leaned in, ever so slowly, and touched the open page.

'What's happening?' Cas asked, in a voice which seemed to come from a long way away.

Aran didn't even want to breathe for fear of breaking the spell. 'I don't know,' he said. 'I think it's magic.'

Then Peregrine let out a cry, and his eyes were suddenly lit with wildfire. '*Learned scholar*,' he said, tracing a line on the page with one finger. '*Bound herein is the lore and wisdom of the eldest, as practised by the sisterhood of the Albion line of Lyonesse, generation to generation since the waking of the world*.' He looked up, his eyes alight. 'It makes sense!'

He turned the book to face Aran. All Aran saw was the usual jumble of signs and runic symbols. 'I don't . . .' he said.

'I can read it!' Peregrine cried out, his voice filled was glee. 'I don't know how, but I can read it. The writing is the same, but somehow . . . Here, there's a list of chapters . . . let me see. *Of the earth . . . Of the river . . . Of the sky* . . . and last of all, *Of darker matters* . . . Well, maybe we'll save that one for later. But still! It makes sense, Aran. This is the moment I've been waiting for. My mother's gift!'

Suddenly he started, his face aglow. 'Aran, the sword!'

Excalibur was vibrating violently on the table, causing the glasses and pots to rattle. Aran reached out, and this time the sword almost leaped into his hand. It whipped upright, Aran struggling to hold on, the blade pointing directly at the ceiling. He could feel waves of power radiating from it.

Peregrine laughed aloud and slammed the book. 'I feel it,' he said, his voice trembling. The room hummed with intense mystical energy, strong and strange and indescribable. Peregrine pressed both hands to his head. 'Mother, I feel it. Oh, how could I have been so blind? I doubt you no more. And you're right, Aran, of course you're right. We have to follow them. We have to get them back. The sword wants it. The Island wants it. And the King wants it.'

Cas looked confused. 'What does he mean, *King*?' he asked Aran in a low voice.

'I'll explain later,' Aran promised.

Peregrine pulled on a dry coat and boots, strapping a knife around his ankle. He thrust his Marauder axe into his pack along with some day-old food and a length of strong rope. He looked amazedly at the book in his hand, then he stuffed that in as well. 'Aran, get yourself some dry clothes,' he said. 'We need to ride out immediately.'

Aran nodded and started for the door.

'But . . .' Cas began. 'What about me?'

'You must stay here and keep watch,' said Peregrine. 'They may yet come back.'

Cas's face fell. But Aran shook his head. 'No,' he said. 'There's something more important you need to do.' He held Cas by the shoulders. 'Are you strong enough to ride?' Cas nodded.

'Aran,' Peregrine protested, 'it's not safe for him to—'

'He's not coming with us,' Aran told him. 'He's going to Barton. To fetch the militia.'

'But by the time they get here we'll be miles away,' Peregrine objected. 'They'll never catch up with us, let alone the Marauders.'

'They don't have to,' Aran said. 'Because we know where they're going.' And he reminded Peregrine about the farmstead where the Marauders had taken food and shelter the night of Carny. 'What did Kira call it?' he asked. 'Eskirk? It stands to reason they'll go back there on their way to the sea. Cas can bring the soldiers. We'll follow Akmid and the others. Even if we don't get there in time to intercept the Marauders, at least we'll have a better chance of stopping them when we do.'

314

Peregrine was looking at Aran with a gleam in his eye. 'All right,' he said. 'Let's move.'

Aran hurried up to his bedroom, wriggling into a set of dry clothes. By the time he reached the surface, Cas was waiting by the smouldering stables holding three skittish horses, saddled and bridled with scorched tack. A pall of smoke still hung over the courtyard and the paving stones were slick with black ash. Snow was falling, lying in a thick blanket on the empty fields where the stray cattle wandered, aimless and afraid.

Aran felt weary to his bones. He was awake and alert, but for how long he couldn't say. He felt a deep pit of dread inside him, clawing at the edges of his conscious mind. What if they were too late? What if his parents and his brother were already dead, and Mohanna on her way to a life of slavery? He clutched the handle of his sword, strapped to his belt in an old scabbard he'd taken from the armoury. He felt a flicker of its power and his heart lifted, just for a moment.

He clambered onto his horse, slipping his feet into the stirrups. Cas seemed tinier than ever, perched atop a snorting black stallion. 'If we're late, don't wait for us,' Aran told him. 'We should be there before you, but if not you have to keep on to the sea.'

Cas nodded. He swallowed down his fear and smiled grimly. 'I'm not afraid,' he said, and just for a moment it was true.

CHAPTER TWENTY-FIVE

Ghosts

The Marauder band was easy to track. They tended to keep to the open, hacking and burning whatever they couldn't go around. The trail skirted the edge of the wood below Hawk's Cross, crossed a few barren, muddy fields, then joined another road which led up onto the treeless heath, and east towards the sea.

The sun had long since set and the wind came gusting out of the darkness, bringing down flurries of stinging snow. Aran pulled his cap down over his face, shielding his eyes. He was soaked through, freezing and frightened. But the sword at his side gave him reassurance. He was sure that before the next day was through it would taste blood.

Reining in his horse, Peregrine dismounted. A bank of earth kept part of the road sheltered from the wind, but a deep snowdrift had blown up against it, burying the tracks. Aran slipped down from the saddle. 'What is it?' he asked.

'I'm not sure,' Peregrine answered. 'The cart tracks follow the path that way.' He pointed into the darkness.

'But there are others. Here, coming down the bank. As if somebody rode over the top and down onto the road. And here's more, leading off in that direction. Just horses.'

'But it's the carts we're following,' Aran argued. 'Who cares about the horses?'

'I just think it bears examination,' said Peregrine. 'If we don't find anything, we turn back. But I don't want to miss something important.'

The tracks were hard to follow, but they seemed to be leading towards a shallow gulley, where jagged rocks jutted from a fast-flowing stream. Aran pulled his mount to a halt. 'We can't go down there,' he said to Peregrine. 'The horses might slip. We can't afford a broken leg.'

'Someone managed it,' Peregrine argued. 'These are horse tracks.'

'That could have been hours ago, before the snow got so deep. I'm not—'

He broke off. Peregrine had tilted his head, listening. All Aran could hear was the howling of the wind. Then he heard it, faint in the distance. A clang, like metal on stone. It was followed by a shout, only audible because the wind had briefly dropped.

'What do you think it is?' he asked.

'Honestly,' Peregrine said, 'I think it's your brother. I think those marks on the bank were an ambush. The Marauders left men behind to waylay Akmid and the others, and they drove them down into the valley. I assumed we'd only find bodies. But now we know that at least one of them is still alive.'

'We have to go to them,' Aran said without hesitating.

'Are you sure?' Peregrine asked. 'We'll have to go on foot, and we don't know what we'll find. If there are fifty Marauders against one man, what will you do? Risk your own life to help him? And the lives of your family?'

Aran shook his head. 'No, I . . .' He screwed up his brow. 'We heard fighting: that means somebody's alive. They're right there, and we have the chance to help them. Even if it's only one man, we have to try.'

They tethered the horses and descended, their packs on their backs, slipping and sliding their way to the bottom of the gulley. The swollen stream cut through a dense cluster of pines, then turned aside at the low edge of a broad, untended pasture which sloped gently up ahead of them. At the top of the field stood the remains of a stone farmhouse. A fire flickered on the muddy grass, and huddled around the blaze were thirty or more black-clad Marauders. Their shouts and harsh laughter echoed through the chill air.

'I know this place,' Aran realized. 'My father told me the farmstead was abandoned before I was born, though nobody knows why. They say the tunnels are haunted.'

They could see very little of the farmhouse, just broken walls and empty windows. 'Akmid and the others must be inside,' Peregrine observed. 'Perhaps we can sneak around the back.'

'They'll have lookouts posted,' Aran said. 'Maybe we can create a diversion. Is there anything in that book of yours that might help?'

'That's risky,' Peregrine argued. 'I wouldn't have the

faintest idea what I was doing. It might be like trying to light a campfire and burning the whole forest down.'

'All right, maybe something non-magical.' Aran turned back. The Marauders' mounts were tethered in the shadows at the edge of the clearing. 'Maybe we could untie the horses. Then while they're getting them back, we slip inside.'

Peregrine frowned. 'Well, first we have to get up there without being seen. Then we have to untie the horses without being seen. Then we have to hope every one of the Marauders goes after a horse, so we can get into the farmhouse without being seen.'

'Details,' said Aran. 'We'll work it out as we go along.'

They circled the clearing, keeping to the shelter of the trees. They could see more Marauders in the shadows behind the farmhouse, standing guard.

'I told you they'd have lookouts,' Aran whispered.

'And yet you think this ridiculous plan will—' Peregrine's voice was suddenly cut off.

Aran turned. His tutor was nowhere to be seen. 'Peregrine?' he whispered, as loudly as he dared. 'Where are you?' The shadows seemed to deepen. Aran clutched the hilt of his sword. An owl hooted softly, somewhere in the dark.

'Aran!' came a voice from somewhere nearby. 'Help me!'

Aran froze. 'P-Peregrine?' he stuttered. 'Are you invisible?'

'Down here!' said the voice. It seemed to be coming from

inside a thorn bush. Aran knelt and pushed the branches aside. Peregrine's fingers were just visible, straining for purchase.

'It's a vent shaft,' observed Aran.

'I know what it is,' said Peregrine angrily. 'Get me out of it!'

'How deep is it?'

'I don't know, and I don't want to find out!'

Aran took Peregrine's wrist, pulling him up. Then he looked at the shaft, wondering. 'Did you bring any rope?' he asked.

Peregrine nodded. 'Of course I— Oh, no. Forget it. We have no idea what's down there. The shaft might be a hundred feet deep. The tunnel could have caved in. There could be ghosts, like you said.'

Aran looked at him. 'You don't believe in ghosts,' he said.

'Two days ago I didn't believe in women who live underwater,' Peregrine shot back. 'Now I don't know what I believe. Besides, what's Carifax going to say when I tell him I got you home safe then managed to drop you down a vent shaft?'

Aran sighed with frustration. 'What do you think he'd say if he knew we had a chance to save Akmid, and we didn't take it?' he demanded. 'Now, do you have any rope in your pack or not?'

Peregrine handed it over. 'I strongly disapprove,' he said.

Aran tied one end of the rope to a tree and flung the

rest into the hole, then he began to climb down. To his relief the shaft was barely twenty feet deep, opening in the west wall of what seemed to be a large, empty room.

Aran dropped to the floor. It was utterly black. He heard Peregrine land softly behind him. There was a rustle and a scrape, and a candle flared. There was a dry scrabbling all around them. Eyes glittered in the shadows.

'Rats,' said Peregrine. 'I've always hated rats.'

The candle did not illuminate very far. They could see the wall behind them, the floor at their feet, and very little else.

Aran felt along the wall until he found an opening. They stepped out into a narrow passageway. They tunnel ran straight for a hundred feet, then turned sharply left.

They descended a short flight of steps into an open hall. Aran's eyes were gradually adjusting to the dark. There were rows of tables with dusty plates and metal cutlery still set out. A pig's skeleton lay on the table, a nest of white bones picked clean by the rats. Above their heads a low chandelier hung with intricate ribbons of dripping wax from a hundred half-melted candles.

'What do you think happened?' Aran whispered. There were no signs of a struggle. It was as though everyone had simply been spirited away.

Peregrine shook his head. 'I wouldn't like to guess,' he said. 'But it's been years. Look at all this dust.'

'It gives me the creeps,' Aran admitted. 'I wish I'd never said that about ghosts.'

They moved on, up another flight of steps on the far

side of the hall. Here were two passages, and they chose the left-hand way. Another staircase led them up to what felt like the first level.

'We must be near the farmhouse now,' said Aran.

Turning the corner, they came upon a last flight of steps. Peregrine held up the candle. 'Damn,' he said. The ceiling had fallen in, bricks and earth blocking the exit.

Aran pressed a finger to his lips. He could hear voices on the other side of the rubble pile. And not Marauder voices; they were speaking quietly, cautiously.

Aran began to carefully remove the fallen bricks, handing them back to Peregrine. He could feel cold air slipping between the stones, and the voices grew louder. Now he'd made a gap wide enough to peer through. He could see nothing on the other side. The voices stopped. Aran listened, holding his breath.

Suddenly a sword was thrust through the gap, inches from Aran's face. He gasped and pulled back. 'Hey!' he said.

'Who's there?' said a voice. 'Explain yourself.'

'It's me, Aran,' he said hurriedly.

There was a brief silence, then Akmid's voice came through the gap. 'Aran?' he said. 'What are you doing down there?'

'Trying to get you out,' Aran said. 'Shut up and help me dig.'

Together they widened the hole until it was big enough for Aran and Peregrine to squeeze through. Akmid pulled Aran up the last few steps.

Snow was drifting down upon the exhausted troops who

huddled, shivering, in the roofless ruins of the farmhouse. There were sixteen remaining from the thirty who had ridden out the day before. Their eyes were sunken, their armour spattered with frozen blood.

'What in God's name are you doing?' Akmid demanded, pulling his brother down behind a heap of bricks and rotted beams. 'And where have you been? Father was worried sick. Of course he blamed me . . .'

'It's a long story,' Aran told him. 'Here, look at this.' He pulled Excalibur from its scabbard.

Keller laid a gloved hand on the gleaming blade. 'Nice,' he said. 'Who'd you steal it from?'

'I didn't steal it,' Aran exclaimed. 'It's an ancient . . . well, it's sort of a magic sword, and it told me to come after you . . . . Well, it didn't exactly . . . The thing is, I'm supposed to be the King, you see . . .'

Akmid's eyes widened. 'Did you say King?'

Aran nodded quickly. 'It's this whole prophecy thing, Peregrine knows the details. But anyway, this sword . . .'

Akmid shook his head, turning to Peregrine. 'So this idiot's the King now as well, is he? I thought my father hired you to keep him safe, not fill his head with crazy delusions.'

Peregrine shrugged. 'If he's crazy, we both are,' he said.

Akmid nodded. 'Exactly.' He turned back to his brother. 'Well, I hope you know how to use that new blade of yours, wherever you got it. They've got us pinned down; we're going to have to fight our way out of here.'

'No, we're not,' Aran corrected him. And he explained

about the tunnels beneath them, and the vent shaft hidden in the woods.

Keller curled his lip. 'What about the horses?' he asked, indicating a group of skittish nags clustered against the far wall, chewing on a crop of nettles which sprouted from the empty fireplace.

Aran told them about the Marauder mounts tied to the trees not far from the opening. 'We'll be halfway back to the road before they know what's happening.'

Keller frowned. 'It's risky,' he said.

'We can't stay here,' Akmid argued. 'We'll either freeze or starve to death.'

'There are plenty of rats downstairs,' said Peregrine helpfully.

'We have the defensive advantage,' Keller pointed out. 'We can hold our ground.'

Akmid shook his head. 'When the sun comes up they're bound to find this shaft of Aran's. They'll attack from both sides.'

But Keller shook his head. 'I'm not going down there,' he said firmly. 'I've heard the tales. Bad things happened here. Unnatural things.'

Akmid's eyes widened. 'You're scared,' he said in disbelief. 'Scared by some stupid ghost stories.'

Keller shrugged. 'You do as you like,' he said. 'I'll not risk offending the damned.'

A man came hurrying towards them, keeping low to the ground. He dropped beside Akmid. 'Something's happening,' he said.

Through the empty windows they could see the Marauders gathering in the light of their dying fire. The sky was pale, the first golden fingers of dawn brushing the eastern horizon. As Aran looked, the sun broke over the white hills and a single shaft of light pierced the shadowed clearing.

Someone shouted, 'Here they come!'

Akmid pulled Aran down as arrows whipped over their heads. One of the soldiers fell back, a bolt jutting from his chest. Aran raised his head and saw the Marauders advancing, grim and relentless. Akmid's men returned fire. One of the Marauders fell to the ground and did not get up.

'Fall back!' Akmid commanded. 'Into the stairway!'

Arrows clattered around them. Keller unsheathed his sword. The Marauders had reached the boundary wall. Aran heard the clang of metal. The militia fought every inch of the retreat, forced back over piles of stone and rubble.

One by one the soldiers squeezed through the gap between the stones. But Keller and two others were pinned on the surface. Aran saw one of them tumble, a sword piercing his breast. Two of the Marauders fell to Keller's blade, staggering back with blood gushing.

'Aran, move.' Akmid's voice was urgent.

'You first,' Aran insisted. But Akmid shook his head and shoved his brother into the hole. Aran felt strong hands on his forearms, pulling him through. Peregrine was standing there, looking anxiously up into the light.

Akmid joined them. 'Keller,' he shouted. 'Come on!'

They could see Keller standing alone at the top of the steps, his sword lashing. 'Close it,' he shouted. 'I'll hold them.'

'Don't be stupid,' Akmid yelled. 'Come on, you can make it.'

But it was too late. If Keller turned his back they'd cut him down.

Akmid and two others blocked the hole with bricks and fallen beams. Someone lit a torch, then another. They stood in the flickering light, not speaking. They could dimly hear the clash of Keller's sword, then silence.

Suddenly there was a resounding thump on the earth above their heads. Dust ran in trickling rivers between the bricks in the ceiling. Another thud. One of the bricks loosened and fell, shattering on the stones.

'They're trying to break through,' Peregrine told Akmid. 'They'll bring the whole bloody roof down.'

They backed along the corridor. Running cracks formed in the ceiling. There was another earth-shaking thump. This time the entire tunnel groaned and creaked, and Aran tasted dust. He didn't dare look back. There was another ear-splitting thud, followed by a crash like the sky falling in. Faint daylight flooded the hallway. Sounds followed — heavy footfalls and cries of anger, metal clanging against stone.

They began to run, forced into single file by the narrow corridor. Peregrine led the way, bounding down the steps, looking for the passage to the great hall. The soldiers followed, the wounded men staggering as fast as they could.

Aran brought up the rear. He could hear the Marauders in the tunnel behind him. Curses and cries rang out. Feet pounded on the stone floor. Swords scraped and screeched against the tunnel walls, sending out flashes of electric blue light.

'They're gaining!' Aran shouted.

He reached the stairway that led into the hall. Peregrine was already at the top of the steps on the far side, hurrying the men forward.

Aran threw himself down the steps and across the hall, weaving around the dusty furniture. The Marauders were so close, he could hear them breathing. He couldn't help himself, he had to look back.

He glanced over his shoulder and there they were, swarming down the steps, swords drawn and gleaming. At the forefront was a hulking brute four times Aran's size, with a two-foot steel-bladed axe in his hand. He looked at Aran and his lips drew back in a hideous sneer.

Aran backed away, stumbling, terrified. He struck a chair, almost falling. The huge Marauder raised his bloody axe.

Then Aran heard the *swip* of a bow, and another. The Marauder looked down at his chest in surprise. Two arrows jutted there, piercing his armour and his heart. He looked at Aran in astonishment and fell with a crash. The other Marauders tripped over his fallen body and went flying.

Akmid grabbed Aran by the collar and pulled him

up the stairs. Militia soldiers stood on either side of the archway, reloading their longbows. They fired a parting shot then ran from the hall as the Marauders gathered themselves and continued the pursuit.

Akmid stopped at the last bend in the passage, calling three of his men to his side. 'There's too many of them,' he said through ragged breaths. 'If they keep coming they'll cut us down as we try to climb out. We have to hold them here, take them one at a time.'

The soldiers drew their swords. They could hear the Marauders coming closer, recovering their strength and blood lust.

Akmid pushed Aran away. 'Go,' he ordered. 'Get moving.'

'But—' Aran began.

'Don't even start, Aran,' said Akmid. 'Just do as I say.'

Aran fled down the corridor, hearing the clash as the soldiers engaged their pursuers. He heard cries of rage and pain, and his brother's furious yell, 'Get back! Get back!'

Then he reached the empty room and found Peregrine waiting for him. The men climbed, hand over hand, up the rope and into the light. Peregrine shoved them bodily up the wall, strong hands pulling from the other end. Soon Aran and Peregrine were alone. Aran ran to the doorway, looking out. He could still hear the clash of metal, closer now.

'Akmid,' he shouted. 'Come on!'

He could see the flicker of a torch in the distance, a

figure silhouetted black against the orange light. His blade gleamed in the darkness. Bodies were piled all around him in the hallway, but still the Marauders came, scrambling over the tangled heaps of their fallen dead. Akmid struck out and his opponent fell, another corpse for the pile.

Then he turned and ran, catching up with Aran in the doorway.

'There's just me,' he said. 'The others . . .' He shook his head.

The light in the tunnel was blocked by a wall of advancing Marauders. Aran drew Excalibur, backing into the room. He could feel the sword throbbing in his grip. Peregrine pulled his blade from his belt.

Akmid turned to his brother. 'Go,' he said.

But Aran knew that the last man would be cut down before he reached the safety of the shaft. 'Either we finish them here, or we all die.'

They turned as the last five Marauders lunged through the doorway. Aran swung out with his sword, making contact. One fell back, slamming into the wall and tumbling to the ground. Aran swung again and this time a blade struck his, sparks flying. In the flash he saw a grimacing face towering over him, bearing down. He felt a thrill of fear and took a step back, whipping the sword around in a slicing arc. The Marauder blocked again and Aran was forced back against the wall.

Peregrine stood beside him, two Marauders pressing the attack. Akmid was visibly weakening, a Marauder lunging at him, cutting his coat and bloodying his arm. Aran struck out once more, but his attacker just knocked him aside, moving in for the kill.

The sword fell from Aran's hand and a gloved fist wrapped around his throat. He was lifted off his feet, fighting for air. He reached up, grasping with feeble fingers. His attacker's face loomed into the light, eyes bright with murderous joy. Aran felt the world closing in. He kicked out helplessly.

Suddenly there was a cry above their heads. The Marauders looked up. A figure leaped from the open shaft, striking out with a long blade. Aran felt a warm spray on his face and his attacker slumped against him, then fell to the floor. The figure came to a crouching rest on the stone flags. It was Keller.

He lunged at the Marauder assaulting Akmid and he fell back, shrieking. Keller's blade arced through the air and Aran saw something skitter across the floor, twitching. It was a hand.

The last two Marauders turned from Peregrine to face this new threat. One fell to Peregrine's knife in his back, the other tried to back away, fleeing from Keller's keen blade.

Aran reached down and took hold of Excalibur. The Marauder staggered towards him, already wounded, and Aran raised his sword instinctively. The man stumbled onto it, and his last breath blasted hot and foul in Aran's surprised face. Then there was silence.

Aran pulled Excalibur free, sheathing it. He was breathing hard, weak at the knees. He looked up at Keller's firm, unflinching face.

'All dead up there,' he said. 'And I wasn't finished.'

Akmid climbed wearily up the rope, favouring his wounded arm. Peregrine followed, leaving Keller and Aran alone in the darkness. Keller gestured to the rope, but Aran shook his head, stepping aside.

'Thank you,' he said. 'For coming back. You saved us.'

Keller's eyes narrowed. 'Now we're even,' he said. He looked around the dark room, suppressing a shudder. He glanced at the bodies by his feet. 'They'll find no rest,' he said. 'The stories were right – this is a bad place.' And he took hold of the rope, vanishing into the vent.

Aran stood for a moment, feeling silence surround him. The dust settled back in place and the shadows seemed to deepen, reclaiming their territory. For a moment he thought he heard voices, a distant whisper in the dark. But it must only have been the wind, or the rustling of the rats as they swarmed in to devour the dead.

'Take it back,' he whispered to the darkness. 'It's yours.' Then he grabbed the rope and hauled himself up.

And high on the wall, hidden in the dark, a tiny glass eye turned to follow, a motor whirring silently as it watched the boy climb, hand over hand, back into the light.

CHAPTER TWENTY-SIX

To the Sea

It was a hard ride over rough terrain. Aran slept in his saddle, riding blind through a white and dreamlike shadow-world. He was weak from hunger and stiff with cold, every muscle in his body aching. His horse was ready to collapse beneath him. And it was still snowing.

They reached Eskirk shortly before dusk, and Aran's chest tightened as they passed the tree where the old man had fallen, where Grizelda had made her final stand. It stood bare, branches black against the white sky.

But his spirits lifted as he saw the stone courtyard crowded with militia soldiers, readying their horses for departure. Smoke rose from the chimneys of the hunched little farmhouse, and Cas perched on a bench in front, making short work of a large bowl of soup. He looked up as they approached, his face breaking into a smile of relief.

'I thought we were going to have to go without you,' he admitted.

'I'm sorry,' Aran replied. 'We got held up.'

They went inside and Aran helped himself to supper while Cas told him all about his ride to Barton, how he had almost frozen to death on the high moors. The kitchen was crammed with soldiers. The boys slipped between them, finding a quiet place under a big oak table.

'Where's Law Little?' Aran asked.

Cas jerked a thumb towards the rear door. 'Sergeant Cross is asking him a few questions.'

The door swung open as one of the militiamen came back into the kitchen, and Aran caught a glimpse inside. Law Little was strapped to a chair, his face ghastly in the lamplight. A gaunt soldier drew a curved blade from his belt, pressing it to the old man's white-bristled throat. The Law's eyes stared pleadingly and his mouth worked, spittle spraying the silver knife. The chair rocked back on two legs, then the door slammed shut.

In the corner, seemingly oblivious to all the hubbub, they could see Peregrine, his nose pressed into his book. Cas eyed him uncertainly. 'Was he serious before?' he asked. 'Is that really a book of magic?'

Aran nodded. 'His mother was a powerful witch,' he said. Then, observing Cas's expression, 'What? You don't believe him?'

Cas shrugged. 'I mean, we always knew Peregrine was a bit . . . odd, didn't we? But magic? That's just from stories, Aran. It isn't real.'

Aran looked at Peregrine. His tutor's brow was furrowed as he absorbed his mother's knowledge. 'We'll see,' he said.

Sergeant Cross emerged from the back room and

Aran got his first clear look at the militia leader. He was broad-shouldered and muscular, with sandy hair turning to grey. He had flashing blue eyes and a nose like a spear point.

The sergeant called his men together in the courtyard, scanning their faces in the torchlight. 'It's as we thought,' he said. 'They're making for their ships. The old man says it's less than a day's ride. We just follow the road, straight to the sea.'

'How many?' Keller asked.

Cross frowned. 'He's tight-lipped, but I get the feeling it's a major force. Seven, eight hundred, maybe more.'

Akmid swallowed hard. 'How many do we have?'

'Counting your lot, not even half that,' Cross admitted. 'But they don't know we're coming. That'll work in our favour.'

The militia rode at nightfall, their armour gleaming blood-red in the last light of the setting sun. As the darkness deepened, torches were lit, tall brands flickering in the salt wind which whipped towards them across the wold. Heavy clouds boiled overhead, hiding the moon and the stars. The road was broad between leafless hedgerows topped by a hard cap of snow. The earth was frozen and their hoof beats rang in the midnight silence. Aran was awake now, and ready. There may be foes ahead, and immeasurable danger. But he had an army at his back and a sword at his side. Whatever may come, let it come.

As dawn broke they reached the shore and the road turned sharply north. Aran had never seen the sea, but he had always dreamed of it. The stories made it sound so grand and romantic. But the sun was just a pale disc swimming in an ocean of murk, and it was impossible to make out the dividing line between grey sea and dull sky. Snow fell intermittently and an icy wind cut in from the coast. They covered the last miles in shivering silence, each one wondering what dangers might lie ahead.

It was Cas who saw it first. A black shape in the distance, bobbing on the water. He pointed and Cross raised his fist, slowing the army to a trot. Coming closer, they could make out a vast dark ship moored in a narrow harbour beneath a wall of white cliffs.

'We have to get off the road,' Cross advised. 'They'll see us coming.'

'If they haven't already,' muttered Keller.

They turned inland across open fields, swinging around in a wide arc and coming on the harbour from the north-west. There, a sandy hill offered a sheltered vantage point. Aran followed Akmid, Keller and Cross to the summit. The sea-wind stung their faces as they lay on their bellies in the grass, peering over the edge.

'Scar Harbour,' muttered Cross darkly. 'Now there's a place I hoped I'd die without ever seeing again.'

The harbour was little more than an inlet, sheltered from the elements by limestone cliffs on either side. A small town stood in the lee, twenty or thirty shacks crowding the banks of a shallow river which emptied into the bay. A stone sea wall kept the tide back, and a number of wooden fishing boats were moored to the dock.

But these were dwarfed by the mighty Marauder ship, tall and black and terrible. It was over three hundred feet long, the mast towering above the upper deck and the dark sails whipping in the freezing wind. The ship was being loaded through the wide-open bow, a yawning mouth-hatch that lifted on a rope and pulley. The hatch was lined with pointed iron spikes like rows of jagged teeth, making the ship look like a great sea beast, rising and falling on the water.

Aran saw three cages standing on horse-drawn carts on the dock. A Marauder approached, lashing at the horses with his whip. The cages rolled forward, vanishing into the bowels of the ship. Aran felt a stab of fear. They had no time to lose.

'It's tricky,' said Cross as they retreated back down the hill to rejoin the others. 'As soon as they know we're coming they'll cast off. That valley's wide open and we can expect no help from the locals. Smugglers and reprobates, the lot of them.'

'The Marauders will leave their own men behind if it comes to it,' Akmid said. 'And as soon as they set sail we've lost them.'

'What about the fishing boats?' Aran objected. 'We could go after them.'

Akmid looked down at him. 'You really think we could mount a serious offensive against that monster? Grow up.'

Aran looked away, his cheeks flushed.

'There's nothing else for it,' Cross admitted. 'We'll just have to ride, and hope we can reach the ship before they

336

have the chance to cast off.'

'Hope?' Aran said bitterly. 'My family's down there.'

'You saw what we saw, Aran,' Akmid said. 'Do you have a better idea?'

'Stop them from leaving!' Aran replied.

Akmid scowled. 'Haven't you been listening? We can't get down there without them seeing us.'

'Not you,' Aran said. 'Me. And him.' He pointed at Cas. 'You look like soldiers, you'd be spotted right away. Whereas the two of us . . .'

'Spotted doing what?' asked Cross.

'I don't know, hanging around, looking inconspicuous,' Aran said. 'We make our way down, wait by the ship. Just local kids coming to see the sights. Then you lot ride in, making a big noise. The Marauders jump aboard. But they have to leave someone behind to untie the rope. And that's where we come in. We stop them.'

'How?' Cross asked in incredulous tones.

'However we can,' Aran replied. 'By the time the Marauders realize they're not going anywhere, you'll be on them.'

'What if they just cut the rope?' Cross asked.

Aran laughed. 'Did you see the size of that rope?' he asked. 'It'd take a week.'

Cross smiled grimly, shaking his bristled grey head. 'You've got sack, boy, but that's the most ridiculous thing I've ever heard. No, I won't allow it. You're just kids.'

'We can take care of ourselves,' Aran protested. 'Can't we, Peregrine?'

Peregrine shrugged. 'Probably not,' he said. 'But don't worry, I'll go with them.'

'Oh, well, that makes more sense,' said Akmid, rolling his eyes. 'Two idiots and a lunatic against a shipful of savages. Much better odds.'

Aran felt his anger rise and turned on his brother. 'If you can think of a better plan, we'd all love to hear it. Come on, brother, impress us.'

Akmid flushed and his mouth worked silently. Aran saw a couple of soldiers smirking at one another, shaking their heads.

'This is the only way,' Aran insisted, facing Cross. 'I won't abandon my family, and I won't risk letting the Marauders escape.'

'Can't we just send someone else in your clothes?' Cross suggested.

'Do you have any dwarfs in this army?' Aran replied. 'You can try and get Peregrine to strip, but I wouldn't recommend it. I've seen him thrash men twice your size, three at a time.'

Cross looked at Aran, sizing him up, the doubt plain on his face. Then he sighed. 'All right,' he said. 'We'll try it your way. But tell the little one's family I was against it.'

A sandy cattle track led through a steep defile towards the harbour. They were halfway down when Cas turned on Aran. 'Thanks for volunteering me,' he said bitterly. 'I'm the one who just tinkered with his crossbow while you

338

were learning to fight, remember?'

Aran shrugged. 'I had to think of something,' he said. 'I hope no one noticed I was making it up as I went along. Where is your bow, anyway?'

Cas frowned. 'In my pack,' he said. 'Not that it'll be much use in a battle. It still takes for ever to load. But Sergeant Cross gave me this.' He pulled his jacket aside, showing Aran the stubby blade strapped to his belt. 'I haven't the faintest idea how to use it.'

'It's easy,' said Aran. 'The pointy end goes in the other person.'

'I can't stab someone!' Cas protested. 'I can't even step on a spider – I have to put it outside so it can go back to its family.'

'What about that Marauder at the falls?' Aran pointed out.

'That was different,' Cas said. 'I was saving your life. And besides, he was a long way away. I didn't have to see the look on his face.'

'Try shutting your eyes,' Aran suggested. 'What's up with that Cross character anyway? D'you think he's like that all the time, or does he just act all grumpy so people do what he says?'

Cas shrugged. 'I don't know,' he said. 'You should try telling him a joke, see how he reacts. That one about the librarian and the Law's daughter always cracks my dad up.'

Peregrine walked behind them, engrossed in his book. Aran slowed, drawing alongside. 'What are you cooking up?' he asked.

339

Peregrine squinted at him. 'It's a surprise,' he said. 'It probably won't work. First time and all. But I may as well jump in at the deep end.' He placed a firm hand on Aran's arm. 'Just promise me you'll stay out of trouble,' he insisted. 'Remember your training. And keep Excalibur with you at all times.'

Aran nodded. 'I promise.' Then he frowned. 'Do we really have to call it Exca . . . whatever?'

Peregrine's eyes widened. 'It's a proud, ancient name. That sword was known all over the world.'

'But don't you think it's a bit . . . I don't know . . . silly?'

'But a sword has to have a name. What would you prefer?'

Aran shrugged. 'How about Headsplitter? Or, I know, Bonecrusher!'

Peregrine sighed. 'You call it whatever you want. Its name is and will always be Excalibur.'

They passed a rough chapel with an iron roof that clattered in the wind. An inn stood beside it, the name on the sign unreadable. A group of swarthy fishermen stood eyeing the newcomers suspiciously, but they didn't dare speak for fear of attracting the Marauders' attention.

Aran slowed his pace, mooching along the sea wall, flipping a flat stone and catching it again. His heart was pounding so hard it was almost painful. The Marauders swarmed around him, loading cattle, hay and crates through the open mouth-hatch. Their raucous language grated in Aran's ears, and the smell of them turned his stomach – a mixture of sweat, fish guts and cheap liquor.

The size of the ship was breath-taking, like a floating black mountain, casting the entire town into shadow. It groaned ominously, canvas snapping like whips as the sails tightened in the breeze. It was tied to a massive stone bollard with a rope four times as thick as Aran's arm, running to a porthole high on the starboard side. Aran clambered up and perched atop the bollard, the rope winding beneath his feet. He whistled to himself, and waited.

A man stood by the open hatch, barking orders. With a start, Aran recognized the third of Karik's bodyguards, his already impressive height topped by a headpiece made from the bleached skull of a stag, complete with branching antlers. He stood with his massive arms folded, gazing proudly out across the bustling harbour as if he owned the place. Not yet, Aran thought. Not if I have anything to do with it.

Cas lingered nearby, chewing his fingernails. He didn't dare look up, sure that if a single Marauder made eye contact he'd just turn and run, or throw himself into the sea. Just the sounds were bad enough. The ship's hold reverberated with the bleats of cows and sheep, men shouting orders and insults, and screams and moans from the prisoners crushed into the cages. The noises collided together and Cas shuddered in horror.

Then to his surprise he thought he heard another sound. A bellowing chorus, lifted on the wind. He plucked up his courage and cast his eyes aloft. The song seemed to be coming from the ship's upper deck. Then the wind changed direction, and the song faded.

Beyond the ship, Peregrine crouched by the stone sea wall, facing the water. Aran could see the book lying open on the ground between his feet. He closed his eyes and held out one hand to the sky. The fingers trembled. The wind seemed to pick up, and dark clouds covered the watery sun. White-capped waves lifted the ship and dropped it back with a splash.

Aran fingered the hilt of his sword, glancing back towards the valley where they had come. The track sloped sharply, then about half a mile up it turned east and vanished out of sight behind a rocky outcrop. Aran knew that just behind those bluffs, the militia were massing for the charge.

But time was running out. The Marauders were beginning to make their way aboard. Aran heard a rolling creak above his head, and saw the hatch start to grind shut. The wailing of the prisoners intensified.

A distant rumble began to build. On the dockside people looked around, trying to locate the source of the sound. Boulders shook loose from the high cliffs, tumbling into the water. Aran felt the bollard vibrate beneath his feet. The clouds blackened.

Then the militia thundered into view, sweeping around the bend in the road. Their armour gleamed. The ground trembled beneath them. The soldiers' eyes were wild with righteous fury.

The villagers fled for their homes or the safety of the inn. The last few Marauders stood frozen to the dock. Men on the ship shouted, calling them back. They broke from their stupor, leaping aboard. Gangplanks were hastily retracted and the hatch closed with a boom. Aran could hear hell breaking out on the upper deck.

The Marauder in the horned mask strode towards Aran and Cas, grabbing for the rope. He'd paid the boys no mind, thinking they were just a pair of curious village brats. But now one of the brats was advancing, a golden sword gleaming in his hand. The smaller boy drew a short blade and joined his friend, his hands trembling violently.

The Stag drew back, his eyes narrowing. He was unarmed, and these boys had murder in their eyes. Aran lashed out and the Stag was forced to retreat. The sound of hoof beats intensified and Aran almost laughed. This was going to be too easy.

Then he saw the rope twitch. Someone came shinning down and dropped catlike to the cobbles. Aran turned, and his mouth dropped as he recognized the white-haired Marauder boy who had given him such a beating that night in the woods. He was bigger now, almost a man, lithe and muscular. He was shirtless, and in the murky light Aran could see a network of scars criss-crossing his body. The boy looked at Aran and recognition flashed across his face. He grinned, his knuckles cracking as he clenched his fists.

'Keep the big one occupied,' Aran told Cas. 'Don't let him near the rope.'

Cas nodded grimly. There was no time to argue.

The Stag moved in, seeing Aran distracted. Cas swallowed hard, gripping his little sword with both hands, trying to hold it steady. The Stag advanced and Cas struck out, but there was no power in his thrust. He felt weak and terrified, and he knew the big Marauder could sense it.

The Stag swung his fist. Cas tried to block, but too slow. The hand caught him on the side of his head and he stumbled, dropping the sword. It skittered away across the cobbles. To his horror, he saw Aran's opponent pick it up, tipping him a sly nod of thanks.

Aran saw Cas slip, but there was nothing he could do. The young Marauder was advancing, brandishing Cas's short sword. His eyes were filled with hate.

Aran hefted Excalibur. It was alive in his hands. Aran swung it but the young Marauder blocked. Sparks flew. The sky flashed white and the clouds rolled overhead.

Cas struggled to his feet and hurled himself at his opponent. But the Stag lashed out again, a savage open-handed slap that nearly knocked Cas unconscious. He fell to his knees, his ears ringing. Then he felt himself being lifted off his feet. The Stag flung Cas over the side of the dock into the sea.

Aran's heart seized as he saw Cas fall. The Stag turned his attention to the rope, heaving it loop by loop over the huge bollard, his muscles straining.

Aran's young opponent moved in, striking with his stolen sword. Aran parried just in time. But the boy was already lunging again, knowing that all he had to do was keep Aran occupied until the rope was untied. The big man was almost there – three more loops, now two. Aran swung Excalibur, trying to drive his opponent out of the way before the rope came loose for the last time. But the boy would not yield, snarling and lashing with his sword.

And then, suddenly, it was too late. The rope slid free of the bollard, over the side of the dock and into the water. The sails filled and the black ship began to move out into the harbour. A heavy sleet started to fall. The Stag stood on the quayside, a satisfied gleam in his eye.

Cas dragged himself out of the water, landing in a dripping, shuddering heap. He watched in horror as the ship picked up speed. Aran heard hooves striking stone. The militia had reached the dock. But it was already too late.

The young Marauder backed away, looking first at Aran, then at the departing ship, then at the advancing soldiers. Finally he broke and dashed for the road, dropping Cas's sword.

Aran let him go. He didn't think one Marauder would make any difference, not now. He had failed. His parents were gone, and Mohanna with them. All this distance, all this effort, for nothing.

Then he heard a sound, and turned. Peregrine stood at the end of the dock, his hands raised to the sky. He let out a cry, and although his lips did not move there were words within it, rising and falling to some unpredictable rhythm. Peregrine's robe lashed around him and a pall of darkness fell over the land.

A bolt of lightning sliced through the clouds, striking the mast of the fleeing ship. The beam split down the middle and the mainsail burst into fire. Waves began to smash against the hull and the great ship tipped and reeled. Then the wind suddenly shifted, howling inland with punishing force. The Marauders on board looked aghast, running from one bow rail to the other, screaming curses as the ship shook and shuddered, driving back towards the harbour.

The Stag stood open-mouthed as the ship drew closer. Then his gaze fell on Peregrine, and a mixture of wonder and rage came over his features. He started to move, striding purposefully along the sea wall with death in his eyes.

Aran saw his chance. He stepped into the big man's path, and raised Excalibur.

The Stag stopped. Reaching down, he lifted Cas's discarded sword from the cobblestones. Aran stood firm. The Stag towered over him, sweat pouring down his chest, black eyes gleaming beneath the branching horns. Aran felt Excalibur trembling in his hands, ready to cut this Marauder down. The rain streamed into his eyes.

Then a vast shadow fell over them, and the Stag turned.

The black ship came careering towards the dock, driven by the waves and the screaming wind. Aran staggered back as it struck the sea wall, timbers shattering. The great hatch tore loose from its bindings and crashed to the cobbles. The Stag vanished beneath it. Aran heard a wet popping sound, and rivers of red splashed across the stones. Broken white horns poked through the planks like bony fingers.

The ship listed to port and water began to pour in through a hole in the bow. Through the open hatch Aran could see swarms of men massing for the attack. Somewhere behind them, in that cavernous darkness, his people were waiting. He vowed not to let them down again.

The Marauders on the top deck gathered three-deep against the rail, scraps of burning sail cloth raining down upon their heads. Arrows began to whistle through the air. Aran backed away, running for the safety of the militia ranks.

The wind howled and the clouds darkened. A heavy sleet fell. The militia horses began to whinny and buck as the air became thick with electricity. Sergeant Cross sat back in his saddle, looking up in disbelief. 'What's happening?' he shouted.

Aran gestured towards Peregrine, who stood silhouetted against the sea, his robes whipping. 'Don't worry,' Aran told Cross. 'He's on our side.'

The big man frowned doubtfully.

Aran gestured towards the ship. 'The prisoners are inside,' he shouted.

'The Marauders will be ready for us,' Cross told him. 'They won't let their bounty go without a fight.'

'We can't back down now,' Aran pointed out.

Cross nodded. 'True enough,' he said. Then he raised his fist. 'On my signal!'

The Marauders stared down from the railing, their weapons drawn. The militia dismounted.

Their trap had been sprung. The ship had been prevented from leaving. But now the real fight was about to begin. Aran held tight to the sword in his hand and waited for the word to attack.

CHAPTER TWENTY-SEVEN

On the Black Ship

The Marauders stampeded across the gangway. On Cross's orders the militia retreated three paces, forming a semi-circular wall of shields and armour. The Marauders broke against them, a seething tide of wild aggression, driven onto the swords of the militia by their own men pushing from behind.

But they quickly drew back and re-formed, then attacked again. This time they made a wedge, driving at the centre of the militia barricade. The defensive wall was broken, and any sense of order or strategy vanished with it. The Marauders swept through the lines and it became a pitched battle, every man for himself.

Aran looked around for his brother or Sergeant Cross, but they had already vanished in the chaos. He was lost in a sea of pounding feet, swinging fists and crashing bodies, slamming into him and past him and on into the fray.

A young soldier tumbled into him, skidding across the blood-slick stones. A burly, black-bearded Marauder threw

348

himself at the soldier, slicing down with a thin blade, going for his throat.

Aran struck out blindly with Excalibur. The Marauder fell on the point, his knife inches from the helpless militia-man's windpipe. Aran pushed the Marauder aside, yanking Excalibur free. The soldier looked up gratefully, and Aran helped him to his feet.

Then another Marauder lunged towards them and the soldier turned, blocking the attack. Aran was knocked aside, losing them.

He kept low, his sword raised, as screams of pain and anger erupted all around him, men fell and got up again, or lay still and did not move. He ducked as an axe came whistling past his ear, the blade matted with blood and what looked like human hair. A spear missed him by inches, the shaft shattering on the stones at his feet. Arrows clattered, fired from the upper deck of the Marauder ship. The sound of metal striking metal rang in his ears until his whole body was vibrating like a bowstring.

He forced his way through, his head spinning, thinking he was making for the ship. But to his surprise, he emerged just a few feet from the inn. The same group of emaciated fishermen still clustered by the doorway, watching the battle keenly. They seemed to be laying bets.

A massive, bare-chested Marauder followed Aran out of the mêlée. He had seen the boy, alone and unprotected, holding a very expensive-looking gold-handled sword. He grinned, exposing rotten teeth.

Aran turned and gulped. The Marauder loomed over

him, dripping sweat mixed with blood. Aran backed up to the inn, the window frame pressing into his back. He struck out with Excalibur but the Marauder reached down with gloved hands, catching the blade between them. The impact shook Aran to the bone. Then the Marauder kicked, knocking Aran backwards through the window. Glass shattered all around him. He crashed to the floor of the inn, looking up to see the big Marauder smiling proudly at his new sword.

Aran picked himself up. The Marauder had vanished back into the crowd, taking Excalibur with him.

The inn was deserted but for a cluster of raggedly dressed young women who crowded around the back entrance. One of them held a screaming baby in her arms. Chairs and tables lay toppled and scattered, and the floor was slick with spilled beer.

'What are you doing down there?'

Aran turned. Peregrine was slumped on a stool by the bar, a mug clutched in both hands. His face was even paler than usual.

Aran climbed painfully to his feet. 'What are *you* doing?' he asked.

'Having a pint,' said Peregrine. 'Magic is thirsty work, as it turns out.' Another rumble of thunder shook the walls of the little inn. 'Not bad for a beginner, though, don't you think?'

'It's amazing,' Aran said. 'But look, we don't have time to just sit around—'

'One second, I promise,' Peregrine held up a finger,

taking a long swig. 'I just need to get my strength back. Besides, I always fight better with a couple inside me.'

'But the Marauders took my sword!' Aran told him.

Peregrine looked aghast. 'Excalibur?' He drained his mug and hurried to the door. 'Well, come on, then,' he barked. 'We've got to get it back.'

As they emerged from the inn a bolt of lightning struck the chapel, sending out a spray of metallic sparks. For a moment, everything was outlined in white.

From end to end the dock was crammed with bodies, but it was impossible to tell who was winning. Aran could see Akmid and Keller, back to back in the centre of everything, a ring of Marauders hemming them in. He could see Sergeant Cross rallying the troops to him, fighting a valiant rear-guard action. The ship was ablaze, sending out a thick pall of black smoke. The hatch hung wide, Marauders still swarming across the gangplank.

But the one who had taken Excalibur stood head and shoulders above the rest, the sword shimmering in the half-light. 'There he is,' Aran said, pointing.

'Right,' said Peregrine and vanished into the crowd. Aran could track his passage by the sudden appearance of flying bodies and the sound of terrified screams.

He saw the big Marauder stop, looking down. He raised his fist and brought it down, then he just disappeared. A leg was briefly visible, and his terrified face rose to the surface for the briefest second before being dragged back under.

A minute later Peregrine emerged, clutching Excalibur.

'Here you go,' he said, wiping blood from the blade. 'Big lad, wasn't he? Well, he's a bit shorter now.'

Aran tried to peer over the heads of the crowd. The frozen rain fell and the wind battered down upon the rolling sea. Then he caught sight of Cas on the far side of the battle, against the sea wall near the grounded ship. There was somebody standing over him, taking his arm. Aran recognized Cas's father. He pulled his son close, his eyes streaming with tears.

Peregrine cleared a path, one arm wrapped around Aran's shoulders. Marauders came at them from all sides, their eyes filled with berserk fury. Aran clutched Excalibur, ready to defend himself. But before any foe could get close they were driven back by Peregrine's flying feet or his swinging staff. Bones cracked and bodies flew as they cut a swathe through the very heart of the battle.

At the harbour wall they met up with Cas, wet and shaking but seemingly unharmed. His father gestured towards the ship, which lay listing and swaying in the thundering swells.

'I saw your parents, and your friend,' he said before Aran had the chance to ask. 'A man took them up to the deck. That leader, Karik. I think he knew who they were.'

Aran was not surprised. Karik would know to single the Law out as a bargaining tool if events turned against him.

'Tell them what you told me,' Cas insisted.

His father looked awkwardly at Aran. 'They made your friend change her clothes,' he said. 'There was food.

And they were singing.'

Aran was confused. 'Singing?'

Cas's father frowned. 'I just think you should hurry,' he said.

Aran strode towards the mouth of the ship. He paused on the gangway, looking down into the hold. It was so vast that the far end was lost in shadow. Rows of wooden ribs stretched out of sight, and the din of battle echoed back faintly, as though from a great depth.

Two of the cages were still locked, more prisoners trapped inside. They gasped for breath as the water rose around them, pouring through breaches in the hull. Cattle and horses struggled towards the hatch, their legs kicking wildly in the blood-red tide.

Cas stepped up beside Aran, brandishing a broadsword he'd taken from a fallen soldier.

'You don't have to . . .' Aran began.

Cas shook his head. 'I'm fine,' he said. 'I want to find them too. Mohanna's with them.'

They waded through knee-deep water, pushing flotsam and floating bodies out of their way, making for a steep wooden gangway which seemed to lead to the upper deck.

'The cages,' Peregrine called from the hatchway, gesturing towards the sinking traps.

Aran nodded. 'Get them out,' he said. 'You can catch up to us.'

Aran and Cas scrambled up the ladder onto the upper deck, emerging into an inferno. The mainsail was engulfed in rippling flames and the mast lay in shards. The ship

353

was becoming increasingly unstable, listing dramatically to port, waves pounding against the hull and spitting flecks of white foam across the smouldering deck.

Aran ran to the bow, looking down. Peregrine was helping the dazed prisoners out of the hold, his efforts hampered by the livestock crashing blindly past on either side. The dock was piled with dead and wounded. Aran saw his brother and Keller, still fighting hard in the midst of the battle.

Akmid looked up and his face fell. 'Get down from there!' he shouted.

Aran shook his head. 'I'm trying to find Father,' he yelled, but his voice did not carry over the noise. He turned frantically to Cas. 'I don't see them,' he said. 'Your dad . . . are you sure he . . .'

'He said he saw them brought up here,' Cas said. 'They must be back that way. On the other side.'

At first glance it had appeared as though the entire stern of the ship was ablaze, but now Aran saw that the fire had formed a barrier, cutting the deck in two. Dark shapes moved beyond the flames. Cas was right – there was nowhere else they could be.

A rope drew taut against the railing, then another beside it. Cas ran to the bow. Two Marauders were climbing up, rusty knives clenched in their teeth.

'You'd better go,' said Cas. 'I'll try to hold them off.' He pulled out his crossbow, slipping an arrow into the cradle.

Aran ran towards the stern. The wall of fire blocked his path. He could not tell how wide it was, or how long it would burn. But he had no choice. He took a few steps back, then leaped into the flames.

For a moment he thought he had made a terrible mistake. The fire raged all around him, smoke filling his lungs. He could feel his hair beginning to singe as he forced himself through, ducking around the crooked stump of the mast and finally bursting out into the open. He stopped, beating at his clothes.

Between the fire and the ship's stern was a broad expanse of open deck. Law Carifax knelt against the far railing, his shirt torn open, a bloody gash running almost from shoulder to elbow. His face was raw with scrapes and bruises, his wrists were bound and his legs were tied at the ankles, hobbling him. The Lady knelt at her husband's side, protecting him with her body. She too had fresh cuts on her face and arms.

Over them towered a slender shape, one that Aran immediately recognized. It was Karik, standing with his back to the flames. Black smoke wreathed around his skeletal limbs and his white skin was darkened with soot. The shark's jaw rested on his brow, and the steel spikes in his white-blond braid gleamed dully.

Beside him stood a figure in white. Or, at least, her dress had once been white. Now it was ragged and smoke-stained, patched with scraps of different colours. Her ankles were bound with twine and one hand hung limp at her side, black with bruises. The other was clasped in Karik's, his grip so tight that her fingers were almost blue.

Hearing Aran approach, Karik turned, pulling his

captive with him. It was Mohanna. A rope was bound across her mouth, forcing it open. Her lip was split and there was a fresh scar on her cheek. But her eyes flashed with grim determination, showing no hint of the fear Aran knew she must be feeling.

Karik drew his blade, but smiled when he saw it was only a boy. 'Welcome,' he said, his voice as dry and guttural as a crow's. 'Welcome indeed. Another guest for the party.'

CHAPTER TWENTY-EIGHT
The Golden Sword

Aran advanced, brandishing Excalibur. 'Let her go, you monster.'

'Aran!' Lady Carifax got to her feet, stumbling forward. 'No, it's too dangerous.'

Karik kicked back with one black-booted foot, striking the Lady in the stomach. She fell against her husband, the breath knocked out of her.

Karik grinned, showing tiny pointed teeth. 'Monster, is it?' he hissed. 'Gods and little fishes, you interrupt a man on his wedding day, try to murder his guests, and you call me monster?' He cackled at his own wit.

Law Carifax tried to climb to his feet but the ropes around his wrists were lashed to the gunwale. 'Let the children go,' he cried. 'Let them go. They mean nothing.'

Karik glanced back and raised an eyebrow. 'On the contrary,' he said. 'This girl was promised to me. Her father drives a hard bargain. But when I see her, I know it was worth it.' His hand brushed against Mohanna's neck, her red hair slipping between his fingers. Her eyes widened but she could not cry out.

'Of course, I didn't tell him that I already have . . . how many wives?' Karik counted on his fingers. 'Nine. Or is it eight? I think one of them may have drowned last month. What was her name? She was always weak. Not like this one.'

'I won't let you take her,' Aran promised.

Karik sighed in mock sadness. 'Then who will warm my bed on the voyage home?'

'There's not going to be any voyage,' Aran told him. 'Your ship is sunk and your men are dying.'

'Then we will swim together in the sunken halls,' Karik snapped back. 'With all my fathers and their watery wives. But, boy, if your militia are going to kill me, I wish they would hurry. I grow bored.' He pushed Mohanna down beside Law Carifax and his wife. 'Perhaps I should pass the time with these prisoners. If what you say is true, they're useless now. The old man put up quite a fight before we tied him down. Do you think I could make him beg before I kill him?'

Aran knew he had to draw Karik away from his parents. 'You'll have to kill me first,' he promised.

Karik bared his teeth. 'That should not take long.'

They circled, the boy and the pale-faced man. Karik loomed over Aran like a predatory insect, his leather robes black and gleaming, his arms weaving like pincers. His sword was dull and notched but it was thicker than Aran's arm and twice as long.

358

Aran held up Excalibur and Karik whistled appreciatively. 'Nice sword,' he said. 'So shiny. I will enjoy gutting you with it.'

He struck out, and there was strength in that skeleton body. Aran blocked but Karik swung the other way, catching him off guard, smacking him in the small of his back with the flat edge.

Karik grinned, showing his teeth. 'That was just to get you in the mood,' he said.

Aran backed away, shaking his limbs, trying to loosen up. He held Excalibur at arm's length, a challenge. The blade was humming, almost audibly. Aran felt its power.

He tried to remember all that Peregrine had taught him. He studied his opponent. Karik was strong and he was fast, light on his feet like a dancer. But it was this very lightness that would work to his disadvantage. One good blow might knock him off balance. Aran was determined to make a chance.

Karik held up three fingers, beckoning. 'Come on, boy,' he said. 'Give it your best sh—'

Aran struck before he was finished, and the attack almost made contact. But Karik was too swift. He caught Aran's arm in his own, pulling him forward. They faced one another at close range, their arms locked. Karik laughed in Aran's face, and the stench was appalling. Then he pushed the boy away. 'Good, good!' he murmured gleefully.

Aran fell back against the railing, breathing hard. He made eye contact with Mohanna, who beckoned surreptitiously. Aran blinked once to let her know he understood.

Then he leaped at Karik, lashing out blindly. The Marauder chief was momentarily surprised by the ferocity of the attack. The sword sang in Aran's hands, seeming to move on its own. Karik was forced back towards Mohanna, who crouched silently.

As Karik came within range Mohanna sprang up, grabbing him by the neck and clinging to his back. He whipped round, trying to shake her loose, but she grabbed his braid with her one good hand, wrapping it tight around his neck, throttling him. The spikes dug into Karik's pale flesh, and a desperate cry rose from Mohanna's gagged mouth.

Aran moved in, slicing with his sword. Karik avoided Aran's blow, but only barely. He reached up with his free hand, trying to prise Mohanna free. But her grip was too tight, her eyes squeezing with exertion as she attempted to choke the breath from Karik's body.

Again Aran swung, and again Karik ducked out of range. His face was beginning to blacken as the noose tightened. Aran struck out for a third time, and this time the sword connected, cutting a bloody gash across Karik's chest. Aran drew back, ready for the killing blow.

But even with his strength draining Karik was ready. As Excalibur swung in, Karik flung himself backward. He dropped to the deck, flattening Mohanna and driving the breath from her body. His head slammed into hers, shattering her nose and breaking her grip once and for all.

Then, before Aran knew what was happening, Karik had flipped acrobatically back up onto his feet.

'She won't be as pretty,' he smiled as Mohanna dragged herself back to the rail, blood pouring from her smashed nose, her broken arm hanging black at her side. 'But they say it's what's inside that counts. Let's see what's inside you.'

And he struck out so forcefully that Aran was knocked off his feet. He hit the deck hard, the wind knocked out of him. Excalibur left his hand and scudded across the boards. Karik towered over him, raising his weapon like a spear pointed right for Aran's heart.

But before he could strike there came a cry and the sound of running feet. Karik whipped round just in time to see Akmid come crashing through the flames, hotly pursued by Keller. Aran had to suppress a cry of relief.

Karik backed towards the railing, assessing this new threat.

'Put up your blade,' Akmid demanded, his voice hoarse. 'The battle's over. Your men will soon submit.'

Karik's black eyes hardened. 'More will come,' he said. And he held his sword out, challenging them to attack.

Akmid and Keller hesitated. They raised their swords but did not advance.

'Leave him, son,' said Law Carifax from the stern. 'He's finished.'

Aran could see the exhaustion on Akmid's blood-spattered face, the slump in his shoulders. Carifax was right. Where was Karik going to go?

The pale-faced Marauder smiled thinly. 'Yes,' he said, in a false, pleading voice. 'Do as your father tells you. Let me go. Don't think about all the friends I've killed. The innocent lives I've stolen away. The bodies you've seen. Forget all of that. Let me live.'

Akmid shook his head, rivers of sweat pouring from his scalp and running into his eyes.

'Akmid,' shouted Carifax. 'Don't listen to him. It's not worth it. He—'

But before he could finish, Akmid lunged. Karik blocked, Keller advanced, and battle was joined.

Aran pulled himself up, recovering Excalibur and backing up to the starboard railing as the three warriors swept back and forth across the deck, slicing and blocking, the hammering of metal ringing loud above the roar of the fire and the howl of the wind. Akmid and Keller moved in formation, their years of training creating an unspoken connection. Their swords seemed to interlock, a whirling wall of double-bladed steel.

But Karik was faster than either and smarter than both. He used the environment to his advantage, ducking behind the smouldering mizzen-mast, using his fast-flying feet to knock crates and clutter into their path. His sword sliced through a tightly wound rope and the sail un-ravelled, raining blazing scraps of cloth onto his startled opponents.

Aran could see Keller getting angry, his blows powered by frustration rather than sense. Each time he lashed out Karik ducked or retreated, or created another diver-sion intended to wear them out. 'Stand and fight!' Keller roared, the veins bulging in his neck.

Karik nodded curtly. 'As you wish,' he said.

He feinted with his sword, forcing Keller to block, then he lashed out with one fist, catching Akmid unawares and knocking him back into a pile of barrels.

Before Keller knew what was happening, Karik lowered his head and charged. Keller was thrown back against the railing, his sword slipping from his fingers. Karik reached down and took him by the ankles, pitching him over the side of the ship. Keller vanished into the waves.

Akmid picked himself up, swallowing hard. He had never seen Keller bested before. He ran at Karik but his strokes were weak and easily blocked. Akmid's strength was waning, but it seemed as though Karik could fight all day and not tire. He toyed with Akmid, bloodying his chest, his cheek, opening thin grazes with the point of his blade. Akmid blundered back across the deck.

Aran strode forward, brandishing Excalibur. 'Fight me!' he commanded, driving Karik back towards the fire.

Karik nodded. 'I did promise to kill you quickly,' he said.

As he faced the Marauder chief for the final time, Aran knew he didn't stand a chance. Karik was faster, stronger and far better trained. Weapons would not avail Aran here, even mystical swords.

Then a thought came to him. If he could get his hands on Karik, he might prove easier to overcome. There was strength in him, but no weight. On that score, the two of them were more evenly matched.

So Aran ducked, throwing himself at Karik as hard as

he could, feeling the heavy blade whistle over his head. Karik stumbled, surprised. Aran held on, his fingers locking around the trinkets, bones and metal studs attached to Karik's robes. He pushed again, forcing his opponent back into the flames. Karik let out a cry as he felt the heat on his back. His hair began to smoke.

Aran dragged Karik down, tumbling to the deck with him. He could smell their clothes burning. Aran clambered on top of Karik, slamming his elbow into his enemy's face, forcing his cheek down onto the smoking beams. Karik let out a cry as his braid set ablaze, the blackened steel spikes tumbling free.

Then Aran felt his own skin beginning to blister. He jumped up, and Karik rose in front of him. They were trapped in a ring of flames. Karik reeled, visibly weakened. His clothes were smoking and the skin on his cheek gleamed like melted wax.

Then he gathered his strength and swung at Aran, his stroke still deadly. Fury shone in his eyes. He struck again, using his sword like a hammer, his blows heavy and relentless. Aran stepped back, holding Excalibur over his head in an effort to protect himself. But Karik's sword battered down, forcing him to his knees.

Aran saw a shadow move. It was Akmid, staggering through the fire. Karik had not seen him – he continued to pound on Aran's sword, beating the boy into submission. Then he must have caught a movement in Aran's eyes, because realization dawned on his face.

'No!' Aran cried out as Karik broke off his attack and

swept backward, knocking the sword from Akmid's hand and removing two of his fingers. Akmid cried out.

Karik turned back to face Aran. This would be his final strike. He would end this child's life without mercy. He had toyed with him long enough. He reared up, his sword aloft, ready to strike the killing blow. And for the briefest moment, he was exposed.

Aran felt Excalibur jump in his hands. It seemed to move on its own, faster than Aran could strike, and right on target. He felt the blade pierce through Karik's leather coat, through the shirt beneath, through the skin and into his heart.

Karik's eyes filled with disbelief. His sword plunged down, piercing the boy's side. Aran felt the hot steel slice through his flesh and plant itself in the timbers below.

Then Karik toppled back, stumbling through the flames, Aran's sword protruding from his chest. Blood gushed from his open mouth. He fell to the deck and lay still.

Aran pulled Karik's sword from his side, looking down at the ragged wound, gushing blood. He staggered to the stern, the world spinning hazily. He slumped to the deck beside his mother, laying his head in her lap.

Akmid tottered out behind him, clutching his ruined hand. He stood over the corpse, nudging it with one nervous toe.

There was movement in the flames. Keller came leaping through, his clothes soaked and his eyes alight. Sergeant Cross and Peregrine were close behind. They looked at Karik's lifeless body, at Akmid standing over him.

Cross stepped forward, putting his hand on Akmid's shoulder. 'You did it,' he said.

Akmid looked at Aran and opened his mouth to speak. Then he closed it again, and nodded slowly. 'Yes,' he said. 'I killed him.' He held Aran's gaze for one long minute, then turned his face away.

CHAPTER TWENTY-NINE

The Laws' Council

It was still a moon until Carny, but the streets of Barton
were already teeming. Under the shadow of the
Marauders all trade and travel had ground to a halt,
and even after the victory at the harbour there had been
no time for celebration – winter had drawn in, a longer
and a crueller winter than most could recall, and all efforts
were bent towards the simple act of survival. At Hawk's
Cross, Exmus dinner had consisted of watery broth and
dumplings, with snowmelt to wash it down.

Now, though, everything had changed. Spring had
come to Barton, and the whole town, the whole Island
was alive with relief and release. The crisp cloudless skies
and unseasonably warm sunshine buoyed every spirit, and
in every narrow winding street there was a hectic, happy
atmosphere. The threat was lifted, and life could begin
again.

The courtyards and markets rang with the shouts of
auctioneers and carnival barkers.

Given the sheer volume of people and cattle and carts, all of them in a hurry to get somewhere, Barton should have been all but impossible to navigate. But Aran had a secret weapon.

For wherever Peregrine went the crowds parted, like water around the prow of a ship. Wagons swerved, horses shied, even the livestock seemed to sense his presence and huddle close, lowing nervously. People ducked into doorways or under canopies, nudging each other and muttering. News of his exploits at the harbour had spread far and wide, and the town was abuzz with stories, some true, some false, all mysterious.

'It's like he doesn't even notice,' Cas observed, jogging along at Aran's side so as not to be left behind. 'It's like he just expects everyone to get out of his way.'

'He notices,' Mohanna said admiringly, striding beside them. Her face was almost back to normal now that the bruise had faded. Her nose would always be crooked, but somehow it suited her. 'He just doesn't care. That's power, Cas. You wouldn't understand.'

'And you would?' Cas rankled. 'Just because you're always ordering us about doesn't make you Queen of the world, you know. Besides, that'll be Aran's job soon, if everything goes to plan.'

Mohanna chuckled. 'I don't think the prophecy said he'd be Queen, did it? Not without some sort of terrible accident first.'

Aran tried to laugh with her, but his jangling nerves wouldn't let him. He fixed his eyes on Peregrine's hurrying back, his thoughts returning to the moment just a few days before when they had revealed the truth to Aran's friends and his family.

Mohanna had almost hit the roof in her excitement – this was everything she wanted, a chance for action, to be a part of something great. Cas had asked question after question, about the sword, the lake, about Peregrine's mother most of all. Law Carifax had wrestled with his doubts, his natural scepticism battling with a desire to trust in his son's word.

Lady Carifax had been the most intractable. It wasn't a question of belief – Aran was simply too young, she said, and too inexperienced. He was still her son, and it was too much, too soon. But Peregrine had been insistent, and Carifax had ultimately taken his side. The Laws had worked together to defeat the Marauders; now they could work together for the betterment of all. There might never be a better time.

And yet, in his mother's doubts Aran had heard his own misgivings reflected. Could it be true? The prophecy, the magic, all of it? She was right; he was just a boy. And now, as they hurried through the muddy, madding streets, Aran looked at the people all around them, the farmers and croppers and traders. And the familiarity of those faces, of these streets, of this sky, made what they were about to do seem all the more ridiculous and unreal.

As they rounded the corner towards the Trader's Rest, Aran saw that Peregrine wasn't the only new celebrity in town. A knot of people had gathered around the doorway, and in their centre he could just make out a familiar face, one he hadn't seen in three months. His legs weakened and he felt the wound in his side throb.

'Dirty sneak,' he heard Mohanna mutter. 'Still playing the big hero.'

'Well, there's nothing to stop him, is there?' Peregrine countered, glancing back pointedly at Aran. 'Not until someone tells everyone the truth.'

Akmid had not been home since the battle, returning directly to Barton with the militia and leaving his parents' increasingly desperate messages unanswered. In his absence, Aran had been reluctant to reveal the truth about what had really happened to anyone besides his three closest friends. He wasn't even sure why. Perhaps, he thought, he was still hoping that Akmid would do the right thing. Hoping that his brother still knew what that meant.

'Come on, what does it matter, really?' Aran sighed. 'What's done is done. And besides, think of the song-makers, all those ballads in his honour. They can't very well start again from scratch.'

'Ballads are not the issue,' Peregrine said sternly. 'We're about to go in there and try to persuade everyone you're supposed to be their leader. And you're not making it easy.'

They had to push past Akmid's admirers to reach the front door of the inn. The majority were female, their cheeks flushed, reaching with trembling hands to touch his polished armour or the handle of his sword. The rest were eager boys, marvelling at the stumps of his missing fingers, healed over now but still raw.

Akmid lapped up the attention, kissing the women and patting the boys. As they passed, Aran thought he saw his brother's face darken, the most fleeting of shadows. Then Akmid's smile returned, plastered falsely across his tight, rigid features.

Keller stood in the shadows, observing everything with a blank, expressionless face. But he glanced at Aran as they pushed inside, and nodded his head almost imperceptibly.

The main hall of the Trader's Rest was as packed as the streets outside. Broken sunlight slanted through the big bay window, driving the shadows back into snugs and corners. The bar had been polished to a dull gleam, the stools and smaller trestles arranged so they all faced in one direction – towards the vast, circular oak table in the centre of the room, where fifty or more Laws and their families were now jostling for the best position. But as soon as Peregrine entered, the banter abruptly ceased. Every corner of the low-ceilinged room was filled with an unquiet, expectant hush.

Aran followed his tutor through the mob, spotting his father on the far side of the table. Law Carifax's face sagged beneath worry-lined eyes and his wrinkled brown pate was covered with a fine white fuzz. Hawk's Cross had been repaired, his family rescued, but the trials of the past year had taken their toll.

Lady Carifax sat at her husband's side, the discomfort plain on her face. Her one condition for condoning all this was that she be allowed to sit in on every meeting concerning Aran's future. Now she grabbed her son's arm, pulling him close and glancing mistrustfully up at Peregrine, who stood over them, his face rigid. Mohanna and Cas took up positions nearby, bickering in low voices.

There was a tapping on the table and Law Walden climbed from his chair. 'It's good to see so many of us here, and in one piece,' he said. 'As you know, this is Law Carifax's meeting. But before I hand over, I just wanted to take a moment to remember those who will not be joining us, and acknowledge those whose bravery and fortitude allowed us to weather this most terrible of storms. A moment's silence seems appropriate.'

He bowed his head. The other Laws did the same, and for a long minute all was silent, but for the muted sound of traffic and cattle in the street outside. Aran felt the tension in the air, felt his mother's trembling hand on his arm, and hoped to the Gods that Peregrine knew what he was doing.

Then Law Carifax got to his feet. Every eye was on him as he cleared his throat and gathered his thoughts, and turned to them with a look of forced confidence.

'My Laws,' he began, 'and Ladies. This meeting was called for a number of reasons.' He sounded stiff and over-rehearsed, sweat glistening on his brow. 'First, we need to decide what to do about those friends and family members taken on Marauder raiding parties. There must be a way to get them back. Then there's the question of our Marauder prisoners. We can't just keep them locked up indefinitely.

Finally, we have to discuss whether to continue funding our militia.' He nodded at Sergeant Cross, who stood pensively by the window, one hand on his sword hilt.

'But all of these questions boil down to one issue. The future.' Carifax's voice steadied, his confidence growing. 'These are treacherous times. The Marauders may have been vanquished, but who knows what tomorrow may bring? To the north are the hill people. What would happen if their tribes were united? They may be backward, but as the northernmost Laws can tell you, they can still be a threat.'

Law Hitchens nodded. 'Those unwashed blighters aren't much for conversation,' he agreed, 'but they'll fight like cats in a pinch.'

'And to the south,' Carifax continued, 'there are other farmsteads, other Laws. New trading partners, perhaps, if we approach them correctly. But I can't be the only one to have heard darker rumours. These Queensmen, what do we make of them? Are they simply bandits, as the stories say, or is there more to it?'

Aran had been hearing tales of the Queensmen since he had arrived in Barton, assuming they were merely the latest trick to scare misbehaving children now that the Marauders were out of the picture. Rumours spoke of a bandit gang who gave everything they stole in tribute to a mysterious woman whom they worshipped like a god. No one had ever seen her and lived to tell about it.

'And there may be other threats we cannot predict,' Carifax went on. 'Other tribes, other invaders seeking to take what's ours. Who knows what may be out there, beyond the sea? The militia has been a success, we can agree on that. But I and others believe that the time has come to go one step further. We cannot go back to the way things were, every farmstead for itself. We must act together if we want to survive. The choice is clear. We need a government, and we need a leader.'

He stepped back. The Laws looked at one another and each face registered a different emotion. Some were clearly inspired by Carifax's words, ready to follow wherever he might lead. Others were sceptical, and more were downright angry.

'Pray tell us, Carifax.' A derisive voice cut through the hubbub, and from an alcove at the back of the room emerged a black-clad figure. 'Who is this leader to be? Some great warrior, no doubt.'

Law Darnell had gone to ground following the defeat of the Marauders; no one had heard a word from Crowdale all winter, and even Mohanna had begun to wonder if something terrible had happened at home. But now he was smiling, exuding an air of absolute confidence, running his hands through his greasy mane. He knows something, Aran thought suddenly. Something he thinks can save his neck.

Carifax clenched his fists. 'Darnell,' he said. 'I was worried you wouldn't make it.'

Law Darnell grinned, showing yellow teeth. 'Oh, I wouldn't have missed this for the world,' he said, his voice dripping with sarcasm. 'The chance to be there at the birth of a glorious new era.' He stared expectantly at Carifax.

'Come on, then, don't keep us in suspense. Who is it to be? This great hero who will lead us into your bright future?'

Law Carifax drew himself upright and gritted his teeth. 'Very well,' he said. 'It's no secret.' He turned and gestured to the boy standing behind him. 'It's going to be him.'

The room erupted. Darnell began to laugh. Some of the Laws hurled insults at Carifax, while others called for calm. Most simply looked at one another in disbelief.

Law Walden leaned forward, casting a piercing gaze towards Aran and his father. 'Carifax?' he asked. 'What is all this? Isn't this boy your son?'

'Adopted,' said Law Carifax with an apologetic frown. 'His father was Tarik Karn.'

Again there was a clamour of voices, each expressing a conflicting opinion.

'You can't expect us to believe this,' Darnell's voice cut through. 'Where's the proof? And even if it's true, so what? Karn's reign ended, so his son has no claim over us.'

Carifax nodded. 'That is correct,' he said. 'But there's more. Peregrine, tell them.'

So Peregrine once more told the full tale, from his own birth right up to his final revelation. The Laws listened in silence, their eyes growing bigger with each twist in the tale. When he reached the lake, Aran began to hear snorts and mutters of disbelief.

Peregrine ended by laying Excalibur on the table. 'My Laws, this sword is my proof,' he finished. 'I've felt its power. I believe my mother knew what she was doing when she set me on this path. I believe this boy has been chosen.'

There was a long silence. Then Darnell chuckled. His eyes were little dark coals in his white, fleshy face.

'I'm stunned,' he said. 'I'm amazed that this . . . man would come up with such an elaborate story just to seize power. And I'm amazed that our friend Carifax would go along with it!'

Law Carifax flushed. 'You of all people should know about seizing power.' He pointed a trembling finger at Darnell. 'My Laws, this man is a traitor. He sold his own child to the Marauders in exchange for land and protection. He should be under arrest.'

'On whose authority?' Darnell bristled. 'You're not the King's father yet, Carifax.'

'On the Council's authority,' Carifax replied. 'Which you agreed to respect. I demand a trial.'

Sergeant Cross moved towards Darnell. But as he did so a tall figure stepped into his path, and everything fell into place. Aran heard his mother gasp, heard his father groan, and heard Mohanna muttering the darkest of curses.

Sergeant Cross stopped short, looking at Akmid with dark, betrayed eyes. Akmid said nothing, but took up a protective position in front of Darnell, gripping his sheathed sword.

Darnell clapped his hands together. 'You see, Carifax, you're not the only one with friends in the militia.'

Law Carifax dropped back into his seat, his mouth agape. Akmid stood at Darnell's shoulder, his eyes fixed on Sergeant Cross. He did not acknowledge his father, or Aran.

Darnell licked his lips. 'So, Carifax. Let's hear your proof of my treachery.'

Carifax wrenched his eyes from Akmid. 'I heard it from Karik's own lips,' he said. 'So did my wife and Aran, not to mention your own daughter.'

'So a dead man claimed he made a deal with me,' Darnell said. 'And the only evidence is testimony from a Law and Lady who despise me, and two children who, I regret to say, are clearly under the influence of this' – he waved his hand at Peregrine – 'creature here, who has used Ala knows what power to turn my beloved child against me.'

Aran heard Mohanna choke – a furious intake of breath – but she said nothing.

Darnell turned to Akmid. 'You were with Karik at the end. In fact, you killed him. Did you hear or see anything to back up your father's accusations?'

For the first time, Akmid glanced at Law Carifax. 'I did not,' he said flatly. The other Laws murmured.

Darnell turned back with a smile. 'So there you have it. The word of a true hero.'

Peregrine squeezed Aran's shoulder apologetically. 'I'm sorry, my Laws,' he said, stepping forward. 'But Akmid is no hero. He did not kill Karik. Aran did. Akmid just took the credit.'

Akmid's face tightened but his smile stayed fixed.

But Darnell was prepared, and he snorted derisively. 'Do you take us for fools?' he asked. 'You're saying this untrained child achieved something which his brother, a seasoned soldier, could not? I suppose he used his magic sword to do it?'

Laughter rippled around the room, but was abruptly silenced when Lady Carifax got to her feet, fixing Akmid with a stare that would have cut steel. 'Son, is any of this true?' she demanded. 'Please, tell me Peregrine is mistaken.'

Akmid shifted awkwardly, mumbling under his breath, unable to match her gaze.

The Lady looked away with an expression of disgust. 'Boy, you've done some foolish things in your short life, but this . . .'

'Is this really the issue?' Akmid spat, recovering his nerve. 'Are we really going to argue about one little misunderstanding after all the nonsense they just told us?' He jerked his thumb at Peregrine and Aran.

'Your brother is no liar,' the Lady said.

'Unlike me, is that right?' Akmid's voice was shrill with frustration. 'Mother, I can't believe you're listening to this. Witches and floods and women handing out swords to small boys? It's a story, that's all. A story this Peregrine has made up so he can put my poor idiot brother on the throne, so he can control us all. I can't—'

'Akmid, that is enough!' Her voice was as hard as an axe blade. 'Don't use this as an excuse to attack your brother.'

Akmid's eyes darkened. He looked cornered, his defences weakening. 'Even if Aran did kill Karik, that'd be one Marauder. How many have I killed? I've lost count. We were out there for months, fighting those monsters wherever we found them. The things I've seen, you wouldn't believe. But just because Aran killed the leader, just because he's got this mad magician on his side, he gets to be King? Why him?'

'Instead of you?' his mother replied. 'That's what this is really about, isn't it? Oh, Akmid, look at yourself. Look at who your friends are.' She gestured at Darnell. 'Do you honestly think this is all there is to life – steel and stone, and blood and power? Peregrine has opened up a whole world to us, a world of miracles, but all you can see is your own petty jealousy.'

Akmid opened his mouth to speak but then he faltered, unable to withstand his mother's onslaught. A look of angry resignation came over his face. 'It's just lies,' he said in a tone of quiet desperation.

Darnell stepped forward. 'Poor Akmid,' he said with a hollow snicker. 'But I don't think it reflects too badly on a man if he's a little afraid of his own mother, am I right?' There was a murmur of appreciative laughter.

The colour rose in Lady Carifax's cheeks. 'Darnell, I warned you what would happen if you crossed me,' she said. 'If you pit my sons against each other you will pay for it in blood, I swear.'

Darnell spluttered, struggling to maintain his composure. He looked around at the other Laws. 'Did you hear that? She threatened me. This woman is a hellcat, she's not fit for such a gathering. I want her removed.'

Law Carifax got to his feet, his face scarlet with rage. 'Just try it,' he said.

Aran felt the mood in the room shift. The Laws began to mutter amongst themselves, some voicing their support for Darnell, others seeming to side with Carifax and Peregrine.

'He has the sword,' said one.

'What sword?' another retorted. 'I could make you a sword like that in a week.'

'But the boy killed Karik!'

'Which one, the warrior or the midget? I won't trust my fate to a lad younger than my own son!'

Law Walden banged his cup on the table, his whiskers quivering. 'Stop this,' he barked. 'I didn't come all this way to watch two proud families go at each other.' He turned to Darnell. 'We all heard the tales from the harbour,' he said. 'I do not know this Peregrine but I respect his power, and I respect the trust Carifax places in him. He, at least, has never given us reason to doubt his honour.' Darnell's eyes narrowed. 'And what he says is true. We need a leader, that you must acknowledge. You don't believe we can continue on as we have?'

Darnell shook his head. 'Perhaps not,' he said. 'But why trust our lands and livelihoods to an untried boy when there's a perfectly good alternative standing right in front of us? Carifax has picked the wrong son, I say. Akmid is the hero of the Island, and I for one would be proud to call him my King.'

There was a rumble of assent from around the table.

But Peregrine sighed, shaking his head. 'Aran will rule,' he said. 'With or without your support. It has been foretold.'

'It could be written in fifty-foot letters of fire and still I would resist,' Darnell shot back. 'I don't trust him, or you.'

'Then what do you propose?' Peregrine demanded.

At this, Darnell could not keep from smirking. With a sudden, cold clarity, Aran realized that throughout this entire discussion they had been walking into a trap. A trap which Darnell was now ready to spring.

'Law Carifax demanded a trial,' he said. 'So do I. A physical trial. A test of riding and swordsmanship. If your boy is successful, if he can prove that he's a worthy warrior, I'll drop all of my protests.'

'A joust,' said Peregrine thoughtfully. 'I suppose it's appropriate, historically speaking.'

'If he killed Karik,' Darnell said. 'If he is indeed meant to be King, he will pass the test and rule.'

Peregrine nodded. 'Of course,' he said.

'And naturally the same would go for his opponent,' Darnell continued, barely able to keep a straight face. 'Akmid, do you accept the challenge?'

'Wait, what?' Peregrine held up his hands. 'No, you don't . . .'

But it was too late. The Laws were looking at one another and nodding eagerly. Darnell was laughing, cruel and bitter.

Akmid looked at his brother and smiled through thin lips. 'Of course I do,' he said.

CHAPTER THIRTY

The Trial

'This is insane,' Aran protested, hefting the breachpole in his hand. 'There's no way I can beat my own brother.' He could hear the crowds out in the Longball grounds. Word of the challenge had spread and the stands were crowded with onlookers. Dark clouds gathered and there was a smell of rain on the air.

Mohanna knelt before him in the small wooden enclosure, binding his hands in white cloth. 'You beat Karik,' she said. 'And he beat Akmid. Stands to reason you can do this.'

'But when I was fighting Karik I was fighting for you, and for my parents,' Aran protested. 'I had to win. I didn't have a choice.'

'Well, you still don't,' said Mohanna. 'Now you're fighting for your future. For all our futures. What do you think will happen if you lose and Akmid becomes King? It means my father rules this Island.' She shook her head. 'Oh, Aran, you should have seen this coming, you and

Peregrine. Akmid's always been jealous of you, we could all see it. You should have known this Karik business would tip him over the edge.'

'But . . . running to Darnell, it doesn't make sense.'

'It makes perfect sense,' Mohanna shot back. 'My father is the only man in the world more bitter and power-hungry than your brother. And now he's had weeks to scheme, to bribe as many Laws as he could into coming over to his side. And of course he told them that these accusations about him and the Marauders were just Peregrine and Carifax trying to discredit him. It all fits, you see.' She tied the last bandage. 'But it doesn't matter, anyway, because you're going to win. I believe in you, even if you don't.'

She looked up with a hopeful smile. Aran placed one hand over hers, lacing their fingers together. The crowds in the arena seemed to have fallen strangely silent. Mohanna's eyes widened and Aran gazed into them, feeling just a little unsteady. She leaned forward, and now their faces were just inches apart. Aran took a breath.

Then the rear gate swung open and Aran's head snapped round instinctively. He snatched his hand back and Mohanna dropped onto the bench.

'The bookies wouldn't be placing such good odds if they could see the look on your face,' said Peregrine, walking into the enclosure. 'Word got out about the prophecy, you see. Gamblers are superstitious people. Normally they'd back Akmid because he's, you know, bigger. But now they think you're destined to win. And they're right, of course.'

He stood behind Aran, placing his hands gently on

the boy's shoulders. He murmured something under his breath and Aran felt a warm, tingling sensation spreading through his upper back.

He jerked forward. 'What are you doing?' he asked.

Peregrine shrugged. 'Just a little protection charm,' he said. 'Something to toughen you up, give your muscles a little extra oomph.'

Aran's eyes widened. 'Oh, no,' he said. 'No, no way.'

Peregrine squinted at him. 'You don't trust me?' he said. 'I'm getting pretty good at this now. I haven't disintegrated anything in almost a week. And besides, no one will be able to tell.'

'I don't care!' Aran protested. 'I'm not going to go out there and cheat! How can I be King if I come by it dishonourably? This has to be a fair fight, or what's the point?'

'The point is to wipe the smirk off Darnell's face!' Peregrine shot back. 'We already know you're going to win. All this will do is ensure you don't get seriously wounded in the process. Nowhere does it say the King will have both his legs, or all his vital organs.'

Aran scowled at him. 'It's a question of honour,' he said.

Peregrine rolled his eyes. 'Oh, for God's sake,' he said. 'The most overrated concept in human history. The number of good men I've known brought low because they insisted on fighting with honour.'

Aran stood his ground. 'I won't cheat.'

Peregrine threw up his hands. 'Fine!' he said. 'But when they drag you back in here, battered and bleeding . . .' He shook his head. 'Of course, I'll heal you no matter what. But be careful.'

Cas entered, hauling what appeared to be a large pile of scrap metal. He dropped it to the floor with a crash. 'Is this cheating too?' he asked.

Aran looked down, poking at the metal with his toe. 'What is it?' he asked.

Cas picked up a curved steel sheet with holes in either end. It bore the marks and dents of repeated hammer blows. 'This is a breastplate,' he said. 'These are for your arms. And here, a helmet.'

'It's armour!' Aran realized. 'Did you make it yourself?'

'Not exactly,' Cas admitted. 'It's practice armour for the militia. Sergeant Cross lent it to me. But I had to adapt it to fit someone your size.'

He heaved the breastplate over Aran's head, tightening the straps. It was followed by the huge, thickly padded helmet. Aran could see little and hear less, but there was no question he'd be well protected.

'There's no way he'll get me in this,' he said, his voice loud in his ears. He dragged off the helmet. 'It's great,' he told Cas.

'Your poor horse,' Mohanna pointed out. 'You'll flatten him.'

'Rather him than me,' Aran replied.

The gate opened for a third time, and Aran was surprised to see Keller's gaunt face peering through the crack. He entered, his eyes fixed awkwardly on his boots.

'Did my brother send you?' Aran asked.

Keller nodded. 'He says to call it off,' he said. 'Doesn't want to hurt you. Just forget the whole thing and let him have the victory.'

Mohanna spat in the earth. 'Well, you can go and tell that treacherous little—'

'It's all right,' Aran said, touching her arm. 'Keller, who are you working for now? Darnell?'

Keller looked away. 'Law Carifax hired me to protect your brother,' he said.

Aran nodded. 'Keep it up,' he said. 'No matter what happens.'

Keller met Aran's eye for a long moment, his face struggling to maintain its stony expression. 'You need to win,' he said flatly, and marched from the enclosure.

Out in the arena a bell began to ring. Mohanna and Peregrine helped to shove Aran up into the saddle. He grasped his breachpole tight in one hand, the enormous helmet under his arm. His heart thumped beneath the steel breastplate.

Then he dug his spurs into the horse's flanks and rode out through the slowly opening gates. The audience clapped politely as he made a quick lap of the field, dust kicking up beneath his horse's hooves. Aran craned his neck to look up into the steeply sloping stands, and wondered how many of the onlookers understood the full significance of what they were about to witness.

The far gate creaked open, and the applause became deafening. Akmid wore a tan leather jerkin and arm guards, but no breastplate or helmet. He twirled his breachpole and Aran saw young women fainting, overcome with the excitement. Others attempted to clamber over the barriers onto the pitch, only to be intercepted by teams of Darnell's men.

Aran and his brother rode side by side to the head of the field. The Laws sat in unsmiling rows, dressed in their grandest finery. Law and Lady Carifax sat at the front, their faces pale and their hands clasped together.

Law Walden climbed to his feet. 'We've come here to witness a fair contest,' he said. 'Both these warriors have proven themselves in battle. May the best win.' He took his seat.

Law Darnell stood. 'Fight well, my champion,' he said. 'Become the King you were born to be.'

The response was rapturous. Akmid spurred his horse down the field, the sound of applause ringing and reverberating around the arena.

Aran looked one last time at his parents, then he shoved the helmet down and rode to his mark. He could see Akmid in the distance, just a dot in his narrow vision.

Aran waited. He could hear nothing but the beating of his blood and the din of the crowd, distant like the sea, rising and falling. He heard the faint clang of the bell and kicked his spurs.

He lowered the breachpole, gripping tight with his legs. He could see sweat standing out on his horse's neck, its eyes wild, its mouth open and panting. Akmid pounded towards him, just thirty feet now, and closing.

Aran braced himself, swinging the pole outward, looking for a torso strike, low enough to knock his brother off his horse. Twenty feet.

His heart thumped. He tightened his grip on the reins. Ten feet. He planted the pole firmly against his side and gritted his teeth.

He felt the impact knock him sideways but held on, putting out his arms for balance. Akmid had struck him hard, of that he was certain. He didn't know if he had managed to do the same.

He reined in the horse, wheeling round. He could see his brother now. They were both still mounted. Aran's breachpole lay in pieces on the ground.

Cas ran forward, offering a replacement. Aran lifted the helmet. 'Did I hit him?'

Cas looked uncertain. 'It sort of glanced off. A bit lower next time and you'll have him.'

Aran rode back to his mark. Akmid was waiting, his pole held aloft. Aran felt a sharp pain in his side and tried to ignore it. At least he'd managed to stay on the horse.

Once again he heard the dim clang of the bell and started forward. He held the pole upright and drove on, knowing his weight must be torture for the poor horse beneath him. But he was thankful for Cas's armour. It had saved him once, and probably would again.

When they were within ten feet of each other Aran lowered his pole and braced. This time the impact was twice as powerful. Akmid's blow struck him on the side of his breastplate, knocking him back. He felt his breachpole shatter in his hand. He toppled backwards, clutching at the reins.

Aran hit the ground hard, the armour digging into his sides. He rolled three times before finally coming to rest. He let out a cry, knowing nobody could hear him.

Then he struggled upright and looked around. His heart rose. Akmid was lying in the dirt a few feet away. Aran picked himself up.

Cas came running with Excalibur, placing it unsheathed in Aran's hand. 'I don't know if it makes any difference,' he said, 'but he hit the ground first. Oh, look out.'

Aran turned to see Akmid climbing to his feet. He gripped Excalibur with both hands and planted his feet in the earth. He would let his brother come to him.

He eyed Akmid as he moved in, looking for any sign of weakness. Aran had watched his brother all his life. Somewhere inside his head must be the key to beating him. But now all he saw was Akmid's towering size, his muscles rippling under the leather shirt. All he felt was a childlike fear of his older, stronger, angrier big brother.

He shook his head, trying to drive away the negative thoughts. He had to believe – that was the only way he would be successful. He couldn't lose. A thousand-year-old dead woman said so.

Akmid rushed at him, his sword held high. Aran sidestepped. This should have taken him well out of range, but he was carrying twice his normal weight and was considerably wider than usual. Akmid's sword struck him on the arm, knocking him aside.

Aran looked around desperately. His brother was nowhere to be seen. He turned as fast as he could and saw a blur disappearing out of his field of vision. Akmid was behind him.

Aran felt a foot in his backside and toppled to his knees. He could dimly hear the laughter of the crowd. Another foot struck him, knocking him on his side. The weight of the armour held him down. He could see nothing, do nothing. He struggled up but again the foot came in, pitching him down on his face.

Now Akmid retreated, giving Aran a chance to stand. He loosened the straps and shuffled out of the armour. He heaved the helmet off, gasping for air. Now he was exposed, but at least he was mobile.

Akmid advanced once more. But he kept his sword lowered, looking at Aran with furious eyes. 'You can't win,' he said, his voice seething with threat. 'Just give it up and I promise not to hurt you.'

Aran shook his head. 'You know I can't,' he said.

Akmid growled. 'When did you get so stubborn?' he asked. 'Maybe we're not so different after all. But I'm still bigger, and stronger. And I will beat you, Aran.'

Aran circled, staying out of range. 'Remember when we were little, we used to fight all the time?' he asked. 'You always won. But you would always apologize afterwards. I think that was when I loved you most. Because you knew it wasn't fair. Because you cared enough to say sorry. What happened to you?'

Akmid's eyes flashed darkly. 'I grew up,' he said. 'You'll

understand, one day.'

'No, I won't,' Aran said flatly. 'Father wanted you to be tough so you could protect us all, keep Hawk's Cross safe. But he was wrong. All it did was make you angry, make you mean, make you think that kindness is weakness. You're like a Marauder.'

Akmid blanched. 'You take that back,' he said. 'Take it back or I really will hurt you.'

Aran sighed and gripped his sword. 'All right,' he said. 'If we really have to do this, let's do it. All I want is to get my brother back. The brother I love. But maybe he really is gone.'

There was a long, aching silence. Then Akmid lowered his head and charged, his sword aloft. Aran swung upwards, deflecting Akmid's blow. Their blades clashed.

They drove back and forth, striking and blocking, advancing and retreating. The clang of metal on metal rang from the high wooden walls. The dust rose in clouds beneath their booted feet, and the crowd bayed their approval.

But something was wrong. Aran shifted his grip on Excalibur's hilt, but the sword was like a dead weight in his hands. He tried to clear his thoughts, waiting for its power to fill him. But the sword would not comply.

It began to rain, big warm droplets that drummed on the earth, turning the field into a mud bath. The water streamed off Akmid's bald head. He took a breath and drew himself up to his full height, then he began to drive forward. Aran blocked, but barely. He clutched the sword, begging it to respond. There was nothing.

Akmid spun and lunged, and this time their blades locked. Aran felt his grip on Excalibur's hilt weakening, his arms trembling with the strain. Akmid towered over him, their swords grinding together. Aran's feet struggled for purchase in the deepening slime. Desperately he tried to push back, to force Akmid to yield.

Then his feet slipped and he crashed to his knees, his clothes and skin turning black. Akmid's blade sliced down, cutting a gash in Aran's chest. Aran's hands opened and Excalibur flew from his grasp. Akmid kicked it away.

Aran felt fear overtake him. This was wrong, this wasn't how it was supposed to be. He was destined to win. He *had* to win.

He began to pick himself up but the mud seemed to suck him back down. Akmid's boot came out of nowhere and knocked him to the ground. He fumbled for Excalibur, staggering on his hands and knees, lost in confusion. It was all happening too fast.

Akmid's final kick caught him under the chin as he was climbing to his feet. Aran flew head over heels, splashing down in the dirt. He felt the wound in his side rip wide and unbearable pain shot through him. He tried to stand but the agony was too great. He could feel the blood running freely beneath his jacket.

His brother loomed over him. Aran could see triumph in Akmid's eyes, and behind it a look of desperation, the fear of what might happen if this was allowed to continue.

'Stay down,' he pleaded, and this time Aran did as he was told. Akmid placed one foot on Aran's chest, signalling his victory.

Aran lay in the dirt. He had lost. It was impossible, but he had lost. The rain filled his open mouth and washed away his tears. The crowd screamed their approval but Akmid hung his head, letting the water course down his back.

Aran saw Cas and Mohanna running towards him, their feet splashing in the mud, looks of horror and disbelief on their faces. He closed his eyes and listened to the rain.

CHAPTER THIRTY-ONE

The King's Justice

Aran stared down from the high window of the inn. The road was becoming a river, washing away to the lake beyond. A reluctant horse dragged a heavy cart, water rising around the wheels. A man whipped the horse mercilessly. Aran watched. There was nothing else he could do.

Golden lamplight was reflected in the warped glass. In it he could see his friends – Cas, Mohanna and Peregrine – sitting stunned and disbelieving on the bed. Aran could not look at them. He had failed them. Failed everyone.

'I don't believe it,' said Cas for the twentieth time.

'There's been a mistake,' said Peregrine, his voice bereft of hope. 'Something's gone wrong.'

'Maybe we—' Mohanna began. Everyone looked at her. 'Never mind.'

'It's all Darnell's fault,' said Cas. 'That filthy traitor.'

'It's Akmid's fault as much as anyone's,' Mohanna retorted. 'He could have killed Aran.'

'It's my fault,' said Peregrine. 'I should have protected him. Why would I have been given this magic if I wasn't supposed to use it?'

'It's nobody's fault,' Aran said, turning to them, the bandage uncomfortably tight around his waist. 'It was a fair fight and Akmid won. Besides, I don't think you could have done any good once the sword refused to help me.'

'Where's Excalibur now?' Peregrine asked. 'Perhaps I could . . . I don't know. Fix it, or something.'

Aran shrugged. Darnell's men had taken the sword when they had grabbed him at the Longball grounds. For the King, they said. The spoils of victory. Akmid's prize.

But somehow, Aran couldn't bring himself to be angry with his brother. The only person he wanted to blame was himself. He wasn't ready, he knew that now. A madness had possessed him. He was just a boy.

'What made me think I could do it?' he said. 'How did I think I could be King? I thought I wanted it, but now . . . Maybe it's for the best.'

Peregrine smiled sorrowfully. 'But that's precisely the point,' he said. 'That's why you were chosen, and not someone like Akmid or Darnell. Power should never be entrusted to someone who actually wants it. That was your father's weakness. He became corrupted by his own ambition. But you, Aran . . . you're not perfect, I think we're all aware of that. You have wild ideas, and encourage others to go along with them. But you never threaten, you never use force. I really thought—' His voice broke off, choked with emotion. 'I really thought we could make a difference.'

'Perhaps it isn't time yet,' Mohanna argued. 'Maybe in a few years . . .

But Peregrine said, 'No. Akmid may wear the crown, but we all know where the real power lies. Your father will never let go willingly. And I won't start a war.'

He lapsed into silence. Aran could hear footsteps in the corridor, Darnell's guards talking in low voices as the watches changed. And deep below, the sound of laughter and raised voices as Akmid and his supporters toasted their success.

'I wonder what they've done with my parents?' Aran said. 'Akmid wouldn't hurt them, would he?'

Peregrine shook his head. 'Of course not,' he said. 'He's an idiot, but he's not a monster. We'll find them in the morning, I promise. For now, you three should get some sleep. I'll stand watch.' He settled into a chair by the window, uncorking his flask and taking a long drink.

Aran lay back on the bed. His thoughts drifted back to that first night in the woods, when Peregrine had dropped off to sleep, leaving him awake and afraid. But now his tutor sat upright and alert, his eyes bright in the lamplight. Just for a moment, he felt safe.

Aran slept fitfully, his sleep disturbed by the drumming of rain on the windows. He heard the sound of creaking timbers and sails whipping in the wind, and dreamed he was back on the black ship, ringed in flames. He felt the kiss of steel in his side, but when he turned to strike he found Excalibur gone. He clutched his wound, crying for his brother to save him. But when he looked up it was Akmid holding the sword.

Aran snapped awake, hearing footsteps in the corridor. The sky was light. He staggered out of bed, pulling on his trousers. Peregrine sat in his chair, the flask still clasped in his hand. He was snoring loudly.

Aran shook him. Peregrine rose, protesting. 'What is it?' he asked.

'I don't know,' Aran said. 'Trouble. Did you hear voices in the night or did I dream it?'

'I didn't hear anything,' Peregrine said irritably. 'And I don't hear anything now.'

They stood for a moment in silence. Then Aran heard a strange popping noise. It was followed by a high, thin scream like a kettle boiling. He crossed to the window and opened the curtains.

A building in the next street exploded.

Timbers shattered. A convulsive cloud of smoke and dust erupted into the air. People in the street were knocked to the ground by the force of the blast.

Cas and Mohanna scrambled from their beds, running to join Aran and Peregrine at the window. They looked down towards the lakeshore, and Cas gasped aloud. 'Oh, Ala,' he said. 'They're back.'

Floating on the glassy surface of the lagoon were seven dark shapes. Six of them were all too familiar – the rusted metal plating, the jaw-like hatches, the black sails flapping in the wind. But it was the seventh vessel that drew their attention.

It was barely a ship at all, more like a floating town, a vast interlocking network of rafts and wooden platforms dotted with shacks and shanties and canvas awnings. In the centre stood a steel freighter over two hundred feet high and three times that in length, its sides copper-brown with rust. A spider web of ropes and chains snaked down from the upper deck, holding the entire structure together. They were anchored around the base of a cylindrical tower from which a thick black smoke was rising.

Even from this distance Aran could see that the surface was swarming with people; hundreds, even thousands of them.

'Hell's teeth,' Peregrine whispered. 'That's an army.'

The central ship was pockmarked with tiny portholes. There was a flash, and a puff of smoke gusted from one of them. The *pop* reached their ears, followed by that awful screech. A fishing boat in the harbour disintegrated.

Aran's heart raced. 'They're using black magic,' he said.

'They're using cannons,' Peregrine corrected him. 'Nothing magical about it. Still, just as effective.'

A small skiff was approaching the shore, its sails hanging ragged from the mast. It ground to a halt on the rocky beach and a group of men climbed out, perhaps thirty in number. They were robed in black and Aran could see familiar trinkets of bone and bronze hanging from their clothes. But these were not wild like the Marauders they were used to. They seemed efficient and calm. Aran felt a chill of fear.

The door to the bedroom burst open. Aran turned, his heart seizing, momentarily convinced that the Marauders were already coming to take him.

He was almost relieved when he recognized Devin. The big man marched in, grabbing Aran by the arm before he could pull away. Peregrine whipped round, snatching up his staff, but Devin raised his sword, pressing the flat edge against Aran's windpipe so hard that he struggled to catch his breath.

'The King wants him, so he's coming with me,' Devin said. 'You can follow on, if you like. But try any of your trickery and your chosen one loses his throat.'

Aran was dragged down the corridor and into the narrow stairway. 'Haven't you looked?' he cried. 'Don't you know what's going on? Peregrine, tell him.'

Peregrine marched behind, his eyes dark. 'He'll find out soon enough,' he said. 'Then we'll see who's really got the power.'

But in the main hall of the inn there was no sign that anyone knew what was happening outside. Many of Akmid's supporters, the Laws closest to Darnell, sat or lay slumped in various states of disrepair on seats and settles around the hall. The room stank of sweat and alcohol, and the floor was sticky and littered with crockery.

Law Carifax and his wife knelt with Walden, Hitchens, Lady West and several others on the floorboards by the bar, their hands folded behind their heads. A combined force of militiamen and Darnell's personal guards stood over them, swords drawn. The prisoners' eyes were sunken, their faces pale, and Aran wondered where they had spent the night.

Relief flooded Law Carifax's face as Aran was shoved roughly down beside him. 'Did they hurt you?' the Law hissed.

Aran shook his head. 'I'm fine,' he said. 'But you, what did they—'

'We're fine,' his father assured him. 'Just exhausted. But Darnell will pay for this, mark my words.'

'Where's Akmid?' Aran asked. 'Does he know you're here?'

The Law jerked his chin. Akmid was sprawled on a long bench under the bay window, snoring softly. Keller stood over him. Akmid clutched Excalibur to his chest like an infant, and the pillow beneath his head was soaked with wine and drool.

'Hail to the King,' said Peregrine bitterly, kneeling beside them.

Then Aran remembered, and clutched his father's sleeve. 'Has anyone been outside?' he asked. 'Do they know what's happening?'

Carifax shook his head. 'We heard a terrible noise,' he said, 'but nobody thought to—'

'Well now!' a familiar voice interrupted, and they all looked up. 'What a motley bunch.'

Law Darnell climbed the steps from the basement, buttoning his robe. 'Good. We're all here.' He scratched his backside and yawned. 'You must pardon my tardiness, I got a little carried away last night. But it's pleasing to see

400

that my orders were carried out, no matter how drunk I was when I gave them.'

Aran started to his feet. 'My Law, you have to look—'

Devin reached out with one massive hand, grabbing Aran by the neck and hauling him back.

'My Law?' Darnell sneered. 'I'm the King's Second now, boy. Call me Your Grace or something.' He looked around. 'Where is my liege lord, anyway?' Then he sighted Akmid on the bench, and smiled.

Darnell whispered to one of his guards, who hurried over and began to shake Aran's brother roughly. Akmid sat up, blinking and clutching his head. He grabbed a bottle from the floor and tipped it to his lips, wincing in the pale light.

'Well, it would seem the King had a big night too,' Darnell said. 'So until he feels ready to join in, I may as well make a start on the important affairs of state. Now, you're all accused of treason in the highest degree. The sentence for that is probably death, isn't it?' He chuckled, scanning the kneeling prisoners one by one.

Then he spotted Mohanna among them, and his eyes darkened. 'What on earth are you doing with this rabble?' he asked. 'We're the winning team this time, sweetheart. Up you get. All is forgiven.'

Mohanna flushed. 'You mean I'm supposed to forgive you for trying to sell me to the Marauders?'

Darnell's smile faltered. 'I told you that was nonsense,' he said. 'Just a mix-up. Now come here before I change my mind.' And he gestured to Devin, who attempted to take hold of Mohanna's wrist.

Mohanna scrambled free, retreating towards Lady Carifax, who quickly put herself between the girl and the guard.

Darnell glowered. 'Daughter, you're making a fool of yourself,' he hissed. 'Now get over here before I lose my temper.'

Mohanna shook her head. 'No,' she said firmly. 'Whatever you do to them, you can do to me.'

Darnell's eyes narrowed, and for a moment Aran thought he was going to take her by force. But he just sighed and shook his head. 'Very well,' he said. 'The choice is yours.' He looked up. 'In fact, the choice belongs to each and every one of you.' He cast his eyes imperiously over the ragged, weary band. 'If it was up to me, you'd all be swinging already. But your King is merciful.'

Akmid had crossed to Darnell's side, and the Law wrapped one arm around the young King's shoulders, clapping him generously on the back. Akmid grinned proudly, and took another drink.

'He insisted I give you one more chance to save your necks,' Darnell told them. 'It's simple, really. All you have to do is join us. Admit that Akmid is the rightful ruler and you can go back to your families and your farmsteads, safe in the knowledge that your King is watching over you.' Then his voice dropped. 'Some of you may be tempted to turn down this generous offer. But before you do, know this. The consequences will be severe. For yourselves, your farmsteads, and for all those you love.' He grinned coldly, and Aran felt the chill down to his bones. 'There will be no place for the weak or foolish in our new regime. No place for rebels and traitors. But we will do great things together, I promise you. Justice for all. Death to those who threaten us. An ordered society, prosperous and strong.'

A few guards clapped, and Darnell took a self-satisfied bow.

'Pretty speech.' Peregrine got slowly to his feet. Darnell gestured and a sword jabbed at Peregrine's chest. He brushed it away. 'I've heard it before, though. From a thousand and one petty demagogues. And you know what? Every one of them died screaming.'

Darnell scowled. 'You keep quiet, vagr—'

'Or what?' Peregrine interrupted. 'What are you going to do? Kill me? Others have tried. You know full well I'm only here because I choose to be. The moment this gets boring I can snap your neck like a pencil. His too.' He waved a hand at Akmid.

Aran saw his brother blanch. Then Akmid took a deep breath and a step forward, squaring up to Peregrine. Akmid was taller and broader, casting Aran's tutor into shadow. Nonetheless it was painfully clear who had the authority. Akmid's lip trembled, his hands shook. Peregrine simply stared calmly, treating Akmid to a half-smile which could've been either threatening or conciliatory, it was impossible to tell.

'You don't frighten me,' Akmid said at last, his voice quaking. 'I'm sure you know a few moves, but that doesn't make you invincible.'

Peregrine nodded. 'You're probably right,' he said. 'And you managed to beat up a fifteen-year-old boy. But that doesn't make you King.'

Akmid snarled. 'So what does?' he asked. 'A golden sword from the bottom of a lake? Taking credit for a freak storm? Come on, show us your power. Make me disappear. Conjure up a dragon to swallow us all.' And he forced a laugh, his men joining in.

'How about an army?' Peregrine offered. 'What if I made an entire army appear on the doorstep, intent on destroying you and everything you hold dear? Then would you believe me?'

Akmid looked askance, and for a moment he seemed almost convinced by Peregrine's threat. Then he laughed again, more heartily this time, his confidence returning. 'An army?' he said. 'Sounds frightening. When should we expect them?'

Peregrine winked. 'Oh, they're almost here,' he grinned. 'I should say any second . . . now.'

There was a knock on the door.

Everyone gasped. Akmid turned.

In the silence they could hear a voice from outside, weak with fear. 'He should be in here,' it stuttered.

One of Darnell's guards opened the door. A boy stood there, bowing almost to the ground. He stepped aside to admit a wiry, leather-clad man, who strode purposefully into the room. He was tall and raven-haired, with rough brown skin and cracked black lips. A curved blade hung from his belt.

The stooping boy indicated Aran's brother. 'This is him,' he said.

Akmid frowned. 'Who are you?' he asked the stranger.

The man looked at Akmid, at the vomit on his shirt and the wine stains on his face. His nose wrinkled. 'You are the leader of these people?' His voice was faint and rasping, utterly without warmth.

Akmid nodded. 'That's me,' he said. 'Now state your business, as you can see I'm in the middle of something.'

The dark man glanced at the kneeling captives, at the guards standing over them. Distaste flickered across his features. 'My name is Ismel,' he said. 'I represent the Mariner people, the masters of the sea. I believe you call us . . . Marauders.'

Akmid's mouth dropped. 'Wh-what did you say?' he managed.

The Marauder's men filed in, blocking the door. Each of them was armed with a curved sword and a throwing axe, and several carried long harpoons with sharpened hooks. They were all clean-shaven and rough-skinned, and every face wore the same grim, determined expression. These aren't raiders, Aran thought with a shudder. They're soldiers.

Ismel smiled. 'I come on behalf of the great Sion,' he told Akmid. 'He wishes to negotiate your immediate and unequivocal surrender.'

CHAPTER THIRTY-TWO
The Mariners

Akmid swallowed. 'I'm sorry,' he managed. 'Did you say surrender?'

Ismel nodded. His men lined up against the bay window, stern and silent. The shadows deepened. 'All your lands and possessions will become the property of the Mariners and their Sion. You will be permitted to live as long as you do all that we ask, without question.'

Akmid almost laughed, but caught himself just in time. 'Are you serious?' he asked. He looked around, as though expecting somebody to tell him it was an elaborate practical joke.

'If you do not believe,' Ismel continued, 'look outside.'

Ismel stepped to the window and Akmid followed. Through a gap in the buildings they could see all the way down to the lake. Ismel pointed to the six tall ships, and the vast floating city between them. Then he indicated the smoking pile of timbers nearby.

'Unless you wish your whole town to become splinters,'

the Marauder said, 'you will accompany us back to our Sion. Now.'

Akmid bit his lip. 'Might I have a moment to consult with my advisers?' he asked.

The Mariner nodded. 'One minute,' he said.

Law and Lady Carifax got to their feet as Akmid staggered back towards them, grabbing Peregrine's sleeve. 'Do something,' he whispered desperately. 'Open up the earth and swallow them. Rain fire down on them!'

Peregrine detached Akmid's hand distastefully. 'My magic's good enough for you now, is it?'

'He only said they wanted to talk,' Lady Carifax pointed out.

'Mother, he said they want to negotiate our complete surrender!' Akmid's voice was little more than a petrified hiss. 'What's the best way to get people to yield? Kill their leaders! Leave them directionless, without hope!'

'You've only been King five minutes,' said his father. 'I think the people will cope without you. And besides, this Sion might be a reasonable man.'

'He's a Marauder!' Akmid moaned. 'When was the last time you met a reasonable Marauder?' He turned to Keller, who had silently joined them. 'Do you think the militia even know what's happening? Will they rescue us?'

Keller frowned. 'Darnell put half of them in jail,' he said. 'The other half are busy guarding the first half.'

Law Carifax rolled his eyes.

'The best option right now,' said Peregrine, 'is to do as they say. At least until we know what we're up against.

There could be thousands of them on those ships, and we wouldn't stand a chance. Our only hope is to try and talk them down. Take Darnell along – isn't this what he's good for, making deals?'

Akmid's eyes lit up and he turned eagerly. But Darnell had disappeared. Somehow, in the confusion, he had made his escape. The door to the basement steps stood open.

'There you go, son.' Law Carifax let out a bark of cold laughter. 'At least now you know who your friends are.' Akmid's colour drained further still, and even Devin looked betrayed.

The King hung his head. 'All right,' he said. 'I suppose I've no choice. I'll go alone.'

Lady Carifax gripped his arm. 'Akmid, no,' she said. 'I could go with you . . .'

Akmid shook her off. 'What kind of King takes his mother to a peace negotiation?'

'Your father, then, or Keller.'

But Akmid shook his head. 'No,' he said. 'It's too dangerous. They'll be needed here if things go . . . bad.'

'Whatever you do,' Peregrine said, 'I wouldn't keep them waiting. Something tells me this Ismel isn't the patient type.'

The Mariner was watching them through narrow eyes, tapping his foot.

Akmid nodded, and Aran could see the terror in his brother's eyes. For a moment he stood stock-still, as though trying to force himself to move. His lips worked soundlessly, and Aran realized he was muttering to himself, a hopeless prayer for deliverance.

Then he mastered himself, and looked up at Ismel. 'All right,' he said in a faint, cracking voice. 'I'm ready.' The Mariner nodded, and turned to the door.

But as Ismel turned his back, something in Akmid snapped.

His arm lashed out, and Aran saw to his dismay that there was a knife clasped in it. Ismel ducked Akmid's thrust, his hand falling on his scimitar. But Akmid reached around with his free hand, grabbing Ismel and pulling him in.

As one, the Marauder soldiers unsheathed their curved swords. But Akmid held his bright little blade to their captain's throat, crying, 'Stop!'

They stopped.

'I'm not going anywhere with you,' Akmid spat, his voice strained. 'Tell them to fall back. Command them!' And he pressed down with his knife, drawing a blossom of blood on Ismel's neck.

'Very well,' Ismel said. 'I'll command them.' He looked up at his men, and his lip drew back into a sneer of derision. 'There's no King here,' he said. 'Kill them all.'

Time seemed to slow.

The Marauders formed up, their scimitars flashing. Akmid wrapped his arm around Ismel's throat, dragging him towards the bar. The Marauder captain's boots scraped on the wooden floorboards.

Law Carifax took hold of Aran and they retreated into the hall, shoving Cas and Mohanna along with them. The other prisoners scrambled to their feet, piling towards the back wall in a tide of sweat and panic. Militiamen and guards moved in to protect the terrified Laws. Aran saw Devin struggling to yank his sword free from its scabbard.

The Marauders advanced, a solid wall of steel and muscle and leather. One lunged, and Aran saw Law Gorton stagger back into an alcove, clutching his chest. Another flung a gleaming steel harpoon towards Aran, but Peregrine's staff came lashing down, breaking the shaft with a sharp snap.

A small table flipped over almost gracefully, sending cutlery and plates spiralling into the air. Aran glanced back in time to see someone, he thought it was Law Malkum, rebounding off a massive Marauder's belly and into the bay window. Glass shattered as he tumbled out into the street, landing in a bloody heap.

Walden, Hitchens, Lady West and a few others were taking up arms, but most of the Laws stood in a quivering mass at the back of the room, flinching at every advance. Keller and Devin fought to protect them, working back to back, their blades flashing.

Law Carifax grabbed a Marauder by his coat and threw him across the bronze bar top. He crashed to the floor on the far side, landing in a sodden pile of smashed wine jugs and crockery. Carifax's shirt was torn and his face ran with blood. His wife ducked, wrenching a sword from the hand of a fallen militiaman. Aran saw fire in his mother's eyes.

But still the Marauders came, clambering over the furniture, their eyes alight with murderous intent.

'Tell them to stop!' cried Akmid in desperation, pressing

his knife to Ismel's throat. 'Tell them to stop and I'll let you live.'

Ismel laughed. 'You don't understand,' he spat bloodily. 'If you kill me, if you kill all of us, you will only make it worse. The Sion will take twenty, fifty, a hundred heads for every man who dies today. You have only one choice. Surrender.'

Aran heard, and knew that Ismel spoke the truth. He balled his fists. He needed to think. Then he saw something, a flicker of reflected light in the shadow of the great oak table in the centre of the room. A feeling moved through him like a bolt of electricity.

He dropped to his knees, and there on the floor he could make out Excalibur, unsheathed and discarded. The only problem was the wall of Marauders between himself and the sword.

He pointed it out to Peregrine. 'I need to get it back,' he said. 'I can feel it. It's awake.'

Peregrine nodded. 'Right,' he said. 'There's something I've been meaning to try.'

He closed his eyes for the briefest second, muttering something under his breath. The Marauders closed in around them and Aran could smell salt and blood.

The foremost Marauder lashed out with his curved blade. Aran pulled back as it swung in towards his face, knowing he wasn't fast enough.

Then Peregrine's eyes were open and he was moving. His staff swung upwards, so fast that Aran heard the air around them pop. The staff struck the huge Marauder in his chest, lifting him clear off his feet. He flew through the air, hurtling into three of his fellows and sending them flying.

'Wow!' cried Peregrine, giving his whole body a violent, exhilarant shake. 'I wasn't sure that was going to work.'

Aran grinned. 'You've been practising, haven't you?'

Peregrine laughed. 'This is just the beginning,' he said. 'Oh, look out, here comes another one.'

Aran flung himself to the floorboards, fumbling under the table for Excalibur. Behind and above him he heard a faint pulsating boom followed by the sound of colliding armour and men hitting the floor. 'If there's one thing I love,' Peregrine cried, 'it's a good bar brawl.'

Then Aran felt metal in his hand, and something travelled up his arm and set his whole body jangling. He pulled Excalibur free and got to his feet, turning to survey the mayhem.

Akmid still had Ismel by the throat, but the look on his face was pure impotence – he had no idea how to make it all stop. Law Carifax was still fighting, his fists lashing out at anyone who got too close. The Lady gripped her sword, five terrified Laws huddling at her back. Cas crouched behind the bar, lobbing mugs and crockery. Mohanna had dragged a Marauder to the floor and was punching him repeatedly, her face a mask of pure, giddy rage. The roar of battle shook the walls.

Aran hefted Excalibur. The blade thrummed in his hands, making every nerve sing. He had no doubt that if he took it now into battle, he would be victorious. The Marauders would be defeated.

But then he remembered the ships, and the men on those ships. Thousands, tens of thousands. And he remembered his fight with Akmid, how the sword had let him down. And suddenly, like a shaft of light piercing through dark clouds, it all made sense. He knew what he had to do.

As soon as he lifted Excalibur over his head he could feel the change in the air. The voices faded, the din subsided, and one by one every head turned.

Aran stood for a moment, feeling waves of power rippling along his arm, through his body and out into the still air. Then he brought the sword down in a straight, clean arc. The huge oak table split down the middle with a great crack. Everyone took a step back.

Slowly the dust cleared.

Aran stood in the wreck, the sword singing in his hands. His heart was racing but his mind was clear; he felt sharper and more alive than he ever had before.

His doubts were gone. It was all true, all of it, the visions and the legend, the words in Peregrine's books. It had always been true. Who was he to go against the will of destiny, of prophecy, of the Island itself?

'I'll go,' he said to Ismel, as Akmid's grip slackened and the Marauder captain got to his feet. 'If you'll take me, I will treat with your Sion.'

'Aran, no!' Lady Carifax stumbled forward.

Aran looked at her. 'Mother,' he said. 'It's time. Who else?'

Ismel rubbed his neck and his lips drew back over fine white teeth. 'Boy,' he said. 'By what authority do you claim this right?'

Aran sheathed Excalibur. 'By this sword,' he said. 'My brother is not the King. I am.' As he spoke the words, he felt their truth.

Ismel stepped clear. 'I will take you to the Sion,' he said. 'But you understand what will happen if your claim is found to be baseless? Your people will be enslaved. Everyone in this room will die, slowly, and in pain. Believe this.'

'I believe,' Aran assured him. Then he turned to Peregrine, a gleam in his eye. 'I understand now,' he said. 'Why I couldn't beat Akmid. Why the sword refused to help me. It's like you said. Violence breeds violence. We have to break the cycle. That's what the sword wanted, all this time. That's what the Island wants. We can't win by fighting, not with the people we love.'

Peregrine smiled. 'Of course,' he said. 'That's the lesson Arthur learned, the lesson my brother taught him. To achieve peace we have to practise it. But what if this Sion won't listen?'

'I have to make him listen,' Aran said. 'I don't have any choice.'

The soldiers stood aside, Marauders and militiamen alike averting their eyes as Aran passed, following Ismel to the door. He paused, glancing back. His parents stood with Akmid, their faces filled with uncertainty. Mohanna crouched by the bar, Cas clutching fearfully at her arm. Peregrine looked at Aran and a slow smile spread across his face. 'I believe in you,' he said. 'For what it's worth.'

Aran nodded once, and was gone.

CHAPTER THIRTY-THREE
The Sion's Answer

Ismel led Aran down to the lakeshore. The world seemed to hold its breath, frozen in perfect stillness, all except for the dark clouds overhead and the hawk which cried, circling among them.

Aran could see a line of ragged carts and cattle on the main track out of Barton. People dragging their life's possessions, seeking sanctuary. He knew it was hopeless. If he failed, the Marauders would find them wherever they tricd to hide.

Ismel's skiff lay on the rocky beach. He climbed aboard and Aran followed. The sails filled, ropes creaking as they swung out into the lagoon. Aran peered over the side. His reflection was blurred by the falling rain. The silent town receded behind them.

The black ships loomed up on either side. It was like moving through a forest of vast, dark, creaking trees. Men peered down from the bow rails as they passed. Aran could see derision in their eyes – this was the best the Island could come up with? One frightened boy? He pursed his lips and tried to look as if he was meant to be there. But his heart was hammering under his ribs, and he had to grab the side to stop himself from falling.

They drew closer to the floating city. On the near side was a wide opening, a harbour of sorts, lined with small boats and fishing vessels. The jetties on either side were crowded with people, and Aran was amazed to see women and children among them, watching him with guarded fascination. Their skin was weathered and tanned, their clothes dark and gleaming, and many of them wore headdresses and necklaces made of bone and feathers. But otherwise, they looked just like the people of the Island – he saw mothers with suckling babes, toddlers peering from behind their grandmothers' skirts, even boys and girls his own age. Some kept pace with the little craft, moving with a steady, loping gait as the linked platforms bobbed and rocked beneath them.

Ismel guided his skiff into the shadow of the central ship. The metal hull was encrusted with stones and shell-fish, right up to the waterline. It had been repaired and patched up countless times, sheets of steel bolted over rust-edged holes.

Massive ropes with iron hooks were flung from the upper deck. Ismel threaded the hooks through rings on the bow and stern, and the little craft began to rise, tipping back and forth as the ropes tightened, inching up the sheer side of the enormous freighter.

Aran leaned over the side and saw the great raft city

spread out below him. Everywhere he looked it was swarming with people, as the Mariners made their final preparations for invasion. Aran couldn't help but marvel at their warlike efficiency. There were battalions of bowmen, and foot soldiers with swords, spears, axes and harpoons. There were rows of armoured gunships, each fitted with a single cannon. There were even animals on board, warhorses with broad backs and iron-shod hooves, clad in burnished armour.

Then they reached the deck and strong hands pulled the little boat in. The ship was so vast Aran could barely feel it moving beneath him.

Ismel took him by the arm, leading him across the deck and down a flight of flaking steel steps until they came to a bolted door. The Mariner knocked hard with his fist. 'Enter,' said a voice, and the door swung open.

Pale emerald light enshrouded them as they stepped into a huge storage bay hung with coloured cloth and carpeted with rough canvas. Far above their heads a small hatch stood open, allowing in a single beam of light. Beneath it stood a raised platform, and on the platform was a wooden chair. In the chair sat the biggest man Aran had ever seen.

His chest was the size of four barrels and his legs and arms were like pillars. Except, Aran noticed, he had only one arm – the left ended in a twisted stump of scar tissue just above the elbow. His face was a mass of cuts and contusions, his lip drawn into a permanent sneer by an ancient scar which ran from his chin to his overhanging eyebrows.

His hair grew in sparse grey tufts and he had no ears, just ragged holes.

A pair of guards stood at either shoulder, looking down at Aran with undisguised contempt. They each carried long blades and Aran had no doubt they would cut him down if he lifted so much as a finger.

The Sion beckoned to Ismel and they spoke for a moment, the big man spitting his words from the corner of his mouth, slurred by the disfiguring scar. Then Ismel was dismissed and the Sion peered down at Aran.

'Step forward,' he said. 'And give me your name.'

Aran did as he was told. The Sion gestured with his stump to a small canvas chair. Aran sat. 'My ambassador tells me you have replaced your own brother as King,' the Sion said. 'I wonder how this could be, a boy so young?'

'I was chosen,' Aran replied.

'By the people?'

'By the Island.'

The Sion's eyes narrowed. 'Indeed?' he said. 'Ismel tells me you possess a strange power, one he has not felt before. And I have heard other tales on my way here, of a man who can control the sky itself. Is any of this true?'

'It is.'

The Sion frowned. There was no sound but the faint patter of rain on the roof.

Then the big man shook himself. 'I should tell you my reasons for coming here,' he began, filling a cup with sweet-smelling wine. 'Since the time of the Great Accident, we Mariners have wandered the oceans. There are fewer of us than there were. Many have taken to the dry life and their great raft cities have fallen into disuse. But those of us who choose the sea, we thrive. We are slaves to no man, and the world is ours to roam.

'The Mariners you encountered, the ones you called Marauders, were under the command of Karik, my sister's son. I never liked the boy, he was wilful and stupid. But my sister wished him to succeed, so I agreed to cut loose a portion of my city and give it over to him, so that he could make his own way as I had done.

'Over the years, rumours reached my ears. Karik had found a place rich in land and cattle, where he could live like the Kings of old, with wealth and servants under his command. He began taking slaves to work his forges. He stole children, training them to fight. Once he had enough men and arms, he planned to invade this country and take it by force.

'It seemed a wild dream, but I let him have it. It kept him occupied, stopped him from threatening my own position. But then, some weeks ago, a fishing boat arrived, carrying the last survivors of Karik's army. The pitiful dregs. And my suspicions about him were confirmed. He was reckless, and now he had paid for it with his life.'

The Sion paused, shaking his head. Red veins stood out on his cheeks. 'I have no wish to rule your land, but neither can I let this go unpunished. Karik was my sister's son and his body lies in a dry grave. His men are held in your jail. They must have their freedom.

'And so I have come to crush the last spark of rebellion

419

from your people. If Karik had never come, we would not be here. If your people had not challenged him, we would not be here. It is regrettable, but the honour of the Mariner people is at stake. You must surrender to my rule. These are my terms. Submit, and keep your lives.'

He sat back. Aran was silent for a long moment.

Then he reached down and drew Excalibur from its scabbard, laying it across his knees. The guards edged forward, but something held them back.

'Great Sion,' he began, and his voice sounded small in the vast space. Then he felt the power of the sword beneath his palms, took a deep breath, and began again. 'Great Sion. This is the sword that killed Karik. It is an ancient and mystical blade, and I draw upon its power now just as I did when I slew your nephew. Karik was a murderer and a thief. He had taken the people I love and was holding them prisoner. I killed him and took them back. Would you not have done the same?'

The Sion nodded. 'But I would do so knowing that the consequences could be severe.'

'Your nephew was cruel,' Aran said. 'And you are right, he was a fool. Don't make the same mistakes he made.'

The Sion's eyes narrowed. 'Get to the point,' he hissed.

Aran swallowed. 'In one way, Karik was right,' he managed. 'We are an innocent people, compared to you. We had little experience of war until the Marauders came. We fought amongst ourselves, petty squabbles that amounted to nothing. We were unprepared. But that has all changed.'

His grip on Excalibur tightened. Despite the fear in every fibre, somehow his voice was steady. 'For we are powerful, my lord. We do not suffer our friends to be killed, our families taken. We do not suffer our possessions to be stolen, our homes ransacked. And so, in answer to your terms, I say no. You cannot have our loyalty. You cannot have our people. You cannot have our land.'

He rubbed his eyes, then looked back up at the Sion. 'Instead, I present a different set of terms. You can take back your men as soon as you return the slaves. We give them freely. You can go back to your raft cities in peace. When you return you can bring goods to sell and trade, and you can teach us warcraft and shipbuilding and other such skills. In time of need you can call upon us and we will send men and arms. If we are threatened you will do the same.

'I know,' Aran shook his head. 'It sounds like weakness. Why collaborate when you can conquer? But I promise, you will never conquer here. Our army may be pitiful compared to yours, but they will fight to the last man to keep us free. And when all the men are dead, the women will fight. When the women have fallen, the children will stand. You will never break us down.

'And if that is not enough, let me tell you this. The stories you have heard are all true. My friend Peregrine has powers you cannot even imagine. If your army comes ashore they will find the earth opening up and their swords turning against them. The very sky above their heads will drive them back.'

As if on cue, they heard a distant rumble of thunder. The Sion looked into the sky with an expression of deep uncertainty. Then he looked down at Aran.

'You dare to threaten me, boy?' he said.

Aran shook his head hurriedly. 'I'm just asking that you do what's best for us all,' he said. 'We will resist. Your men will die. That's not a threat, it's a fact. Work with me, I beg you. There's so much we can learn from one another.'

The Sion stared at him, but did not speak. The rain continued to fall, and the floating city creaked softly on the water.

At the inn, an uneasy silence had descended. The militiamen and Mariners stood in restless ranks, eyeing one another uncertainly. The Laws huddled together at the back of the room, debating in hushed voices.

Cas, Mohanna and Peregrine stood by the window, watching as the clouds gathered overhead. High above, they could see the lone hawk soaring on moist air currents, scouring the earth.

Peregrine looked up and smiled. 'Merlin,' he said, identifying the bird. 'That must be a good sign.' Then he sighed deeply. 'I wish my brother were here. In the stories, Merlin always had the answers.'

'You've done all you can,' Mohanna said. 'It's up to Aran now.'

'I hope he's all right,' said Cas.

A cart passed, piled with crates. A child sat on the

backboard, sucking her thumb and staring at the black ships which rocked silently on the lake.

'You could go,' Peregrine said. 'Both of you. Get somewhere safe.'

Cas shook his head quickly. This was his place, at Aran's side, or as close to it as possible.

Mohanna frowned. 'Run away?' she said bitterly. 'Who do you think I am, my father?'

At that moment, they heard a ruckus from the back of the room. Parry bustled in, followed by the blacksmith who kept the forge behind the inn. He was dragging a third man by his collar. Law Darnell's clothes were black with mud, his face red with fury.

'Let me go!' he shouted.

The blacksmith ignored him. 'I caught him trying to pinch one of my horses,' he said to Law Carifax. 'Funny thing was, he seemed to think it was his. Like he had a right to take it or something.'

'I do have a right,' Darnell spat. 'I am the King's Second. If I tell you to do something, you do it.'

'Begging your pardon, sir,' said the blacksmith, 'but nobody tells me what to do except my missus. And far as I can tell, you're not her.' He looked up at Carifax. 'I'll turn him over to your care, my Law, if that's all right.' Then he leaned close and whispered, 'If you ask me, he's not quite right upstairs.'

Carifax nodded. 'You may have a point,' he said.

Darnell glared around the room, his cheeks flushed. 'What are you all staring at?' he demanded. Then he

423

spotted Akmid, slumped on the floor between his mother and Keller. Confusion flooded Darnell's face. 'What's happening?' he asked. 'Why isn't he . . .'

Carifax smiled thinly. 'Akmid is no longer in charge.' He gestured to Devin, who took great pleasure in binding Darnell's hands tightly behind him. 'But don't worry. I'm sure that when the King returns from treating with the Mariners, he'll be happy to hear your case.'

'The . . . the King?' Darnell asked.

'That's right,' Carifax said. 'You remember Aran.'

Suddenly Cas cried out, 'Something's happening!'

He led them out into the street. Shielding his eyes from the glare, he could see a line of small ships approaching over the water.

Carifax broke away, hurrying down towards the shore. The others followed, spreading out along the beach. Some had weapons drawn, others stood poised to flee at the slightest provocation. Peregrine stood in the centre, the children close to him.

They could see the boats clearly now, five steel gunships, narrow and fast. On the prow of each stood a masked warrior, upright like a figurehead, maintaining balance despite the choppy water.

In the centre came the boat that had taken Aran, the ragged sail flapping. A guard stood at each corner. Between them sat an enormous warrior in a bearskin robe, carrying a long wooden spear. Some fled when they saw him, breaking for the road.

But beside the giant sat a tiny figure. He held a gleaming

sword, and as the craft reached the shore he began to wave it in the air, sending splinters of reflected sunlight glancing out across the surface of the water.

'Aran!' Mohanna cried, and she began to run. Cas and Peregrine were right behind her, and soon the line of people broke and rushed forward to greet the boy returning. The boat ground onto the stony shore. The crowd waited breathlessly.

The Sion heaved himself over the railing, his huge bulk casting a long shadow. He took his wooden spear and held it above his head.

'People of the Island,' he began. 'I came here to avenge the death of my nephew. But my spear, poised to strike the killing blow, has been turned aside.' He brought the spear down, breaking it over his knee. He handed one part to Aran. 'Let this be a symbol of the friendship between our peoples. Long may it last.'

Aran took the spear and bowed low. 'Great Sion,' he said. 'Your strength is matched only by your wisdom.'

The Sion looked down at him, and slowly his face broke into a smile. 'You young pup,' he said. 'Your courage is matched only by your cheek. If my nephew had half your wit we wouldn't have been in this mess in the first place.'

Aran held out a hand. 'Come,' he said. 'I don't think either of us have had breakfast.'

The Sion nodded. 'I have eaten,' he said. 'But I am always ready to eat again. Lead on, King Aran.'

They entered the town, the crowd closing ranks behind them. The Sion's guards fanned out on either side, keeping pace with their leader. The clouds were beginning to break and the sun shone through, glinting off a river of puddles in the muddy street.

Aran paused and turned, squinting into the bright sky, white with a single patch of blue. A black speck circled there, the hawk spiralling in the sunlight. It let out a cry and dropped from sight, vanishing into the clouds.

Aran turned away, following his friends back to the inn.

CHAPTER THIRTY-FOUR
The Road Ahead

Aran was invested at a simple ceremony in the courtyard by the chapel in Barton, the old librarian reading a document which Peregrine had cobbled together from scraps of memory. Law Carifax lifted a silver crown – forged by a local smith to Peregrine's exacting specifications – and placed it on his son's head, grinning proudly as a great cheer went up from the crowd. Aran felt himself blushing, the crown slipping over his eyes.

The coronation was followed by a sumptuous feast, to which everyone was invited. Places of honour and first pick of the food was given to the returned prisoners from across the sea. Looking at their haggard faces, Aran knew that they would never be fully healed. He vowed not to let such a thing happen again, as long as he was alive.

He looked along the head table. The King's table, he reminded himself. Law Carifax sat on his right, gesturing with a chicken leg as he debated fiercely with the Sion, who sat opposite.

Before the ceremony, the Law had taken his son to one side. 'No matter what happens,' he'd said. 'No matter how grand you get, you'll always be my boy.' And he had taken Aran in his arms and held him.

To their left sat the Lady, picking uninterestedly at her food. She had not been the same since they had taken Akmid away to the militia brig, and her doubts about all this had not abated. But she had chosen to support Aran nonetheless.

'Don't question yourself,' she had told him. 'You've been raised well, and you have all the good qualities we could beat into you. Trust your instincts. And remember, we'll always be with you.'

Aran had listened, and knew that she meant every word. But still he felt strangely alone. From now on, no one would be able to comprehend the burden he carried, the choices he would have to make.

Except, he thought to himself, there was one. But who knew what had become of Law Karn since he had fled Hawk's Cross, fifteen moons and a lifetime ago? By now his bones might have been picked clean by dogs and wild birds.

What would Tarik say to his son if he could see him now? What would his advice be, presuming his mind wasn't utterly broken? Aran wasn't sure he wanted to find out.

The eating and drinking, the dancing and carousing, promised to drag on into the early hours. So just before midnight the new King slipped away, ducking out of sight and making his way down to the lakeshore. He could just make out the distant lights of the Mariner city, low on the horizon. The moon left a silver track on the water and Aran was tempted to follow it, to throw off his clothes and dive into the lagoon, to swim out as far as he could and never return.

But he sat instead, taking off his shoes and paddling his feet in the water. His mind was heavy with thoughts of the future. He had been chosen for a reason, and he couldn't believe it was just to fight the Marauders.

He turned, hearing footsteps. Three figures came striding out of the darkness. Aran's hand strayed to the hilt of his sword.

'Don't worry,' said a friendly voice. 'We're not assassins.'

Cas, Mohanna and Peregrine emerged from the shadows. Cas carried an entire leg of lamb, dripping grease down his chin. Peregrine handed Aran a mug of wine and they sat together, staring out across the water.

'What were you thinking about?' Mohanna asked.

Aran shrugged. 'Everything that needs to be done.'

'Like what?' asked Cas between mouthfuls.

'Like *everything*,' said Aran. 'We need a proper army and a government, and somewhere to put them. We need to feed the poor and house the homeless. We need to do something about the Laws – too many of them have done exactly what they wanted for too long. And we need to pay for all this, so Peregrine says we need taxes. But how much is too much? What if people don't like the way I do things? Are they going to start to hate me? What if they hate me, but I don't know about it? And what if there's another war, and we're not ready? Everyone will blame me. And they'll be right to blame me. And what if—'

'All right,' said Peregrine loudly. 'You're making my head hurt.'

'Well, now you know how *I* feel,' said Aran. 'It's not as easy as it looks, being King.'

Peregrine laughed. 'I'm sure that's true,' he said. 'But you're fifteen, Aran. No one expects you to be perfect right away.'

'But I'm responsible. If I make mistakes, people could die.'

'Then we'll have to make sure you don't,' said his tutor. 'Listen, part of your responsibility is to find the right people to look after the right things. Take the militia. You can't recruit new men, arm them, pay them, and breed horses and build barracks all by yourself. Someone needs to make the day-to-day decisions. Your responsibility is to pick the right people, people you can trust. If you do that right, the rest falls into place. Do you see?'

'I think so,' said Aran uncertainly.

'So who would you pick? To run the militia?'

'Erm . . . my father?' he suggested.

Peregrine smiled. 'I think he'll be a bit busy keeping an eye on you. And besides, you should try not to seem like you're favouring your family.'

'Sergeant Cross, then. And Keller.'

'That's better,' Peregrine nodded.

Aran thought about it. 'Cross can run things,' he suggested. 'Keller can find recruits, and train them.'

Peregrine clapped. 'Perfect,' he said. 'You now have the first two members of your new government. Apply the same logic to all your problems and we'll start to get somewhere.'

'What about me?' Cas asked. 'What do I get to be in charge of?'

Peregrine looked annoyed. 'This isn't a game,' he said.

Cas's face reddened. But Aran said, 'No. You said pick people I can trust. There's no one in the world I trust more than these two.'

Cas and Mohanna looked at him in surprise, blushing.

'Cas, I know what you can do,' Aran said enthusiastically. 'Get a team together. Carpenters, blacksmiths, inventors, anyone who wants to help. I want you to start making things, like the Ancestors. Horseless carts and hard roads, and towers up to the sky. Peregrine can help you.'

Cas's eyes lit up. 'Well, I don't know about the towers, but there's always my irrigation system. There are lots of people who don't have enough to eat.'

'Perfect,' said Aran. 'This time next year I want every farmstead to have one. I don't want anyone going hungry.'

'What about me?' Mohanna asked. 'What's my task?'

Aran thought for a moment. Then, in a flash, the answer came to him.

'The most important job of all,' he said. 'You can be my bodyguard.'

Mohanna glared at him. 'Don't joke,' she said.

'I'm not,' Aran insisted. 'Borrow five or six good men

from the militia and form a royal guard. You'll need costumes, really fancy ones, like the Sion's spearmen.'

'Do they have to be men?' Mohanna asked.

'They can be whoever you want,' Aran told her. 'As long as they're tough. But you won't just be my bodyguard. You'll need to be my eyes and ears. Watch everything that happens and give me your opinion.'

'In my brother's time,' Peregrine told them, 'the King's counsellors were called knights. They all came together at a big round table and discussed the needs of the land. They were the bravest men the King could find.'

'Sounds like a good idea,' said Aran. 'So how do I make this lot into . . . what you said.'

Peregrine thought back. 'It had something to do with kneeling in a church overnight, then having a bath.'

'That sounds awful,' Aran said. 'Never mind, we'll think of something. We can make up our own ceremony.'

'Whatever it is,' said Cas, tossing his bone into the water with a splash, 'it should definitely involve feasting. I like feasting.'

'You'd never guess,' said Peregrine archly.

'Well, Peregrine,' Aran said. 'You deserve to be the first.'

Peregrine smiled and shook his head. 'I don't think so,' he said. 'The knights swore fealty unto death. I value my freedom too much for that.'

'You're going to leave?' Aran asked, dismayed.

Peregrine shook his head. 'I don't plan to. But one day you'll be experienced enough to do all this by yourself, and you won't want an old troublemaker like me hanging around.'

'That's not true,' Aran protested. 'I'll always want you hanging around. This is as much your kingdom as mine. You made it possible.'

'No, I didn't,' Peregrine said softly. 'You were the one who understood what the Island was telling you. You broke the cycle.'

'But there may be more fighting still to do,' Aran countered. 'I can't believe it's going to be so easy.'

Peregrine raised an eyebrow. 'Easy?' he said. 'I don't call that easy. But you're right, I can't see the road ahead. There may come a time when you're forced to wield Excalibur again. Just remember everything you've learned. Violence leads only to violence. It must be your last resort.'

Aran looked out across the water. His fears had been calmed, for now. Suddenly he turned to them, his face serious.

'There's one more favour I need to ask,' he said. 'It might be the most important of all.'

They looked at him uncertainly. Mohanna put a hand on his shoulder. 'Go on,' she said.

Aran was silent for a moment, trying to put his thoughts into words.

'I need you to keep me the same,' he said at last. It was clear from their faces that they didn't understand. 'Just because I'm King,' he said haltingly, 'doesn't mean I'm not me. And it's important that doesn't change, no matter how much everything around us changes. I need you all to promise. Keep me *me*. All right?'

He looked at them each in turn. Mohanna squeezed his shoulder. 'Of course,' she said. Cas nodded.

Peregrine raised one eyebrow. 'It's an impossible task,' he said. 'But I'll do my best.'

The distant sounds of revelry came drifting down through the warm night air. Aran felt secure and confident, ready to look into the face of the future without blinking. He had an army and a royal guard, and a team of engineers and a round table of knights, and his very own wandering wizard. Whatever may come, let it come.

'Well,' he said. 'What's next?'

Geographical note

The landscape of *The Waking World* is essentially that of North Yorkshire, Lancashire and Cumbria, but major artistic licence has been taken. Just as the names of some farmsteads are corruptions of existing place names – Skipton, Harrogate, Scarborough – so the places in the story are corrupted future-cousins of the real-life locations which inspired them. The valley of Hawk's Cross and the landscape around it are vaguely based on my childhood memories of Arncliffe and Wharfedale; Crowdale has a loose connection to the moorland roads between Slaidburn and Hornby; and the stone circle was inspired by the ancient ring near Keswick – there's no lake there at the moment, but who knows what effect 1,000 years and a shift in global weather patterns might have?

The map was based – loosely – on projections for a global water-level rise of approximately fifteen metres, which I found online at **www.geology.com**.

Acknowledgements

This book would not exist without the encouragement and inspiration of many, many people. Elizabeth Fraser and Steve Huddleston read me all the right stories. William Watson taught me to tell my own. Jean Fraser showed me that normal people can write books. Margie Fraser was my first and most enthusiastic reader.

Rebecca Saunders got the ball rolling. Antony Harwood took a chance I wouldn't have taken under the circumstances. None of it would have meant a thing without the patient perseverance of David Fickling, who kept insisting it could be better, and was right every time. And huge thanks are also due to Matilda Johnson and Bella Pearson, who saw it through to the end.

Chris Power never doubted for a second that this was possible. Jamie Crewe drew amazing pictures. Pat Long was kind and not too critical. Mark Wilson gave the most useful notes (which neither of us expected). Steph Cole gave positive reinforcement at a time when it was badly needed.

Thanks to Scott Eastlick for getting me writing, among many other helpful things, and to my travelling folk-rock support network The No Sorrows, who at various times have been Sean Berry, Iqbal Birdi, Nicola Calvert, Colin Greenwood, Adam Hill, Tom Hughes, Tom Paterson (honorary), Steven Pih, Sandra Rehme and Robin Rochford. Thanks to Evan Manifattori and everyone on 'The Surprise', to Lee (Law) Gorton and Ray Smith for movie nights and funkiness, and to David Jenkins, Dave Calhoun, Wally Hammond, Derek Adams, Cath Clarke and Adam Lee Davies because, to misquote *Throw Momma from the Train*: a writer writes, always, even if it's the Top Ten Hat Movies.

Then there are those family members and friends who have made this whole process bearable: Daisy, Alfie & Pete Brown, Joan, Mike, Jim, John & Viv Huddleston, James Hindle, Benedict Giovine, Jackie Hendrie, Victoria Yeulet, Ella Seebacher, Lucy Evans, Richard Olson, Meaghan Thurston, Jemma Cullen, Malcolm Skene, Alice Lloyd, Emma Tricca, Jenny Carey, Catherine Ince, Dottie Alexander, Amy White, Nikki Hirst, Abigail Lapell, Naomi Robinson, Iker Olabarria, Rosie Greatorex and far too many more to even begin to mention.

Finally, as the very last draft was being completed, my dear friend Nick Clark passed away. Without his shining example, I'd probably still be asleep.